AF820236

Praise for *Lola in the Mirror*

'Unpredictable, fantastic … It takes a charged narrative, like Dickens achieves, and as Dalton does too, to reach the heart and the brain – writing that is able to carry both stories, the individual and the political/personal … To tell you more would spoil this complicated and surprising story. You should read it'
Sydney Morning Herald

'Trent Dalton's third novel reminds me of the 1980s advertising slogan for the author's home state of Queensland: Beautiful one day, perfect the next … *Lola in the Mirror* is a bold, big-hearted, hopeful, humorous, dark, reflective, truthful, superbly written novel that confirms Dalton's place in all the shimmering skies (to borrow the title of his second novel) of Australian literature. He is not a rising star but a star full stop' *The Australian*

'Wonderful … An original, heart-thumping novel … you are right there with the protagonists, feeling and believing every word and every raindrop. It is the type of novel you read filled with pure hope and sorrow for the characters. You want to believe that everything is going to work out just fine, and that there will be dancing, and art, and delight. You won't know until the end, and by that time you, too, are running through the streets, turning the pages, and trusting that love wins' Readings

'Dalton holds a mirror up to the darkest corners of this Australian life and reveals every bit of beauty, magic and calamity it has to offer' Booktopia

Praise for *Boy Swallows Universe*

'The best Australian novel I have read in more than a decade … The last 100 pages of *Boy Swallows Universe* propel you like an express train to a conclusion that is profound and complex and unashamedly commercial … A rollicking ride, rich in philosophy, wit, truth and pathos' *Sydney Morning Herald*

'*Boy Swallows Universe* is a wonderful surprise: sharp as a drawer full of knives in terms of subject matter; unrepentantly joyous in its child's-eye view of the world; the best literary debut in a month of Sundays' *The Australian*

'The book is plotted like a murder mystery, with the requisite twists and turns providing illuminating surprises right to the last page. Scenes are rendered in intimate detail, the characters are as real as your family and the writing is glorious' *The Advertiser*

'A towering achievement. It is the *Cloudstreet* of the Australian suburban criminal underworld' *Herald Sun*

'One of the best Australian novels I've ever read … The characters are human and complex, the writing is fast-paced and heartfelt, and every sentence is surprising … This book will stay with me for a long time' *The Guardian*

'*Boy Swallows Universe* hypnotizes you with wonder, and then hammers you with heartbreak' *Washington Post*

'Filled with beautifully lyric prose … the characterization, too, is universally memorable, especially of Eli and August. At one point Eli wonders if he is good. The answer is "yes," every bit as good as this exceptional novel' *Booklist* (USA)

Praise for *All Our Shimmering Skies*

'I think *All Our Shimmering Skies* is even better than *Boy Swallows Universe* … There's a whiff of southern gothic here, with Molly reminding me of Scout Finch from *To Kill a Mockingbird*' Stephen Romei, *The Australian*

'A work of shimmering originality and energy, with extraordinary characters and a clever, thrilling plot … unputdownable' Toni Jordan, *Sydney Morning Herald/The Age*

'His keen eye for detail and vivid sense of place take us on another tumultuous and ultimately beautiful Australian journey. It is a novel Molly Hook herself would hail poetic and full of grace' *Herald Sun*

'A spellbinding saga of survival and transformation in WWII Australia … This is a wonder' *Publishers Weekly* (starred review)

'Achingly beautiful and poetic in its melancholy, *All Our Shimmering Skies* is a majestic and riveting tale of curses and the true meaning of treasure' *Booklist* (starred review)

'The book is alight with joyous candour, extravagantly beautiful writing and a series of intriguing jungle-set pieces' *The Advertiser*

'A magical realist epic grounded by a vividly evoked sense of place and a cheeky sense of humour' *West Australian*

GRAVITY LET ME GO

Also by Trent Dalton

Lola in the Mirror

All Our Shimmering Bodies

Boy Swallows Universe

Love Stories

GRAVITY LET ME GO

TRENT DALTON

THE BOROUGH PRESS

The Borough Press
An imprint of HarperCollins*Publishers* Ltd
1 London Bridge Street
London SE1 9GF

www.harpercollins.co.uk

HarperCollins*Publishers*
Macken House, 39/40 Mayor Street Upper
Dublin 1, D01 C9W8, Ireland

First published by HarperCollins*Publishers* 2026
1

A catalogue record for this book is available from the British Library

Hardback ISBN: 978-0-00-881083-2
Trade Paperback ISBN: 978-0-00-881084-9

Printed and bound in the UK using 100% Renewable
Electricity at CPI Group (UK) Ltd

THE GECKO STREET GAZETTE

Volume 1, Issue 12

Clementine Cork | *Editor-in-Chief*

Well, dear readers, it seems spring has sprung in the best street in the world and you loyal geckos have leapt into action. Thanks for all the letters and photographs you sent in to Gecko HQ letting us know what's been happening in your little patch of paradise.

Our cover story (page 3) this month profiles Gecko Street's oldest resident, Celia McIndoe from number 7. Would you believe me if I told you that Celia was born Celia de Boissieu in Lyon and at the age of 15 became known as the feistiest member of the French Resistance? Celia was once even a copygirl for the clandestine French Resistance newspaper *Combat* and worked for six months under the guidance of the esteemed editor-in-chief, Albert Camus. Read it here first!

Thanks to Harry and Miriam Barker from number 21 for their photo essay capturing the rare sighting of a prized regent honeyeater from their back deck. The endangered regent honeyeater hasn't been spotted by twitchers in Jubilee for at least two years. Turn to page 7 now to see why Harry and Miriam consider it the 'Olympic gold medal of Brisbane birdwatching'.

Recipe of the Month features Rita Munro from number 39 (also known as my amazing mum!), who shares her famous and ever-reliable Chunky Chicken Pot Pie recipe for your dining pleasure. And, keeping it in the family, don't miss this month's Street Beat (page 9), in which we exclusively reveal the cover and publication date of my dad's first book, *Anonymous Source: The Disappearance and Discovery of Tamsin Fellows*. At last, Noah Cork reveals the true story of how he came to be a key figure in the twisted murder mystery Australia can't stop talking about. The book is certain to set the true-crime genre alight and show everybody why my dad is the bravest crime journalist in the world!

ONE

Sometimes the trickiest thing about the digging is actually finding what you were looking for.

– Professor Lionel Rutledge, *Journalism Practices and Principles,* Second Edition, 1996

Feels like a medieval coin bag sewn from the skin of a forest witch. I'm forty-four years old but my scrotum must be eighty-eight. Zoom in on all my naked panic, if you think you can stomach it. Use that satellite-eye view from outer space. Zoom through that layer between humanity and the universe, look through that exosphere where atoms skip loose from the earth's embrace, see through all that blue-hued illusion and the shifting ghost clouds veiling Asia and North America, look further south, look all the way down here to the northern suburbs of Brisbane, Queensland, Australia – and find me in the thick of it, in the snowballing consequences of breathing, standing in the shower with the water off, fumbling for the pea-sized lump I've long accused of wanting to end my journalism career. I woke in the night with a knuckle-biting pain that felt like a fire ant was gnawing for seven seconds on my right testicle. Oh, this mid-life carnage. Oh, this puzzling pantomime. For the love of God, zoom out, zoom out, zoom out!

'You decent, Dad?' asks Erin, my fifteen-year-old daughter, fingernails tapping on the bathroom door.

'Far from it.'

'I left my brush on the sink.'

'Got my hands full, E.'

'With what? Wait. Backspace. *Deleeeeete.*'

Satisfied the southern Australian doom pea has neither grown nor shrunk, I open the shower door and reach for my towel. Four steps to the bathroom sink, face buried in a towel that smells like my gym socks. I run the towel through my hair and spot Erin's purple detangler brush resting by a crowded ceramic toothbrush holder. Stare at the bathroom mirror. The bathroom mirror makes no sense to me. Condensation formed by the heat from my morning shower reveals four words written across the glass by the finger of someone I love.

Gravity

let

me

go

*

In my bedroom now and it's a difficult choice between two lint-balled sports jackets hanging in a tightly packed built-in wardrobe. Lambrusco problems. The mission-brown one with elbow patches that my sister, Meg, calls 'professorial', or the navy-blue one with blue and white striped lining that Meg says makes me look like a 'keytarist' when I roll the sleeves up? I slip the blue jacket from its hanger and then I see the skeleton that is standing against the back wall of my closet. Breathe. The skeleton's white-grey dome-headed skull. At once dead and alive. Remain calm. Black voids for eyes. Exposed tooth roots fused to the jawbone. Don't panic. I slam the wardrobe door shut. Breathe. Step two paces to my right and open another wardrobe door. A full-length mirror hangs inside the door that opens to four storage shelves where Rita, my wife of twenty-three years, keeps her walking hats and her make-up boxes and her purses and a whole shelf up high reserved for bagged Christmas presents for Erin and her twelve-year-old sister, Clem. I slip the blue jacket on, sleeves down.

Do not look at her over there in the bed.

Do not look at her over there in the bed.

I scan my nose for skin cancers. Two years ago, a Canadian-born dermatologist named Roly Hudson carved a basal cell carcinoma from the centre of my nose, the way a forest witch might carve a worm from a poisoned red apple.

'Queenslanders,' Roly said with a sigh.

Things I pushed aside to write my first book: skin-cancer check-up; pea-sized scrotum-lump assessment; prostate check; taking time to remember Mum while I stand on the shores of Woorim Beach at sunset; wedding anniversary date night;

blood-sugar test; cholesterol test; Dad's birthday; bowel-cancer screening; eye test; hearing test; long-feared and increasingly urgent mental health assessment.

Look at her over there in the bed.

Look at her over there in the bed.

I slowly turn my eyes to my right and see a living skeleton lying on the queen-size bed that I share with my wife. The white sheet pulled up over the skeleton's bony kneecaps. Breast bones and ribs slowly moving up and down. This is an apparition, of course. Visible white-grey lumbar vertebrae bending to rest the spine on a pillow propped up against the bedroom wall. This is a curse. As my head turns to see it, the skeleton's head turns to see me. This is obviously some form of post-book-publication mental breakdown. Black and hollowed and pear-shaped orbits where its eyes used to be. Nothing for a nose. And then the skeleton tries to speak. It always tries to speak.

'*Ssssss ...*'

A single word. An 'S' word.

'*Ssssss ...*'

But the skeleton cannot speak. No muscles in her face. No skin. No throat. No voice.

'Tamsin?' I enquire.

Her mandible drops and her mouth opens and it can't close back up again and, almost embarrassed by her impairment, she sheepishly raises her bone right hand and forces her mouth to say the word she cannot say.

'*Ssssss ...*' she tries again and fails.

And I turn back to the wardrobe mirror. Slap my face. 'Youuuuuu. Fucking. Nuuuuuut.'

I whip my head back to the bed and the skeleton is gone. Just a white sheet curled across the mattress. White pillow propped against the wall.

I'm in phase four of the publication process, after writing, editing and publishing: full and private psychological disintegration. My publishers told me to expect a certain sense of upheaval in my life. But nobody said anything about skeletons in my bed. And in my car and under my writing desk and, yes, in my fugging closet.

Her name is Tamsin Fellows. The subject of my debut. The subject of my concern. Six months ago, I chose to follow a trail of breadcrumbs dropped by a cold-blooded killer, which led me to Tamsin's skeletal remains. It was the scoop of a lifetime. I've been seeing her skeleton in my head ever since. Just seein' things, I suspect. Just feelin' things. Fear and uncertainty and what's that dreadful 'G' word again? Rhymes with wilt. Rhymes with spilt. Rhymes with everything bad and good *you built.* Natural on-the-job post-trauma response, I suspect.

I only work freelance, so no PTSD pension plan for yours truly, I'm afraid. I once interviewed a Rat of Tobruk for *Wartime*, the Australian War Memorial magazine. Two-thousand-word profile, $1.20 per word. This veteran recalled the sticky Egyptian midnight he spent in a desert outpost. His unit spotted a German ammunition transport at the bottom of a valley and quickly obliterated the vehicle with an extended blast of anti-tank gunfire, which saw the truck combust in an ammunition fireball that blew the young German driver's body to within thirty metres of my wearied magazine subject. Our thoughtful Rat spent fifteen interminable minutes of that night at his post pretending not to hear the hopeless wailing of the German driver as he called for his mother: '*Mutter, Mutter, Mutter*'. The Rat could not bring himself to let the German soldier die alone in the dark. He shouldered his rifle and scurried out from his post to the voice in the night and found a young man, no older than eighteen, whose entire pelvic region had been blasted into three or four pitiless strips of skinless flesh connecting his torso to his legs. The boy had been severed. Almost perfectly halved, thought the Rat. He held the boy's hand until he mercifully died, repeatedly whispering something that started with 'S'.

'Sssssshhh.'

For his compassion, the Rat was rewarded with a curse. Every time he cut something in half, every time he saw something perfectly severed in two – a chicken breast, an orange, a sponge cake, a plank of wood – he would see that German boy's eyes staring at him from a desert valley floor in Egypt.

My curse was once a fifty-two-year-old mother of two who was raised in Goondiwindi and prayed in the Jubilee Uniting Church at least twice a week. I think she's upset with me. I think she's upset because I obsessively and publicly explored every facet of her ordinary suburban life and extraordinarily macabre murder in my first book, which hit the shelves three days ago and retails for $34.99 in all good bookstores across Australia and New Zealand.

I tug on a jet-black nose hair that's hanging from my left nostril like the rope on a church bell and whisper necessary words to the wardrobe mirror, fearlessly eyeballing the blue-eyed man solely responsible for all that is terrifying and wondrous in my life.

'Noah Cork, you jittery, loose-tongued kook,' I say. 'You're just seein' things. No big deal. People see things all the time.

She's just a vision in your head. The phantom sum of your fears, is she not? So stop fearin' things and you'll stop seein' things. Do not pussy out on me now. You have done nothing wrong. The scoop of your lifetime landed in your letterbox and you did what you were supposed to do. You did your job. So you go out there now and tell the truth. The palatable truth and nothing but the palatable truth. No more skeleton chat, you hear me? No more descriptions of how dry and brittle her bones were. They can't stomach that shit. You can't either. You ready? You ready, you witch-sacked, pipsqueaky, scaredy-cat hack?'

I summon a response to myself.

'No.'

*

Erin stands at the kitchen bench in her school uniform reading *Frankenstein* for her Year 10 literature class and eating a slice of toast with cream cheese and cut crescent moons of an avocado that hasn't fully ripened.

'Victor Frankenstein is a douche,' she says.

'Why?' I ask, wrapping my fingers around a stainless-steel cafetière resting by the toaster. It's still hot: Rita left enough brewed coffee this morning for me to pour into my favourite mug, the big white one that Clem bought me for Father's Day. Darth Vader raising a celebratory pint of beer: *Best Dad in the Galaxy*.

'Total deadbeat dad,' Erin says. 'Guy wants to play God. Guy makes himself a monster-slash-son. Then he abandons the monster the moment the monster starts acting a little monstrous.'

'Not the first bloke to create something he was repulsed by,' I say.

I step across to the fridge for milk. Clem's stuck the latest edition of the *Gecko Street Gazette* to its door with a One Direction magnet. Poor kid's got the journo bug. The story habit. She collects stories the way other kids in our street collect seashells and Barbie dolls. Kid's got it bad. I still remember the look on her face when I told her about the little newspaper empire I created from my own bedroom as a boy on Bribie Island. The *Bega Street Bugle*. The first three editions were handwritten in blue Kilometrico pen. Then I found my first typewriter, a $15 Lifeline thrift shop 1978 Olympia SM9, and the *Bugle* went pro. 'So many suburban stories, Clem,' I said. 'So little ink.'

The *Gecko Street Gazette*. Volume 1, Issue 12. Thirteen typed and stapled A4 pages of feel-good stories exhaustively sourced from the neighbours in our street. Fresh off the press, which is to say I can't imagine how much of our printer ink she's wasted publishing that World War II–era grainy black and white cover shot of Celia McIndoe, who lives alone in the red-brick cottage down the street.

'You read Clem's latest edition?'

'Bravo, Daddio,' Erin says. 'Looks like you made yourself a monster, too.'

'I think it's inspiring what she's doing.'

'Just what the world needs,' Erin says, 'another nosy journo.'

'She's reminding us what a beautiful street we live in,' I say. 'Poor kid's had to hear about a few of the darker realities of the world lately. Maybe she's reminding herself what a beautiful place the world can actually be.'

'Beauty is a lie,' Erin says.

Sometimes over breakfast Erin likes to pretend she's Sylvia Plath.

'Beauty might be the only truth we humans have left in this world,' I suggest.

'Not the whole truth.'

'And what, pray tell, is the whole truth, according to Erin Eliza Cork, age fifteen years and seven months?'

'The world is sick and dying and cannot be saved, and anybody who doesn't see this truth is either wilfully ignorant or profoundly stupid.'

'So pessimism equals intelligence?'

'All the smartest people in the world are miserable. All the dumbest people in the world are rapturous.'

First sip of coffee. I briefly consider whether raising a pessimistic teenager is a parental job well done or yet another sign of my fatherly wheels falling off. Second sip of coffee.

'We see what we believe, Erin,' I say. 'Sometimes it's impossible to see the truth of the world as it is, because we can only see the truths of ourselves.'

'Says the guy who found a dead woman's bones in a kitchen oven and then spent six months putting together a book about it so the world could be further reminded of how sick it truly is.'

Erin smiles, pats my left shoulder on a job well done. There's a fifteen-year-old's humour in there somewhere and I'm sure I'll find it after midnight when I can't get back to sleep.

'Is that what you think I've done?' I ask, sounding more urgent than I intended.

'What?'

'Do you think my book only feeds the nation's insatiable hunger for darkness?'

'I dunno, Dad. You're assuming I read it.'

'I gave Tamsin a voice.'

'And I'm sure she appreciates it.'

My daughter snaps her *Frankenstein* shut and places it face-up next to another book resting on the kitchen bench. Her dad's book. Her father's first published work of longform non-fiction. *Anonymous Source: The Disappearance and Discovery of Tamsin Fellows* by Noah Cork. The book's cover features a red tin suburban letterbox beneath the title. We, the Corks of number 39 Gecko Street, Jubilee, Brisbane, in fact, have a canary-yellow tin letterbox. Same shape as the cover's letterbox, a thin yellow pole supporting a rectangular container the size of a shoebox – with a keyless rear mail flap and an arched, open-ended compartment on top, where, every month, neighbourhood kids stuff a rolled Harvey Norman catalogue big enough to keep a baby warm in winter. The book's publishers wanted to feature our real letterbox on the cover but, in the interests of privacy, Rita insisted on a stand-in, coloured red.

'Is it not enough that the world knows what suburb we live in?' Rita asked. 'Now you're gonna tell them what our letterbox looks like, so every creepy true-crime obsessive across Australia can come crawling through Jubilee in search of Noah Cork's life-changing letterbox.'

I remember what I said about that. 'I won't bend for this butcher, Rita,' I replied. 'A journalist never retreats from the truth. He charges towards it like a knight on horseback, knowing truth is an armour too strong to be penetrated by fear.'

'I fear the hole in your arse was just officially penetrated by your head,' Rita shot back.

Rita knows I don't actually believe that stuff about journalism and truth and fear. Rita knows that relentless hunger-quashing fear is the reason I rise in the morning.

'A red letterbox will work,' my publishers reasoned. 'You know ... red like Tamsin's blood.'

It's not the letterbox on the book's cover that draws one's eye. It's the object shown resting ominously inside it that's supposed to stir the average bookshop browser's imagination. A small wind-up music box, no bigger than a box of matches. The music box's rust-coloured machinery is uncased and exposed: the spring housing, the winding shaft, the hand crank that even a child's fingers would struggle to grip, a metal drum dotted with strategically placed protruding pins that spin and pluck at a small vibration plate that reminds me of the stainless steel comb Rita used to remove Clem's head lice in Year 2. What can't be shown on the cover, of course, is the giddy music box tune that severs my brain and freezes my tempered-glass heart every time I lay my eyes upon that book cover.

Truth is no armour.

Fear walks through walls.

Like memories.

Like curses.

Erin says something that I don't catch because I'm taken again by the miraculous existence of my book, allowing myself a moment to reflect upon the speed with which the book was put together in six brief months and the blurred fever-dream transitions between thinking and typing and editing and printing.

'Whassat, honey?'

'I said I was thinking about the meteor shower.'

'What meteor shower?'

'*What meteor shower?*' Erin repeats. 'Last night's meteor shower.'

I remember now. The biggest meteor shower to ever soar across the Australian continent. An asteroid the size of San Francisco Bay was cracking and shattering as it swung by the fierce sun, leaving a burning dust trail that the planet I call home passed through last night. Rita and the girls were going to lie on their backs in the yard to watch it.

'Weren't you lying beside Mum when it showered?' Erin asks.

'No.'

'That's so funny,' Erin says. 'I assumed you were there and were just being quiet.'

'I wasn't there, Erin.'

'Where were you?'

'I don't know.'

That's not the whole truth. I suspect I was flipping through a copy of *Anonymous Source*. I suspect I was marvelling at how quickly I'd written it. I was lost in it. Who knows how long I lay on that bed before I nodded off?

A broken asteroid orbiting the sun.

A scotch grey mosquito circling my big fat head in my sleep.

I slide Erin's *Frankenstein* five centimetres across the bench so its paperback edge rubs the spine of *Anonymous Source*.

'How about that,' I say, gently elbowing Erin's ribs. 'Mary Shelley and Noah Cork, united at last by the time-hopping miracle of literature.'

Erin scoffs. 'Settle down, Dickens. Let's see if anyone's still reading your book next week, let alone two hundred years from now.'

Erin scrapes the crumbs from her toast into the waste bin beneath the sink. 'Ants, Dad,' she announces. 'We got ourselves a whole ant civilisation. They're building 7-Elevens an' shit down here.' The bin liner has been fashioned from a bag that once housed twelve rolls of two-ply Sorbent toilet paper, and it's brimful this morning of used tissues and lamb forequarter bones and plate-scraped peas and carrots covered in cold gravy. The colony of tiny honey-coloured ants is busily building its empire out of its headquarters in a cup-cake wrapper encrusted with hearty boulders of uneaten choc-banana muffin.

'Weren't you on clean-up last night?' I ask.

'No, I did a double on the weekend,' Erin replies. 'It was Clem's turn.'

I tie the bag, hold it out from my waist, slugging my coffee. A fat cockroach leaps from the bottom of the swollen bag onto the polished wooden kitchen floorboards and runs for its life. It's half a metre from the sanctuary of the crack beneath our fridge when the rubber sole of Erin's black leather Clarks school shoe squashes it into a glob of caramel-coloured insect gut paste that looks, I realise, like the crunchy peanut butter resting on the middle shelf of the fridge.

'When are we gonna dynamite this house and build a new one?' Erin asks.

'Where do you suppose I might acquire six-dozen sticks of dynamite in Brisbane?'

'I know a guy in Logan.'

'What sorta house did you have in mind?'

'I dunno, something with taste and two bathrooms.'

'You'll get your second bathroom.'

'When?'

'I'm guessing about six months after you move out.'

I pat my book the way one might pat a boy scout who has just received a bugling badge. 'I'll get this book out,' I say. 'Then I'll pay a draughtsperson to draw us somethin' with taste and two bathrooms.'

Erin reluctantly accepts a goodbye kiss on the thick brown hair that hangs over her right ear and I dig my right hand into the purple glass fruit bowl that holds everything from car keys to USB sticks to coins to a pair of black 3D cinema glasses.

'Mum take the Corolla?' I ask.

'She's parent helper for Clem's excursion to Pioneer Village,' Erin says.

I hate myself for forgetting this.

A whole truth splitting through the world as I see it. You forget such things because you are as ambitious as you are self-absorbed. You have placed your lurid and public exploration of Tamsin's demise above all other facets of your own existence, from physical health and mental stability to school excursions and pest control. Bravo, Noah Cork, you made another monster. You are the modern Prometheus. You're basically Victor Frankenstein without the flair for science. But don't let this truth interrupt your busy morning. Hurry now. Don't wanna be late for your special book event. This book matters!

I take the keys for the Yaris and tuck the copy of *Anonymous Source* under my arm.

'You on the 804 bus?'

Erin nods.

Remember the rules for life, kid. 'Be kind and don't do drugs,' I say, one foot out the front door.

'I promise to be kind,' Erin says.

A thought strikes me and I turn back to Erin, a fist on the front door handle.

'Hey, by the way,' I say. 'The words on the mirror this morning. That a Boygenius song or somethin'?'

'What words?'

'The words on the bathroom mirror when it got all fogged up by the heat. *Gravity let me go.*'

'I have no idea what you're talking about,' Erin says. 'I didn't have a shower this morning. What did you say the words were?'

'*Gravity ... let ... me ... go.* One of Clem's singers maybe? Taylor got any songs called that?'

'Don't think so. Maybe Mum wrote it?'

I ponder this possibility for three seconds. 'Nah, doesn't sound like Mum,' I say.

'Oh, is that right, Dad?' Erin replies. 'And what exactly does Mum sound like?'

TWO

The stories are everywhere. In the cracks of the crowded cities, in the empty deserts of the outback. There are a thousand stories up and down your street. Which story do you want to tell?

– Rutledge, *Journalism Practices and Principles*

Hercules and his Monday morning shit on my slice of the Gecko Street grass verge. Nothing about my presence inhibits the dog's seamless bowel flow. Eyes on me, big rear legs bent to punch out two thick bars of solid bullmastiff monster dog dung. I look around for signs of his owner, Jim England, my neighbour three doors down. Nowhere to be seen, of course. Between the first and second bar, I take two fast steps towards the dog, like some desperate Yosemite hiker trying to scare off a bear.

'Git,' I spit.

The large and imperious man-dog snarls and lifts the right side of his mouth to show three canine teeth the shape of Sydney Opera House. He's a beast so at ease I almost expect the smug reprobate to pull out a *New Yorker* and settle in for a third turd emancipation. Mercifully, he finishes up and saunters back, head down, towards his home.

'Manners, Hercules,' I say, as he ambles by me. 'It's a simple matter of *manners*. I don't shit on your dog mat. You don't shit on my lawn.'

Hercules refuses to speak, as always.

'Spoilt brute.'

Monday is bin day in Gecko Street. By the left side of our carport are three garbage bins on wheels. The recycling bin with the yellow lid, the garden waste bin with the green lid and the black general waste bin with the red lid, into which I drop the Sorbent bin bag full of ants. When I wheel the general waste bin out to the gutter, I see three cars parked in front of the home of our neighbour at number 37, Carol Myers-Ryan. Carol's daughter marches from her mum's open garage, carrying an old red ceramic bedside lamp, something from the 1970s, shaped like a butternut pumpkin. Carol is a widow with three daughters all aged in their fifties and all possessing names starting with the letter 'D': Daphne and Dominique and the woman carrying the red lamp. Her name is something like … *Dale*? She slides into the driver's seat of a silver Audi and rests the lamp in the leg space of the front passenger seat. Dale doesn't start the car. She rests her head back and closes her eyes for roughly ten seconds. When she opens her eyes, she stares through the Audi's windscreen directly at me. She gives me a half-smile and starts her car. She's halfway through a U-turn when she brakes the Audi and lowers her window to address me.

'Just so fuckin' unfair, isn't it?' she says.

I don't know why she says this, but there is an intensity to it that forces me to offer a face of sincerity and understanding.

I follow my heartfelt nod by folding forty-four years of collected wisdom and experience into one brief verbal expression. 'Mmmm,' I say.

Dale nods appreciatively and slams her accelerator. The Audi's tyres screech as she completes her U-turn. She's driving well above acceptable suburban speed limits when she passes a visibly dismayed Jim England, Hercules' owner, who's walking in a casual grey business suit and tie to the silver Triton utility parked in his driveway. Jim has a lump on his forehead that looks like a marble has embedded itself in his skull. He's a lifer cop, so I guess it could be a bullet slug. A tall, rangy man in his late-fifties, he's got a salt-and-pepper flattop haircut and thick gym-toned arms and legs. As he slips into the driver's seat, he catches my eye.

'Your Demigod of Doo-doo just shat on my lawn again, Jim,' I shout.

'Accidents happen, Cork,' he says, shrugging and doing his best not to smile.

'Care to inspect the crime scene, Detective?'

'Relax, Cork, I'll grab it when it's dry,' England says, pulling out of his driveway. 'And please tell Rita that her chunky chicken pot pie was sublime.'

*

Hercules didn't always shit on my lawn. Me and that beast used to be buds.

I met Jim England two days after we moved into Gecko Street. It was sunset and Jim was walking Hercules' near-identical roid-munching brown and charcoal bullmastiff predecessor,

Samson – rest in peace. Rita saw him from afar and told me that Jim was a cop of some twenty-plus years who'd served Jubilee for fifteen years before rising to the role of Senior Detective, Homicide Investigation Unit, Queensland Police Service.

'So our little "Pillar of Jubilee" has come back home!' Jim said, still holding his dog's leash as he hugged my wife.

'You know how it is, Jim,' Rita said. 'No one ever really leaves Jubilee.'

'Jim,' he said.

'Noah,' I said.

The grip of Jim's handshake could have cracked a coconut.

Jim told us that if we ever had any concerns in our street we should drop his name to the good people of Jubilee Police Station, down where tea-coloured Teaneck Creek runs under Drake Bridge and Wicker Road, the main route into Jubilee if you're driving from the Brisbane CBD. 'Not like you'll ever need to,' Jim said. 'Safest suburb in Brisbane. Not just because we got the best cops.' He laughed, running his right hand along Hercules' smooth, short coat. 'We got the best people, too. People like our Rita here.'

Jim told us he'd been raised a cat man. Samson, he said, had been the idea of his husband, Hua England, a gifted sports therapist at the Jubilee Health and Racquet Club. 'Now I'm your standard suburban doggy daddy who spoils his kid rotten,' he said. 'At home, at least, I'm always playin' "good cop".'

Jim asked me what I did for a living, while forgetting to ask Rita the same question.

'Journalist,' I said.

'Yeah, who ya write for?' Jim asked.

'I freelance,' I replied.

'What sorta things you write?'

'All sorts of things. Crime, mostly.'

'Oh yeah,' Jim said. 'Would I have read anything of yours?'

I shrugged my shoulders and shook my head.

Rita spoke for me. 'You remember the series the *Courier-Mail* did on the Mary Younger murders?' she asked.

Mary Younger was a Sunshine Coast beautician who'd served her two children, Ashlee and Samuel Woods, aged eight and six, bowls of choc-chip ice cream laced with ground temazepam pills before suffocating them in their sleep.

'Yeah, read every word,' Jim said.

Rita pointed at me. 'He won a Walkley for it.'

I was the first journalist to link the Mary Younger murders to a Eumundi-based charismatic leader named Mason Frears, who had penned several self-published books that drew loosely upon the beliefs of the Church of Jesus Christ of Latter-day Saints to speak of an impending global apocalypse. Frears had convinced a growing group of Sunshine Coast hinterland followers – including Mary Younger – that a great war of good and evil was about to be waged between two opposing armies, one named 'The Clean' and one named 'The Infected'. Interviewed extensively by investigating police, Mary Younger continually gave the same rambling and unhinged explanation for her actions: 'All clean now, all clean now, all clean now, all clean now.'

After the popularity of the Younger series, the newspaper offered me a double-page spread every second Saturday, devoted to the investigation of any long-cold murder case connected to my state: 'True Crime Uncorked with Noah Cork'. See what we did there? If it was bleeding, it was leading in my pages.

Ariella Tucker, murdered, age twenty-nine, 1996. Somebody fed her body to a fenced pit of saltwater crocodiles in the Proserpine Reptile Park. Dennis Nicol, murdered, age sixty-six, 2003. A Rubyvale, Central Queensland, gem fossicker who was found sitting in his armchair with a beer by his side and his right temple crushed by the ten-pin bowling ball that was sitting half a metre from his blue and swollen bare feet. Saanvi Ghosh, murdered, age thirty-three, 2001. A glamorous married Holland Park real estate agent with two lovers, both acquitted. Stabbed seventeen times in her home and left for dead on her living room floor. The killer used Saanvi's blood to paint a rough sketch across the living room wall of a man with six arms holding balls of fire in his palms. Police believed this man to be Agni, the Hindu god of fire, protector of humanity with a special responsibility to safeguard the home. The 'True Crime Uncorked' pieces were grisly, sensational and widely read, and covered the payments on our new home in Jubilee.

'Well, you won't find no crime stories here in Jubilee. Us cops drive to Glen Forrest for those,' Jim said, pointing towards Salem Road, which connects Jubilee to its neighbouring suburb.

'Thanks for the tip.'

Jim smiled at Rita again and nodded back at me. 'You married a very special girl, Noah.'

Something about his tone made that line sound less like an observation than a revelation.

'Don't I know it, Jim,' I said, nodding back.

Jim made a clicking sound with his tongue that caused Samson to shoot his head up at his owner.

'Samson?' Jim said, smiling. 'Can you say, "Welcome to the best street in Australia"?'

Samson appeared to nod to Jim, then turned to us and barked a seemingly considered sentence that might be transcribed as: *Worrrrlf worrrrlf hurrumph growwwlk worrrrlf.*

'Gooood boy,' cooed the big strong cop.

The canine poop paddies only started appearing on my lawn about three years ago. Around the same time Jim stopped talking to me. Around the same time I broke the Brandon Curtis story.

Nothing sensational about my pieces on Brandon Curtis. Those pieces were plain ol' flat and tragic. First Nations man, age nineteen, arrested for public drunkenness after exiting the Spotted Cow Hotel in Toowoomba, in Queensland's Darling Downs. Six hours later he was found dead in a watchhouse cell, with signs of bruising to his neck and skull. My investigations, detailed in a story I wrote for the *Courier-Mail* that paid a healthy one dollar per word, led to the two attending police officers, Constable Craig Auster and Constable Kurt Lawson, being dismissed from the police force. It was also around this time that every contact and not-so-anonymous source within the Queensland Police Service that I had spent years – and countless long-lunch pints of beer – cultivating, suddenly clammed up like a Russian spy fresh out of kill-pills.

A crime journalist lives and dies by their police contacts. There were no more firsthand source quotes from retired cops who'd once been happy to talk to me about cold cases. It seemed like the entire Queensland police community had taken an unspoken collective vow to let my freelance journalism career slowly bleed to death. My lucrative bimonthly true-crime spread in the *Courier-Mail* died with it. When I lost my crime pages, an online weekly Australian media-diary-slash-digital-jizz-rag named *The Spike* – edited by a man called Brian Solomon, who physically resembles Tasmanian cricketer David Boon, or Joseph Stalin if you squint – placed an item in its 'Whispers and Moans' page suggesting fallout from my Brandon Curtis pieces had caused influential and unmerciful ex-journo colleague and Queensland Police Chief Media Liaison Officer Georgia Long to send a group email to every station commander across the state, unofficially outlawing all police communication forthwith with one Mr Noah Cork.

'It seems the Long arm of the law has put a cork in Mr Cork's career,' Solomon squealed.

The same day that piece dropped, I found four thick brown dog lumps on my nature strip entwined in such natural and grand architectural balance that I should have boxed them up and mailed them to the Guggenheim Museum.

*

The sound of a nail gun fired twice draws my gaze to the house directly across the street from ours. The Cavendishes of number 40 Gecko Street – Jonathan and Rose and their only son, Sebastian – are building upwards and installing an in-ground swimming pool in their backyard. Builders in hi-vis polos and Balmain Tigers football shorts with tanned legs and steel-cap boots splattered with paint and grouting and cement mix surround the structure.

A lanky sixteen-year-old punk with a schoolbag emerges from Jon and Rose's garage. A walking Clearasil ad. Dyed blue curtains of hair and a black T-shirt that features a fist giving the world the middle finger above the words 'FuKKK AmeriKKKa'.

'Seb,' I say, by way of morning greeting. The kid doesn't turn his head, just places his AirPods in his ears and walks right on by. Thought as much. No harm in trying.

Sebastian Cavendish used to be the best and only friend Erin had on our street. Five years ago, he knocked on our door so often that we had to talk to his parents and arrange a system whereby Rita would text Rose Cavendish and tell her when Erin had completed her homework and was free to skate, sing, shoot hoops and trace clouds with her fingertips in the middle of the street. I was wary of Seb at first, but then he told me that he'd enjoyed one of my crime features in the *Courier-Mail* and I immediately told Rita that eleven-year-old Seb Cavendish represented a positive future for post-Snapchat Australia. Then Erin, in her first year of high school, spent the majority of her September school holiday break with her new best friend from school, Holly Ricketson. Seb met Erin and Holly in the street one day and suggested the three of them ride their bikes to the Sunrise Grocer on the corner of Wicker Road and Cedar Street because he wanted to buy a family box of the grocer's borderline-miraculous chips with chicken salt and gravy. After they'd devoured the family box of chips, the youthful and adventurous trio sneaked into an apartment-block construction site six doors up. I've only ever heard Erin's side of the story about what happened next, and Erin's side of the story is the one I believe.

Seb was feeling left out of a conversation Holly and Erin were having inside a half-built unit, so he climbed up some scaffolding to an exposed and unwalled second floor, where he found a stack of bricks and began building a kind of Jenga tower. Holly and Erin sat cross-legged on the concrete slab directly below the scaffolding, Holly looking up over her shoulder occasionally at Seb as she giggled about him crushing on his longtime neighbour across the street. Erin was staring straight into the eyes of her new best friend when she saw a falling brick slice Holly's right ear open then smash her right collarbone. Erin glanced up and saw a look on Seb's face that she later described to her mum and dad as 'zombie sorrow'.

Holly needed surgery on her ear. The collarbone injury caused her to miss selection trials for the Queensland junior representative hockey team, for which her parents believed she was a walk-up start. Seb maintained that it was all an accident, that he'd pushed over the Jenga tower of bricks just to see how they would fall and hadn't considered how far the bricks would spread. Holly's parents – both lawyers – didn't believe that story and embarked upon a breathless legal investigation into the matter, in the hope of proving it was a senseless act of attempted murder by a deeply disturbed young man. Unfortunately for Seb and his family, the investigation revealed that Seb had recently been referred to a psychiatrist for possible signs of childhood schizophrenia.

Rita didn't share my anger at Seb's parents for not previously disclosing this information to the parents of Seb's closest street friend. 'What did you expect them to do, Noah,' Rita reasoned, 'put a sign on the front gate saying, *Beware: possible schizophrenic child inside*?'

The families settled out of court. Jon and Rose Cavendish covered the heavy costs of ongoing cosmetic surgery while Holly mercifully clung to her dream of becoming the world's first palaeontologist-slash–*Vogue* cover model by the age of twenty-five. Jon and Rose were running a small cinema advertising videography business – CineFix – and the surgery costs very nearly wiped that business out. Holly stopped talking to Erin over the incident. In turn, Erin stopped talking to her old friend Seb.

'Maybe it's best you don't come around here anymore, Seb,' I said, the last time Sebastian Cavendish knocked on our front door. The kid was fighting tears in his eyes when I closed the door on him. Rita came home from work two hours later and we poured ourselves white wines and sat around our dining table and dutifully commenced arguing about my handling of that moment as we stared at the grey polished-concrete apple table ornament that has been an abiding presence during all of our largely unsolvable marital conflicts.

'So, another door closes on another Aussie kid with a tricky brain?' Rita said. 'Is that who we are, Noah?'

'No, Rita, that's not who we are. But we're also not the kind of parents who leave their children exposed to dangerous relationships.'

'Dangerous?' Rita said. 'You honestly think Seb is dangerous? What if it really was just a stupid accident?'

'Yeah, well, I guess we'll never know,' I said. 'Whatever the case, Seb Cavendish's tricky brain is not my problem to solve, and it's not my daughter's problem to solve. Poor Seb is a Cavendish family problem, Rita. He's not a Cork family problem. We've already got enough problems for one family!'

I slugged my wine and concluded another triumphant closing argument for the defendant left of the concrete apple. 'Can't choose yer family. Can't choose yer neighbours. But you can choose your bloody problems, Rita.'

The nail gun fires twice again and I'm drawn back to the hi-vis labourers in the house across the street. I wonder how many extra bathrooms the Cavendishes will be able to fit in all that newfound space between all those posts and joists and studs and trusses. I turn to study my own house for a moment, and wonder in which aisle of Bunnings one might locate six dozen sticks of dynamite.

*

We live in a three-bedroom, low-set renovator's night-sweat in a cul-de-sac that slopes up towards a high-fenced Queensland Urban Utilities water tank, a round concrete structure the size and shape of an Ancient Greek amphitheatre, overlooking a small patch of grassed public parkland with a lone brilliant red poinciana tree shading an army-green timber picnic table.

Technically, our home belongs to Rita's parents, Deborah and Bill Munro. Deb and Bill still live in the two-level, five-bedroom brick home on Birch Street, Jubilee, that Rita grew up in, a four-minute drive from our house. Deb and Bill bought the Gecko Street house in 2005 as an investment. I told Rita I was not at all the type of insecure and prideful husband who would take issue with making interest-free house payments to his parents-in-law every month, and approximately ten seconds after saying this realised I was exactly the type of insecure and prideful husband who would take issue with making interest-free house payments to his parents-in-law every month. Rita – ever-wise, ever-prescient – was worried I would grow to resent her parents. 'Don't be silly,' I said. 'When do we move in?'

Rita and I tell people the house is 'post-war', but 'post-habitable' is a truer descriptor. 'Mid-shit' is truer still. We always told ourselves we were lucky to buy into a suburb as leafy and safe as Jubilee. This, given certain events of the past six months, now feels like an awfully funny thing to have told ourselves.

Our box-shaped house is on the high side of the street. When it storms, our flat tin roof feels the full force of heavy summer rain. Rita and I moved in two months before what people in Jubilee simply refer to as 'The Storm', the suburb's infamous microburst of 13 December 2009, which damaged four thousand homes and turned at least thirty to useless mountains of bent tin, broken brick and splintered timber. This all happened, mercifully for us and them, pre-kids. It was a Sunday afternoon and I was almost at the end of *People of the Book* by Geraldine Brooks when the biblical storm barrelled into Jubilee like a drunk and vengeful gunslinger bursting through a set of swinging saloon doors in search of the outlaw who shot his mum in the heart. The thing was malicious and horrifying. Loud and violent and bullying. Nobody makes repulsive monsters better than God.

The first wave of the blast shattered three of our windows and pushed a leopard tree onto the roof of our backyard garage. I thought the storm was easing when I shuffled momentarily out of the bathroom where Rita and I had taken shelter. I walked to the sliding glass doors that opened from the living room onto our backyard and used my phone to film a kind of swirling storm dome that seemed to have encased the entire suburb. Our house appeared to be in the eye of the storm, where all was oddly and briefly silent and still. It was as if God had instructed the storm to leave our house alone for the remainder of the blast.

Rita said later that she thought she was standing in a waking dream. The interior walls of the dome were a strange and alien blue-green colour, and it looked like numerous spotlights were flashing at us from deep within the grey storm. Rita studied the scene from behind my left shoulder. She whispered two words: 'It's beautiful.' Then we heard what I later named 'the devil thrum'. A sound that was at once silent and deafening, it reverberated in your soul, not your ears. *Thrrrrrruuuuuuummmmmmm*. It was the sound of Mother Nature losing her temper, like she was reverting back to her rebellious teens, all her awkward elemental limbs made of electricity and fury waking on the wrong side of the bed. *Thrrrrrruuuuuuummmmmmm*. And that was precisely when the storm intensified in an instant and tore our old roof from its fixings. Peeled it off right above our heads like it was the lid of a yoghurt tub, leaving it curled and hanging carelessly from one side of our first and only home. Our home without a ceiling. Our shoebox without a lid.

Then hail and wind and rain and sticks and twigs and leaves and missile-like gumnuts swept into our living room via the open roof, smashing glass in family photo frames and ripping cheap art prints from the hallway walls like a disgruntled interior decorator whose bill we forgot to pay. I watched an olive-coloured vase – a wedding gift from my Aunt Leanne – as it was lifted from the dining room table and thrown across the kitchen before shattering against the pantry door. It felt like our home was being terrorised by invisible poltergeists. We ran to shelter in the bathtub, but it was occupied by a thick branch from a snapped and now potentially deadly eucalypt. We ran to our main bedroom and commando-crawled under our bed, praying the storm wasn't powerful and angry enough to upturn our queen-size Tasmanian oak frame and hefty latex mattress. Fortunately, it was dark and safe under there and we stayed put for fifteen minutes as the storm banshee-screamed around us. I remember Rita and I were lying flat on our bellies, under the bed, with our arms down by our sides, rubbing shoulders. Sardines in a can. I was five centimetres from my wife's face as the storm of the century swirled above us and I realised at one point that Rita's eyes were the same blue-green colour I had just seen inside the storm that was destroying our home. I remember how she shook her head and laughed at that terrifying storm. And I remember what she said.

'I love you so fuckin' much, Noah Cork.'

*

From the nature strip I pick up four fallen leaves that once belonged to the ageing frangipani tree that has spread over our letterbox and one wall of our carport. The undersides of these leaves are covered in a yellowy-orange dust that looks like curry powder. I will get this book out and then I will find out which mysterious disease causes frangipani leaves to be dusted in curry powder.

I stuff the dead frangipani leaves in the green waste bin that's already filled with the palm fronds that keep falling off the trees that form our garden's front boundary. Turn my head up to a set of black motion-sensor spotlights affixed to the top right corner of our carport's white timber fascia board. Hidden at the base of these lights is a surveillance camera that captures a 150-degree view of the area surrounding our canary-yellow letterbox, twenty-four hours a day.

I stand beside the letterbox and wave at the camera. 'You there, Constable Baker?' I say. 'Top o' the mornin' to ya.'

I breathe deep and exhale, then turn to the letterbox. Three small pot plants circle the pole beneath it, each holding a white and yellow glossy-leafed peace lily rising to my kneecaps. What our house lacks in space and comfort and expensive furniture, we make up for in pot plants. Rita loves them and we have more than fifty dotted inside and outside the house. I honestly don't know what she sees in those plants or why she needs so many. Fuchsia sun kisses by the sliding glass doors off the living room. Port-wine magnolias and elephant-ear plants fighting for space on the red-brick porch. Potted pink and green flamingo flowers lining the thin concrete path that splits the backyard lawn on its way to the rusted Hills Hoist. Potted fiddle-leaf figs by the dozen. Rita says there are few troubles in this world that can't be soothed by tending to a potted fiddle-leaf. And we do have our share of troubles. Money troubles. Marriage troubles. Good ol' fashioned anonymous murderer troubles. Ain't no troubles quite like those.

Most years, I have trouble clearing $50,000, even though I supplement my freelance journalism with occasional work as a real estate copywriter who can describe rear deck views to Mount Coot-tha in no less than forty-seven ways: sweeping, grand, panoramic, boundless, scenic, commanding, commandingly scenic, scenically commanding, and so on. Rita earns roughly $60,000 a year working three days a week as a communications officer for the Australian Red Cross while shouldering the lion's share of Erin's and Clem's school needs. She makes most of the school lunches. She does more school runs than me. She told me she was happy to be the parent helper on excursion day to Pioneer Village. I told her I would make it up to her one day. I told her that one day I was going to write something long and important that was going to land with a bang and not a boing or a blah or a thud. Something that was going to hit big and pay off our house and maybe pay for an extension to our main bedroom. We could have a parents' en-suite with his and hers sinks, and Erin and Clem wouldn't have to rub elbows with their dad when they brush their teeth on school mornings.

When the police leads and leaks dried up, Rita encouraged me to move away from true crime. Rita wears the rose-coloured glasses, just like Clem. She said it was a good thing the leaks had dried up. She said all those ghastly murder stories were taking their toll on me. She said the stories were changing the way I saw the world. She said she'd seen a sense of child-like wonder in me when she'd first met me. She said I had a spark. A certain light inside me that she worried might go out for good if I spent too much time barging into shadows with my Spirax notepad. She said one day all that darkness was going to swallow me whole, drag me down into some place black and deep that I wouldn't be able to crawl back out of. She challenged me to write about subjects that interested me and did not feature murder or death or blood or bloody murderous death.

Every spare moment I had in our daughters' early primary school years was devoted to the writing of two non-fiction books, never published. One book was called *Cloudbuster* (with apologies to Kate Bush) and was the true story of a crippling seven-year drought in the western Queensland town of Charleville that climaxed in 1902 with the arrival of an eccentric English meteorologist named Clement Wragge, who promised to make the heavens weep by 'busting' gathering clouds with the force of six eighteen-foot-tall conical 'vortex' cannons firing flasks of gunpowder at the sky. The other book, *Serious Moonlight*, was a microscopically detailed history of the week in 1983 when David Bowie visited the small sheep-farming town of Carinda, in western New South Wales, to shoot the video for 'Let's Dance'.

Funny how life works. Funny how a rainbow can burst once in a lifetime from a busted cloud and lean down to plant a kiss upon your pale white Australian arse. We fell behind on our house payments around Christmas last year. The most embarrassing moment of my adult life was telling Bill Munro over a schooner of XXXX Gold in the Jubilee Tavern sports bar that I was flat broke and would need a pause on the house repayments for the whole October-to-December quarter. I managed to sell a two-thousand-word story in early December to the *Courier-Mail* about a loose theory that Jack the Ripper was buried in Brisbane's Toowong Cemetery. The seventy cents per word I received covered Christmas presents for the girls, with enough left over for half a leg ham from Aldi. By February, Rita and I were talking seriously about selling the house back to her parents. Bill offered his own advice. 'You got the gift of the gab, Noah,' he said. 'You're a born snake charmer. A natural salesman. How else could you get all those stories outta people the way you do? For years you've been sellin' invisible spaces in a newspaper. People were once happy to buy those spaces from you, but now they're not. So what does a salesman do when his product stops sellin'? Well, he finds another product to sell. Bloke like you could sell anything. Real estate. Used cars. Persian rugs. You just gotta swallow your pride and pick up the megaphone.'

But then, six months ago, two days after Clem's twelfth birthday, at approximately 9.20 a.m. on a warm and silent autumn morning, I walked to our letterbox and opened the rear mail flap to find a small bronze music box sitting upon an anonymous letter penned by a killer. And I guess it was in that precise moment that a home renovation suddenly seemed possible for us.

This morning, the letterbox is empty. I'm as disappointed as I am relieved by this, and I hate myself for feeling this way.

A voice travels along the nature strip and lands in my right ear.

'No surprises this morning I hope, Noah?'

It's our next-door neighbour at number 41, Ellis Towers. He's out on the nature strip forcing a bag of rubbish down inside his general-waste wheelie bin so that its red lid can fully close.

'No, Ellis,' I say. 'No surprises this morning.'

Ellis takes this comment, as he always does, as an invitation to engage in neighbourly conversation.

'Any updates from the boys and girls in blue?' Ellis asks, tip-toeing across the nature strip to stand beside me at my letterbox.

Ellis still talks with a faint northern England accent, despite the fact he moved from Leeds to Brisbane with his family when he was six years old.

'Nothing lately,' I reply.

My neighbour wears blue and red plaid slippers, striped blue and white pyjama pants and a tourist T-shirt for the town of Albany, Western Australia, featuring the silhouette of a humpback whale breaching before a half-circle of orange sun. The slightest bit of morning sunshine turns Ellis's seventy-three-year-old face tomato-coloured.

'Had a visit from a friend of yours yesterday,' Ellis says.

'What friend?'

'An old journo friend of yours,' he says. 'Ricky Waverly.'

'Ricky Waverly isn't my friend, Ellis,' I say. 'He's a muckraking freelance web writer who would trade his mum's beating heart for a scoop on the Tamsin Fellows murder.'

Ellis pinches his bottom lip. 'Oh dear,' he says. 'Seemed nice to me. You weren't home, so he came knockin' on my door, wonderin' when you'd be back.'

Ellis's thick mop of grey-white hair has been slicked back by a fine-tooth comb. That hair was copper-coloured when we first moved into Gecko Street. Maybe Ellis combed all the copper out of it. Clear, thick plastic spectacles with square frames. Big row of front teeth, like he's tucked six pieces of Juicy Fruit under his top lip.

Ellis and his wife, June, recently returned from a caravan trip across Australia. Their twenty-foot Snowy River caravan with bathroom and queen bed is now for sale on Facebook Marketplace and sitting on blocks in their front yard.

'You didn't tell Ricky Waverly anything did you, Ellis?'

Why do I see the worst in Ellis? Why do I see the worst in people? Didn't always. Just lately, I guess. Ellis is the biggest gossip in our street. Ellis is kind and thoughtful. In the sixteen years we have lived beside them, Ellis and June have been nothing but informative, protective, generous with cake and beef burgundy, frequently wary of neighbourhood thieves posing as tree loppers, and deeply loving of our two daughters, whom they babysat regularly before Erin was old enough to babysit herself. Ellis is a bigoted bore.

Ellis shakes his head, confidently. 'We did get talkin' about that dreadful Tamsin business, but my lips were sealed, Noah.' He runs an imaginary zip along his lips, gives me a thumbs-up. 'Well, mind you,' he continues, 'I did share with him my own personal theory as to who's the who in our beloved suburb's very own whodunnit.'

'And what theory is that, Ellis?'

'Freddy Mercer,' he says, nodding his head.

'Tamsin's brother?' I ponder aloud. 'You think her brother did it? He was driving an earthmover in a Kalgoorlie gold mine in November 2022.'

Ellis leans in, whispers, 'So he says.'

We've got one genuine detective in our street and a dozen amateur sleuths, keyboard gumshoes like our dear ol' Ellis here, convinced he's gonna crack the big Jubilee murder case and bask in the warm afterglow of a thousand digital raised thumbs.

'You and Ricky speak about anything else, Ellis?'

'Nah,' he says. 'All I told him was what a joy it's been to have you and Rita and the girls as neighbours for the past sixteen years. Don't worry, I told him there was slim chance of tying Noah Cork down for a natter. "Busiest man in Jubilee," I told him. He had a laugh when I told him that in *sixteen* years you've never once had the time to come downstairs and see my suburbs.'

Ellis finally retired last year from part-time lecturing in social sciences at the University of Queensland. He calls himself a human geographer. He says he specialises in anthropogeography. 'Anthropology meets geography,' he explains. 'We study the spatial relationships between human communities, cultures and economies.' This fondness for spatial relationships has driven Ellis to spend some three decades plus change of his life creating the most extraordinary dioramas of every Brisbane suburb he has ever lived in.

I should come clean. Ellis, I have not visited your workshop to see your dioramas because I am not the slightest bit interested in your life. You are, in fact, the very representation of everything I am afraid of becoming if I live the rest of my life in this street.

In sixteen long years of neighbourly small talk I have heard – some might say endured – Ellis Towers' breathless descriptions of his supposedly uncannily lifelike miniature models of four different suburbs, apparently occupying every bit of floor space in the downstairs workshop of the sprawling six-bedroom, two-storey brick house that he and June have called home for forty-one years. The Sandgate of his youth was recreated on a painted polystyrene foam base the size of three ping-pong tables, complete with a Sandgate Town Hall filled with teenaged dancers in 1950s swing dresses, plastic-model barefoot boys feeding bread to black ducks in the Einbunpin Lagoon, a pair of hatted lovers kissing goodbye at Sandgate train station, and old women in the Woolworths carpark pushing miniature shopping trolleys filled with miniature bags of potatoes and frozen peas and corn. He donated the Sandgate diorama to the Sandgate Historical Society, then set about building a diorama he entitled *Stafford 1972–1976*. Stafford is where Ellis and June – a fellow student and rising star of the University of Queensland's School of Social Sciences – bought their first home in 1974. He spent half an hour one afternoon by our wheelie bins describing the miniature Our Lady, Queen of Apostles Church, Stafford, where he married June in 1972. A week later he told me about his miniature re-creations of the Stafford Skate Centre, where June had sold hot dogs and popcorn part-time and taught kids how to roller-skate backwards and not break their tailbones, and the red-brick heritage-listed Stafford State School, where three of Ellis and June's seven grandkids were educated.

'Of course, I did tell him how busy you've been lately with the Tamsin business and the stress it's put you under,' Ellis says.

'You told Ricky Waverly that I was stressed?'

'Well, I just mentioned how difficult it's been for June and me to witness the strain you and Rita have been put under by all this murder-mystery-notes-in-the-letterbox stuff and how hard it's been for us to hear you and lovely Rita having your barnies every second night.'

Out with it, Cork. Spill the beans. Gimme a fucking break with your goss, Ellis. Gimme a fucking break with all your hokey suburban myopia, Ellis. You have spent your whole life walking in a fabrication of an illusion unfolding inside a collective Australian dream that died on arrival. You are living in a past that your memory paints prettier than your present. You are a figurine in your own living diorama, pinned to this manicured nature strip by the nails in your feet. You are a piece of plastic with foam where your blood and guts should be. You are ornamental. You are décor. Would you even have the slightest awareness of the darkness that lives in the cracks of your nostalgia?

'It actually sounds to me, Ellis, like you and Ricky Waverly had quite the chinwag,' I say.

Ellis allows himself a chuckle. 'Yes, well, we did have quite a laugh about the time you and I tried to remove that nasty

Chinese elm from your backyard and couldn't get it out and I had to pay to get it removed because you were so skint.' He gently elbows my shoulder. 'Guess you won't be so skint when that book starts sellin', huh?'

Ellis laughs and the laughter makes him fall into a brief coughing fit that swells his neck and reddens his face. There's a chesty wheeze in that cough that I haven't heard before. I look at his eyes and see, for the first time, the pink-purple bags under his lids.

'You don't look the best, Ellis,' I say.

He wipes his mouth with the back of his right hand and collects his breath. 'Well, you're no Robert Redford yourself, Noah, if we must discuss looks.' He cleans the edges of his nostrils with two fingers. 'Got some kinda chest thing I can't shake. June said I've got long Covid. I said it must be pretty bloody long, indeed, because I've had a gammy chest since the nineties.'

Ellis donated the Stafford diorama to the Chermside and Districts Historical Society, then set about recreating the suburb of St Lucia, home of the University of Queensland, where he studied and worked for more than half a century. Much to Ellis's dismay, I'm yet to visit his workshop to stand with him and enjoy a tawny port as we soak in the wonders of what he has regularly assured me is his masterpiece: an ongoing miniature-model re-creation of our very own suburb, Jubilee.

'But I can see the real thing every day, Ellis, just outside my door,' I told him recently.

'But nobody sees Jubilee like I see it,' Ellis said. 'You won't believe your eyes, Noah. The whole suburb is down there.

Eight by seven metres of tireless replication. Spearwood Reservoir to the edge of Hazel Park. Every street, every corner store, every school classroom, rendered in microscopic, dioramic detail.'

He told me about the many hours he'd spent recreating Gecko Street. Scale-true. Colour-true. Window-true. Every house in the street. He told me about the trouble he went to finding the right paint colours to create the little plastic pumpkins for the thriving backyard pumpkin patch that Ellis and June have tended for decades. He also told me about the extra time he'd spent on his miniature version of our house.

'Wasn't easy,' he said. 'Not a whole lot of house to work with is there, Noah?'

'No, Ellis,' I said. 'Not a whole lot.'

I turn to walk towards my car. Ellis places a gentle hand on my arm.

'Noah, do you mind if I ask you something?'

He seems to be keeping his voice low so other neighbours in the street can't hear him.

'Sure, Ellis, you can ask me anything.'

For forty-one years, from the living room window of his home at number 41 Gecko Street, Jubilee, Ellis Towers has studied the spatial relationships of the neighbours up and down his street. 'Ordinary non-academic types have another term for such anthropogeographic study,' Rita once said. '*Snooping*.'

Ellis leans in to me. 'It's about Rita,' he whispers.

A brief and alarming pulse of rage shoots through my belly like electricity at the thought of Ellis Towers having anything whatsoever to tell me about my wife that I do not already know.

'What about Rita?'

Ellis adjusts his spectacles at the top of his nose and the frames brush his bushy auburn and grey eyebrows that are so wild and untamed they remind me of a rockhopper penguin Rita and I saw during our honeymoon in New Zealand. He's then momentarily distracted by something over my left shoulder.

'Good morning, Dale,' he says. 'We wish you every comfort at this difficult time.'

I turn to find another of Carol Myers-Ryan's daughters carrying a cardboard box marked *Photo albums/newsletters* to a parked forest-green Kia Sorento.

'Thank you, Ellis,' the woman says. 'And thank you all for the flowers.'

'One couldn't have wished for a finer neighbour,' says Ellis.

The woman nods in agreement and we watch her slide into her car and drive down the street towards Wicker Road.

'I thought her name was Daphne,' I say.

'Who's Daphne?' Ellis asks. 'There's Dale, Dominique and Diana.'

'What the hell happened to Carol?'

'You mean you haven't heard?'

'Well, I've been a bit distracted with … you know, Tamsin and everything …'

'Of course,' Ellis says. 'Tamsin and everything. You know, Noah, someday you might consider focusing as much on the living as you do on the dead.'

'Thanks for the advice, Ellis. What the hell happened to Carol?'

'She's dead,' he says, matter-of-factly. 'Perhaps you'll find her more interesting now.'

Ellis resets his spectacles on the bridge of his nose, leans in close to my ear. 'Hit an' run,' he whispers. 'Can you believe it? Thursday morning. She was staying at Diana's house in Indooroopilly. Doing her morning exercise, a simple sunrise stroll. She crosses Lambert Road, heading to the golf links. Boom. Clipped by a speeding car. Bastard left her for dead in the gutter. Honestly, this city has had it. An unequivocal, inextinguishable bin fire of a place.'

'Jesus,' I whisper. 'They find the driver?'

'Nup,' Ellis says, lifting his pyjama bottoms an inch up his waist. 'But I'd be looking for the next car full of black kids souped up on meth and heading for Goodna.'

'What the fuck, Ellis?' I exclaim.

'What?'

'Or the next pale, white, coke-snorting lawyer from New Farm? Or the next white alcoholic kindergarten mum from Sherwood?'

Ellis sniffs. 'Adult crime, adult time, I say.'

I scratch my head and turn towards Carol's house. Gone for a walk. Gone forever. 'It's just so fuckin' unfair, isn't it,' I say.

'Precisely, Noah,' Ellis says. 'It's deeply unfair. That's precisely the problem. The balance is out. Too many humans not playing by the rules of life anymore. Morality cheats. I've made my peace with it. Evil prevails. Darkness took home the chocolates. The world is an unequivocally monstrous place and I honestly don't know why anyone would even walk out of their front door these days.'

Rainbows, Ellis. Rainbows. Rare regent honeyeater birds appearing after two years to tell you they exist. Dragonflies that land on your left shoulder just to hear your secrets. A leather

sky with a population of one fluffy cloud shaped like Africa. 'Did you speak to her at all this morning?' he asks.

'I had gym this morning. She was gone before I got home.'

Ellis again squeezes his bottom lip between two fingers.

'She went jogging early this morning,' I say, breaking my rule about never elaborating on our personal lives for gossips. 'She runs all the way to Glen Forrest sometimes. She was probably just exhausted, catching her breath.'

Ellis scratches his head. 'Yes, probably,' he says. 'Except there was something so peculiar about the way she had her arms out. She reminded me of a little girl making angels in snow. But her arms weren't moving. She was just lying perfectly still in her joggers.'

'Stretching,' I say. 'She was stretching her arms after exercise. Don't see what's so concerning about this, Ellis.'

'Yes, but then she stood up,' Ellis says. 'I watched her put her arms out by her side. She looked for a moment like Christ on the cross or something. And then she looked slowly down at her feet as though she was waiting for them to do something.'

'To do what exactly, Ellis?'

'I don't know,' he says. 'I have no idea what she was thinking. That's why I'm telling you what I saw.'

I slip into the Yaris. Ellis steps further into our carport.

'I think that's something her physio told her to do,' I say. 'She's got a crook neck.'

'No, I really think this was something entirely different, Noah,' Ellis says. 'This was something far more … *mystical*.'

I laugh and shut the car door, then start and rev the engine as I bring my window down. 'Mystical,' I say, considering the word for a moment. I shake my head and start to reverse out of the driveway. 'Nah, that just doesn't sound like Rita.'

'Oh, is that right, Noah?' Ellis replies. 'And what exactly does Rita sound like?'

I slam the brakes, lean my head out the window. 'What did you just say?'

THREE

Dig deep, but please dig lightly. In digging up aspects of the story, it is not uncommon for the journalist to dig up long-buried aspects of themselves.

– Rutledge, *Journalism Practices and Principles*

The blue and yellow council bus. The moss-green council bus stop. The red and white post office box. The black and green climbing fort in Thornberry Park. The sunburnt builder mixing concrete on Marg Hancock's front lawn. His apprentice in black sunglasses rolling a smoke. Something wrong with that young man's face when he stares at me. It's a skeleton's face. He puts his smoke between his skeleton teeth and lights it with a skeleton right arm, his hi-vis orange and silver work shirt hanging loose over flimsy skeleton limbs. The boy takes a long drag and the smoke rises out of his eye sockets.

Ellis is wrong about this world. He has to be. We see what we believe. So what if I keep seeing skeletons everywhere I look?

A young mum wheeling a mountain bike out of her garage, clipping a bicycle helmet to her own chalky grey-white skeleton head. Her daughter flashes by her on a BMX, schoolbag slung over her skeleton shoulders and her skeleton spine, skeleton feet pushing hard on the pedals.

A butterfly with iridescent blue wings flies from the shelter of a swamp she-oak on the corner of Jaffa Street. Rita said something to me about butterflies the other day. I was thinking about Tamsin and the book and everything else, so I didn't quite hear all of what she said, but she was making some random observation about how I used to be the kind of guy who would look at a butterfly and ponder how many wonders that butterfly would see today. Now I'm the kind of guy, Rita said, who looks at a butterfly and wonders how many days the butterfly has left to live.

The yellow and black Bobcat in the yard of that house on the corner and the ridge of raw soil waiting for a retaining wall. For less than seven seconds, as I turn right out of Gecko Street into Hartnell Street, I ponder the meaning of it all and what it's all for and where it's heading. What are we all trying to achieve here in this sunbaked idyll? Some eighteen thousand Australians starring in a suburban daydream unfolding in the valley between Mount Parsons and the Baker Range. Only twenty minutes' drive from the Brisbane CBD, but only fifteen minutes' drive from waterfalls and wombats in the mountain forests that fringe our suburb to the north. Jubilee was once a residential locality named Spearwood. In 1977, the Queensland Place Names Board renamed it Jubilee in honour of Queen Elizabeth II's Silver Jubilee marking twenty-five years in the big gold chair. It was the links with Her Maj that caused every 1970s wag living outside Jubilee to suggest its residents walked with antique sterling-silver spoons wedged between their arse cheeks. Of course that's ridiculous because everybody knows that most long-term Jubilee families replaced all their antique cutlery years ago with the Villeroy & Boch twenty-four-piece setting for six.

The Jubilee Laughter Club is in hysterics this morning in Clifton Hill Reserve, and it's a busy morning at the community shed on Burralong Street. Beginners Mahjong, 10 a.m. Dovetail wood joinery class, 11 a.m. Classics book club, noon till tipsy. Rita and the girls adore this place. Erin once told me out of nowhere – we were skipping stones at Flatrock, the name we've given to a quiet corner of Teaneck Creek, not far from our house, where a cathedral of bamboo trees bend and sway over a white-grey bedrock so smooth and flat that you could host a dinner party on it – that she looks forward to the time when she's a hundred years old and she returns to Jubilee and sits in a swing in Jefferson Park and reflects with her aged but still handsome and attentive husband, Harry Styles, on the happiest days of her life. Rita says the only reason the endless trees don't speak in this place is because they don't like to brag. Rita says Claude Monet turns up in Jubilee every day at 5 p.m. to paint us a pink-orange sunset over Mount Parsons. Rita says Boreas, Greek god of the north wind, turns up at 5 a.m. in winter to blow crystal-coloured dew across the park grass so that 6-a.m. kids in quality leather soccer boots can write messages with their heels: *Jubilee Diamonds r 4 eva.*

Kind and decent people here in Jubilee. Not the murdering kind. Clean cars and consciences here. Not the killing and chopping up bodies kind. Big hearts and open arms and minds. Eat, love, vote and pray to a god half the suburb still believes in. House pride, green pride, rainbow pride, First Nations pride, even if your best chance of seeing a real-life blackfeller in Jubilee is still at the local Catholic school during NAIDOC Week. The neighbourhood Facebook page – The Jubilee Junction – is in a pickle this week. Tonia in Poplar Place thinks she just inherited an Arthur Streeton landscape painting from her dead grandfather, Connell. Or is it a Walter Withers? James Reynolds in Primrose Close is once again cursing the single greatest threat to Australian social and cultural life: skinny and drunk white kids aged thirteen to seventeen on skateboards. Brad Lofthouse in Willow Street has another strange request: 'Anybody got a metal detector or a bayonet I can borrow?' It's Hazardous Waste Week at the Ferny Grove Resource Recovery Centre. Kerry Updike wonders if Mr Sheen is hazardous. 'Mr Sheen never hurt nobody,' says Greg Ford from Chidgey Street. 'He's a fine, upstanding man.' Henry Kneebone in Ball Close has a bottle of homemade orange whisky marmalade to give away to the first person who can answer this riddle: 'I am the beginning of everything and the end of everywhere.' Jan Ford in Duhig Street has found a deadly eastern brown snake in her laundry sink. And the 'Who Killed Tamsin Fellows?' chat thread is alive and kicking.

> Travis79: *My second cousin was a homicide D in Fortitude Valley for 24 years. His unit had a motto they used to live by – eleven times outta ten, it's the husband. Anyone else sense that Neil Fellows' alibi is about as dependable as my sharts after a night at Taj Bengal? He says he was in a forest in Maleny looking for tree wood to carve one of his tables from. But the only person to corroborate this is his own younger brother. Three words: Blood. Is. Thicker. #thingsthatmakeyougommmm.*

SarahKMartinez: *Got this homicide data straight from the Uniform Crime Reporting (UCR) Program of the FBI: 'Of the offenders for whom gender was known, 89.3 per cent were males. In incidents of murder for which the relationships of murder victims and offenders were known, 54.3 per cent were killed by someone they knew (acquaintance, neighbour, friend, boyfriend etc); 24.8 per cent of victims were slain by family members. Of the murders for which the circumstance surrounding murder was known, 42.9 per cent of victims were murdered during arguments (including romantic triangles).' Stats don't lie, folks!*

CSIrene: *Why's nobody talking about all the satanic material found in that horror house? Numbers on the walls. The devil signs and the book on the kitchen bench? The number 764 painted everywhere? Look into it people. Online global predator cult with proven links to satanism.*

LadyGagGag: *RE: Linedinchalk98's thread from yesterday about why Tamsin's killer chose Noah Cork to communicate with. Hot take: Noah Cork orchestrates the whole horror show. Bum journo. Career in the toilet. He gets a bright idea. Kill some random woman. Bury the body. Two years later, dig the body back up. Leave a trail of breadcrumbs to the body for yourself to find. Write a bestseller! Boom. Now there's a story!*

Murder was found six months ago in Jubilee and now it can't be unfound. It was me who found it. A faceless murderer helped me find it. My one-way pen pal. My anonymous source. Finding murder in Jubilee is like finding an anchovy in your strawberry sundae. A worm in your wedding cake. Murder now lingers in our town like a travelling-circus freakshow that won't leave until the townsfolk square a debt they know not how they accrued. Instead of dancing elephants and bearded ladies we got thick-lensed cameras and attractive TV journalists and front-page newspaper headlines. Instead of tightrope walkers and acrobats we got street-corner crosses to a national news anchor. Tamsin has changed my town. Tamsin has changed me.

I play the message Georgia Long, police media liaison officer, left on my phone: 'Are you fucking insane? I just read your little three-car-pile-up of a book. Please rest assured I'll be using the pages to wipe my arsehole after my morning coffee shit. Do you have any regard whatsoever for police process? Did you guys even legal this thing? You need to call me immediately. If I have any say in the matter, you will never speak to another Queensland police officer again in your life. You are hereby banned from all my pressers. Don't even bother turning up. You are fucking done writing crime in the state of Queensland. Call me right fucking now, you absolute fucking moron. I am going to bury you, Cork ... supposing this fucking psycho butcher pen pal of yours doesn't bury you first.'

I delete Georgia's message and focus on the road.

As I drive through my suburb, I see it all in painted and glossed polystyrene. The trees, the houses, the people. Each and every one of us just another painted resin figurine in Ellis Towers' sprawling basement diorama. I picture my little red Yaris moving among diecast Honda Civics and Ford Rangers parked along fake plastic streets, and passing fake plastic dogs barking behind fake plastic fences. I see my miniature self through the open driver's-side window of that miniature model

Yaris and I see that my face is horrifically distorted. Ellis has painted only one eyebrow over my eyes and hasn't bothered to paint a mouth on my pink-cream face.

My phone rings and *Megatron* flashes on its screen, my childhood nickname for my older sister, Meg, based upon the deadliest antagonist in the Transformers universe, Megatron, tyrannical robot leader of the Decepticons, whose delightful motto is 'Lesser creatures are the playthings of my will.'

'Hey, Megs.'

'Hey, sailor boy.' Meg's childhood nicknames for her little brother, Noah, were always boat themed. 'Any updates from the cops?'

'Nothing lately.'

'How are my girls?'

'They're good. Erin thinks Victor Frankenstein's a douche. Clem and Rita are panning for gold in Fernvale. What's up?'

'Dad's crook.'

'He's got emphysema, Meg. He's perpetually crook.'

I turn left out of Burralong Street into Boodua Street.

'More crook than usual, I mean. It's flu or somethin'. Not Covid, but he sounds awful on the phone. Was wondering if you had a chance to drive up to Bribie and see him?'

'Not the best timing for me, Meg. You know … Tamsin and everything.'

'Of course, Tamsin and everything.'

'I'm trying to get this book out there now, you know. Give it a chance to take off. You know, I think this one could really fly. Do you think you could go up?'

Meg sighs the way she sighed in our teens whenever I asked to borrow her *Nevermind* cassette.

'Noah ... like ... fuck, bro, I get busy, too, you know. I can't carry all Dad's shit on my own.'

'I know. I know. I'm gonna get this book out and then I'm gonna get back to all the things I've let slip over the past six months, I promise. Trust me, sorting Dad's shit is very high on my to-do list.'

Meg leaves a long pause before speaking again. 'You all good, little bro?'

Her serious voice. That's the do-you-ever-think-about-Mum voice.

'Yeah, I'm good, Megs.'

'You still seein' skeletons in your closet?'

I ponder the question for a moment. Tell her, Cork. Spill the beans, ya big weirdo. Tell her it's worse than ever. Tell her it's getting to the point where you considered mentioning it to Dr Cracknell but you chickened out because you knew he'd tell you to stop. You knew he'd make you let it all go and take a trip to Burleigh Heads with Rita and the girls. And you couldn't possibly let it all go, could you, Cork? Because how will you ever know how the story ends, if you let the story go?

'Nah,' I say. 'I was just being silly about all that. Just talkin' in metaphor, probably. Like, sometimes I think about Tamsin so much that I feel like I can see her skeleton everywhere I look.'

'Yeah, right,' Meg says. 'Metaphor. Well, just remember to take a break every now and then. Probably not healthy to be thinking about a dead woman every second of yer life.'

I turn right out of Boodua Street into Lamb Street and that's when I nearly kill Jean Rooney.

I slam the brakes and study eighty-seven-year-old Jean through my windscreen as she walks barefoot in her nightgown along the very centre of Lamb Street.

'Fuck,' I say.

'What is it?' Meg asks.

'Jean Rooney's gone walkabout again.'

'Who's Jean Rooney?'

'I'll tell you later. I gotta go, Megs.'

'Yeah, of course you do, Captain A-hole. Later.'

Meg's line drops abruptly from the car's Bluetooth connection. I check the time on my phone. It's 8.53 a.m.

'Fuck,' I say, pulling the handbrake on the Yaris. I leave the car running as I race to catch up with Jean Rooney, who's walking wide-eyed and smiling in the middle of the street.

'Jean,' I say, placing a gentle hand on her right shoulder. 'Jean. You're walking in the middle of the road again. *Jean*.'

Jean stops, turns to me. Her face is pale yellow in places and her sapphire-blue eyes are wet and glistening. She has the hazel-grey-coloured messy hair of a preschool boy rolling in a sandpit. Hanging by a black strap around her neck is a silver and black Canon Rangefinder camera from the 1970s.

'You're a nice man, aren't you? What's your name, nice man?'

'Jean. It's Noah Cork. We met last week. We had this exact conversation six days ago. You said you were walking down to the creek under Drake Bridge. You said Kenneth was waiting for you down there. You said you were gonna take his portrait with your camera.'

'Kenny,' Jean says. 'We call him Kenny. He's waiting for me under the bridge. He made scones. He's wearing his wedding suit.'

'I'm sorry, Jean. Kenny's not down there today. Come on, let's get off the road.'

Jean holds her camera up with both hands and points it at me, trains her eye through the viewfinder and adjusts the manual zoom on a device that possibly stopped working three decades ago. 'I'll take your photo, if you like?' she says.

I smile for the camera, my head tilted to the left side, eyebrows raised. She taps the shutter-release button with her right forefinger, but the camera doesn't go click, only Jean's mouth does. 'Click,' she says.

I lead Jean off the road. Feels as if the bones in her wrist could crack like honeycomb between my fingers. I'm glad she follows willingly this time. We shuffle back the way she came, some four houses back along Lamb Street to her small dark brown brick and timber home at number 14. I scroll through the contacts on my phone to the name *Gwyn Rooney*.

'Yeah, Gwyn. It's Noah Cork here. I called you last week about your mum. Yep. Yep. I just nearly ran her over in the middle of Lamb Street.'

It takes me five minutes to convince Jean Rooney to follow me up three brick steps, through her front door and into her kitchen. Her walls are covered in framed black and white photographs. Travel pictures. Portraits of old men in India or Nepal, maybe, their faces covered in holy ash and sandal paste. Italian coastlines and cafés. Beautiful people on mopeds. A series of framed photographs of suburban Australian corner shops.

'You're a great photographer, Jean,' I say.

She stares into a framed black and white image of an altar boy walking down the aisle of a church with an open Bible in his palms.

'Pictures speak a language anyone can understand,' she says.

It takes me another five minutes to eat the Iced VoVo biscuits she hands me on a thin ceramic saucer and drink the weak black tea she pours me. Jean asks me why I can't stay long, and I tell her that I have to get to an important event this morning for a book I've just had published. She asks me what the book is about and I say it's about a music box that I found earlier this year in my letterbox.

Jean says Kenny likes music. She says he likes the songs of Loretta Lynn and Karen Carpenter. I tell Jean that 'Superstar' is quite possibly my wife's favourite song, but Jean doesn't remember it, so I hum the tune for her and then she says she's now even less familiar with the song than she was thirty seconds ago. We're discussing Kenny's favourite spread for scones – homemade rosella jam – when Jean's youngest daughter, Gwyn, hurries down the hallway into the kitchen.

'Gwynnie,' Jean says, beaming.

Gwyn turns to me and grips my right shoulder with a firm hand. 'Thank you so much,' she says.

'All good,' I say. 'Listen, I've got a pretty important book event to get to … so … I'm just gonna …'

'Of course, of course,' Gwyn says. 'This is the Tamsin book, isn't it?'

'Yeah … Tamsin and everything after,' I say.

'Any new leads from the police?' Gwyn asks.

I shake my head.

'Have they looked into Alejandra Ruiz?' Gwyn asks.

'The house cleaner?'

Gwyn's eyebrows rise as she nods her head and fiddles with an earring in her left ear.

'I strongly doubt her picture's on the police cork board,' I say.

Gwyn nods her head. 'Hmmm,' she offers. 'She cleaned our place for six months. Never trusted her. We think she stole my engagement ring.'

I stare at Gwyn for a long moment, pondering her sanity as I move towards the hallway entrance.

Jean's voice breaks the silence. 'We need to find that killer,' she insists, banging her fist on the dining table so hard she spills her tea. 'We need to find him. We need to find him for Greer's sake.'

Gwyn places a calming hand on her mother's shoulder. '*Tamsin*, Mum,' Gwyn says. 'Her name was Tamsin Fellows. She lived in Fletcher Street. Not far from Mary's house, remember?'

'No, Greer lived in Todd Street.'

'Oh, Mum.'

I wave at Jean and Gwyn with two open palms. 'I'm off,' I say. 'All the best to you both.' And move to make my exit.

'Noah,' Jean calls after me.

I turn back to face her.

She stands from her seat. Smiles at me. 'You do know Kenny's dead, don't you?' She looks at me as she places the lid on the Tupperware container full of Iced VoVos. I picture a resin figurine miniature of Jean walking along the middle of Lamb Street in Ellis's workshop diorama.

'Yeah, Jean. I know.'

*

I take Wicker Road, Waterworks Road and then Musgrave Road almost all the way into the Brisbane CBD, my eyes frequently turning to the time on my phone. The State Library of Queensland is hosting a national true-crime writing and podcast festival called 'Crime Scene Australia', featuring a mix of local and international true-crime writers and, new to this year's festival, victims of crime and relatives of criminals. One of the biggest drawcards this year is Shannon Schmidt from North Dakota, the only daughter of Herman Schmidt, aka the Beast of Bismarck, who was jailed for life for bludgeoning seven people to death with a pickaxe across the course of eight months in 1998. Shannon commands an entry fee of $55 to hear her talk about what her father was like around the family breakfast table and how much he adored watching his daughter open presents beside the Christmas tree.

Festival organisers have kindly found space for a free Q & A event to mark the launch of *Anonymous Source: The Disappearance and Discovery of Tamsin Fellows*. It's scheduled to start at 10 a.m. and it's now 9.48 a.m. as I drive down Countess Street to take the William Jolly Bridge to the south side of the Brisbane River, where the State Library is tucked between the Gallery of Modern Art and the Queensland Museum. I was supposed to meet the Q & A's facilitator, Chelsea Lasrado, Professor of Media and Cultural Studies at the University of Queensland, in the green room at 9.15 a.m. for our introductions and a session debrief. I pull into the State Library carpark, running over some dot-point mental notes I've prepared in anticipation of several inevitable questions from Professor Lasrado.

Noah Cork, first things first, please allow me to express my gratitude for what I consider to be the most compelling true-crime book I have read in at least a decade.

Be humble with such praise. Grateful, but not hungry-cavapoo grateful.

Noah, please tell us why it was so essential for you to tell the story of the disappearance and discovery of Tamsin Fellows?

The scoop of a lifetime landed in my lap. Well, my *letterbox*. (Pause for laughter.) Public's right to know etc. Darkness beneath the suburban inner-north daydream. Stealing back the narrative for Tamsin? A voice for the voiceless? Careful, dickhead. Not good to speak for the dead.

Your family must be so proud of you, so bravely dropping yourself into the story the way you have. Why is it so important for journalists to put themselves into their stories in situations such as this, however reluctant they may be?

The reader must come first. Self-preservation be damned. A journalist never retreats from the truth, Chelsea. He charges towards it like a knight on horseback, knowing that truth is an armour too strong to be penetrated by fear.

How wonderfully put. So powerful and true. Well, Noah, could you please take us back to the beginning? How was it exactly that you came to be used like an innocent pawn in the sick and twisted game of a cold-blooded killer?

Start at the letterbox. Then Spearwood Reservoir. Then church. Then Monaco House. The kitchen. The cops. The consequences. Go easy on the descriptions of the bones. They can't stomach that shit. I don't think you can, either.

*

The Crime Scene Australia program co-ordinator Veronica 'Ronnie' Bird is waiting for me at the entrance to the library auditorium. She wears a pink and black Childish Gambino T-shirt tucked into a tiered white cotton peasant skirt with sky-blue Doc Martens boots. Ronnie hugs a folder of papers to her chest, holds a wireless microphone in her right hand.

'You always cut things this fine, Mr Cork?'

'I'm so sorry, Ronnie. I couldn't seem to get myself out of Jubilee.'

'My Aunt Maeve never could, either,' Ronnie whispers. 'She died there, aged ninety-one.' She rushes me through a side door that leads to the auditorium's backstage area.

'You've got a full house. Well done, you!'

'Full house? No shit?'

'People can't get enough of this Tamsin Fellows stuff. You sure you know what you got yourself into?'

I'm sure I love Rita Munro.

I'm sure I love Erin and Clementine Cork.

I'm sure of nothing else in my life.

'No,' I say, weaker than I intended.

'Well, you're next in to bat,' Ronnie says. 'Just keep your eye on the ball and watch for the bouncers. I'm gonna go introduce you guys. You'll find Professor Lasrado standing side of stage.'

As Ronnie takes the stage and welcomes the auditorium audience to the festival, I circle behind a royal-blue stage curtain and silently step up behind Professor Lasrado just in time to hear her speaking to a young male sound technician manning a lighting and sound monitor, left of stage. 'I wanna shoot my past self for agreeing to do this,' she says to the young man with the headphones around his neck. 'Compelling story, no doubt about it. But the writing is simply awful. Reminded me of one of those woodchopping competitions at the Royal Show. Hack, hack, hack, hack!'

The professor's words are a momentary axe through my softwood heart. I cough once before making my introduction. 'Professor Lasrado,' I say. 'So sorry I'm late.'

She wears a smart chocolate-brown suit with a lavender scarf around her neck. Her perfume is her scarf in olfactory form. She bumps my fist instead of shaking my hand.

'Traffic?' Professor Lasrado asks.

'No,' I say, taking a deep breath, 'long story.'

She holds up her uncorrected proof copy of *Anonymous Source*. 'Not as long as your book, I hope.'

Ronnie Bird hollers into her microphone on stage. 'Please welcome to the stage … Noah Cork and Professor Chelsea Lasrado!'

Ronnie wasn't lying: full house. The audience applause is welcoming and affirming. Chelsea beams a smile and I beam one just like it. We sit in aqua-blue armchairs that look better suited to a Swiss alpine chalet.

'Well, Noah Cork,' Chelsea says. 'First things first. Let me ask the question that's surely on the tip of everyone's tongue.'

I turn sharply to the audience for clues as to what this question might be. Through the stage lights I can just make out knowing half-smiles and nods. My busy mind processes a list of potential burning questions prompted by my first book of non-fiction. The questions are spat from my brain like white strips of text from a handheld label maker.

Who … did … it?

Why … did … they … do … it?

Will … they … do … it … again?

Why … did … the … killer … choose … you … Noah … Cork?

I have prepared compelling answers for these questions, so I relax into my seat.

'Please, ask away, Chelsea,' I say.

Chelsea smiles. 'How do you sleep at night?' she asks.

I did not prep for this question. It's at this precise moment, while resting in my guest speaker's armchair with my right calf propped upon my left knee, that I once again feel a dull throbbing sensation radiating from the central core of my right testicle.

'I'm sorry, come again?' I reply, shifting awkwardly in my seat.

Chelsea turns her head to the audience and finds connection with several guests in the first three rows who are nodding their heads in appreciation of the question.

'How do you sleep at night?' Chelsea repeats.

The auditorium falls so silent that I feel the only thing to be heard is the vibration of my throbbing right testicle. This vibration seems to me – and thankfully no one else – to generate a sound, something like the sound Luke Skywalker's light sabre makes when he waves it in meaningful semi-circles. *Vwooomp. Vwooomp.*

'I'm afraid I don't know what you mean,' I reply.

'How long has this book been out now?' Chelsea asks.

'Three days.'

'That's enough time, wouldn't you say, for Tamsin's killer to have purchased a copy from their local bookshop?'

'I guess so.'

'Which means there's every chance that Tamsin's killer has already reached page 317 of your book?'

My right testicle throbs. *Vwooomp. Vwooomp.* My memory scrambles back over the feverish three-month period in which I fearlessly and breathlessly wrote *Anonymous Source* in the small asbestos-walled garage that's slowly disintegrating in the rear left corner of our backyard. I remember the pages I typed about my frenzied hunt for evidence surrounding Tamsin's murder. Two chapters devoted to Tamsin and her family. Their summer holidays to Tin Can Bay. Where Tamsin got her hair cut. The schoolboys who broke her heart. I interviewed the Jubilee Plaza butcher about which cuts of meat she bought most often. I interviewed the Jubilee newsagent about the magazines she liked to read. I remember the endless condensing of police interview transcripts, the way I turned the cold coroner's report into something readable, something rollicking. Detail after detail on comparable crimes from near and far; Jubilee crime statistics and facts and Jubilee whispers and rumours that skated ever so lightly upon the thin ice of defamation law. I remember every last page I wrote about my speculative theories regarding Tamsin's final hours, the ghoulish place where I found her body, the killer who led me to it. But why can't I remember page 317?

'Page 317,' Chelsea prompts. 'You remember page 317, don't you? The very last page. The one on which you stunningly ridicule Tamsin's killer as, I quote, a "worm-ridden coward" and a "deranged and perverted monster who somehow crawled from a bucket of evolutionary slime to end the life of a good and loving Brisbane mother of two teenaged children". You further challenge Tamsin's killer to, quote, "find the courage to quit playing games for your fifteen minutes of fame and start confessing to your crimes for the sake of Tamsin Fellows' family".'

The dull ache in my scrotum sharpens to a pain possessing a rare kind of needlepoint focus. The fire ant has returned for another feast. It feels as if someone has stuck a syringe directly into the soft marinated olive that is my right testicle and is now thumb-compressing a thick and lava-hot liquid directly into it.

I turn to face Chelsea Lasrado. She is a skeleton now. A frame of bones in a chocolate-brown suit, with her cervical spine wrapped in a lavender scarf. She has become my curse. Surely this ache is my curse, too, the manifestation of all my bad decisions and all my guilt and all my shame and all my insatiable ambition, physicalised and localised into a ball of knuckle-biting pain in my right testicle.

The Chelsea skeleton speaks. 'I wholeheartedly commend you for your bravery, Mr Cork, but are you at all concerned that this potentially aggravated and embarrassed cold-blooded killer is out there somewhere right now, tracking your every move?' She casts her cold bone right hand over the wide-eyed audience. 'I mean, who's to say Tamsin's killer isn't sitting with us today in this very auditorium?'

Several audience members suck air deep into their lungs. My face winces as I fight to swallow a destructive wave of stabbing pain from the fire ant chewing on my testicle. I feel woozy. Dizzy and vulnerable and exposed. My eyes scan for faces in the audience, but all I see through the stage lights are the whites of eyes.

'Who's to say,' the Chelsea skeleton ponders further, 'that Tamsin's killer is not staring at you right this very second?'

The stage lights seem to brighten. I feel the heat of those lights on my scalp, and the eyes of my audience cruelly and invasively zeroing in on my face. Feverish beads of sweat are rallying like soldiers on the anxiety-bombed battlefield of my forehead. A lightning bolt of pure pain shoots from my balls to my brain and I rise abruptly from my chair in an effort to ease the physical impact of my unfortunate situation.

'Uuuuuggghhh,' I wail. I slap my face. Turn back to Chelsea. She's normal again. Full-bodied, I mean. Of flesh and blood.

'Are you okay, Noah?' she asks. 'Are you feeling unwell? Was it something I said?'

'Uuuuuggghhh,' I wail again, involuntarily, something like an old man trying to pass a kidney stone.

I stare into the stage lights, close my eyes and bend forward at the waist, submit to the full pain of the relentless fire ant. I look like I'm bowing to my audience. 'Arrrrgghhh,' I howl. I couldn't keep that one in.

A collective gasp echoes across my audience.

'Noah, are you okay?' Chelsea asks again, panicked, darting her head to the stage wings.

Purely on instinct, I kneel on stage, with my left knee propped up and my right leg fully extended behind my body, like a sprinter at a starter's block. This peculiar stretching movement momentarily – and mercifully – eases the zapping bolts of agony exploding from my scrotum. I turn to Chelsea with a reassuring palm out. 'Just gimme one second,' I say, breathing hard in through my nose and out through my mouth. 'I have … an answer … to the … question.'

I spin around on the stage floor like an aged and awkward breakdancer, then lie flat on my back on the stage floor.

Professor Lasrado leans over me from her chair as if she's a wartime surgeon inspecting a wounded infantryman.

'Just one second,' I say. 'I'm really quite fine.'

And then the ache eases. I cautiously bring my knees to my chest and I realise that, miraculously, the pain has disappeared. It has left my body as quickly as it so rudely arrived.

I take one more long breath and squeeze it out slowly between the gaps in my gritted teeth. Sheepish and sweaty and confused, I stand to address the momentarily stunned audience. Release a nervous laugh. 'Sorry about that,' I say. 'Some kinda cramp, I think. Comes and goes. Nothing to worry about.'

Offering a reassuring smile, I return to my seat. Place my hand on my heart, which is beating too fast. Deep breath. Relax. Relax, you buffoon. You are a professional writer. This is not professional behaviour.

'My apologies, Chelsea,' I finally manage to say. 'I do have an answer to your question.'

Chelsea turns to her audience, then turns her head to the side of the stage, where Ronnie shrugs her shoulders before giving an uncertain nod to continue with the event.

'We can take a break if you'd prefer,' Chelsea says.

'No,' I say. 'This book is very important to me. Would you like to hear my answer?'

'Yes, of course,' Chelsea says.

I turn my face to the audience. 'I will not bend for this butcher, Chelsea,' I say. 'A journalist never retreats from the truth. He charges towards it like a knight on horseback, knowing that truth is an armour too strong to be penetrated by fear.'

Chelsea laughs. A single chuckle that slips from her lips like a stray coin from a closed purse. The chuckle turns to belly laughter.

'What's so funny?' I ask.

'You don't actually believe that, do you?' she asks.

'Of course I do,' I reply. 'I will not be intimidated by some lonely and twisted psychopath who saw my name in a newspaper and decided to make my life a misery.'

Chelsea sits up in her seat. 'Is your life a misery, Mr Cork?'

'Well … no … but—'

'I remember the press conference you gave when the news broke of Tamsin's discovery. I couldn't help but feel you seemed somewhat … *enlivened* by the attention.'

'Enlivened? I don't think that's a fair description … Energised, maybe … shaken …'

'What if you have no say in the matter?' she asks.

'In what matter?'

'The matter of your death, Mr Cork. Sure, the very principles and protections inherent in a functioning and free First World press afford any journalist a kind of invisible shield, philosophically. But how do you truly protect yourself from an anonymous killer who remains, most assuredly, on the loose? A killer who, may I remind you, Mr Cork, knows exactly where you live?'

In my mind's eye I see an image of the wood and glass front door to our home. I have a sudden urge to call Erin and check she locked it.

'There has been nothing threatening in the communications from my anonymous source,' I say. 'He's not interested in doing me harm.'

'So you think the killer's a *he*?'

'My apologies. *They* are not interested in causing me harm.'

'What are *they* interested in?'

'Same thing as me,' I say. 'Seeing where the story goes.'

'Why haven't you moved house yet?'

'Because I will not bend for this butcher. And also because we can't afford to move anywhere else. Have you seen the housing market lately?'

Pause for laughter.

'What protections have you put in place to ensure the safety of your family?' Chelsea probes.

'Listen, I'm not the first journalist to have found themselves in a one-way dialogue with a killer. But, rest assured, there are protections in place.'

'Such as?'

'Well, for a start, our home is now under twenty-four-hour police surveillance.'

'That's all well and good,' Chelsea says, 'but what happens when you're out and about? I don't see any police SWAT teams standing in the wings right now. I don't see any security whatsoever. Honestly, what the hell was going through your mind when you wrote that page?'

I stare out at the audience for ten long seconds in silence. Soon my eyes adjust to the lights and I begin to make out several faces in the first eight or nine rows. A mix of women and men, more women than men. Most of them over forty years of age, many of them over fifty. These people are newspaper readers. True-crime lovers. They have more than likely read my crime pieces in the *Courier-Mail.* When the police detectives asked me who I suspected Tamsin's killer was, I told them that I felt it could be anyone, man or woman, who has ever read one of my crime pieces in the *Courier-Mail.* That newspaper has a combined print and digital monthly audience of three million people, so I told the police that I thought Tamsin's killer could be one of three million people.

My eyes settle on the face of a young man at the edge of the sixth row. This man is maybe nineteen or twenty and he has a ginger goatee and long ginger hair tied back in a ponytail. He wears a black T-shirt. A death metal rock band shirt with a name I can't make out because of the shirt designer's chosen font, which might well be called Scalpel Black or Blade Gothic or Guillotine Bold. As Chelsea's comments about the suburban killer on the loose linger unchallenged in the still auditorium air, I focus on this young man's mouth because I can see that he is saying something to me. I lean forward to try to read his lips.

'Count mummy,' I think he's mouthing, at first. But that's not it.

'Can't memory,' I make out next. But that's not it.

And then I understand the two words this man is noiselessly communicating: 'Cunt money,' he is saying.

He repeats these words three more times. 'Cunt money. Cunt money. Cunt money.' Then he fashions a pistol shape out of his right hand and places a two-finger gun barrel in his mouth and releases his right-thumb pistol hammer. And it feels, now, as though there are only two people sitting in this whole auditorium, me and the young ginger-haired man in the sixth row mouthing a haunting couplet that I remember last seeing scrawled in white spray-paint on the door of a broken oven. I know this young man, and I know there's something not right with him.

Chelsea's voice snaps me back to the Q & A. 'Noah,' she continues, 'what I'm trying to say is that, as compelling as these pages are, I wonder if you ever thought about the possible consequences of writing this book?'

I stare at Chelsea's face for a moment. Her left eyebrow rises briefly and settles back in place. I turn my head back to the audience and meet the eyes of the ginger-haired man in the sixth row.

'You want to know the truth, Chelsea?' I ask.

'Always.'

'I think the truth protects a journalist from nothing and no one,' I say. I shake my head, keep my eyes on the ginger-haired man. 'But who among us is ever truly protected from the broken and the willing? I sleep terribly at night. I'm terrified of the consequences of writing this book. Sometimes I wonder if there's twice the amount of darkness in this world than there is light. I'm genuinely worried that every word I've ever written as a journalist has only ever added to the darkness. Sometimes I'm filled with so much fear that I can't move the joints in my bones. All I think about these days is Tamsin. All I think about is how that despicable person left her bones there for me to find them like that. Tamsin comes to me in my dreams. I see her when I sleep. I see her when I wake. She's a skeleton. She's death. She's all the darkness of this world, standing in the back of my bedroom closet.'

I look at Chelsea. 'I honestly don't know what I was thinking when I wrote this book, Chelsea,' I say. 'Something came over me. The story, probably. The story was just so extraordinary. I couldn't *not* tell it. My wife, Rita, told me not to write it, but I said it had to come out. I told Rita it was the story of a lifetime and I was a central part of it. I told Rita the story had landed in my lap for a reason. How could she deny me this opportunity? I told her it was my job to tell this story. I told her I had to tell the story right. I told her I had to do it for Tamsin.

Then the cops told me not to write this story. But I told them I couldn't not tell this story. I told the cops I had to do it for Tamsin. And the cops told me to stay quiet. They wanted me to bend. Bend to their rules. Bend to their beloved *process.* I told the cops that I'm never gonna bend for them and I'm certainly never gonna bend for no butcher.'

I pause for a moment. Look up at the stage lights shining in my eyes.

'I really don't know what I was thinking,' I say, shaking my head. 'Maybe I was just thinking about a second bathroom for my daughters to brush their teeth in.'

Silence in the auditorium.

'Are you serious?' Chelsea asks. 'You did it for a second bathroom?'

All I offer Chelsea is a faint nervous smile.

She raises her eyebrows, then runs her eyes over the three sheets of stapled A4 paper that hold her questions.

'Well, before we go any further, let's rewind a bit,' she says. 'Take us right back, Noah. Tell me how this all began. How was it exactly that you came to play a central role in the twisted game of an anonymous killer?'

I gaze again at the ginger-haired man in the sixth row. The question has made him smile. I want to punch his teeth in.

I hold his gaze as I answer the question. 'I opened my letterbox,' I reply. 'That's all I did, Chelsea. I didn't ask for any of this. All I did was open my letterbox.'

FOUR

Follow your leads. Follow your logic. Follow your nose.

– Rutledge, *Journalism Practices and Principles*

Hello lemon drop,

Big fan. Miss yr collums in the newspaper.

You still doin the journo thang?

Might have yarn for u.

Seems I left my ruby slippas by the reservoir.

Could u find them for me, lemon drop?

I wanna go home.

TF

That's what the note said. The note itself is now police evidence. But that's what it said. I must make do with screenshots of it now. Blue ballpoint pen, words seemingly scrawled in a rough child's hand or the hand of a grown-up idiot. Misspellings and awkward spacings between words, but the cops say that means nothing, because anybody can write like an idiot, including idiots and people pretending to be idiots. The words were scribbled on a yellowed page torn from what I figured was a child's activity book, one the police later confirmed as a 1979 edition of *The Brownie Annual*, published by the Girl Guides Association of Great Britain. Page seventy-five. The words were scrawled across a child's maze. A farmyard theme. Sun-bathed farmhouse at the top of the maze, wooden farmyard fence at the bottom. 'WHICH WAY?' asked the two words in bold black capitals across the top of the page. *Can you find your way to the house on top of the hill, after going through the stile?* On the flipside of this torn page was half of an illustrated short story, entitled 'Caroline Joins the Sprites', which appeared to be about a hopeful aspiring Brownie whose widowed mum couldn't afford to buy her daughter a uniform.

The torn page had been laid flat inside my letterbox by someone, but there were two uneven creases across the page, indicating it had been folded twice. The page itself was frayed and worn, which made the cops later suggest that it had been carried in someone's pocket for some time. The cops told me that mentally unstable offenders often carry notes inside their pockets for extended periods, but they also told me not to read too much into that because it could have been a case of someone just pretending to be a mentally unstable offender.

I stood at the letterbox that day turning the note over in my hands and glancing up and down my street. There was nobody but me, it seemed, in all of Gecko Street. I laughed at first. I thought it might have been part of some strange game that Erin and Clem were playing. They weren't home to ask. I wanted to show the note to Rita, but she had a Red Cross shift that day, working in the city. I read the note twice before I played the small novelty music box that accompanied it. My right thumb and forefinger gripped the tiny hand crank and tentatively set the box's spinning drum in motion. The pins on the drum plucked the teeth of the vibration plate and a soft melody echoed through the still morning air of Jubilee.

'Over the Rainbow'. A song about lemon drops and chimney tops and things that wait for us beyond clouds and rain. The music box version was a lullaby. A cradle song. Not to be confused with a grave song. I saw Judy Garland's perfect farmyard face in my head. Dorothy and the dog and the wizard and the heartless guy and the brainless guy and the lion full of piss and wind. A singing sixteen-year-old angel and all her wide-eyed, pep-pilled promise. Beautiful song when it's sung by an MGM marvel. Kinda bone-chilling when it's played on a music box that some creepy weirdo placed in your letterbox, more than likely while you and your family were sleeping.

I should have thought about danger in that moment. I should have thought about calling the police and maybe suggesting that an unhinged reader of my newspaper columns had found my address and was now playing some kind of bizarre reader–writer puppet-on-a-string game designed to make me rush off to see my own mystery wizard behind the curtain. But all I thought about in that moment was copy. All I thought about was how much this felt like the beginning of a good newspaper feature story, no matter where it went from there. The mysterious 'TF' in the note: it was a call to action, a challenge to embrace my investigative journalist powers, find the 'ruby slippas' by the reservoir and help this person get home.

A good story is like a good Sunday roast: you smell it first. This was one of them garlic-and-rosemary-lamb-smelling good stories. This was a red-wine-gravy good story. You smell a good story first and then you feel it in your problematic balls.

You get the hots for it. Every good story is like a good first date. You might have a preferred ending in mind, but the real thrill is not knowing where it's all going. The real thrill is in the intoxicating and irresistible *unfolding*. Event to event to event to an inevitable end. Like music. Like a song. C chord to A minor to E minor to F to somewhere over the rainbow.

I should have thought about danger, but all I thought about was how I was going to write the very moment I was standing in. I thought about my clothes – blue rubber flip flops, black denim shorts and an old Cranberries T-shirt emblazoned with lyrics from 'Zombie'. I noted the sky – grey and darkening with rain on the way. I noted the hand I held the music box in. I noted the creases in the paper. I noted the weirdness of the Brownie annual pages on which my mysterious correspondent had scribbled the message. Question one: who the hell had put this note in my letterbox? Question two: why would someone need me to find their slippers? Question three: why on earth would anyone expect me to jump straight in my car and embark on a fool's errand of unknown origin and outcome? Answers: copy, copy, copy.

I scurried back into the house and found a pair of old blue Chuck Taylor sneakers – the nearest thing I had to walking shoes – and I slipped them on my feet and ran into the kitchen for the car keys. I drove to Spearwood Reservoir at the end of Wicker Road, where it starts its serpentine journey up Mount Parsons. Rule number 17 of investigative feature writing: start at the simplest solution to the puzzle and hope for the best. Not quite Occam's razor. More like Occam's prison shiv, which he fashioned from a sharpened decking nail, a strip of electrical tape and the handle of a ping-pong paddle. Slippers by the reservoir? Spearwood Reservoir is a four-minute drive from my house. Couldn't hurt to take a squiz. A story can start wherever you want it to start. Sometimes you just gotta hop in your 2012 red Yaris with the dodgy clutch and drive.

Spearwood is the second oldest reservoir in Brisbane, 2,500 metres long, 630 metres wide. A lily pad and pink and purple and red flower lake that would not be out of place in the wetlands of the Northern Territory, just twenty minutes' drive from the Brisbane CBD. I used to jog the five-kilometre Hickory Wattle walking trail that circles the lake and rambles through towering hoop pines and red cedars and acacias and ironbarks. The trail was empty and silent that day. Most people come to the reservoir on the weekend to swim and kayak the still lake waters, usually with binoculars for close-up views of painted button quails and crested shrike tits and white-eared monarchs and dusky wood swallows and the kings of the reservoir, the white-bellied sea eagles. This was mid-morning on a Wednesday that had just turned rainy. I hadn't taken an umbrella but the tall native trees above the well-trod dirt walking track blocked much of the falling rain. I gripped the letterbox note in my left hand and the music box in my right, as the track twisted through the peaceful forest. If there had been white-bellied sea eagles dancing across the lake, or even cameo appearances by the lake's rare and spectacular regent honeyeater, I wouldn't have noticed them, for my eyes were fixed to the ground, scanning the sides of the walking track for signs of ruby slippers.

The deeper the track wound through the forest, the darker the forest canopy grew beneath the grey sky, and the more I realised how alone I was. I was about one kilometre along the walking track when I started looking back over my shoulder, under some false, spine-prompted suspicion that someone was following me. Just a jumpy instinct thing. The rain was light enough that I could still hear lizards and scrub turkeys pushing through the undergrowth bordering the track, and the whizz of bellbirds and forest kingfishers darting between trees that were standing in the mid-1800s when the reservoir was built. I leapt over puddles and small mud baths and stepped awkwardly on tree roots, never taking my eyes off the path. I came to a thin stream crossed by a small rock and concrete bridge and I got down on my hands and knees and looked under the bridge in case the slippers were there, but saw nothing but mud and an empty Corona bottle.

A hundred metres on, I passed a clearing where someone had built a kind of teepee out of branches and sheets of fallen paperbark. I checked inside the teepee for a pair of ruby slippers and found nothing but two half-used crayons, one green and one red, and a smooth, flat rock upon which someone had drawn a smiley face in yellow crayon.

The rain hardened. The puddles spread. The track thickened with mud. There was no grip on the soles of my old Chuck Taylors, so every ten metres or so one of my feet would slip sharply out of rhythm. The track arched left and the track arched right and then followed a soft incline uphill. My head was down when my view was abruptly filled by a pair of blue and white Nike running shoes. I stopped and lifted my head to see that the shoes were filled by a pair of feet belonging to a man roughly my age who was sitting on the second step of a small rock and concrete staircase at a steep bend in the trail. The man wore a hooded, black all-weather running jacket, and had his hands tucked into its front pockets. He looked more like a monk on a silent retreat than a trail jogger. A distance in his face. There but not there. Seemingly concentrating on nothing – not me, not the rain, not the muddying track before him – but the thoughts in his head.

Then I recognised him. 'Miles,' I said.

The man looked up at me from the rocky step, rain falling on his face. Miles De Jonge. Runs a mobile, environmentally friendly nappy-cleaning service for new parents who consider disposable nappies as dangerous as asbestos and Putin and other toxic materials. His daughter, Sienna, had been in Clem's Year 6 class at Good Shepherd Catholic Primary School on Salem Road. Miles and I had manned the putt-putt golf stall together at the school fête, three years earlier.

'Miles, you right, mate?'

He wiped water from his eyes and studied my face.

'Noah,' he said. 'What are you doin' here?'

'Thought I'd go for a walk.'

'It's pissin' rain, Noah,' Miles said.

'Yeah, Miles,' I said, 'guess it is. You good?'

'Yeah,' he said. Then a tear fell from his right eye and he closed his lips and puffed his cheeks to stop more tears from following it. 'Yeah, nah. Not real good, mate.'

'What's wrong, Miles?' I asked.

'Steph says she's leavin'.'

I tried to picture Steph De Jonge in my head. I gave her straw-coloured hair, but I couldn't give her any facial features. I couldn't remember what she looked like. Wasn't sure I'd even met her.

'She called me vanilla,' Miles said.

'Vanilla?'

'Yeah, like, fuckin' colourless. Boring. Not blue. Not red. Not yellow. Vanilla. Do you think I'm colourless, Noah? Do you think I'm vanilla?'

'No, Miles,' I said. 'I think you're a regular rainbow.'

I looked down at the music box tucked inside my right fist. I turned the hand crank and the mesmerising tune for 'Over the Rainbow' split the rain and landed in Miles's ears. He smiled like a four-year-old boy seeing a yo-yo for the first time. For a moment, I thought he was gonna cry again. Instead, he laughed.

'What the fuck is that?' he asked.

'Found it in my letterbox this morning.'

'Why was it in your letterbox?'

'Dunno. Found a note sitting under it.'

'What did the note say?'

I read Miles the note that had been rolled up in my left fist.

'Are you fuckin' serious?' Miles exclaimed. 'Ruby slippers by the reservoir?' He was beaming now and his right thumb was pointing over his right shoulder towards the trail behind him. I could tell he wasn't thinking of Steph anymore. He stood up so fast he nearly slipped on the wet step. 'Follow me,' he said.

There were a dozen or so more steps running up the incline and Miles ascended them in three-step leaps. Then he paused on a crest in the track to wait for me to catch up, urging me forward with a wave of his hand.

'Where the hell are we going?' I asked, catching my breath.

'You're not gonna believe this,' he said, darting off again along the trail, which sloped gently down and bent left and bent right before coming to a long leaf and mud straight section of track that stretched to a public viewing seat set on a horseshoe-shaped outcrop overlooking one of the more majestic corners of the reservoir. The viewpoint was enhanced that morning by the presence of six blue-winged forest kingfishers perched on the leafless branches of a fallen tree half-submerged by the rain-dappled lake waters. I guess, come to think of it, one could have called those birds *bluebirds*. Happy little bluebirds.

Miles ran to the wooden bench, which was about the width of a council bus-stop seat. He pointed under its right edge where, sitting as neatly as if they'd been placed in a princess's shoe cabinet, there was a pair of women's flat red leather shoes. They looked to me like ballet slippers, but for the single strap across the top of each shoe, which connected to a circular chrome buckle.

'Nuthin' vanilla about your life, Noah,' Miles said.

I picked the shoes up. They were soaking wet, and their toes were scuffed and curled with age and wear.

'I was gonna pick 'em up myself,' Miles said. 'But then I thought the owner would probably come back for them soon.'

There was nothing under the shoes. I looked inside them and saw only the last four letters of a half-faded brand: *—dler.* Then I turned them upside down to examine their soles and something fell out of the right shoe and landed on my wet and muddy right Chuck Taylor. A piece of paper. Folded twice.

Miles watched me unfold it. It wasn't plain old notepaper, but an order docket, the kind a fish 'n' chip shop worker might use to scribble down an order of crumbed cod and potato scallops. There was a red number, *33*, and a series of words had been scribbled roughly across the docket in blue ballpoint pen. I read the first two and knew it had been written for me.

Hello bluebird.

FIVE

There is no money in journalism. There is no glory. There is no fame. There are no awards that matter. There are no speeches to be made about the witnessing of history. There is only the witnessing. There is only the story. Your name has nothing to do with it. The byline at the top of the story is nothing more than proof that the story was written by a human in pursuit of the truth.

– Rutledge, *Journalism Practices and Principles*

Sitting forward in her aqua-blue armchair on the stage, Professor Chelsea Lasrado looks at her watch. 'I'm sorry, it seems time has slipped away from us,' she says. 'We probably only have time for one or two questions from the audience.'

The main lights in the auditorium go up and Chelsea casts her eyes across the still and silent audience. 'Don't be shy,' she says.

Nobody moves. No hands go up. Then a woman in the third-last row of seats stands.

'Good for you,' Chelsea says with a smile. 'Speak up so we can all hear your question.'

'Hi, my name's Bec,' the woman says. 'Thank you, Noah, for being so candid with, you know, all the details on how this book came about. It was fascinating to listen to, if a wee bit creepy.'

Laughter runs through the audience.

'That bit about the shoes under the seat ... and then the bit where you went to Monaco House in Jubilee. I often drop my husband off at golf on a Saturday at the Jubilee Golf Club and we drive past that abandoned building and we've always wondered what was in there. I'm a bit like your friend, Miles. I wouldn't step into that place for a million bucks.'

Chelsea Lasrado interrupts Bec's monologue.

'Do you have a question for Noah, Bec?' she asks. 'We're just a little time-impoverished right now.'

Bec nods. 'Yes, sorry, sorry. Ummm ... what I wanted to ask was ... See, I'm a nurse at the Wesley Emergency Centre ... and I just wanted to ask Noah if he's feeling okay because the way he keeled over at the start of your chat ... well ... it looked a lot like what I see patients do when they come in for emergency appendectomies. Have you had yourself checked for appendicitis?'

'Thanks for asking, Bec,' I reply into my microphone. 'I had my appendix taken out when I was twelve. I'm fine. Honestly. Just the odd ache, here and there. Might be cramping or something.'

'Would you say the pain is localised more in your abdomen or your groin?' Bec asks.

I cast my eyes over the hundred or so people sitting between Bec and me, their ears clearly attuned to this impromptu and unnecessary medical assessment.

'Well, it feels just a little further south, Bec, but I'd prefer to focus on the—

'It's in your testes, isn't it?' Bec barks across the auditorium. 'Men never get their testes checked like they should. Testes don't cramp, mate, just sayin'. Is it a sharp ache or a dull ache?'

An elderly woman in the third row hollers her suspicions. 'Could be cancer in the goolies?'

Another woman calls out from the middle rows of the audience. 'Could be an STD. My ex-husband came home from Ko Samui with aching taters. Turned out to be chlamydia.'

Chelsea interrupts again. 'Thank you for everyone's concern for Noah's health,' she says into her microphone. She turns to me. 'I'm sure he's going to be visiting his doctor about these mysterious pains as soon as he is able. In the meantime, does anybody have a question that's not related to Mr Cork's testicles?'

A woman stands, nine rows back, dressed in a blue woollen pullover.

'What happens now, Noah?' the woman asks. 'Are you and your family just expected to get on with your lives while Tamsin's killer is still out there? I mean, what's next for you?'

'Well, you're exactly right,' I reply. 'We're gonna get on with our lives. I'm gonna let the police do their job. I think it's fair to say I've let a few things slip in my personal life over the past six months. What's next for me? School drop-off. Making lunch for my kids. Being present again for my wife and two daughters.'

'Unless ...' Chelsea Lasrado says into her microphone. She lets the word hang in the auditorium air.

'Unless what?'

'Unless Tamsin's killer leaves another message in your letterbox.'

I shake my head. 'That's not gonna happen.'

'What makes you so sure?'

'The killer doesn't need me anymore. I've played my part.'

'And what part was that?'

'To get us all talking about him.'

'Him?'

'*Them.*'

Chelsea smiles, turns to her audience. 'Any more questions?'

Nobody raises their hand. Then the young ginger-haired man on the edge of the sixth row stands.

'I had a dream about you last night, Noah,' the young man says. 'You were sitting in a room in hell.'

The audience draws a collective breath. Whispers and murmurings ripple up the banks of tiered seating.

'I'm sorry, sir,' Chelsea says. 'Could you say your name and, please, if you don't mind, keep any personal feelings out of your questioning.'

'My name's John Fellows,' the ginger-haired man says. 'I'm Tamsin Fellows' son.'

More gasps and whispers among the audience.

'John,' says Chelsea. 'I'm so sorry for … ummm … all that you and your family have endured in recent times.'

Chelsea turns to me. 'Have you two met before?'

I nod. 'Yes, Chelsea,' I say. 'I tried to interview John for my book.'

'I see,' Chelsea says, turning back to John Fellows. 'Mr Fellows, why did you want to come here today?'

John squeezes his eyes shut then opens them again, like he's waking himself up. 'I wanted to tell Noah about my dream last night,' he says.

Chelsea turns to me. 'What do you think, Noah?' she asks. 'Do you mind if we hear about John's dream? I assume it is relevant to our discussion.'

I look at John. 'Sure, John,' I say. 'Let's hear about your dream.'

'Well … it's kinda hard to explain,' he says. 'But there was this big red room, Noah. Red walls. Red desk. Big red chair. I think … well … I know … this was a room in hell, Noah. You had been sent to hell. And this room was … like … Satan's office or somethin'. And there was this red and black typewriter sitting on the desk. This musta been Satan's typewriter. And you were sitting at the writing desk, Noah … and you were writing your ugly little book about my beautiful mum … except … except … you were scared … you were scared of writing it all because Satan was standing right behind you as you wrote and there was blood all over the typewriter … and the white pages that you were typing on were all covered in blood, too … because every time you typed my mum's name Satan would slice one of your fingers off with a carving knife.'

An elderly woman seated beside John sucks air sharply into her lungs and clutches her handbag to her chest.

'That's a very … *dark* … dream you describe, John,' Chelsea says.

John Fellows grips his right ear lobe with his thumb and forefinger. His fingers are shaking. He nods his head.

'Why do you think you are seeing such scenes in your dreams, John?' Chelsea asks.

John laughs. Points at me. 'Because while he was busy putting this book together over the past six months, my sister, Helen, and I were walkin' in and out of therapy rooms, trying to process the trauma of our mum's disappearance and subsequent discovery by *him*. Then he went ahead and described this discovery in microscopic and graphic detail in his so-called book. My dad, Neil Fellows, lost the job he'd held down for twenty-two years. He's a full-blown drunk, Noah. Last week he dipped into his superannuation to buy a six-bottle box of vodka. He's drinking himself to death, Noah, and I don't blame him because half the country thinks he killed his wife. Helen is only eighteen years old, and she has tried to take her own life twice since 2022, when Mum disappeared. I climbed outta the hole for a bit. I had a job as an apprentice baker. I was makin' sourdoughs an' shit. Gettin' by ...'

John Fellows points his right forefinger at me again, his arms shaking now. 'And then this ... *cunt* ... goes and writes a book and drops me straight back in the hole.'

Fellows weeps. Drops his head and wipes his eyes.

'I don't mind tellin' ya I turned to the gear, just to cope with the pain,' he continues. 'Anything to get those images of my mum's skeleton outta my head. He put those images there. He gave me that shit. That's what his words done to me.'

The critical eyes of audience members, dozens of them, are drilling into me. Questioning my actions. Questioning my words. *Look what you have done to him, Cork. Look what you did to Tamsin's boy. Well done, Frankenstein, you made another monster!*

'With all due respect, John, you were a known amphetamines user well before—'

Chelsea hovers a hand in my direction, cutting me off. 'Please, Noah,' she says, 'let's allow John to speak his truth.'

Chelsea turns back to John. 'Please, John,' she says, 'do you have a question for Noah?'

'I don't have a question,' says John Fellows, fighting more tears. 'I just have a statement.'

He pauses to take a long breath, composes himself. Eyes of the audience on him.

'Um ... John ... maybe we can talk about this after,' I quietly suggest.

Chelsea Lasrado speaks into her microphone with the soft and calming voice of a counsellor. 'Please, Mr Fellows, feel free to speak your truth,' she says.

Fellows cries some more, nodding his head. One more deep breath and then ... 'Cunt money!' he screams. 'CUUUUUUNNNNT MONNNEEEEEY!'

He points his forefinger at me once again. 'He wrote those words for you, Cork!' John fumes. 'Cunt money! The killer knew what you were gonna do. You didn't care about my mum. You just scribbled your ugly little book and took the money. Cunt moneeeey!'

He keeps repeating that foul phrase. He's in a mad loop with the words, spit and tears streaking his rabid face. He starts kicking the seat in front of him. His right forefinger stays on me, but his left fist beats his own chest. Eyes alight. The terrifying noise of his barking abuse forces everybody around him to flee their seats. Some older guests shuffle out the exits of the auditorium in fear. *It's alive. It's moving. In the name of God, it's allliiiiiiive!*

'Please lower your voice, Mr Fellows,' Chelsea says.

'Cunt money,' Fellows spits, louder than ever. 'Cunt money. Cunt money. Cunt money. Cunt money.'

'Yeah, I get it John,' I say, not leaving my seat. 'Can we please talk about this outside?'

'Cunt money!' he wails.

In a matter of seconds, half the audience has left and only John Fellows is left standing in the first ten rows. Some guests at the back sit watching this strange expression of decidedly brutal reader feedback, mouths wide open with astonishment and can't-turn-away-from-a-train-wreck interest.

'Cuuuuuuunt,' Fellows screams again, 'mooonnneeeeey!'

Chelsea turns her head to the stage wings, finds event coordinator Ronnie Bird speaking frantically into her phone.

'You people got any security in this place?' Chelsea bellows.

*

Ronnie Bird's now walking me across the State Library forecourt, past the library café and bookshop, towards the stairs that will take me down to my car.

'I'm so sorry you had to endure that,' Ronnie says. 'Please rest assured that we managed to calm him down. He's sitting with our security staff, sipping a green tea. He's okay, it seems. Think he just had to get it all out. You good?'

'Yeah, I'm good.'

'Have you two met before?'

'Just once,' I say. 'I went to the family's home in Jubilee. I asked John and his sister and their dad if they were interested in being interviewed for my book.'

'What did they say?'

'Well, young John back there had just two words for me.'

'Lemme guess,' Ronnie says. 'Cunt money?'

'Good guess.'

'Like the words on the oven, right?'

I nod my head. Ronnie ushers me through the library's underground carpark. I start the Yaris and Ronnie hands a parking voucher through my window.

'Just wave that against the sensor thing,' she says.

'Thanks.'

Ronnie bends down to the window, rests an elbow on the door.

'Hey, listen,' she says, 'don't worry about that guy. I read your book. You had every right to write about what happened to you. If something crazy like that ever happened to me, I wouldn't hesitate to spill the beans about it. Every last fuckin' detail, no matter who I pissed off. Did you see the review on the weekend?'

'Yeah, I saw it,' I say. 'I was particularly glad I stayed with it for that final summary line: "Somehow Cork delivers a genuinely compelling and unputdownable true-crime page turner, despite possessing about as much literary dexterity as a Bowen mango."'

Ronnie laughs. 'Hey, some writers would trade a lung for an endorsement like that.'

'Be honest, did you like my book?'

'Yeah, I did,' Ronnie says, sincerely. 'I devoured it. Like a Bowen mango.'

She smiles, taps the car door twice and walks back towards her office. I press the button to raise my window and it's almost fully closed when a man appears, from where I cannot tell, and taps his knuckles against the glass.

The man smiles. Pure white hair. Bowl cut, parted down the middle. He looks sixty, going on six. White eyebrows matching the hair. Northern European, maybe. Swedish. Danish. The tip of his tongue hangs out his mouth when he smiles at me. He points down to the ground. He wants me to wind my window down. I wave at him instead. Tap my fingers on my left wrist where a watch would be if I owned one. *Sorry mate, gotta fly. Pressed for time, see. That's why I'm tapping my wrist. Beat the clock before it beats us to death.*

But he won't take sorry-I-don't-feel-like-this-right-now for an answer. He continues to smile and point at the ground. I bring the window down.

'Hi,' the man says, waving his right hand at me so that it can say hi as well. He's wearing a grey suit with a white business shirt and a green and white paisley-patterned tie. An open brown soft leather briefcase, stuffed with papers and books, hangs off his left shoulder.

'Hi,' I say.

'Great presentation,' the man says.

'Thanks.'

'Bit weird at the end there.'

'Yeah. Bit weird.'

'Who was that guy? Gave me the creeps.'

'Didn't you hear what he said?' I ask.

'I was sitting up the back. We missed what he said first up.'

'It was John Fellows. Tamsin's oldest child.'

'Oh, shit. That's why he was so angry.'

I nod twice.

'Poor bastard,' the man says. 'God knows how many times he's wondered if his own father was the one who did it.'

The man reaches into his briefcase and retrieves a copy of *Anonymous Source* and a fountain pen. 'Would you sign it for me?' he asks.

'Sure,' I say, pulling the handbrake on the Yaris.

I open the book to the title page. 'What's your name?'

'My name's Axel,' he says. 'Axel Olsson. Could you please make it out to "Axel and Deirdre". And, if you'd be so kind, could you please write something about the greatest suburb in Australia, our beloved Jubilee?'

I give him a half-smile, raise my left eyebrow. 'You live in Jubilee?' I ask.

'All my life,' he replies.

I scribble a message across the title page: *Jubilee Forever!*

'In fact, I thought you might recognise my name,' Axel Olsson says.

And the tingle down my spine tells me that now I do. 'The Olsson family,' I say. 'The house on Kidwell Street.'

Axel nods. I don't know why he's smiling, but he is. In 1983, in a two-storey red-brick home in Kidwell Street, Jubilee, mother of two Abigail Olsson crept after midnight into her darkened main bedroom with a torch in one hand and her husband Birger's fish-filleting knife in the other. She stabbed her sleeping husband twenty-three times in his head and back, before proceeding to the room where her daughter slept. Astrid Olsson never saw her thirteenth birthday. Abigail Olsson then went to the kitchen sink and washed the filleting knife clean. Next she took an apple from a bowl of fruit in the centre of the kitchen table and, with the filleting knife she had just used to murder her husband and daughter, cut the apple into quarter wedges, of which she ate three before slicing her wrists and stabbing herself twelve times in the vicinity of her slow-beating heart. Newspapers reported that Astrid's sixteen-year-old brother was, mercifully, away on an interstate school ski trip. What was his name again? Started with an 'A'. André? Anders? Anton?

'Jesus, I'm so sorry, Axel,' I say.

He shrugs his shoulders.

'I did have to laugh when that cop in the book, Jim England, welcomed you to Jubilee by saying nothing bad ever happens in our suburb,' Axel says. 'I think your readers, Mr Cork, would actually be very surprised by the number of ghastly crimes that are crawling through the cracks of our beloved Jubilee.'

I nod, hand Axel's now-signed book back to him.

'Kinda what I was getting at in my book,' I say. 'No suburb is immune to human darkness.'

I release the handbrake.

Axel nods at several papers and books in his briefcase. 'I've written multiple books about human darkness,' he says. 'Horrific real-life murders across suburban Brisbane that nobody talks about anymore. I published them all myself.'

'I'd love to read them some time, Axel,' I lie, looking into the Yaris's rearview mirror and preparing to reverse the car.

'Why don't you come around our place for supper,' he says. 'We're only a stone's throw from Gecko Street.'

I turn my eyes sharply to Axel. 'What did you say?'

'Why don't you come around to our place?' he repeats. 'We're on Barley Close, about two blocks from Gecko.'

'How do you know I live on Gecko Street, Axel?' I ask. 'I've never said what street I live on.'

'You sure about that?'

'Yes, Axel, I'm sure about that.'

'I could swear I read it in one of your columns,' he says. 'Maybe I read it in a police report.'

'The police have never publicly stated what street the note was dropped in,' I say. 'As per my repeated requests.'

'Maybe we saw you on one of our afternoon walks,' he says with a shrug, smiling. 'Anyway, small world, I guess. Even smaller Jubilee.'

I study his face for a moment. The tip of his tongue again, every time he smiles. I try my best to end this encounter. 'Well, I best get g—'

'I'm curious, Mr Cork, what conclusions did you reach regarding motivation.'

'Whose motivation?'

'His,' Axel says. 'The man who killed Tamsin.'

'We're not sure it's a man.'

'Ninety-five per cent of all global homicides throughout history were committed by men,' he says.

'Your mum was quite the trailblazer, then.'

Axel stares blankly at me for three seconds.

That was careless of me. I may be strangled by this man now, though it's hard to tell what he's thinking.

Then Axel's laughter echoes through the underground carpark. 'That's actually the very thing I would like to talk to you about,' he says. He squats, rests a hand on my car door. 'Do you really think for a second that my mother would have been capable of doing what the police claim she did to my father and sister?'

'I'd need to look at the case again, but my understanding is that the police were not the slightest bit confused about who did it, Axel,' I say.

'I thought you of all people would understand the fallibilities of the Queensland Police Service,' Axel says.

'A few bad apples don't spoil the box.'

'I think it's disgusting the way the police have shut you out of your own story,' he says. '*You* receive the messages. *You* find the body for them. And they thank you by shutting you out of their investigations?'

'What, you expect them to throw me a badge and a gun, Axel?'

'No,' he says. 'But I would expect them to keep you abreast of developments. And certainly not pass all their off-the-record leads to that amateur, Ricky Waverly.'

Three days ago, Ricky Waverly published an exclusive on his Patreon page – 'Chain of Evidence with Ricky Waverly' – stating that police had been contacted by a key witness who claimed to have been the last person to see Tamsin Fellows alive.

Axel leans in to the window space. He's so close to me that when he talks I can smell coffee on his breath. 'What if I told you that the man who killed my family is the same man who killed Tamsin Fellows?'

I have no response beyond an awkward half-chuckle. I look around the underground carpark for signs of other humans. Sane ones.

'I wanna help deal you back in, Noah,' he says.

'How exactly would you do that, Axel?'

He digs into his briefcase, finds a thin, softback self-published book, then hands it to me through the window. *Improbable*

Cause, by Axel Olsson. The book's cover features an illustration of Themis, goddess of justice, with a bandage around her eyes, holding her scales of justice. On one scale rests a knife, on the other a pistol.

'That's an account of the twenty-plus years I have spent investigating unsolved murders and multiple inexplicable disappearances across Brisbane, including the brutal unsolved murders of my sister, my father and my mother.' He taps the book cover. 'I've left a note inside the cover with some names that I think you might find intriguing,' he says. 'I feel I can help you, Noah. I feel we can help each other.'

I flip through Axel's book. Black and white text pages and poorly printed black and white images of crime scenes and newspaper front pages.

'To be honest with you, Axel,' I say, trying to sound gentle and caring, 'I don't need your help, because all I intend doing from here on in, as soon as my publishing commitments are over, is spending as much time as I can with my family.' I hold the book up. 'But thanks so much. Can't wait to dive in.' I place the book in the glovebox.

Axel studies my movements. 'You won't forget it there, will you?' he asks.

'No, mate,' I reply. 'I won't forget it.'

He looks into my eyes. His chin rises for a moment. He smiles. 'Very well then.' He stands, steps back from the car. 'I'm glad to hear that about your family plans. I'd certainly never begrudge a father his wish to spend more time with his family. I'd give anything to spend more time with my parents.'

He walks away. Then he turns back to me once more, when

he's eight paces from my car, and holds up his signed copy of *Anonymous Source*.

'Thanks for signing my book,' he says. 'Who knows, might even be worth somethin' after he kills ya.'

He stares at me blankly for three seconds, then his back-bending cackling echoes through the underground carpark.

SIX

Some deadlines are not worth dying for.

– Rutledge, *Journalism Practices and Principles*

It's dark and just past 6 p.m. when I turn back into Lamb Street, Jubilee, where, nine hours ago, my Yaris nearly ended Jean Rooney's life. Almost home. Since lunchtime I've been driving across the city of Brisbane visiting bookshops – as per a detailed map and extensive itinerary prepared by my publisher-appointed publicist, Sherry Sharp – thanking booksellers for doing their best to put *Anonymous Source* before the eyes of loyal customers. West End to Indooroopilly to Mount Gravatt to Carindale to New Farm to Chermside to North Lakes and back home to Jubilee.

Two council streetlights are out on Lamb Street. Only my headlights and the headlights of the car in front of me – a rusting red single-cab Toyota Hilux ute – appear to be illuminating the street. Almost home, and hungry and tired. I rub my eyes and curse the red Hilux for driving five kilometres an hour below the speed limit. Then, curiously, the Hilux stops in the middle of the street. Engine still running. Brake lights glowing.

I figure the driver's looking for an address, so I give them thirty seconds, then sixty seconds, then ninety seconds to find the place they're looking for. There's no space for overtaking between a parked hatchback on the left of the street and the gutter to the right.

I beep twice, barely pressing down on the horn, something like the Road Runner's *meep-meep*. The Hilux doesn't move. Another thirty seconds. Fuck this guy. Long blast of the horn. Less Road Runner, more Viking invasion. The Hilux motors on, mercifully, but only for some fifty more metres. Then it stops again. Another long blast of my horn and the Hilux moves, reluctantly, to the left edge of the street so that I have enough room to pass. I gently accelerate and move up parallel with the Hilux. Small red Yaris. Big red Hilux. I look through my passenger-side window and see the driver of the Hilux – a heavyset woman wearing a vibrant pink turtleneck sweater – laughing uproariously at me. Her hair is grey and wild and curled and long.

Just as I'm about to pass her, she drives forward. She keeps laughing at me, head turned towards me, eyes not on the road but on me. It's as though we're racing, but only at a pace of ten kilometres an hour. I raise an open left palm in a 'What-the-fuck-is-your-malfunction-lady?' way. She quickens her pace and I quicken mine and we're side by side when she has to stop suddenly to avoid running straight into the rear end of Gwyn Rooney's parked Hyundai Tucson.

She turns right sharply and falls in behind me, riding my bumper as I take a left into Boodua Street. Then she switches her high-beam lights on and her aggressive white light drowns me and my Yaris. She revs her engine threateningly and almost nudges my bumper. I turn right into Burralong Street and realise how close to home I am. I don't want this woman anywhere near my house, so I slam on the brakes. She does the same, stopping her car mere inches from my rear licence plate. I stare at the woman for a moment through my rearview mirror. She revs her engine hard, three times.

I pull the handbrake on the Yaris. Step out of my car with my palms held up and open to the sky. I repeat, verbally this time, 'What the fuck is your malfunction, lady?'

More demented laughter. Then her window descends and she sticks her head out and licks her lips, preparing to speak. With her right elbow resting casually on the door, she wags her right forefinger at me in admonishment. 'Cunt money,' she says.

Then she reverses, wildly and recklessly. The hulking rusted Hilux almost smashes into two parked cars on Burralong Street as it drives backwards for some fifty metres. The tyres burn and screech when the woman slams on the brakes. She puts the car in neutral and revs the engine three more times. Then she turns her headlights off. I fumble for my phone in my pants pocket and type the Hilux's licence plate number into the notes page: *985 TL—*

I don't have time to finish typing because the Hilux is now accelerating rapidly towards me and my Yaris. I think she wants to kill me. I run that thought through my brain again. *I think she wants to fucking kill me.* The Hilux speeds up, still heading straight towards me and my waving arms. Faster. Faster. Not stopping.

I run for the safety of the nature strip and fumble for the video button on my phone because a journalist always needs proof when he or she stumbles upon the impossible. But I don't have the time or focus to hit the big red video button because all my attention has been stolen by the big red terror car about to turn my soft-purring and vulnerable Yaris to scrap metal.

I'm breathless, voiceless. She's really going to do it. *She's really going to fucking do it.* But moments before impact, she yanks right on her steering wheel and the Hilux bounces violently up the street's right-side kerb and fishtails momentarily across the grassy nature strip, nearly clipping a thick eucalypt, before bouncing back onto the Burralong Street tarmac and, with a sharp right turn, disappearing into Hamlyn Street.

I breathe once. Breathe twice. Walk off the nature strip into the middle of the road. My eyes scan up and down the street in the hope that someone was watching all this through their living room window.

Nobody to be seen. Nobody to see me. I tilt my head to the stars and the black night sky, in case anybody up there just saw what happened all the way down here in this suburban paradise we call Jubilee.

*

I pull the Yaris back into our carport at 39 Gecko Street. Breathe. Breathe again. Slip out of the front seat and open the boot and lift an open cardboard box from the car with both hands. The box is from my publisher: twenty complimentary copies of *Anonymous Source* for any friends and family members who might have asked for one. Nobody's asked for one.

I close the boot with my right elbow, then turn around in the darkness of my street and find myself standing face to face with a witch.

'I've spoken with her, Noah,' says Anushka Burman.

I nearly toss my box of books at her in fright. 'Jeeesus, Noosh,' I say. 'You scared the life outta me.'

'Fear not the witch, Noah,' she says. 'Fear the ones who burned her alive.'

She has long curled black hair that falls to her hips. A beauty spot below the right edge of her mouth. She's wearing her purple silk nightgown and black slippers. The words 'Resting Witch Face' are written in cobweb-font across the nightgown. Anushka lives at number 36 Gecko Street. She advertises her therapy services on the back of her purple Mitsubishi Mirage hatchback, which is currently parked in her pebblecrete driveway: *Psychic medium, psychotherapist, modern witch and healer.*

'I saw your car pull in,' she says. 'I had to see you. She spoke to me, Noah.'

'Who spoke to you, Noosh?'

'Tamsin.'

'Tamsin spoke to you?'

'She witnessed my clairaudience last night.'

'Your what?'

'My clairaudience. Some nights I open my mind to *seeing* the guidance. We call this clair*voyance*. But other nights I go to my sacred dark and take guidance from what I hear. A whole host of voices from the beyond realms. My personal clair*audience*.'

'I see.'

'Last night, Tamsin joined my audience. She spoke to me, Noah.'

Call the funny farm, Cork. Tell 'em to fix a room for your neighbour here. You might wanna book a room for yourself while you're at it.

'What did she say, Noosh?'

'She just kept repeating the same name over and over again.'

Anushka takes a step closer to me. Her left palm cradling her right palm at her waist, like she's offering some form of invisible Buddhist almsgiving. 'Helen,' she says, mystically.

She waits for my face to turn white, but it doesn't. 'Does that name mean anything to you?' she asks.

I pause for a moment to check if she's joking. 'Helen Fellows. Tamsin's daughter, Noosh. Her name's all through the papers.'

The good witch of Gecko Street nods twice. 'Tamsin worries for her,' she says.

Tell her, Cork. Tell this nutbar she's not the only one in the street who interacts with the daisy pushers.

'I saw her in my closet, Noosh,' I whisper.

Anushka takes another step closer. 'Who?'

'Tamsin,' I say. 'I saw her in my bed. I saw her mowing the lawn. I saw her riding a bike to Jubilee Plaza. She's just a skeleton.'

'Tamsin's ghost?'

'It's not a ghost. It's just something my brain is making me see.'

'Uh-huh,' she says, as casual as she might respond to me telling her that I've switched from Omo laundry powder to Radiant. 'Did this … sacred *something* … manage to communicate anything to you?'

'She keeps trying to get a word out, but she can't say the word. Her mouth keeps falling off when she tries to speak. She's got no flesh, no tissue on her body to help her talk. She's trying to say an "S" word … *Sssssss* … but she can't get it all the way out.'

'An "S" word?' Noosh says. She bites her bottom lip, deep in thought. 'The letter "S" has great significance in the spiritual realm. It stands for *serenity* and *strength*. But it can also mean the serpent, Noah. The snake.'

'I hate snakes,' I say.

'You shouldn't. The snake is all-knowing and all-powerful. The great temptress but also the sacred feminine. Think of the curvature of the letter "S". The flow of energy in it. Like the flow of water, is it not?'

'Well, it seems like a bit of an over-reach, but I guess—'

'It's the water element, Noah. Tamsin is leading you to water.'

'You can lead a hack to water but you can't make him—'

Noosh draws breath with the realisation of something.

'After Tamsin said that name to me, Noah' – she grips her bottom lip, pondering the meanings in the whispers buried in her head – 'I spread my tarot cards face down across my bed. The first card I picked up, Noah: *the hanged man*.'

'That doesn't sound good,' I say, swallowing a sigh.

'Well, the hanged man is many things, Noah. Many "S" things. Surrender. Sacrifice. Selfishness. Sometimes it just means … *stop*. A suspension of … *actions*. A letting go.'

Some kind of dark shadow swirls through the modern witch's gaze. Something that makes me pause, makes me momentarily suspend my actions.

'Is there anything you can think of that you might need to stop doing, Noah? Is there anything you might need to suspend?'

Aside from this conversation … 'Well, I guess I've been going a bit hard on this Tamsin yarn for a while now, truth be told.'

'Maybe you need a break from it all? All that darkness?'

'I'm going to take a long break from it all and attend to all the things I need to attend to, just as soon as I get this book out there.' I hold up the open box of books. 'You want a complimentary copy?'

Noosh studies the book's cover for a moment. 'No, thanks, Noah, I don't care for that book's energy. Sorry.'

'Mmmm … you just said another "S" word.'

Noosh turns and walks back towards her house. 'Look for the water, Noah,' says the good witch of Gecko Street. 'Look for the water.'

*

I lug the book box through the front door. Erin sits on a stool at the kitchen bench, tapping on her laptop. A calculator and her tube pencil case holding three pens rest beside the computer.

'Hey bro, how was your day?' she asks, eyes not moving from the laptop.

'Eventful.'

I scan the kitchen and the living room off the kitchen. Dishes piled by the sink. Clem's schoolbag and hat resting on a living room armchair.

'Where's Mum?'

'In her room,' Erin says.

'Where's Clem?'

'In her room,' Erin repeats. 'They're total weirdos.'

'Why are they weirdos?'

'Mum's not speaking to me.'

'Why? What did you say to her?'

'Nothing,' Erin says. 'I didn't do nuthin', bro. I didn't say nuthin'. Clem says Mum's not talking to anyone. Hasn't spoken to anyone since lunchtime.'

'What? That's ridiculous.'

'I think something happened at the excursion today. Clem says Mum was attacked by a bird or something.'

'A bird?'

I drop the box of books on the kitchen bench and my wallet and phone and the keys to the Yaris in the purple fruit bowl. Hurry down the hall. Clem's bedroom door is closed. Our main bedroom door is half-open. Rita's lying flat on her back on the bed, head on a pillow. Her arms are by her side, palms flat on the sheets. Sunburn on her forehead. The smell of sun cream on her skin. A dark green linen shirt, tucked in, sleeves rolled up to her elbows, bringing out the emerald in her eyes, which stare at the bedroom ceiling. Blue denim jeans, low-cut mint-green Converse sneakers still on her feet.

'Hey, are you all right?' I ask. I sit down on the bed, leaning over her face. Run my thumbs across her cheekbones, checking for signs of scratching. 'Erin said you were attacked by a bird or something?'

Rita nods.

'What happened?'

She takes a deep breath. Her left hand finds my thigh and rests on it for a moment. She smiles weakly.

'What happened?' I ask again. 'What happened with the bird, Rita? Are you all right? Just tell me you're okay?'

She pats my thigh. Nods her head twice.

'What is this? Erin says you're not talking? Is this a joke? Did Clem tell you to do this?'

Rita turns her head slowly to the left and then slowly to the right.

'All right, this is all very funny, Rita,' I say. 'But, honestly, hon, I've had a *very* strange day and I really can't deal with this right now. Honestly, Rita, I *cannot* deal. What's goin' on?'

Only her eyes now, staring so deep into mine that I feel love for her, and then warmth and protection and devotion and awe and wonder. Then all these beautiful things turn to confusion and frustration. 'Don't be silly, Rita,' I say. 'It's not funny. You're scaring me. Stop it.'

Her head tilts slightly towards her right shoulder. There's pain in her face. Seriousness. Sorrow. Then a single tear pools in the bottom of her right eyelid, breaks its flesh-formed levee and rolls down her cheekbone dusted with the freckles that reveal themselves whenever Rita spends too long in the sun.

My left thumb gently wipes the tear away. 'Why the hell are you crying?' I whisper.

She shakes her head, smiles. Her left hand squeezes my left hand.

'Just … say something,' I say. 'Just tell me what's going on. What the hell happened today, Rita? Were you harmed in some way? Were you hurt? What happened with the bird?'

Clem's room is across the hall from ours. I look towards her closed door. 'Clem,' I call, 'can you come in here a minute?'

Something in the way I just turned my legs causes a familiar shooting pain to surge like an electrical charge inside my recently embattled scrotum.

'Ugggghhhh,' I howl. I stand and move my legs to mitigate any further bolts of agonising and mysterious pain in my acorns.

Rita sits up on the bed, a look of concern across her face.

I breathe and shake my head at her. 'Don't worry, it's nothing,' I say. 'Just a little burning sensation … um … you know … down south. Started last night. It's probably nothing.'

I call out to Clem again. 'Clem, can you please come in here?'

Her door doesn't open. I shuffle to her bedroom, tap my knuckle three times on the door. 'Clem? Can I come in? Clem? You decent?'

I knock three more times. Nothing. I open the door to find Clem lying on her bed with her wireless headphones on, chunky pink and purple ones with cat ears that change colour in time to the beat of any given song. Eyes closed. Her twelve-year-old head bobbing to the music, beneath a shrine of wall posters and stickers and badges unsubtly indicating her devotion to the gospel of her lady and saviour, Taylor Alison Swift.

'Clem,' I say. No response. I lift the earphone from her right ear. 'Hey … Miss Americana … sorry to interrupt.'

Clem sits up on her bed. 'Hey, Dad,' she says, smiling. I kiss her on her forehead, right arm pulling her in for a brief hug.

'What's going on with Mum?' I ask, sitting on the edge of her bed.

'Yeah, she's not talkin', ay,' Clem says.

'When did she stop talking?'

'I don't know exactly, Dad,' Clem says. 'I thought she was just being quiet, but then we were driving home from the excursion and she just stopped talking to me. Like, she wasn't answering any of my questions. She was just nodding and shaking her head. And I just came right out and asked her if she was gonna stop talking for a bit and she nodded her head and kept her eyes on the road and I just said, "That's okay with me, Mum, if that's what you need to do." Because I thought about how I don't like talking sometimes, either. I figured Mum has to talk all the time to everyone. To you, to me, to Erin, to Nan and Grandad, to her friends, to the teachers at school, to Ellis and June and all the other neighbours, to the people at the phone company and the electricity company and the hot water comp—'

'Clem, slow down for a second,' I say. 'Was there anything you can recall that you said to her or maybe someone else said to her that might have made her stop talking?'

'I dunno. Nobody said anything to her. I think it was the birds, Dad.'

'What birds?'

'All the birds around the creek,' she says. 'I reckon there must have been twenty birds coming for her.'

Clem hangs her headphones around her neck and starts making flapping wings out of her hands. 'They all just came flapping around her. Flap, flap, flap, flap—'

'Wait, Clem. Take me through it, as slowly as you can. Where were you when these birds turned up?'

'The whole class was panning for gold,' she says. 'This old man from the pioneer village, who called himself Curly – I don't think that was his real name – he showed us all how to pan for gold in the creek. You gotta start by putting some creek dirt into the pan and then you add some water and then you gotta slosh it around just right so the gold can settle on the bottom. Gold settles on the bottom of the pan because it's heavier than all the other sand and the tiny bits of rock. But the trick is sloshing out the lighter sand without also sloshing out your life's fortune. Curly said he once sloshed a Porsche 911 straight into the drink.'

'Sweetie, when did the birds come?' I ask.

'Well, the rest of the class was all crowded at one end of the creek and I said to Mum that we'd have more chance of striking it rich if we went around this quiet little bend in the creek where we could be by ourselves. It was so pretty this spot, Dad. Big pine trees surrounding us and the water looked like Coke Zero when you pour it over ice. We were kneeling by the edge of the creek. Then I'm all distracted because I think I've found my fortune in the pan – if not a Porsche 911, then at least a new Mitsubishi Outlander for us. And I turn to show my pan to Mum and I see her staring into the creek water. She's about three metres from me, just staring at her reflection in the water. Or maybe, I thought, she was staring at the sky that was reflected in the water. And then I went and stood beside her and I stared down at what she was looking at, because I wanted to see what was so interesting. And then, in the reflection in the water, we started to see all these birds circling in the sky above us. Big black crows and magpies and other birds with beautiful colours that I can't remember ever seeing before. I looked up and it was so amazing to see all these birds making this one big circle in the air above us. Mum turned her eyes to the birds, too, and then she spread her arms out like she was a scarecrow or somethin'. "Mum," I said. "Mum." And she didn't answer me, she just closed her eyes. Kept her arms out. And then suddenly all these birds up in the sky came right down to us and started flying around us. I stepped back because I was scared and all the birds just hung around Mum. They were flapping around her and I started to worry that they were gonna attack her. So I wrapped my arms around Mum's waist and I kept my head down and started waving my arms around, screaming, "Go away. Go away." But they wouldn't go away and I got so scared, though I wasn't as scared by the birds as I was by the fact that Mum was just standing there letting the birds fly around her. She didn't do nuthin', Dad. She just let them fly around her and then some of them birds landed on her outstretched arms and some of them birds landed on her shoulders and dug their feet hard into her skin, and she just let them do that. There must have been ten birds on her at one point and it looked like they were all pulling at her shirt. Pulling at her skin. The only reason the birds flew away was because Mrs Holloway, our teacher's aide, came along and started waving a big umbrella at them. And I've been thinking about it all day, Dad. I can't get it out of my head.'

I wonder for a moment if Clem's not making all this up, as she's got a big imagination. But she's no fabulist.

'What have you been thinking about, Clem?' I ask. 'Go on, please.'

'It's stupid,' she says.

'Clem, nothing that's ever come out of your head has ever been stupid,' I say. 'Clementine Cork doesn't *do* stupid.'

Clem chuckles. Looks up from under her fringe. 'I do weird a bit, though, Dad, don't I?' she asks.

'Just a bit,' I say. 'But a bit of weird is always good for a twelve-year-old kid.'

She smiles. Fingers massaging her knuckles. She moves her body closer to mine. Talks in a whisper. 'I don't think the birds were trying to attack Mum at all,' she says. Even softer whisper now. Clem's letting me in on a secret. This is how she spoke when she was nine and she told me about the crack between the wooden floorboards of her bedroom, through which she would slip letters to a pen pal named Jemima Starhopper who lived in a parallel dimension beneath our house, a joyful utopia that had replaced its roads and footpaths with bouncing trampoline material.

'The birds were trying to take her away, Dad,' she whispers.

On second thoughts, maybe the poor kid has a little too much weird in her.

'Where were they trying to take her, Clem?'

'I dunno,' she says. She thinks for a moment and looks to her ceiling. Points her finger up. 'Up there, I guess. Up into the sky.'

A zapping pain shoots up through my body, from the burning source that is my right testicle.

'Mmmmmmphhh,' I wail, gritting my teeth to absorb the pain.

'You okay, Dad?' Clem asks.

I nod my head twice. 'Yes, honey, I'm okay. Been getting some kind of spasm or cramp or something.'

I stand and shuffle gingerly into our bedroom. Another bolt of blinding pain explodes from my balls.

I raise my voice to Rita. Too loud. Too angry. 'Stop this nonsense right now, Rita,' I say. 'You are scaring me and you are scaring your daughter. She's in there thinking all sorts of crazy things because you're carrying on with this silent-treatment bullshit. Honestly, I don't know what the hell is going on here, but we'd all very much appreciate it if you could hurry the hell up and tell us what's got into you.'

Rita remains silent.

'I'm not fuckin' around, Rita,' I say. 'I can't deal with this right now. I have had the worst day, possibly, of my life, and I don't need to come home to this bullshit. Say something. God damn it. You're being a child. *Sayyyyyy somethiiiing.*'

A thought enters my brain, a termite of a thought crawling through the information-carrier tubes of my mind. There's a Sydney hotel hallway in my head. A hotel room door off the hallway. A number on the door: 617. The door opens and I enter this room. Open wine bottle on the sideboard against the wall. A woman's red overcoat hanging from a desk chair.

Don't look at her over there on the bed.

Don't look at her over there on the bed.

I turn my head in this scene and find a female skeleton lying on the room's queen-size bed. A skeleton in a one-shoulder silver sequin mini dress. No shoes on her bare bone feet. Glass of white wine in her right bone hand. Her left bone hand patting the space on the bed beside her. The space this skeleton left just for me.

I turn to Rita in the real world. 'Is this about Georgia Long?' I ask.

Another bolt of pain in my balls.

'You can't stop thinking about her, can you? Jesus fucking Christ, Rita.'

And another bolt of pain. The brutal jolt of it forces me to my knees. I try to move my legs and flex my knees and bring my knees to my chest, but nothing makes the burning vanish down there.

'Mmmmmphhh,' I swallow. 'Arrrrgghhh.'

Eyes back to Rita. She's sitting on the edge of the bed.

'Please … Rita … just … say … something,' I plead, but the words aren't coming out right. I'm feeling dizzy. Light-headed. Struggling to form sentences, because the blinding pain in my balls is drawing too much focus from my brain.

'Please … Rita … stop … doing … this …'

Feeling faint now. Need to sit. I move towards the edge of the bed, but I don't make it that far. And then I let go. Feel myself falling. It's okay because I'll land on the bed. Yes, I'll just drop like a stone right here. This feels good. This feels right. The collapsing. The dissolving. Falling, falling, falling into the void of my blissful unconsciousness.

SEVEN

Look and look and look. Listen and listen and listen and listen again. Now write.

– Rutledge, *Journalism Practices and Principles*

Hello bluebird
Thanks for finding my kicks.
Now click your heals together three times.
'There's no place like Jubilee! There's no place like Jubilee!'
Seems I left my Bible beneeth Dot in the bone orchard.
Could you find it for me, bluebird?
I wanna go home.
TF

That's what the second note said. The actual note itself is police evidence now, but that's what it said. I read it by the birdwatcher's seat on the reservoir walking track and handed it to Miles De Jonge, who'd already read it over my shoulder. The rain made the flimsy docket soggy in Miles's fingers.

'What's all this about, Noah?' he asked.

'Kicks,' I said. 'Someone's getting their kicks by sending me on a treasure hunt.'

'What's the treasure?'

'I don't know yet. A yarn, I guess.'

'You gonna keep hunting?'

'Don't see why not.'

'Mind if I hunt with you?'

'Don't see why not. But if you stay on the hunt, then I'm gonna have to mention you when I end up writing a feature about this. Fair warning.'

'You can mention me. I'd love to be part of a Noah Cork true-crime yarn.'

Miles ran his finger under the final lines of the note. 'You know anybody with the initials TF?'

I pondered the question for a moment. 'Tracey Feldman,' I said.

'Who's Tracey Feldman?'

'A girl I kissed in Year 5.'

'She the note-writing type?'

'No. I think she develops flu vaccines at the Queensland Institute of Medical Research. You know any TFs?'

Miles lifted his head to the grey sky. His eyes widened. He clicked his fingers triumphantly. 'Tim Flannery,' he said.

'The environment guy?'

'Yeah.'

'You think Tim Flannery's leaving me messages in my letterbox?'

Miles scratched his head. 'Seems unlikely,' he said.

The rain intensified. I took the note from Miles and slipped it inside my wallet to keep it from being destroyed. I walked back along the twisting trail and Miles followed, unpicking the clues in the note, like some chirpy and excitable Watson to my more reserved Holmes.

'What the hell's a bone orchard?' Miles asked.

'Graveyard,' I replied.

'And what about the name,' Miles pondered aloud. 'Dot?'

'Short for Dorothy,' I said.

The name didn't register with Miles.

'As in, Dorothy Gale,' I said.

'Who's Dorothy Gale?' Miles asked.

'Dorothy and the dog and the yellow brick road,' I replied.

'Wow!' Miles said. 'You do this detective stuff a bit do ya, Noah?'

'No.'

'We off to see the wizard now?' Miles laughed.

'Nah, Miles,' I said. 'We're off to church.'

*

It was still raining hard when the Yaris pulled into the driveway of the Jubilee Uniting Church on Wicker Road.

'So what are we doing here?' Miles asked.

Miles was soaking wet. The heater in the Yaris was turned up fully so we could dry our clothes, but the downside of this was the smell it drew from beneath Miles's jogger's armpits. No doubt I didn't smell much better.

'The only cemetery in Jubilee,' I said, pointing at a large silver cross fixed to the wall of a sprawling red and yellow brick church that could pass as a large-scale work of cubist art.

High and neat garden hedges surrounding the church. Flame-coloured ornamental plants lining the pavement.

'There's no cemetery in Jubilee,' Miles says.

'There's a very small one right behind that church,' I replied.

'Bullshit? Really?'

'Rita's great-great-uncle Bill Blair is buried there. Scottish cabinetmaker who came out here in 1911. Fought for Australia. Was taken prisoner in the Battle of Bullecourt. Repatriated to England with shrapnel wounds. Met a Scottish nurse named Fifer. They sailed off to Australia, via the moon, and landed smack-bang in the middle of what used to be known as Spearwood, before it got pimped up to Jubilee.'

The church carpark was empty. Nor were there any churchgoers inside, praying in the wooden pews. Just a woman in trainers with a vacuum on her back like a jetpack, running the power head across the carpeted altar and stage area of the church, beneath two sky-blue banners, one reading *Peace* and the other *Hope*. Our presence startled her. She switched off the vacuum and I told her that we had come to visit the grave of my wife's great-great-uncle Bill. The cleaner studied our clothes and raised an eyebrow as she nodded to a door at the rear of the church.

Bordered by a low orange-brick fence, the cemetery occupied a space not much bigger than a tennis court. Concrete and white marble burial plots dating back to the 1800s. Weathered headstones browned with age.

To the memory of Henry Heywood, who, after a long and painful illness, departed this life on 8th February, 1873, aged 45 years.

'Tell me if you see a Dorothy,' I said to Miles.

We scoured the cemetery for almost half an hour in the rain. White and grey and bronze-coloured headstones told stories of pioneer migrants who lived to their eighties and newborns who never lived a day. There was no more room in the grass for the newly dead to occupy.

'Found her, Noah,' Miles called through the rain. I turned from a grave by the western side of the yard to find Miles standing by a columbarium running along the eastern side. Hundreds of square metal plates, all the size of a postcard, bearing the names and departure details of cremated loved ones. Dozens of niches waiting to be filled by the remains of new dead. Miles was kneeling, running his forefinger along a plate he'd found.

In loving memory of Dorothy Elizabeth Beane
Departed this life 15 March 1987
Aged 78 years
The Lord gave and the Lord has taken away
Blessed be the name of the Lord

'Ya reckon she's our Dot?' Miles asked.

I shrugged, then kneeled beside Miles at the memorial plate.

'Dorothy Beane?' Miles said. 'What's she got to do with anything?'

'Nothing,' I said. 'Just a name.'

Then I turned my attention to the empty niche below Dorothy Beane's memorial plate. A rectangular void built into the brick memorial wall, waiting for an urn to fill it. I stared into the hole in the wall and saw nothing but darkness.

'Anything in there?' Miles asked.

'Can't tell,' I said.

I reached my right hand into the void, slowly. My fingers found something hard and flat at the end of the hole. A book. A pocket-sized Bible. Black faux-leather cover. Text pages that felt as thin as tobacco rolling papers. I hunched over with the Bible in my hands, shielding it from the rain. Thumbed through it and it opened wide where someone had dog-eared a page – more than likely, I thought, the same someone who had placed the book in the empty niche. Passages from Isaiah, and, on the right-hand page, a roughly scribbled message over the printed text in red permanent marker pen.

Hello   lemon drop
Almost done, ya   wunnerful one
Seems I left my tin   heart in Monaco's place
Could you find it for me,   lemon drop?
I wanna go   home.
TF

On the left page of the open Bible, a line of verse had been roughly circled by the same red marker. Words from Isaiah 2:12.

The Lord Almighty has a day in store for all the proud and lofty, for all that is exalted (and they will be humbled).

I handed the pocket Bible to Miles. Wiped rainwater through my soaked hair as Miles read the note.

'Ummm … yeah … this is getting a little creepy now, mate,' he said. 'In fact, I'm startin' to think this is all a little fucked up.'

Miles read aloud the circled line from Isaiah. 'Is that supposed to be a shot at you? Are you "proud and lofty"?'

'Nah,' I said. 'Most of the time I'm lowly and ashamed.'

'Sounds like a threat to me,' Miles said. 'Who the fuck would leave someone messages like this?'

I had been asking myself that same question. 'Someone who's a true-crime nut, I'm guessing,' I said.

I stood and ambled back across the graveyard in the rain. Miles followed me.

'Someone who's probably read too many of my true-crime pieces in the *Courier-Mail*,' I continued. 'Someone who's familiar with the long and, yes, fucked-up, tradition of criminals engaging the media in their work.'

'What sorta *work* are we talkin' about here?'

'Dennis Rader's sorta work comes to mind,' I said. 'He sent a letter to the *Wichita Eagle* newspaper in 1974, saying he had killed four members of the same family. "The monster goes on", he wrote. Spelling mistakes all through his letter. He gave the paper a series of code words to know him by: "Bind them"; "Torture them"; "Kill them". That's how Rader became known as the BTK Killer.'

Miles shook his head, turned his eyes back to the note in the Bible in his hands.

'Rader killed at least ten people between 1974 and 1991,' I said. 'His day job for a decade was installing home-security alarm systems for Wichita homeowners who were concerned about the very killings he had committed. He kept things from his kills.'

'Like what?' Miles asked.

'Keepsakes,' I said. 'Some sickos like to keep things from their crimes. Reminders of past glories. Mementos. Souvenirs.'

We marched back through the church to my car.

'What sorta souvenirs?' Miles asked across the roof of the Yaris.

I slipped into my seat, reached for my seatbelt. Miles did the same on the passenger side.

'Well, Australia's own Ivan Milat, he kept clothes and camping supplies,' I replied. 'Ted Bundy preferred to keep human heads. Charles Albright kept the eyeballs of his victims. That's why he got called the Eyeball Killer. Dennis Rader kept all kinds of personal items: things like jewellery and clothing and drivers' licences.'

'He ever keep a pocket Bible?' Miles asked.

'Not that I know of.'

I thought for a moment about where I was going to drive to next.

'So, what,' Miles asked, 'you think you got some serial killer communicating with you?'

'No,' I replied. 'Not at all. This is someone, I imagine, with too much time on their hands who's trying to send me on a wild goose chase because I wrote something unflattering about them once in a feature story.'

'Any *someones* spring to mind in particular?' Miles asked.

'Well, I can think of about a dozen someones I've pissed off over the years,' I replied, 'all of whom would love nothing more than to waste my time with a bullshit quest like this.'

'So you go to the cops?' Miles asked. 'Tell 'em some creepy arsehole's dropping notes in your letterbox?'

'Rule number one of the first-person true-crime feature yarn, Miles,' I said, 'is never bring in the cops unless it's absolutely essential to the narrative. Nobody can kill a crime story quite as quickly as a Queensland cop.'

'But what if this weirdo's got something in store for you that's something the cops need to know about?'

'I would say roughly ninety-nine per cent of physical threats made against journalists by the public are never followed through,' I said. 'This right here isn't even a threat. This is a game being played by some troll currently dressed in nothing but a singlet and underpants, stirring a tall glass of Milo chocolate malt drink while he logs into milo-in-my-undies dot com.'

'So, what now?' Miles asked.

'We see where the story goes,' I replied. 'That's my job, Miles. That's what I do. I see where the story goes and then I write about where the story went.'

'It's not what I do, mate,' Miles said. 'I wash nappies most days.'

'Yeah, well, not today you don't,' I said. 'Today you can help me find Monaco's place.'

'Well, that's easy,' Miles said.

He pointed a finger in the direction of the Brisbane CBD. 'Everybody knows Monaco House,' he said.

'What are you talkin' about?'

'The big run-down mansion on Wicker Road. Big fenced-up joint, looks like the place where The Eagles wrote "Hotel California".'

I started the car, put it in reverse.

'Show me,' I said.

*

I'd driven past it a thousand times. A sprawling three-storey hacienda-style architectural marvel left to die beside the Jubilee

Garden Centre and a Mobil service station. Giancarlo Monaco was a property developer who purchased the five-thousand-square-metre block in 1967. By 2016, the home was vacant and a group of other local property developers were announcing plans to turn the site into a luxury sixty-seven-apartment residential building with a rooftop swimming pool and an open-air cinema. It was going to be called Monaco Place, in honour of the site's original owner.

'But the project went south,' Miles explained from the passenger seat of the Yaris, which was parked on a sloping slab of concrete in front of the security fence surrounding what had been Giancarlo Monaco's family home for four decades. 'Giancarlo's fortunes took a dive in the GFC. He had a wife and five kids living there, and one day they all just upped and left the joint. The place was left to rot. People say you go in there now and it's filled with furnishings and household items, just like nobody ever left. Dinner plates and salad bowls. Big shelves with books an' shit. Pots and pans. Televisions and VCRs. It's like a whole family has just been abducted by aliens or somethin'.'

'Why'd they leave everything?'

'Beats me. Maybe they realised that most of the shit we all cart from house to house throughout our lives is ultimately about as valuable as a fart.'

I looked at the site through the car windscreen. The rain had stopped. A gloomy sky backgrounded the abandoned home. Two tall palm trees towered above an arched third-storey balcony. The white brick walls of the building were covered in graffiti tags: *FBS*, *SIKO*, *ZOAR*. I wondered how many deadly eastern brown snakes had slithered from Teaneck Creek into the weedy overgrowth beyond the fence. I unbuckled my seatbelt. 'Let's take a squiz,' I said.

Miles did not move. 'Fuck that for a joke,' he said.

'What's the problem?'

'I'm not goin' in there,' he said with a higher pitch to his voice, like he was refusing an offer to sip from a bottle of engine coolant.

'Why not?'

'The place is filled with meth heads,' Miles said. 'I heard they crank all night in there and sleep all day among the rats and snakes. One of the dads from school works on the front desk at the cop shop. He told me six months ago they found a dead goat in the centre of the living room upstairs. Thing was all cut up inside one of them Satan's pentagrams that someone spray-painted on the carpet. Occult shit. Devil worshipper fuckin' nerds-in-trenchcoats shit. Cops have had to go to all the principals of the schools around here and warn the kids from ever stepping foot inside the place. Nah, fuck that for a joke. You wanna see where the story goes, be my guest. But I'll wait right here, thanks. I can read your story when it's published.' He folded his arms across his chest.

'All right,' I said. 'If I'm not back in thirty minutes, call the cops and tell them I went walking into Monaco House and there's a fair chance I'm being cut up by the children of Lucifer.'

Miles nodded, taking the request more seriously than I'd expected.

Someone had cut a hole in a corner of the security fence. My old Cranberries T-shirt caught on the wire as I crawled through the hole to a front yard filled with weeds and broken wine and beer bottles. Planks of wood and sheets of plasterboard were scattered about the entrance to the sprawling house, along with dinner plates caked in dirt, drawers with no cupboard to slot into. A used fire extinguisher. By the front door sat a basketball cut open at the top, like it had been scalped by Comanche warriors, and filled with dirt and uncapped disposable syringes. Someone had gone to great trouble to make this piece of décor; it looked cared for, like one of Rita's potted geraniums.

A long stretch of copper wiring sheathed in orange plastic was hanging from a balcony above the front door. Some creative soul had tied it into a welcoming hangman's noose.

The green double wooden doors were wide open, allowing free access to an entrance hall and, beyond it, via three small steps, the rest of the house. The hall was silent and poorly lit by window light, but I could see that the house spilled onto many rooms and passages.

I knocked loudly three times on the doors. 'Hello,' I called.

If there were any sleeping meth addicts inside, I wanted them to meet me at the front door, where I figured I would say something about having seen my dog, Hercules, squeeze under the fence and enter their temporary home.

'Anyone around?' I called.

Nothing. The floor of the entrance hall was covered in broken stone tiles and the floor beyond the hall was strewn with paperback books that looked like they once belonged to a property developer. Books on wealth creation. Books on achievement and self-improvement. *How to Avoid Detours on the Road to Success* by Bill Newman. *Don't Tie Yourself Up in 'Nots'* by David P. Schloss. A book about piloting aeroplanes. A TV tie-in book for *Better Homes and Gardens*. A collection of six

British hardback Brownie Annuals from the 1970s. A dozen books about scouting, including *The Australian Scout Songbook*, *The Official Boy Scout Handbook 1978* and *Cub Scout Boomerang Trails*.

Filing cabinets by the walls. Graffiti on the walls. A painted portrait of a man's face with crosses for eyes. A shopping trolley filled with empty boxes in the corner of the hall. A hubcap filled with cigarette butts. Another hubcap, this one filled with disposable syringes. An overwhelming whiff of shit – rat or possum or human – grew more intense with every forward step.

'Hello,' I called again, climbing the three steps that led to a larger hall with three doors opening onto other rooms in the house. One led to a small kitchenette, like something built for guests, where I saw a pot resting on a stovetop, half-filled with tinned spaghetti that had turned the colour of snooker chalk. Another door led to a bedroom that was empty but for two old mattresses covered in dirt and what looked to me like dried blood. A Satanic pentagram had been drawn in black paint across one wall, and in four places across the walls someone had spray-painted the number 764 in black and red paint. Off this bedroom was a bathroom with a toilet bowl filled with a mountain of dried human shit that could not possibly have been flushed.

At the far side of the hall I came to an old wooden switchback staircase that looked like it might fall on top of me if I stood under it for too long, or collapse beneath me if I walked up it.

I thought about my anonymous source's note inside the Bible, and I thought about what a tin heart might look like. I wondered how I might find such a thing in this rundown mess of cockroach-munched, possum-pissed decay and family ephemera. I thought about seeing where the story went.

'Hello,' I called again, from the bottom of the staircase.

The wooden banisters were covered in white and grey bird shit. The ceramic tiles on the stairs were decorated with an Art Deco gold and white pattern that resembled an unfurled handheld silk fan.

I took one step up the staircase. The banister nearly tipped over when I placed my weight upon it. Wallpaper peeling from the walls around me. Two steps up. Three steps up. I heard a rustling sound coming from the room above the staircase. The smashing of glass.

'Helloooo,' I hollered.

No sound in reply.

'Sorry to intrude,' I called. 'I thought I saw … my dog … ummm … He ran into this place …'

Nothing. But the rustling sound continued beyond the stairs.

At the top of the staircase I came to an archway that led into a lounge room with a wooden media entertainment unit built into a corner. There was a television in the centre of the unit and its screen had been smashed in. Dust-covered VHS cassettes and CDs were strewn across the ceramic tiled flooring. A Richard Clayderman CD. A Tears for Fears cassette.

Then the sound of a bottle smashing on hard tiles made my body shudder with vein-freezing fear. I turned right at an opening off the lounge area and came to the home's main kitchen and dining area, where a heavyset magpie was walking through a crowded collection of glass jars and tea and coffee cups on a mud-spattered benchtop. The magpie and I locked eyes for a moment before it flew out of the house via an open set of wood and glass bi-fold doors leading to an ornate balcony off the kitchen.

The floor of the adjoining dining area was covered in burnt paper, as though someone had made an open fire there. The number 764 had been spray-painted several times on the walls here too. The smell of mould and faeces mixed with something new – burnt animal flesh maybe. A bowl of dead roses sat on an island-bench gas cooktop. The exposed floor-to-ceiling kitchen shelves were filled with broken plates and broken sugar bowls and broken Dutch ovens. Between the shelving and the dual-tub kitchen sink was a built-in stainless-steel oven that looked big enough and fancy enough to be used in a restaurant kitchen.

And written diagonally and roughly across the door of this oven in vivid white spray-paint were two words. These words made no sense to me. These words interested me. These words, I thought, would read intriguingly in whatever feature story I would form from the strange couple of hours I had just experienced on this rainy, life-changing morning.

Cunt money.

Each letter in the word 'money' had dripped and the tail of the 'y' in 'money' had run all the way down to the bottom of the oven door, ending at a dome of paint that was rock hard to the touch. These words had not been painted recently.

On the left side of the oven, resting on the kitchen-sink bench beside a red electric water jug, was a stack of three books. The book on the top of the stack was a faded, bent and half-burnt copy of *The Satanic Bible* by Anton Szandor LaVey.

Black paperback cover with a five-pointed star in the centre. The second book was a university textbook: *Journalism Practices and Principles* by Professor Lionel Rutledge. Second edition, published 1996. I'd read that book three times, almost knew it by heart, as it was required reading in my time at the University of Queensland journalism school. Me and my uni mates would make jokes about getting long Rutledge quotes tattooed on our arse cheeks: '*The journalist reports the problems, the journalist does not solve the problems. Never sacrifice objectivity for journalistic glory. There are no victories in journalism and there are no losses. There are only facts.*' The placing of Rutledge in the stack of books seemed pointed and deliberate, some kind of statement the killer was making about modern news media, about the kind of journalist who follows true-crime breadcrumbs into an abandoned building for a story. But it was the third book, the one at the bottom of the stack, that I picked up. *The Wonderful Wizard of Oz* by L. Frank Baum. An old paperback edition from the 1960s. Green and yellow cover with a cartoon image of the cowardly lion wearing spectacles and a bow in his hair. The book's pages were yellowed. I opened the cover to the flimsy front matter and found a message scrawled across the title page.

Ding dong, bluebird !
The witch is dead.
Which old witch?
The one we cooked in the fuckin' oven!
Ding!
Ding!
Ding!

I threw the book on the kitchen bench. Stared at the oven door. I should have called the police then. I should have walked straight out of that nightmarish kitchen and slipped straight back into the Yaris with my dad friend Miles. Me, the struggling and penniless hack, and Miles, the guy who washes nappies for a crust. We could have driven straight to the cops and I never would have had to see what I saw next.

I sure wish I'd never opened that oven door. But I did. I had to see where the story went. And I don't know what part of my brain and my soul so often allows that desire to overwhelm my caution and common sense. And I try to tell myself that I didn't open that door because I'm just another cunt in need of money. I'm *not* a cunt in need of money, I swear. I'm just a cunt who needs an ensuite bathroom off our main bedroom.

I gripped the oven door handle and took a deep breath. The door opened with a rusty creak. I saw the right foot first, when it flopped onto the inside of the oven door as I brought it down. The bones were the colour of ash. Burnt bones. Fire bones. The darkest kids' song ever written entered my head. *The foot bone's connected to the leg bone. The leg bone's connected to the knee bone. The knee bone's connected to … Oh dear God, no.* There were no trays inside the oven. The bent and snapped and distorted skeleton occupied the entire space. The ribcage was intact and pressed against the back of the oven, precariously propping up a skull that was the colour of a wiped chalkboard. High cheekbones. A wide terror smile of charred teeth. A teepee-shaped hollow where the nose used to be. Arm bones not connected to the torso bones but leaning against them, as if the whole skeleton had been artfully assembled that way.

The skeleton was sitting upon a bed of cooled and dusty coals, and there was something shining at the centre of the ribcage. My stomach stirred for a moment and I swallowed air three times to fight a physical urge to vomit up my Weet-Bix-and-sliced-banana breakfast. I pulled my phone from my pocket and tapped on the torch app. Shone a light directly at the ribcage. It was only then I could see the necklace hanging from the black-dust collarbones. A thin silver chain holding a heart-shaped metal locket. A tin heart with a name engraved across it.

Tamsin.

EIGHT

You are a voice for the voiceless. You are not a megaphone for the moronic.

– Rutledge, *Journalism Practices and Principles*

This is where the dream begins: Tamsin's skeleton putting a bone forefinger to her mouth. An 'S' sound: 'Ssssshhhhh'. We must be quiet because it's after hours in the museum of my life. I know this place. I know this building. This is the Noah Cork museum at midnight. Tamsin's skeleton leads me on. I notice now that Tamsin's skeleton is gripping a heavy black crowbar in her left hand. Why is Tamsin holding that black crowbar? What could Tamsin possibly need a crowbar for in the museum of my mind?

The bones of her feet clickety-clack like a tap dancer's shoes on the museum's polished wood floors. Her rickety limbs move through glass display cases holding the technicolour memories of my life. The ceiling lights are out in the museum, but there is enough light bouncing from the maze of glass cases surrounding us. Tamsin doesn't look into them as we move through the museum, but I do. There's me and my mum, Alison Cork.

Scenes of a real life we both lived once, unfolding like a film projected on a screen of air, a memory playing on repeat inside this glass prism in my dreaming. We're in the Bega Street house on Bribie Island. We're in my bedroom and it's raining outside and I'm under my favourite blanket – the one with all the country flags of the world on it – and Mum's reading me *Storm Boy* because I love that book about the kid whose best friend is a bird. There's me at my graduation, in my black gown and cap, with my dad, Phil Cork. He's wearing his fishing flanno, but it's okay because he's wearing it in a formal manner, tucked into his best blue jeans; he's even buttoned the flannel right up to the top button that's pressing into his Adam's apple. 'You're gonna be a shit-hot journo, mate,' Dad says, beaming proudly. Mum kisses my cheek. She can't seem to remove her left palm from the part of my chest that protects my heart. Mum starts to cry. 'You're really gonna make a difference, Noah,' she says.

Tamsin's skeleton walks on through the museum. She doesn't care for all these precious exhibits. There's me and Rita on the first night we met. We're standing on platform four of the Bowen Hills train station. I watch myself leap from the train platform onto the railway tracks below. The next display case shows our house on Gecko Street, with the roof being peeled from its fixings. There's me running for my life. And there's my wife, Rita, staring at the swirling storm like there was some kind of encrypted message written in the eye of it that only she could decipher. Another case has Rita in a hospital bed, sucking in short, sharp breaths and then pushing and pushing and pushing our precious Erin into being. But Tamsin the skeleton has no interest in these scenes. She keeps walking and walking and walking on and I have to follow her. I don't want to follow her, but I have to. We walk all the way to the back of the museum. All the way to the darkest corridor of the museum, where we come to a wall with only one white door built into it, and upon this door is a word that tells me something about what it contains: *STORAGE.* Tamsin's skeleton attempts to open the door but it's locked. She turns back to me and offers me the crowbar.

I raise my palms. 'No, Tamsin,' I say. 'No.'

Tamsin's skeleton shrugs her round bone shoulders. Her fused and exposed tooth-lined jaw seems to smile sympathetically at me. Then she drives the crowbar into the lock, levers the rear end of the crowbar twice, and chips of wood explode violently from the doorframe.

Tamsin grips the door handle once more.

'No, Tamsin!' I scream. 'Please, God, nooooooooo!'

But she doesn't listen to me. She opens the storage door and all the heavy water in the whole of the Pacific Ocean floods into the museum of my life, drowning me and Tamsin the skeleton in a churning sea of flathead fish and mud crabs and sharks and starfish and the cracked glass cases holding every story of my life that was ever worth keeping.

*

Breathe, Noah. Breathe. I wake from the dream with a gasp and suck in air as my eyes take a moment to adjust to a bright white light coming from a fluorescent tube on the ceiling above me. The ceiling is moving. No, wait. The ceiling is staying put and it's me who's moving. I lift my head. Dizzy. Groggy. Nurses on either side of me. Blue scrubs. Blue surgery masks tied around their faces. A trolley. I'm lying on a hospital trolley and these nurses are pushing me down a hospital aisle. A room now. Not as bright as the aisle. Metal bowls and metal trays and machines blinking with numbers in yellow and red. A surgery room. I feel so good. I feel so calm. I'm not at all bothered to find myself in this strange place. A man's hand cups my cheek and a man's head leans over me. I see this man upside-down. A mask across his face.

'Mr Cork, my name's Dr Ben Hong,' he says. 'I'm a consultant urologist at the Royal Brisbane and Women's Hospital. You are experiencing a rather severe case of testicular torsion.'

'Testicular ... *whaaat*?' I mumble.

'Your right testicle has rotated multiple times, twisting the spermatic cord that brings blood to your scrotum.'

'Jesus Christ.'

'Not his fault, I'm afraid,' Dr Hong says. 'In men your age it's usually the result of too much strenuous exercise. You been to the gym much lately?'

'I've been going twice a week,' I say. 'My doctor suggested I go twice a week as a way to relieve stress.'

'Well, Mr Cork, it seems we now need to bring some emergency stress relief to your right plum, which is in a bit of a state,' Dr Hong says. 'Try to picture, if you can, your right nut as a ripe red grape hanging off the stalk on the vine that's bringing it all that good water and sugar that makes a grape taste so sweet. You've twisted your stalk and no blood's getting to your grape and now your grape is rather agonisingly shrinking. Withering on the vine, as it were. In fact, if we don't untwist your testicle right now, we might even have to pluck that poor thing from the vine altogether. But, rest assured, you'll still have the left one making some high-quality merlot. Can you tell me when the pain started?'

'Sometime early this morning?' I reply. 'Three a.m. or something, maybe.'

'Why didn't you come straight to hospital?'

'Well ... I ... I ... I had this really important book event to get to? Kind of a launch thing for a book I've written.'

'Wow,' Dr Hong says. 'Must be one helluva book if you're willing to risk a gonad for it.'

Dr Hong addresses a trio of masked registrars. 'Yeah, people, we best dive in quick-smart if we're gonna save this bloke's stuffed olive.'

He turns back to me. 'Mr Cork, we're just gonna knock you out for a wee while and then I'll make a small cut in your scrotum and I'll get that wound-up little acorn untwisted for you, okay? You good with that, Mr Cork?'

'Yes,' I say. 'I'm good with that.'

'All right,' Dr Hong says, as a nurse places a snug-fitting mask over my face. 'Sweet dreams, Mr Cork.'

'Funny you say that,' I say. 'I just woke from the strangest dreeeee—'

*

Morning now in the RBWH public recovery ward, and Clem stands beside my hospital bed, scanning my breakfast tray for viable food options. A green curtain circles the bed. The sound of nurses making rounds beyond the closed curtain. Families catching up with in-patients. An old man snores loudly in the curtained bay to my left.

Clem eyes an uneaten bowl of Corn Flakes and a sealed tub of orange juice. She points at a plastic bowl of fruit salad. 'You gonna eat this?' she asks.

'Leave me the pineapple and the rockmelon,' I reply. 'You can have all the grapes.'

Erin sits in a white plastic visitor's chair, her right white Nike shoe propped up on my single bed, phone in her right hand, an AirPod in her right ear, nothing in her left ear.

'Sounds like the backyard hose when it gets all twisted and the water stops running,' Clem says.

'Somethin' like that,' I say.

'So did he manage to save it?' Clem asks.

'He did,' I reply. 'Dr Hong gently untwisted the spermatic cord and then he kindly stitched my right testicle to the inside wall of my scrotum so it won't ever happen again.'

'Would anyone object if we changed the subject?' Erin asks.

'I object,' Clem replies.

'Objection overruled,' I say. 'Where's Mum?'

'Some lady from the hospital wanted to talk to her,' Erin says.

'What about?'

Erin shrugs. 'Dunno,' she says. 'Think she wanted to work out why Mum's not talkin'.'

'She's still not talking?'

Erin shakes her head. 'It's so fuckin' embarrassing.'

'Erin, did you really need the F-bomb there?' I ask.

The left edge of Erin's top lip curls. 'I had to explain to all the doctors last night why we were here and who we were,' she says. 'I had to call the ambulance myself. I'm only fifteen, Dad. I shoulda been doing my geography task sheet.'

'Sounds like you stepped up for your mum,' I say. 'Sounds like you did good.'

'Then we got here and they kept looking at Mum like she was crazy or on drugs or somethin',' Erin continues.

'She's not crazy,' Clem says, mouth full of grapes. 'She just doesn't want to talk for a while.'

'It's fucking ridiculous,' Erin spits.

'Don't swear, Erin,' I spit back. 'Please stop that shit.'

Erin rolls her eyes, sinks her head into her phone as it pings.

'That another message from lover boy?' Clem asks.

I study Erin's face for a moment. She reveals nothing. 'Who's … lover boy?' I ask.

Clem's eyes light up. 'She's back talking to—'

Erin knuckles her sister in the shoulder. 'You shut the hell up, Clem,' she barks.

Erin's eyes are back on her phone. Her face goes red and I know that's my sign not to probe. I'm touched to see her wearing my old Echo and the Bunnymen T-shirt and I desperately want to tell her that she looks much cooler in it than I ever did, but I would never tell her that because she would never wear the shirt again if I did.

I turn to Clem. 'Did your Mum tell you that, Clem?' I ask.

'Tell me what?'

'Did Mum tell you that she just doesn't want to talk for a while?'

'No,' Clem says. 'She's not talkin', remember.'

'Then how do you know she just doesn't want to talk for a while?'

Clem shrugs. 'Moon-time connection,' she says and places her hands behind her head.

Fonzie levels of self-confidence. She lifts her legs up and rests her shoes on the bed, mirroring the great never-will-she-truly-acknowledge-it hero of her life, her older sister. The shoes are her pride and joy. Adidas Gazelles, the red suede ones that Harry Styles wears in the live concert poster stuck to the side of her wardrobe. Twelve weeks of pocket money plus a crisp $50 note slipped inside an age-inappropriate birthday card from her grandfather. The card featured a doddering cartoon grandfather with a birthday balloon string wedged in the crack of his bare and hairy arse: 'Hope you have a *cracking* birthday.' I notice that Clem has covered the edges of the thick soles of her shoes with white and purple unicorn stickers. As far as modes of transport go, Clem says the humble unicorn beats any car. More character, unbreakable horn.

'What connection?' I ask my daughter.

'Moon-time connection,' Clem says, popping another grape in her mouth. 'You know, Aunty Flo's chatline. The mysterious ways us Cork women can connect during the crimson tide.'

'What the hell are you talking about, Clem?'

'She's talkin' about her period, Dad!' Erin groans. '*Jeeesus*.'

Clem nods. 'Mum and me and Erin keep getting the girl flu at the same time,' Clem says.

I place a gentle hand on Clem's left shoulder. 'You got your period, honey?' I ask, softly and gently.

Clem turns to her older sister and howls with laughter. Erin nearly throws her phone at me.

'What the hell's wrong with you, *Daaaad*?' she bellows. 'She got her first one a year ago. Do you see anything that happens around our house whatsoever? Honestly, do you ever take the time to come out of your precious little man bubble? No wonder Mum stopped talking to you. Talking to you most days is about as meaningful as talking to a cauliflower.'

I let this mini-speech sit for a moment. Erin breathes. Returns to her phone.

'You done?' I ask.

'Yeah, I'm done.'

'If I'm not mistaken, Erin, Mum's not talking to you, either.'

'Yeah,' Erin says. 'But we all know it's you she doesn't want to talk to the most.'

'Nice to know. I somehow missed that communication.'

Then the old man who is snoring beside us adds a long fart to his one-man symphony. Clem howls with laughter again and Erin and I follow suit.

I turn back to Clem.

'Could you please tell me more about moon-time connection, Clem?'

She pulls at a grape stem that's wedged in her teeth.

'Saw a woman talkin' 'bout it on TikTok,' she says. 'It's a feel thing. Basically, me, Mum and Erin are able to meet each other on a feminine hormonal plane that you could never possibly reach or understand, Dad. Sorry. Don't mean to leave you out or nuthin', it's just girl business. Basically, I can tell what Mum and Erin are thinking and feeling without them even having to tell me how they're thinking and feeling.'

I turn to Erin. 'Is this true?' I ask.

Erin shakes her head twice. It pains her to have to use her neck muscles to shift her gaze to her younger sister. 'That's such bullshit, Clem,' she says. 'What am I thinking right now?'

Clem casually places the fruit salad bowl back on the mobile food trolley.

'You're wondering if Dad loves his creepy bones-in-the-oven book more than he loves you and me,' Clem says, matter-of-factly. 'You're wondering if he cares more about Tamsin Fellows than he does about Mum.'

I turn to see Erin's reaction to this.

She says nothing. Mute. Turns her head down to her phone, right thumb moving haphazardly across the screen.

'Tell me that's not actually something you think, Erin,' I say.

She doesn't respond. Eyes fixed on the phone.

My right foot taps her shoe that's resting on my hospital bed. 'Hey,' I say. 'You can't possibly think that, can you? Erin? Erin? Seriously, tell me you don't actually think that?'

Erin gives a closed-lips laugh that seems to come out her nostrils. She pulls her foot off the bed.

'Well, I can't say it hasn't crossed my mind,' she says.

Well played, Cork. Father of the fuggin' year. You sad and empty vessel. Your stomach is a black hole that could swallow up space junk. Your heart is a cursed stone that could only be softened by the love of three women you share a bathroom with. Look at you now. You can barely squeeze one simple vowel out of your mouth. C'mon, Cork, you can do it. Quick. Fix it. Quick. Fix everything you fucked.

'E,' I say.

Erin smiles, shrugs her shoulders. And that's how I know her feelings are true.

'You wanna know what I think?' Clem asks.

Erin, quick as a flash. 'No, and thanks for asking.'

'I think we finally broke Mum,' she says. Clem points at me. 'Well, more specifically, I think *you* finally broke her, Dad.'

'What are you talking about?' I reply. 'Your mother's not broken. She's just not talking.'

'Nah, she's broken,' Clem says. 'You just can't see it because Mum only breaks inwards.'

'What the hell are you talking about, Clem?' I ask. 'This another thing you saw on TikTok?'

'Nope,' she says, shaking her head. 'This is entirely my own observation. You and Erin break outwards. When you guys get upset, the whole world's gotta know about it. Always stompin' around and slammin' doors. But Mum and me, we break inwards.'

I want to say something now, but nothing comes out. Because this time I break inwards. Kid's too observant. Maybe too observant for her own good.

'Never any visible signs of damage,' Clem says. 'Strictly internal bleeding for Mum and me.'

I study Clem's face. Vast oceans inside that head, deep seas filled with eight-legged monsters of the abyss and flash observations from twelve-going-on-thirteen years of silent domestic anthropological study.

'And what exactly did I do to break her, Clem?'

'Nothing.'

'Exactly,' I say. 'Nothing!'

'Exactly!' Clem says. 'You did nothing. That whole six months when you were locked away in the backyard garage possessed by that book like some kind of a crazed … crazed …'

'Victor Frankenstein?' Erin offers.

'Yeah, like some kinda crazed Frankenstein,' Clem says. 'You just left Mum to do … *everything.* We didn't even see you some days. Meanwhile, Mum's making breakfast and washing the school uniforms and combing out the knots in my hair and French-braiding my hair and helping me make my costume for Book Week. Do you even know who I went as this year?'

I answer quickly and authoritatively. 'Anne Frank.'

'Close,' Clem says. 'Katniss Everdeen. Doing the groceries. Fixing the dinners. Helping with homework. Booking the dentist appointments. Booking the doctors' appointments ...'

Erin dives in, just for kicks. 'Vacuuming the floors. Mopping the floors. Cursing the floors for ever existing. Hanging the uniforms out to dry. Stacking the dishwasher. Unstacking the dishwasher. Sympathetically listening to all the ways Grandma is convinced she's gonna die. Wash the sheets. Fold the towels. Get a breast check. Get an iron check. Ask the doctor why you keep waking up at three a.m. every night and can never get back to sleep. Pay the electricity bill. Pay the water bill. Pay the phone bill. Argue with AAMI insurance about why the home and contents bill went up by one thousand bucks when we haven't bought any new contents as a family for at least three years. Explain to Gemma Leader that you can't do coffee at New Farm Deli this morning because you're sticking the little cushion pads on all the legs of all the chairs in the dining room so they don't scratch the floorboards anymore. Squeeze five days of work into the three days of work you get paid for. Thank your boss for his understanding when you have to leave work early because your daughter's been vomiting and the school receptionist can't get hold of your husband because he's in the backyard garage working on his groundbreaking true-crime book with his phone off so he can concentrate on *every ... last ... precious ... sentence.* Fill the car up with petrol before it dies on Waterworks Road. Snatch another fistful of bills from the letterbox. Check that one of those bills is not actually another piece of correspondence from some anonymous psycho killer. Thaw the frozen steak in the microwave. Try to disguise how cheap and tasteless the steak is by marinating it in honey and soy sauce and turning it into a stir-fry. Set the table. Plate the stir-fry. Wait for your husband to enter the kitchen and tell you what a productive day he spent in the garage and how he feels he *really broke the back* of his precious book. Then try your best to just break inwards as he forks his first mouthful of stir-fry at the dinner table and casually says, "You know, honey, this would have been great with some cashew nuts."'

Clem and me staring at Erin now, dizzied by the details.

'Exactly,' Clem says.

'Where the hell did all that come from, Erin?' I ask.

'It came from opening my eyes, Dad!' Erin replies.

Clem whips a pen and a yellow Spirax notebook the size of her palm from her pants pocket. She runs the pen's ballpoint over a page to make sure it's working and then she asks me a question.

'Dad, has Mum always been strange?'

'Strange? You think your mum is strange?'

'Not bad-strange like Pedo Pete, who's always sitting at the Jubilee Plaza bus stop. Mum's good-strange … You know … like Lady Gaga and Winona Ryder.'

'Well, I don't think she's particularly strange,' I say. 'She's her own woman … she's not like …'

I realise my youngest daughter is scribbling my response in her notepad.

'What's this?' I ask.

'It's shorthand. I'm up to eighty words a minute.'

'Clem, why are you taking notes?'

Clem beams. Leans in to my bed. Whispers like she's sharing her latest scoop in a smoky bar with two old journo friends.

'I'm writing a profile on Mum for the latest edition of the *Gecko Street Gazette*. I was thinking last night about how weird it was that Mum just stopped talking like she did, and then I got thinking about what an intriguing individual Mum actually is. How lucky am I that the most interesting person in Gecko Street actually sleeps in the bedroom right across from mine? Of course, I haven't been able to get a decent quote out of Mum in the past twenty-four hours on account of the fact she's gone all Charlie Chaplin on us. Lucky for me, I also sleep across the hall from the man who knows her better than anyone!'

Clem points her pen at the space between my eyes. 'I thought you and I could work on the profile together,' she says. 'Shared byline. Me first, you second, of course. Just an alphabetical thing.'

'Clem … I can't … I don't have time to—'

'Of course, if you're too busy with Tamsin and everything—'

'I didn't say that, Clem, it's just that—'

'Great.' Clem brings her pen to the pad. 'Where did you guys meet? What made you fall in love with her? Did you know she was strange from the start?'

'Clem, I'm just not sure Mum would want you splashing her life story across the *Gecko Street Gazette*.'

'No, she's totally up for it.'

'She tell you that?'

'No, but she communicated it.'

'Via the feminine hormonal plane?'

'Exactly.'

A woman in a red cardigan pulls the green hospital curtain aside.

'Sorry to interrupt,' she says. Short brown hair, the kind of pixie cut Erin was considering two years ago. A clipboard under her right arm. 'How's everybody this morning?' She smiles.

Clem answers first. 'The grapes are nice and crispy here,' she says. 'But there's no more little white cups at the water fountain.'

The doctor nods, smiling. 'I'll get right onto that,' she says. She turns to me. 'My name's Dr Marcia Khan. I'm part of the in-patient welfare unit. Do you think we could have a quick word in private, Mr Cork?'

'Ummm … yeah … sure,' I say. 'I'll just wait for the girls' mum so she can look after them for a bit.'

'She's grabbing a coffee in the cafeteria,' Dr Khan says. 'Down the hall and to the right.'

I turn to Erin. 'All right, you girls wanna go see Mum for a sec?' I ask.

Erin studies Dr Khan with a suspicious eye, reluctantly stands.

'Is everything all right with him?' she asks the doctor. The tremble in her voice is something new to me, and I suspect to Erin, too.

'Your father's going to be fine,' Dr Khan replies. 'I just have a few quick questions for him.'

The girls slide the curtain across. Clem meaningfully nods her head at me as she exits.

'That's moon-time comms for, "I love ya, Dad",' she says, winking her left eye.

'Thought as much,' I say, winking my left eye back.

Dr Khan smiles at me. 'Sweet kids,' she says.

I nod twice. 'They do have their moments,' I say.

Dr Khan slips into the bedside chair Erin was just sitting in.

'You got bad news, don't ya?' I ask. 'It's cancer, isn't it? They found something else down there, didn't they? An anomaly? A pea-sized lump?'

Dr Khan shakes her head, consults some papers on her clipboard. 'A pea-sized lump?' she asks.

'Yeah, I shoulda had it checked out sooner. I'm an idiot. I just kept putting it off and putting it off. I had this book, you know, it was a real good story and ... something just came over me. I had to get the story out there, you know. I was kinda possessed, I guess. Kept raising my middle finger to fate, and now it's all come back to bite me. Down south where it hurts, too. Fate's literally got me by the ball—'

'Mr Cork, I'm not here to talk about you,' Dr Khan interjects.

'You're not?'

'No, I'm not. However, if it helps in any way, I should tell you that I took a look at your in-patient record and I did notice that our consultants have made note of a fluid-filled spermatic cyst that they have deemed to be benign. You should always remain vigilant, of course, but I think you're in the clear.'

Pulse slowing. Future brightening.

'Nice to know,' I say. 'Thank you for the good news, Doc.'

Dr Khan pulls the curtain fully around my hospital bed and pulls her chair in closer to me. 'I wanted to talk to you about Rita,' she says.

'Rita? What about Rita?'

'One of our intensivists has been somewhat concerned by her sudden refusal to speak, as relayed to him by your daughters,' she says. 'He asked me if I could have a brief word with Rita as a matter of due diligence on our behalf.'

'Must have been a really brief word,' I say. 'The girls told me she's still not talking.'

Dr Khan offers a laugh. 'Well, we managed to find other ways to communicate,' she says. 'In fact, we had quite the discussion.'

'You did? How did you do that, exactly?'

'Well, there are other ways to talk than out your mouth.'

I quickly consider these possible ways to talk and find no more ways beyond talking out of one's arse.

'And there are other ways that I would encourage you to try to listen to Rita than merely with your ears,' Dr Khan says.

'Such as?'

'With your heart,' Dr Khan says. 'With your empathy. With your love for a woman who has seemingly chosen to take a much-needed break from the more traditional forms of human communication.'

I take a deep breath. Slowly exhale.

'I know it seems unlikely on the face of it,' Dr Khan says, 'but I learned a great many things about your wife in the space of an hour, and she didn't have to say a single word to me.'

'What exactly did you learn?'

'Well, that she doesn't appear to have any kind of social anxiety disorder, something commonly associated with cases of selective mutism in adults,' she says. 'I learned that she is not fearful. She's not fearful of you. You are evidently not violent to her.'

'Why would you even need to know that?'

'I've worked with several women in my career who responded to the extreme shock of intimate partner violence with extended periods of self-imposed silence.'

Dr Khan turns to her clipboard, reads from a series of typed notes. 'Rita maintains good eye contact,' she says. 'No particular reluctance to smile or express contentment. No signs of insensitivity to noise or crowds. I'm convinced she's not depressed. She is, in fact, by all admittedly inadequate clinical definitions, presenting as a perfectly normal working mother of two who has chosen not to speak.'

She lets the sheet of paper fall back on her clipboard and rubs her lips. 'Which is why I find your wife so utterly fascinating, Mr Cork.'

'She's always been a bit fascinating.'

'She intrigues me,' Dr Khan says. 'Excites me, even. I've been a clinical psychologist for twenty-four years and I've never come across a patient quite like her.'

Dr Khan is making the same face people make when they see Uluru for the first time or sign for their first Temu delivery.

'Did you ask her about the birds?'

'What birds?'

'The birds that attacked her,' I say. 'Clem and Rita were panning for gold in a creek in Fernvale on a school excursion. Clem said a whole bunch of crazy birds came along and attacked her. Clem says after that she just stopped talking.'

'Birds, you say?' Dr Khan starts scribbling notes. 'Well, I'd be very surprised if that was the cause of this, Mr Cork. I observed no signs of physical harm. No evidence of a lingering trauma of any kind. Of course, I'd like to continue with further treatment, should she be willing to embark on a therapy journey with me, but, honestly, if I was to give you my most candid and speculative assessment, I would tell you that this is something far more ... well ... *poetic*.'

'Poetic?' I repeat. 'With the greatest respect, Dr Khan, what the fuck are you talking about?'

'There seems to me to be something poetic about what your wife is doing, Mr Cork,' Dr Khan says. '*Graceful. Strong.* There is defiance in it. Silence almost as an act of rebellion. Please consider this a hunch and nothing more, a woman's intuition, one might say—'

'Moon-time comms.'

'Huh?'

'Fogeddaboutit.'

'I just have this sneaking suspicion that, in the face of what I have gathered are extended periods of feeling somewhat *unheard* by her husband—'

'Unheard?'

'*Under*heard, perhaps?'

I shrug my shoulders, reluctantly say, 'Perhaps.'

'In the face of feeling *underheard*, I'm wondering if Rita has chosen, instead of talking louder and louder and louder at you, to go deeper and deeper and deeper … *inwards*.'

Dr Khan rubs her lips. 'If I was allowed to speak plainly—'

'Don't let me stop you, Dr Khan.'

'Speaking plainly, this feels to me like Rita is offering a kind of "fuck you" to the world,' she says. 'And I wonder, to send a speculative drill down even further into this mineral-rich rock of a woman, if it is not, in fact, one great big, elegant and utterly defiant "fuck you" to, well … *you*, Mr Cork?'

'Me?'

'Yes, you, Mr Cork,' she says. 'Can you think of any reasons why Rita would want to express such a thing to her husband of twenty-three years? Is there any reason at all why she would want to say one great big "*fuuuuuuck youuuuuu*" to you, Mr Cork?'

At that moment, Clem slips back inside the green bay curtain, holding Rita's hand behind her.

'We found Mum,' Clem says. Rita stands over Clem's shoulder. 'She wants to tell you, Dad, that she's cross at you for not looking after yourself better, but she's very relieved that you didn't lose your right nut.'

Rita almost laughs out loud at this, but turns the laugh into a half-smile that she sends my way.

'Anything you want to say to Mum, Dad?' Clem asks.

And I stare into the eyes of my wife for ten straight seconds and I shake my head once slowly and still my gaze and stare again for ten more seconds and I can feel a tear form in the well of my lower left eyelid and then I feel this tear run down my cheek.

'Wooowww,' Clem gasps. She turns her eyes up to her mum and grips her elbow. 'He just said, *I love you so fucking much, Rita Munro.*'

NINE

You will be invisible in the story. And yet every part of you will be in it. Every failure, every heartbreak, every person you ever kissed, every person you ever loved, every person you ever buried in the ground.

– Rutledge, *Journalism Practices and Principles*

I leapt in front of a moving train for Rita Munro, though the moving train was about a hundred metres away from me when I leapt. That's how we met. Twenty-first of October, in the year 2000. We'd both been at the Livid Festival in the RNA Showgrounds, better known as the place where ribboned cows move in circles at the Royal Queensland Show. That day it was the place where Green Day roared 'Brain Stew' to thirty thousand beer-buzzed and sunburnt Queensland music lovers. Lou Reed made his way from the dirty boulevards of New York all the way to bumfuck Bowen Hills to show us why it was such a perfect day. He was right about that day. I remember the lemon sun sinking over Brisbane and watching Gwen Stefani from No Doubt nearly kill herself as she climbed ten metres up a steel stage framework singing 'Just a Girl'.

But me and Rita only had eyes for The Cure. We'd both left the groups of friends we'd come with and forced ourselves through the crowd to lean against the pit fence about a metre from Robert Smith's black and white Gretsch Silver Falcon guitar. This was in the days when mosh pits were still dangerous. It was no Rage Against the Machine mosh, to be sure, but few modern armies would fail to tremble before the combined heaving force of twenty thousand pale-faced goths fist-pumping to 'Fascination Street'. When the band sang '10.15 Saturday Night' that night, it was genuinely almost 10.15 p.m. on a Saturday night.

I swear I remember seeing Rita on the pit fence, six people along the front row from me to my right. She wore the distinctive floppy black Stevie Nicks sun hat that would later lead to Erin and Clementine Cork being born. I remember I kept looking along the fence at her during 'From the Edge of the Deep Green Sea'. She was doing some rare and endearing kind of street miming to Robert Smith's lyrics. When he sang about the girl in the song listening to her lover like her head was on fire, Rita made her fingers look like there were wild flames coming from her head. When Smith sang about the guy in the song brushing his tears away and pretending that the tears were just rain, she brushed tears from her own eyes and I wondered if her tears were real. When Smith sang about the girl in the song hanging herself in front of her lover, I watched Rita tilt her neck and poke her tongue out the side of her mouth, like her head was caught in a taut noose. It was macabre and hilarious, that mime, and I swear it was just me who saw her do it and I swear she saw me watching her and she smiled at me along the row of sweaty goths banging and pulling on the pit fence. She was half-embarrassed and half-proud of the way I was looking at her with nothing but awe. And we kept looking at each other for a moment and there was something connecting in our gaze, like we were both acutely aware of the fact that when Robert Smith visits your home town he makes the world feel small and intimate and hopeful and beatable. We both knew that if Robert Smith can exist in the city of Brisbane, Queensland, Australia, then so can imaginary friends and unicorns and soft falling snow. We both knew that anything is possible when Robert Smith comes to Brisbane, even true love.

It was after midnight that evening when I saw her standing on platform four of Bowen Hills train station, a five-minute walk from the RNA Showgrounds. I had moved to the far northern end of the platform to get away from the crowds of drunk and high music lovers singing 'When I Come Around' by Green Day. Rita was standing with her arms crossed over her white singlet top, still wearing her sun hat. She had a purse slung over her shoulder, one she still has to this day, the one embroidered with the face of Siouxsie Sioux. A red ruffle-hem skirt and practical high-cut black gym shoes like the ones Robert Smith wore in the 'Friday I'm in Love' video. She was twenty-one years old and sun-browned and solitary and beautiful. I stood about six metres to her left on the platform and hoped she might catch one of about forty sharp glances I threw her way. She caught the forty-first glance and smiled at me as though she recognised my face from somewhere, maybe even the front row of the life-altering Cure concert she had just attended. Then a train pulled hard into platform three and kicked up a wind gust that blew Rita's sun hat clean off her head onto the rusty train tracks below us. I watched the hat settle smack-bang between two tracks and promptly marched towards the edge of the platform with every intention of jumping straight onto the tracks to fetch it.

'Stop!' she said. 'Are you crazy?'

I turned to face her. 'I'm gonna get your hat,' I said. 'The train will crush it if you leave it there.'

'Yeah, well, I can stand to see a twenty-dollar hat get crushed beneath a train. I don't think I could stand to see some admittedly gallant try-hard in an Echo and the Bunnymen T-shirt get crushed beneath a train.'

'Nah, won't take a second,' I said.

'The train could come any second now, ya dingbat.'

'What time's it due?'

'Twelve fifteen.'

I looked at my Swatch watch.

'It's only twelve thirteen. More than one minute to jump down there, grab the hat, jump back up and accept your eternal thanks. At the very least, there's enough time for me to get down there, pick up the hat and fling it to you just before the train squashes me like a bug.'

'What if it's early?' Rita replied.

'Brisbane trains are never early,' I scoffed.

Then a bright yellow light illuminated the bend at the end of platform four.

'Oh, fuck,' I said. 'It's early.'

And then I leapt onto the train tracks. The drop was deeper than I'd anticipated. I scrambled across track gravel and rocks and scooped up the sun hat then scrambled back to the platform. I threw the hat up to Rita, who caught it with two hands, then dropped it immediately by her side so her hands were free to help pull me back up onto the platform just before the train pulled in.

'You're crazy,' she barked, half-furious, half-laughing her guts out.

I gathered my breath as I sat by her feet on the platform.

'Not as crazy as those eyes you were making at Robert Smith tonight,' I said.

Two years later, on that very spot where we'd stood on the platform, I asked Rita Munro to be my wife. She said yes and a month later we got hitched in the old Brisbane marriage registry office on George Street. We were married at 10.15 on a Saturday morning.

*

'Wow!' Clem says, scribbling shorthand notes in her Spirax in the back seat of the Corolla. 'Great story, Dad. That's, like, my second favourite love story of all time, just behind *To All the Boys I've Loved Before*.'

Halfway home from the hospital. Clem's relentless questioning has accompanied us all the way to Ashgrove.

'You ever think about the timing required for anyone to fall in love?' Clem asks. 'Just how lucky it was that you two found each other?'

I turn to Rita, who's behind the steering wheel, eyes fixed on the road.

'Like, what if you were standing on a different platform, Dad?' Clem asks. 'What if you weren't that much of a Cure fan and you didn't go all the way up to the fence and you didn't see Mum in the crowd? It's a miracle. Every single time two people fall in love – think of all the thousands of tiny things that had to fall into place for them to be together. Miracles.'

Clem spots an elderly couple seated at a bus stop outside St Finbarr's Catholic Church. 'See, there's another miracle,' she squeals. She spots two women walking hand in hand into the Metro Radiology centre. 'There's another one!'

Clem taps my shoulder. 'But that's the thing about Mum, ay Dad? Miracles just seem to happen when she's around.'

'What do you mean by that?' I ask.

'The fire in Pike Street,' Clem replies. 'The storm that lifted the roof off the house but somehow left you guys alive. The way you two met like that on the train platform.'

Rita turns to me for a moment, offers nothing.

'Yeah, well, a good journalist would never mistake favourable timing for miracles,' I say.

I keep my eyes on Rita while she drives. We've been talking for twenty-five years. Isn't that what a marriage is? One big talk. One big conversation that pauses and picks up again but never stops. It starts on a train platform and carries on through a bar and a car and a bedroom and a mountain and a grocery store and a cinema house and a labour ward of the Mater Mothers' Hospital in South Brisbane.

I remember talking to Rita on the first night of Erin's life. I was leaning over a clear plastic hospital crib. Erin was swaddled in a pink and yellow striped blanket, the most perfect creature wrapped inside her chrysalis.

'Ssssshhhhhhhh,' I whispered, as Erin fell into a long warm sleep. 'Ssssshhhhh.'

'You give good sibilance,' Rita said, resting from a twelve-hour birth in the bed beside us.

'What the hell is sibilance?' I whispered.

Rita was falling asleep herself. 'It's when people make hissing and hushing sounds,' she said, pulling the hospital blanket to her chest. 'Wooooshhhhh.'

And that word, 'Woosh', became our family goodnight word. So often the last word I'd hear her say before drifting off to sleep. A nighttime raft for all of us, sent down the river of dreams. *Wooooshhh.*

And now I remember the way she talked about her dreams in the morning over Weet-Bix: 'It was you, me and Keanu Reeves and we were on a roller-coaster in the Himalayas.'

I remember the way she talked about the world. She was interested in all of it. Every ant carrying crumbs across a benchtop. Every song on the radio. Every scent in the air. I remember the time she entertained a whole dinner party of twelve with a thirty-minute reflection on the evolution of the anus.

'Before the anus came around, animals had to eat and excrete through the same hole,' she said, as no fewer than five dinner party guests suddenly realised they were full.

She had this thing about stepping. 'You should step back from that, Noah,' she'd say. And that could mean stepping back from anything: grief, anger, regret, tricky relationships.

'You should step into that, Noah,' she'd say. And that could mean stepping into anything: dance classes with Erin when she was eleven, the works of Hilary Mantel, painting, singing, fishing, remembering, forgiving.

My phone vibrates in the central console of the Corolla. The name 'Sherry Sharp' flashes on the screen.

'That's the publicist,' I say, turning my head right to gauge Rita's reaction to this statement. Rita remains silent.

'Hi, Sherry.'

As my publicist, Sherry's role is to help *Anonymous Source* 'punch through' – or, better still, 'organically penetrate' – a crowded spring–summer true-crime book market.

'Noah, just checking you're okay?'

'Yeah, I'm fine, Sherry. Why do you ask?'

'I saw what happened at the State Library event.'

'You did? How did you see that?'

'Everybody's seen it, Noah. You just penetrated America!'

'I'm sorry, what did I just do to America?'

'Bloodstain Bex has become your biggest fan.'

'Who the hell is Bloodstain Bex?'

'Rebecca Baumgart. Username BloodstainBex. She's a seventeen-year-old true-crime BookToker. Three hundred and fifty-eight thousand followers. One of the most influential figures on US BookTok. She was sitting in the front row for your event. Can you believe it?'

Sherry is breathless. Sherry is having a wonderful day. The stitches in my ball throb in protest.

'She did a whole series of edits and dropped them on TikTok,' Sherry rejoices. 'She headlined it: ICYMI THE MOST BATSHIT CRAZY BOOK EVENT EVAAAA! She's got you rolling around on stage in agony and then she goes into how much she loved your book and then she says how shocking it was to see that guy screaming at you from the audience. She got it all on video. "Cunt money! Cunt money! Cunt mo—"'

'Sherry, I remember what he said. Look, I'm just in the car right now with my family, can I—'

'Yes, yes,' Sherry says. 'Listen, the *Today* show has been in touch. They're going to air the viral video on tomorrow's show and they wanna cross to you right after to get a bit more insight into the book and how this all happened.'

I look down towards my recently severed scrotum.

'Listen, Sherry, I don't know if I'll be up for that, but lemme think on it for a bit,' I say.

'Yeah, good, good,' Sherry says. 'Have a think. Come back to me. I have some very exciting thoughts about how we can leverage all this. Well. Done. You!'

'I didn't do anything, Sherry. I just twisted my right testicle.'

'Well, we book folk do love a good twist!' she howls. 'Ciao, legend!'

I place my phone back in the central console. Turn to Erin in the back seat of the car.

'Erin, are you on TikTok?'

'I've already found it,' she says with a sigh, leaning forward from her seat and holding her phone out in her hand so we can all see and hear the video. 'Sherry sounds like a dolphin through your phone,' Erin says.

She taps the screen with her thumb.

*

'Hey guys, Bloodstain Bex here, comin' to you from the Crime Scene Australia book fest. I caught dozens of events this year that I'll be telling all my Blood Buddies about in coming weeks, but first I just have to GIT. SOME. SHEEEEET. OUT. MA. SYSTEMMMM!'

Bloodstain Bex has dyed red hair, the colour of blood. Arms covered in tattoos. I think that's Raymond Chandler's face on her right forearm, or maybe it's Orson Welles'. She appears to be talking to her phone at a desk in a hotel room. She holds up a copy of my book.

'This book,' she says. 'It's called *Anonymous Source: The Disappearance and Discovery of Tamsin Fellows*. By this Australian true-crime hack, Noah Cork, who you've never heard of, but ... *holyyyyyyyyy molyyyyyyyyy* ...'

A computer graphic flashes on the screen. Bex has formed a crucifix shape out of the words 'holy' and 'moly' and it comes spinning at the camera like a ninja star thrown by the 1960s TV Batman.

'So I hadn't read this guy's book,' she says. 'If I'm honest, I thought the cover looked about as interesting as, well, a red letterbox. But then my friend at ZebsDead stands me up for a coffee date and I get this free window and me and my blood-stained boots skip along to this little morning session that I assume will be a snooze-fest and then it starts and this media professor woman just comes out hard with all these questions about how fuckin' crazy this reporter guy Noah Cork is because he's literally called some real-life murderer a big coward because it seems like this murderer has been playing games with him, and Cork's got all pissed off in this book and he's like, "Have the balls to reveal yourself, ya big coward, ya big pervert monster fuck." Then the author starts rolling around on the stage like he's about to die, because he's got some kind of cramp in his stomach. He kinda looks like he's trying to breakdance while squeezing chilli from his butthole.'

Clem howls with laughter in the back seat. 'Daaaaad!' she shrieks. 'Chilli from your butthole!'

Bloodstain Bex continues on screen. 'But then he comes good and sits back in his chair and he starts revealing what the book's about and where it came from and why he was pissed off and I'm front row in the audience thinking, Damn girl, I gots to read me this book. So, guess what, I come straight back here to my hotel room and eat this thing up like a blood-flavoured doughnut!'

The cover of *Anonymous Source* comes flying at the screen like a ninja star thrown by the 1960s TV Batman.

Erin swipes to Bex's next TikTok video. It finds Bloodstain Bex wearing a pair of bookish black-framed spectacles and sitting in an egg-shaped hotel room chair, standing a copy of *Anonymous Source* up on her lap.

'So the book opens with Noah Cork describing how suburban-meh his life is in this cosy little baby-makin' place in Brisbane, Australia, called Jubilee, where *nothing bad ever happens*. Like, this place is supposed to be, like, the safest Brady Bunch neighbourhood in the world … Well, that's until something pretty fuckin' totally bad happens to our friendly neighbourhood crime hack.'

Guess the horse has really bolted now, Cork. This is the reaping, you know. This is cause and effect. This is you. Nobody did this but you.

'He's got a wife named Rita Munro,' Bloodstain Bex continues. 'And he's a father of two kids, but he's flat broke because he burned a bunch of police sources when he wrote about a case of police brutality that pissed off every cop in his home state of Queensland. Now he can't sell a crime yarn to save himself.'

An image of a gothic raven fills the screen and this raven squawks a cartoon 'Fuuuuuck!' from its mouth.

'Then one ordinary-ass day in the suburbs, Cork goes to his letterbox and he finds one of those little mechanical music boxes and this thing plays the tune of "Over the Rainbow".'

The video cuts to black and white footage of Judy Garland singing said song in the Kansas farmyard in *The Wizard of Oz*.

'And there's a note with this music box and it's from this *anonymous source* – remember the title, my dear Bluddies – urging Cork to go down to the local reservoir and find a pair of ruby red slippers that someone's left by the water.'

The video cuts to a shot of Glinda the good witch pointing her silver-star wand at Dorothy's ruby slippers.

'And this is where the creepometer kinda hits the red! Now, I'm sorry, my beloved Bluddies, but if I'm gonna tell this story right, I've gotta just come out and spoil this bit, cuz it's too *forked* to keep to myself, so if you wanna know what happens next, climb up my link tree and get your Tarzan on and swing yourself over right now to my YouTube channel for every spoilerific detail about the craziest book event I ever been to!'

Erin taps the screen, swipes left, searching for the YouTube page.

'I think we've seen enough,' I say.

'I haven't,' Erin says.

'I'll watch the rest when I get home,' I say. 'I don't want Clem hearing this stuff.'

'What *stuff* am I gonna hear, Dad?' Clem asks from the back seat. She's building a bouncy ball – now the size of a cricket ball – out of a box of rubber bands that she keeps in the side compartment by her seat. 'The stuff about the bones? The stuff about the psycho killer who leaves you messages in our mailbox? I'm not scared by that creep. It's like what you said in the book, ninety-nine per cent of these people who threaten journalists never follow through on anything. You were right, Dad, he's just a sicko coward too scared to come out of the shadows and face up to you because he knows you could kick him in the butthole.'

I turn to face Clem, stitched ball smarting with the movement.

'You read my book?' I ask. 'I told you not to read it, Clem.'

'I didn't read it,' Clem says. 'But Kelci Burton's mum did and she told Kelci all about it and then Kelci told me.'

'I never said I could kick anyone's butthole,' I say. I turn back to face the windscreen. Glance across at Rita, whose eyes are fixed on the road home. Blank face. Not a word from my wife. Not a whisper. Not a wail.

'I wish I never wrote that stuff about him being a coward,' I say. 'It was foolish of me. Don't even know what I was thinking. I let my anger get the better of me. Something just … came over me.'

Rita briefly turns her head towards me.

'I think you were being brave,' Clem says. 'You always told us to stand up to bullies. You were just standing up to yours. He comes anywhere near our house again, I'll show 'im why you never mess with a Cork.'

Erin howls with laughter. 'Ohhh, big bad Clem's gonna save us from the Jubilee bogeyman. And what are you gonna fight him with, Clem? Your rubber-band ball?'

'No, I'll fight him with my knife,' Clem says.

I whip my head to face the back seat again. 'What knife?' I ask.

'The one I'm saving up for.'

'What the hell are you talking about, Clem?'

'Ashton Gillan in Year 9 said he'll sell me his old Swiss Army knife for twenty-five bucks,' Clem says. 'It's not just any knife. It's a screwdriver, a can opener, a toothpick, tweezers and nail clippers, all in one.'

'Great, Clem,' Erin says. 'You can now give the bogeyman a pedicure!'

'You do not need a knife, Clem,' I say. 'You will not be buying Ashton Gillan's dodgy pocket knife because you will never need to use it. You do not need to protect your family because the police are protecting us just fine.'

'But don't the cops hate your guts?' Erin asks.

'The cops hate a lot of people,' I reply. 'Doesn't mean they don't protect them.'

Erin swipes left on her phone again. Taps three times with her thumbnail. The YouTube video finds Bloodstain Bex now lying in her hotel room bed, lit only by a bedside lamp. She's wearing a nightgown emblazoned with an image of Freddy Krueger waiting at the end of a sparkle-showered rainbow with his razor-blade fingers raised, above the words 'FOLLOW YOUR DREAMS'. She holds a copy of *Anonymous Source* to her chest and whispers when she speaks.

A flashing red siren appears on screen with the words 'SPOILER ALERT'.

Bloodstain Bex continues her breathless review. 'So this treasure hunt leads Cork to this hella bussin' abandoned mansion place and then he creeps up some stairs and he comes to an old rusty oven and there's two words spray-painted across the oven door,' Bex whispers. 'Excuse the French, but the words are "Cunt money". I know, right! What the flamingo! Don't worry, made no sense to me, either. And there's this note next to the oven urging Cork to open the oven door and he knows he shouldn't open it, you know, but he can't resist because he has the storyteller sickness. He's one of those sorry souls who's just gotta know how it all ends.'

You know what she speaks of, don't you, Cork? You know she speaks the truth. You do have the sickness, don't you?

'Of course, he does open the oven door,' Bex says. 'I mean, what self-respecting crime hack wouldn't!'

Bloodstain Bex breathes, pulls a lock of hair behind her ear, continues her review. 'Okay, like, fair warning, Bluddies, what he finds in the oven might just make you wanna vomit when you read the way Cork gives all the – some might say unnecessarily macabre – little journalistic details about what he sees.'

The video cuts briefly to the contagious blueberry pie vomiting scene from the film *Stand By Me*.

'Bones,' says Bex, talking over the images. 'Burnt human bones.'

You did go too far, Cork. I mean, for fuck's sake, the editor counted at least seven different words for 'burnt'. Seared. Scorched. Charred. Blackened. Roasted. Toasted. Incinerated. You fucking heartless animal. She was a mother of two kids. She played soccer in her teens. She won a high school talent quest singing 'Hopelessly Devoted to You'. She would have done the sorts of things on Christmas Day that your girls will remember Rita doing. She used to make bunny feet out of talcum powder for her kids at Easter. She made a Pokémon cake for her son, John, on his sixth birthday. She was Rita once. She was your mum once. She was Tamsin Fellows once.

'As you may have guessed from the title of the book,' Bex says, 'the bones belonged to a real-life missing person named Tamsin Fellows.'

The video smash-cuts to shaky phone-camera footage of John Fellows screaming at me in the State Library auditorium.

The video cuts back to Bloodstain Bex now seated at a hotel room table at breakfast, still wearing her nightie. She spoons a milky mouthful of Froot Loops from her breakfast bowl and talks while her mouth is full. 'So there I was in the auditorium and it comes to question time and this loosey-goosey metalhead stands up and starts shouting the words "Cunt money", over and over. So who the hell is this guy, you ask? Well, he's John Fellows, the son of Tamsin Fellows.'

A grainy image of Tamsin fills the screen, in which she's at a backyard barbecue, wearing a paper Christmas-cracker crown. The song 'Angel' by Sarah McLachlan begins to play over the video.

Bex is now reading from what feels like a script. Her best newsreader voice. Respectful of the dead. 'Tamsin Fellows was a loving mother of two children, John and Helen Fellows,' she says. 'She was the loving wife of Neil Fellows, this seemingly ordinary, decent dad-type guy who works in luxury wood-flooring sales for a Brisbane timber company.'

So that's all she gets, Cork? That's all she was? Loving mum. Loving wife. What about that kid she saved from the surf in Yamba that time when she was sixteen? What about all those days she volunteered for the church? What about that dream she had to drink white wine and paint watercolours for a month in the Cinque Terre? What about her fear of redback spiders? What about the time she shared a cab with Jeff Buckley?

'Tamsin was reported missing from Jubilee on the night of November eleven, 2022,' Bex continues. 'Police reports stated that she had last been seen saying goodbye to friends in the grounds of St Andrew's Uniting Church on the corner of Ann and Creek streets, in the Brisbane CBD. She had been attending a Uniting Church Remembrance Day fundraising luncheon, raising money for Australian War Widows Queensland, of which Tamsin's mother, Barbara, was a long-standing member. At approximately two thirty-five p.m., by the corner of Wicker and Salem roads, Jubilee, she disembarked from the 804 bus from the city. Tamsin was never seen again.'

The video cuts back to Bloodstain Bex, her whole face now filling the frame of her phone camera.

'Then the shit gets real weird,' she whispers. 'Police find Tamsin's red Hyundai Elantra parked in the carpark at the entrance to this popular nature reserve with a huge swimming hole called Spearwood Reservoir.'

Cue colour shots of families swimming in Spearwood Reservoir's designated swimming area, a space the size of half a football field, with an inflatable yellow fence fastened to yellow buoys. Shots of locals kayaking along the edges of the reservoir. 'Police reports suggest suicide is the likeliest explanation for Tamsin's disappearance,' Bex says. 'Police divers, however, fail to recover Tamsin's body from Spearwood Reservoir, the second oldest reservoir in Brisbane and the third largest dam built in Australia in the 1800s. Tamsin's husband, Neil, publicly refuses to accept suicide as the reason for his wife's inexplicable disappearance, describing her as a loving mother who dedicated her life to her children, John and Helen.'

There it is again. Loving mother. I see now they've got that shit etched across her gravestone in Toowong Cemetery. *Loving mother to John and Helen.* Guess there wasn't more room to explain a hundred other sides of Tamsin. I mean, how does one sum up a fifty-two-year-old life in two words? Loving mother? Ecstatic mother. Euphoric mother. Worried mother. Uncertain mother. Underwhelmed wife. Ignored wife. Underappreciated wife. *Underheard wife.* Debased wife. Hateful wife. Avid reader. Rule stickler. Disappointing daughter. Light sleeper. Big dreamer. Careful whisperer. Stargazing romantic. Soufflé murderer. Crossword killer. Scorched mother to her children, John and Helen Fellows. Dead and buried and dug up and buried again wife to husband, Neil Fellows.

'As police search fruitlessly for clues under the ever-watchful eye of salivating media, whispers and rumours spread through Jubilee regarding the truth of Tamsin Fellows' disappearance,' Bex continues. 'Those who don't believe it was suicide point their fingers immediately at Tamsin's husband, Neil. Teams of media camp outside the Fellows' family home for days, urging Neil Fellows to explain his movements on the day of Tamsin's disappearance. Police then inform the media that, on the day of Tamsin's disappearance, Neil was walking through a forest some two hours' drive from Brisbane. Neil and his younger brother, Grant, have got this hobby where they spend days going into forests searching for just the right tree that they will have chopped down, legally, and delivered to Neil's house, where the two brothers will turn the tree into some piece of handmade furniture.

'A month after Tamsin's disappearance, as police continue to search Spearwood Reservoir for signs of Tamsin's body, Neil gives an interview to a popular Australian investigative journalism program called *A Current Affair.* Unfortunately for the Fellows family, Papa Fellows comes across kinda weird and a little creepy. He's about as natural in front of the cameras as a Yellowstone grizzly looking for a private place to take a long-held shit. Neil does himself no favours when he leads this TV journalist – who kinda looks like Margot Robbie's older sister – through his backyard woodwork shed, which happens to be filled with giant old bandsaws and circular plunge saws which he proudly says can cut through big chunks of the thickest cedarwood and, of course, every true-crime sleuth watching from their lounges at home is saying, "They can also cut through chunks of human arms and legs."'

So she married a wood lover? What, so every bloke in Brisbane with a shed and a panel saw is suddenly Jack the Ripper? She loved his woodworks. He made her a pair of bookends once, out of a slab of rose gum, shaped like two thick hardback books. He made her a jewellery box out of maple, with a wooden latch formed by Tamsin's initials.

'Then a neighbour in Jubilee talks to the press and says she heard Neil and Tamsin arguing viciously on their front stairs one evening,' Bloodstain Bex explains. 'Then our poor papa bear Neil digs himself further into a hole when Tamsin's best friend, Sherilyn Ruskin, posts on Facebook, saying that the reason Neil and Tamsin were having so many arguments that all the neighbours could hear was because Tamsin had recently found text messages on Neil's phone from a woman he was briefly ballin' named Luna Ora, a married mother of three who owned a dance school in Jubilee called The Elevation Academy. Luna then gives a paid interview to *A Current Affair* in which she explains that she ended her brief love affair with Neil Fellows for the sake of her three young children who had already suffered enough by having to watch their father, Ezra Ora – a big-boned New Zealander who looks a bit like The Rock's older brother – move out of the family home, which happens to be three doors up from Tamsin's house on Fletcher Street, Jubilee.'

Honestly, there are upsides to being stone-cold dead, Cork. Namely the fact that Tamsin didn't have to live through the embarrassment of having her closest friends and family reading Neil and Luna's phone sexts in the newspapers and in your precious book: *I miss you in me … I need to plant another seed in your lady garden … I just realised I've been stroking my phone like it's your cock.* Honestly, it's not so bad down there in the dirt. The dead are far more polite than the living.

I turn to Erin. 'Switch it off.'

'Huh?' Erin responds.

'Wait,' Clem says. 'I wanna see how it ends.'

'Why?' I ask. 'What's it going to do for you?'

'What's what going to do for me?' Clem responds.

'Seeing how Bloodstain Bex's story ends?'

Clem scratches her head. 'Because I wanna know how it ends?'

'But the story will never end,' I say. 'Stories don't end, they only stop and start back up again. Even if they catch Tamsin's killer, the story won't end there. The story will go on for Tamsin's family. Her children will carry the story until they are old and grey and eventually buried in the ground. The story will continue down through generations of the Fellows family. The pain of it will never die.'

Silence in the car.

'Jeez, bro, that was quite the reflection,' Erin says.

I reach for Erin's phone but the stretch makes my balls howl with pain and I pull my arm back.

'Turn it off, Erin,' I say.

'Just thirty more seconds.'

'So, eventually, the police have insufficient evidence to support any explanation beyond suicide,' Bloodstain Bex continues. 'It's written up as a missing persons case and the missing persons case goes cold for, like, two and a bit years. Until, of course, the scoop of Noah Cork's lifetime literally lands inside his letterbox.'

Bex has inserted a brief shot of an earnest member of the United States Postal Service giving a hearty thumbs-up.

Bex says, 'And now he's gotta get his answers. He's gotta find out where the story goes. One afternoon, Cork knocks on the door of Neil Fellows' house. Neil Fellows *begs* Cork not to write his book, but Cork says he *absolutely must* write it.'

You remember the conversation, Cork. You remember what her husband was wearing. Red polo shirt, untucked; blue denim jeans. Black rubber thongs on his feet. You were standing in Neil's living room. The two-level place in Fletcher Street, Jubilee, with the wobbly front stairs that you thought might collapse beneath you. You remember all the wooden bowls around the living room. And the wooden cabinets. The hand-crafted wooden armchairs. You remember Neil was drinking and smoking rolled cigarettes. He was drinking a clear spirit from a miserable yellow plastic cordial cup, like one you'd find at a five-year-old's birthday party. You remember the Elvis Presley wall-hanging and how there was so much smoke in the living room that you couldn't tell if the wall-hanging next to Elvis was Ricky Nelson or Bobby Vee.

'Why?' Neil asked.

'Why what?' you replied.

'Why must you write a book about it?'

'Because it's what I do, Neil.'

'But nobody's forcing you to do what you do?'

'It is clear now, Neil, that your wife was brutally murdered by someone or a group of someones who remain unfound and unpunished for their despicable crimes. The police have established with great certainty that someone buried your wife's body soon after her disappearance and, two years later, dug her bones up and stuffed them inside an oven that they wanted me to open for their own sickening brand of personal delight. There is a killer out there somewhere, Neil. A killer who is more than likely planning on killing again. The public have a right to know what happened to your wife, Neil. We owe it to the people of Jubilee. Hell, we owe it to Tamsin.'

'What did you say?' Neil asked.

'What?'

'What did you just say to me?'

'Tamsin would want the world to know the truth about what happened to her, no matter how brutal or uncomfortable that truth might be. Tamsin deserves the truth.'

Neil sucked on a cigarette and stubbed it out in an ashtray crowded with butts and ash. He snarled and spoke through lips that barely made the effort to open. 'Don't you ever fucking tell me what my dead wife deserves,' he said. Tamsin's troubled and flawed husband brought his palms together. 'Tell me, Noah,' he said. 'What do you think those words they painted on that oven door meant?'

You shrugged your shoulders.

'They were nonsense,' you said. 'The police said the words had been there well before I even got there that day. They'd made regular inspections of the area. They're always chasing drug users out of the property. Two local officers from Jubilee recalled seeing those words spray-painted on the oven as far back as a year before I ever walked in there.'

Neil took a deep breath and leaned back in his lounge. 'Cunt money,' he said. He pointed a finger at you. 'Cunt money. Cunt money. Cunt money.'

Bloodstain Bex continues in the video, 'This is kinda where the book isn't like most true-crime stories you'll read,' Bex says. 'There's this deeper, somewhat unexpected thread that Cork's trying to explore. He starts wrestling with the idea of whether or not he should even tell the incredible story that has literally landed in his letterbox. He's really honest about the whole moral struggle of it. The rights and wrongs of it. The cops don't want him to write about what he finds in the oven. Tamsin's family practically beg him not to write about what he's seen; they beg him to respect their privacy. But Cork keeps telling himself that it's not his job to be respectful, it's his job to report the facts. Fuck the consequences. Nothing matters but the truth of the story.'

The video cuts to an edit of Tom Cruise in *A Few Good Men* demanding the truth from Jack Nicholson.

'Then one night his wife, Rita, loses her shit. She's had enough. They have this big fight over the fact he never thinks about anyone or anything but Tamsin. The more he argues with his wife, the angrier he gets with the creep who left the music box in his letterbox in the first place.'

I turn my eyes to Rita. Nothing. Rita remains silent.

Bex continues, breathless and buzzing. 'The whole thing leads to this big explosion of words where he just comes right out and calls Tamsin's faceless murderer every name under the sun and sensationally challenges a murderer to confess to his crimes for the sake of Tamsin's family.'

Bloodstain Bex opens her copy of *Anonymous Source.*

'Listen to this very last page. Cork ends the book with a note of his own, addressed to his anonymous source. This might be one of the most fucked-up and insane ways I've ever seen a book end.

'To my anonymous source,

Fuck you. I'm not your lemon drop and I'm not your bluebird.

You are a deranged and perverted monster who somehow crawled from a bucket of evolutionary slime to end the life of a good and loving Brisbane mother of two teenaged children.

I hope one day that you can find the courage to quit playing games for your fifteen minutes of fame and start confessing to your crimes for the sake of Tamsin Fellows' family.

In the meantime, leave me and my letterbox alone, you worm-ridden coward.

Sincerely,

Noah Cork'

Bloodstain Bex's video explodes with a montage of mic-drop memes. Barack Obama dropping a mic. Prince Harry dropping a mic. Stephen Colbert dropping a mic. An animated Minion dropping a mic.

'Gooooo, Dad!' Clem rejoices, clapping her hands in the back seat.

Erin slaps Clem's left shoulder with the back of her right hand. 'Shuddup, dumbass. Dad's picked a fight with a cold-blooded killer. How's it feel to know your dad has a death wish?'

'I'm good with it,' Clem says. 'How's it feel to know your dad isn't afraid of anyone?'

But when are you going to tell her the truth, Cork? You *are* afraid. You are afraid of everything. And you know what you're most afraid of. Letting go. Not knowing where the story goes. You know why you wrote those words. You know why you ended your flimsy little book like that. The police had shut you out. They weren't letting you in on your own story. They were forcing you to let it go. Then you blew a hole in the side of it so you could crawl right back in.

The Toyota crests a hill on Wicker Road, passing the Jubilee Golf Club. I stare out my window as we pass Giancarlo Monaco's abandoned family mansion. The car takes a gentle bend and I see Drake Bridge and the street beyond it that turns into the Jubilee police station.

'Can you pull into the police station?' I ask Rita.

She turns to me. A crease deepens on her forehead between her eyes.

'Please, Rita,' I say. 'I'll explain when we get home.'

'Why do you need to see the cops, Dad?' Clem asks.

'Just need to report something,' I say. 'Nothing serious.'

There's a shared carpark off the Drake Bridge Reserve playground, next to the police station. In the playground, in full midday sunshine, Jubilee parents watch over children scrambling along wobble bridges and climbing netted forts. Two girls look like they're about to vomit inside a spinning orb that's being pushed by a sadistic older brother. Two teenaged boys are kicking high, spiralling bombs on a patch of lawn with a long-punished Steeden ball. They laugh at me as, trying to protect my tender scrotum, I waddle from my car to the cop shop as though I am carrying an invisible wombat between my legs.

The Jubilee police station looks like the kind of two-level sprawling home families of six or seven live in across our suburb. At the end of the carpark, some ten metres from the entrance to the police station, a local woman is sitting beneath a shade umbrella at a portable camping table adorned with posters and flyers bearing images of Tamsin Fellows' face beneath the words 'Justice 4 Tamsin'. Also on the table are a clipboard holding a list of signed names, a pile of T-shirts and an EFTPOS machine. I've seen this woman many times in Coles.

The woman wears a tennis visor with a green see-through plastic brim that casts a green glow across her sweating face.

'Looks like you've been in the wars,' she says, smiling, as I pass the table.

I give her a half-smile and waddle on by her table.

'Would you have time to sign our petition?' she asks.

I stop on the spot. Reluctantly turn my face to the petition.

'Are you familiar with the murder of Tamsin Fellows?' she asks.

I stare at the woman for a moment and wonder if she recognises me from the twenty or so times my face has been splashed across television screens and newspapers in relation to the subject of her petition.

'Yes, I've seen her name in the news,' I reply.

'We feel the investigating police have dropped the ball,' she says. 'It's been six months since her body was discovered by that journalist, and the police are yet to make a single breakthrough.'

'I'm sure they're doing their best with what they've got.'

'We feel they could do better,' the woman says, pushing the clipboard across the table towards me. 'I'd so appreciate it if you'd sign this petition demanding the Queensland police do more to protect the good citizens of Jubilee.'

I turn my head to a pile of folded T-shirts bearing the grainy photograph of Tamsin smiling under the Christmas-cracker crown.

'How much for a T-shirt?' I ask.

'Thirty-five,' the woman says.

Same price as my book.

'Or two for sixty dollars. All profits going to the Justice 4 Tamsin action group.'

I waddle away from the table. 'Lemme think about it,' I call back.

The automatic door of the Jubilee police station slides open. The young constable on the front desk, Blake Wishart, waves his right forefinger at me before I've even said a word.

'Nope,' he says, standing behind a clear glass screen, a pen in his hand poised above a textbook laid flat on the reception desk.

'Blakey, listen, it's—'

Blake holds up an open palm. 'Not listening,' he says. 'Don't even bother, Cork.' His head goes down to his textbook.

'But I need to report an attempted murder,' I say.

Blake's head shoots up again. 'Whose attempted murder?' he spits, doubtful and indignant.

'Mine,' I say.

'You attempted to murder someone, Cork?'

'No, Columbo, someone attempted to murder me. Last night on Burralong Street, some crazy woman in a red Hilux tried to run me over.'

'Is that right, Cork?'

'Yes, that's dead right, Blake.'

'Your secret admirer, perhaps? Or maybe one of the hundred or so people whose lives have been ruined by your journalising.'

I pull my phone from my pocket. Tap on my notes page. 'Can you just run a check on a plate for me?'

'No, I can't,' Blake says.

'Why not?'

'Because I'm not allowed to talk to you.'

'But I'm reporting an incident,' I say. 'What about all that stuff you guys told the press about ensuring the safety of me and my family at all times?'

'Well, that was before you decided to publish a book about a homicide case you know nothing about.'

'I found her body,' I say. 'Without me, there'd be no case for you all to get pissed off about.'

'I've been instructed by my station heads to ensure any communications from you are directed immediately to Georgia Long at police media.'

'Did Jim England tell you to say that?'

'Yes, in fact, he did.'

'What did he say exactly?'

'You want to know his exact words?'

'Yes, I do.'

'Well, his exact words were, "If that pustular arse boil of a journalist, Noah Cork, comes back in here again, tell him to drag his lowdown dirty rat cunt arse off to Georgia Long's office in police HQ in Roma Street."'

'That's verbatim?'

'Well, he actually said, "rat *fuck*". I subbed in "cunt".'

'Appreciate your candour. Jim still working on the Fellows case?'

'Yes.'

'Has he been working out of this station?'

'Yes.'

'Can I speak to him?'

'No.'

'Why not?'

'Because he's gone for lunch.'

'Where'd he go for lunch?'

'Grill'd.'

'Newmarket Grill'd or Rosalie Grill'd?'

'Chermside Grill'd.'

I shake my head, heave a deep sigh. Look at the plate number in my phone.

'Can you just write this down? Who knows, might just be the breakthrough you boys have been looking for,' I say. 'Red Toyota Hilux utility, licence plate 985 TL …'

A brief silence between us.

'TL what?' Blake asks.

'I didn't get the last letter.'

Blake laughs. 'Some fine police work, Cap'n Cork.'

'Well, unfortunately I didn't have time to read the last letter on account of the fact I was running for my life from the screaming hell machine that was trying to mow me down.'

Mercifully, Blake scribbles the plate number on a large square pad of paper.

I slide the phone back into my pocket. 'I'm sure that's enough to go on,' I say. 'Biggish woman driving the car. Sixty-plus years old. Flowing white hair. She looked a bit like Meat Loaf.'

'Who's Meat Loaf?'

'Never mind.'

I waddle back through the station's sliding door. In the distance, one of the teenaged boys on the playground lawn thunder-kicks his football high in the air. When it comes back down three seconds later, his mate drops the ball. I can see the Corolla in the carpark and Clem's red Adidas sneakers protruding from a side window.

As I pass the woman on the Justice 4 Tamsin table, she beams at me and asks, 'Care to sign the petition now?'

'Not this time, thanks,' I reply.

'Would you like me to tell you more about who Tamsin was?' the woman offers. 'She was such a loving mother.'

'No, thanks,' I say. 'I don't want to hear any more about what a loving mother Tamsin was. And I don't want to sign your petition.'

I keep on walking. Keep on waddling.

'But don't you care about finding the person who did this to one of our own?' the woman asks. 'A callous, cold-blooded killer could be walking among us.'

I ignore her.

'Where's your sense of community?' the woman calls after me.

In my left ear, I hear the comforting thwack of a teenager's right foot making contact again with the well-pumped Steeden. In my right ear, I hear the words of the woman at the table.

'What would Tamsin think about your obvious lack of compassion?' the woman roars.

I stop and turn back to her. She is now a skeleton. A skeleton sitting at the table with a green plastic tennis visor resting upon her bare skull. I stare at this skeleton in silence for almost ten seconds.

I shake my head. I rub my eyes. Now the woman's flesh and blood face has returned.

'Helloooo?' she says. 'You still there?'

I wipe my face with my open palms.

'Yeah, I'm still here,' I say.

'What do you think Tamsin would say to you?'

I want to tell this woman the whole truth. I think Tamsin would say something that starts with an 'S'. I think, maybe, she would say, 'Stop.' 'Stop, Noah,' she would say. 'Just … *stop.*'

'But I can't, Tamsin,' I would say back to her. 'I've never been able to stop digging for a story once I've started. It's something inside me. I just keep digging and digging and digging—'

'Until?'

'Until I can see where the story ends.'

'But do stories ever really end, Noah? Don't stories only pause, Noah? They never really end, do they? You could let this one go, Noah. The story can't stop, but you can. Why don't you try letting go, Noah? Easiest thing in the world. Can't you see what it's doing to Rita? Can't you see? Let it go, Noah. Let *me* go.'

I see four words on my bathroom mirror: *Gravity let me go.*

The thump of a kicked football sounds again, snaps me back to the here and now.

The woman in the green visor speaks again. 'Helloooo? Anybody home?'

I stare at the woman for a moment. Give her my answer. 'I'm sure Tamsin will tell me what she thinks, soon enough,' I say.

The stunned face of the petitioner.

The screaming voice of a teenaged boy echoing across the reserve: 'Heads!'

And me looking up just in time to watch the pointy end of a Steeden football land flush inside my left eye socket.

TEN

Know when to fight for your story. Know when to hold that story close to your chest like it's your newborn child. But, most importantly, know when to let your story go.

– Rutledge, *Journalism Practices and Principles*

Minor surgery made the coin bag swell. Feels like a bloated and toxic puffer fish. Some new and spiky black hairs sprouting from my otherwise bald scrotum. Four dissolvable stitches in my dad sack, four days old and disintegrating between my fingers in the shower. Speaking of disintegration, how's about my marriage? Speaking of decomposition, how's about my psyche? Seeing skeletons in my closet. Seeing skeletons in my pantry. Seeing skeletons in my dreams.

Zoom in on my wet and naked sag, if you think you can keep your Weet-Bix down. Look upon the world with an albatross's eye and fly across the vast Indian Ocean and head east over Australia's slow-beating red desert heart and when you hit the Great Barrier Reef, swing down past the Bundaberg Rum distillery and the Big Pineapple and the Caboolture flea market and take a right onto Gecko Street and fly through the front door of the house in Jubilee with the canary-yellow letterbox and flap your wings to slow your landing as you set yourself down at the end of the Cork family dining table where I usually eat my dinner. Stare if you dare for a moment in confusion and rising intrigue at the opposite end of the Cork family dining table, where my wife, Rita, sits in silence, resting her hand on a grey polished-concrete apple-shaped table ornament. Turn your head down the hallway and see my fifteen-year-old daughter knocking on a bathroom door.

Erin opens the door just wide enough to speak to me in the shower without having to suffer the trauma of seeing me in the shower.

'You gonna be much longer, Dad?'

'I thought you weren't needing the shower this morning?'

'I want to wash my hair before drama prac.'

'You'll have more hot water tonight.'

Our hot water system is old and weary and has only a 125-litre water tank, which can ensure a hot shower lasting between four and five minutes for exactly three out of four members of my family every twelve hours. Our water heater comes on steady, hot and weak.

'Can you leave some hot water for me, please?' Erin asks.

'Yes.'

'Love you, pookie.'

I have no idea what a pookie is.

I turn the hot water off and let the shower run cold for twenty body-shocking seconds before reaching for my towel. Take four steps to the bathroom sink, bury my head in a towel that smells like my gym socks. Feel the black and blue bruising around my left eye. Peer into the mirror to see if it still looks as though someone hit me flush with a right cross.

The bathroom mirror makes no sense to me. Once again, condensation reveals four words written across the glass by the finger of someone I love.

Gravity

let

me

go

I wrap the towel around my waist and march, still dripping, out of the bathroom, down the hall and into the living room, where Rita sits in silence at the dining table.

'Did you write that message on the bathroom mirror?' I ask.

Rita turns her gaze to me, face distant and blank, like it has been for the past four days.

'What's that supposed to mean, Rita?' I ask. 'You tryin' to leave me some kind of cryptic message? Am I supposed to figure out what the hell that means? Is that what would make you speak? Am I supposed to write something back to you? Is this how we're going to communicate from now on? Ridiculous messages scribbled on mirrors?'

Rita remains silent.

I nod three times. 'All right, all right,' I say. 'Two can play at that game.' I point my finger at Rita. 'Don't you go anywhere,' I say. 'We're gonna have a big talk, you and me. I mean, well, maybe you won't talk, but I bloody well will. I'm sick of this shit, Rita. You don't wanna talk, fine. Maybe you can just listen to a few things I gotta say.'

I march back to the bathroom and finger-scribble a message in the mirror's condensation: *And where exactly did you go, Rita?*

*

So begin my stages of grieving the loss of Rita's voice. Anger arrives first. It hits me when I'm driving the girls to school and some arsehole in an electric-blue Peugeot cuts me off on Wicker Road. I foolishly speed up and change lanes to draw parallel with the Peugeot driver. When our eyes meet, I curl the fingers of my left hand and stroke the invisible penis extending from my forehead. The driver shakes his head at me and waves kindly to Erin in the front passenger seat.

'Dad, that's my modern history teacher, Mr Shaw,' Erin says.

'Fuck, sorry honey.'

I drop the girls at stop-drop-and-go and another parent's car beeps at me three times for holding up the turning circle as I'm spit-cleaning a stain on Clem's right school shoe that smells like old dog shit. The anger takes control of my body when I return the Corolla to our carport and realise I've parked too close to the wall to open my door.

On entering the house, I see Rita still sitting silently at the dining table, gripping that ugly fucking concrete apple ornament that her sister, Mardi, bought us as a housewarming present. I take it from her hand and squeeze it in my right hand, and I have to stop myself from throwing it through the glass doors.

I hold the apple up to my eyes. 'I've never liked this apple,' I say. 'I hate this fucking apple. It just sits in the middle of the table doing nothing. What's it supposed to be saying? *We like apples.* Yes. What a groundbreaking concept. Who doesn't fucking like apples, Rita?'

I grip the apple with two hands now as I pace across the living room. Rita studies my frantic and random movements with the kind of empathetic and compassionate face Jane Goodall showed Koko the gorilla.

'It's just so breathtakingly childish, Rita,' I say. 'I mean, is it not the most adolescent way to punish someone you supposedly love? Just stop talking. Oh, very good. Bravo. Real mature.'

I breathe. Pause. Breathe again.

'I'm sorry,' I say. 'I'm sorry. I'm getting angry again. I promised myself I wouldn't get angry. Is that the problem? My fluctuating emotions. I'm sorry. I've been like this all my life. Up and down like a fuckin' see-saw. Splinters in my arse the whole friggin' time. Good ol' splintery-arse me.'

Breathe. Pause. Breathe again. Hug the concrete apple to my chest. A thought lands like an apple landing on my head.

'Perimenopause,' I say. I raise a finger in the air, wide-eyed and hopeful, like I've just struck a seam of gold in Rita's impenetrable sandstone face. 'It's perimenopause isn't it? I've been googling it, you know. I'm not completely ignorant of the inner workings of womankind, I hope you know. You're smack-bang in the age range, Rita. Oestrogen levels about as stable as a rocking chair. Hot flashes. Itchy skin. Night sweats. And that's just the physical stuff. Scientists have barely even scratched the surface of what it does to the female brain. One specialist guy said all husbands should ready themselves for a period of not recognising the person they married. He said some men reported feeling like a stranger had taken possession of their wife's body. He said it sometimes lasts for years. Wildly unpredictable mental health effects. Irritability. *Tick*. Sadness. *Tick*. Hopelessness. *Tick*. The article said if you're experiencing feelings of sorrow and despair for longer than two weeks then you might be experiencing a major perimenopause-related depressive episode. Depression, Rita? Fuckin' depression. This shit's no joke.'

Rita remains silent.

Breathe. Pause. Collect my thoughts. Collect some dots. Join some dots.

'I just realised something,' I say. 'I'm stuck in the eye of a fuckin' hormonal hurricane. I'm the corned beef sandwiched between two teenaged girls processing puberty and a wife neck-deep in a total menopause mindfuck. I get it now. I should have seen this coming. I'm such a fuckin' idiot.'

I walk circles around the dining table. Denial shifts gears and rubs its front wheels right up against the bumper of my anger. Denial is a river in Egypt and it runs through my toes and moves through my feet and makes me move around the living room.

'I didn't do *anything* to deserve this, Rita,' I say. 'What did I do to deserve this? I wrote a book about something extraordinary that happened to me? You said you wanted me to write something great. You said that one day I would write something that landed. Something that made an impact. I was just doing my job, Rita. What was I supposed to do? That book is gonna pay our bills. That book is gonna get our girls through school. That book is gonna get us *a second bathroom*!'

I shake my head. 'Listen to me,' I say. 'See what I've become. Some fuckin' houseproud materialistic bore who measures his good fortune in bathrooms. This is all *your* choice, Rita. This is all on *you*. I can't do anything about this. So, please, go right ahead, Marcel Marceau, do your worst. See if I care.'

I sit down opposite her. I take a long breath. Rub my forehead. Bargaining follows denial.

'Just talk to me,' I say, softly. '*Please*, Rita. Where does silence get us? How can I possibly know what the problem is if *you* don't tell me what it is. Seriously, I mean, you choose to do this to me now? At this precise moment in my life? After everything I've been through in the past six months? I got some anonymous killer out there sending me messages. You don't even know that, the night I went to hospital, some Meat Loaf–lookin' psycho woman tried to run me over. I can't even get the cops to investigate the incident because they all hate my guts about as much as Tamsin Fellows' family hates my guts. And now the one person I care about the most – my fucking sanctuary of a wife – is giving me the silent treatment because, well, I guess, she hates my guts, too.'

Anger returns for an encore. 'If this is about Georgia Long and that fucking hotel room, then I don't know what more I have to tell you.'

I slap my mobile phone on the table. 'You wanna phone her yourself? Her number's in there under "Beelzebub". She can tell you herself. Nothing. Fucking. Happened.'

I lean back in my chair. Rub my eyes. Grip the concrete apple in my right fist.

'That shrink at the hospital seems to think this is some poetic "fuck you" to me,' I bark. 'Some kind of peaceful-Tibetanmonk-vow-of-silence protest bullshit. Well, you know what, you wanna say a "fuck you" to me, Rita, well, I guess I can say a "fuck you" right back. Fuck *you*, Rita. Yeah, that's right. You heard me. *Fuck you.* I love you. I'd die for you. I hope you're okay. I'm worried about you and I pray to God we make it through all this, but, honestly, right now, as far as I'm concerned, *fuuuuuuuck you.*'

I place the apple back on the table in triumph. It's a triumph because I know Rita thought I was going to throw the apple at the living room wall. But I'm not gonna throw the apple at the living room wall because I would never do something so childish and useless and violent and dumb.

Then I pick the apple up again, open our sliding glass doors and throw the polished concrete ornamental apple over our backyard fence and onto the aluminium roof of our neighbour's house. The violent noise of concrete bouncing on metal makes me instantly realise my error in judgement.

'Fuuuuuck,' I scream.

*

I'm holding my steel folding ladder when I ring the front doorbell of the house on 32 Jandowae Street, Jubilee. Ivy Gladstone opens her front door and squints at me through the flyscreen.

'Noah,' she says.

Ivy is a seventy-nine-year-old former naturopath who has lived in Jandowae Street for almost fifty years.

'Sorry to bother you, Ivy,' I say. I search for words that will explain my behaviour in the best way possible.

There is no best way. 'I accidentally threw a concrete apple on your roof.'

Ivy opens the flyscreen door. 'You threw what?' she asks.

'A polished concrete apple,' I reply. 'It's a table ornament my sister-in-law gave us for our housewarming.'

'You accidentally threw a table ornament on my roof?' Ivy replies, pondering the idea.

'Well, truth be told, it was more an act of frustration than an accident.'

Ivy studies my face. 'What happened to your eye?'

'Now that was a genuine accident,' I say, with a weak chuckle. 'A football landed on my face.'

'Is everything all right with you and Rita, Noah?' Ivy asks.

'Yes, Ivy, everything's all right.'

'It's just that … well … I have heard the arguments you two have been having at night.'

'That's just talking. Unpacking a few work–life balance issues.'

'Rather loud talking I'd say, Noah. I was chatting to Ellis and June at Coles the other day. They said they'd heard the arguments from their place, too. Ellis said you told him about the stress this Tamsin Fellows business has put you both under.'

'I didn't say any such thing to Ellis,' I protest. 'In future, Ivy, please take anything Ellis tells you about Rita and me with a grain of salt. Maybe a whole shaker of salt, in fact.'

'Why did you throw a concrete apple on my roof, Noah?'

'Because Rita has stopped talking.'

'To you?'

'To everybody.'

'Why has Rita stopped talking to everybody?'

'I don't know.'

'And that's what made you frustrated? Not knowing?'

I nod.

'So you threw a concrete apple on my roof in frustration.'

Nod my head again.

'Well, that was stupid wasn't it?'

'Yes, Ivy, I guess it was.'

'Is there anything you might have done to make Rita stop talking?'

I stare at Ivy for a long moment before I answer. Anger leads to denial leads to bargaining leads to anger leads to depression leads to truth.

'Well ... I think ... somewhere along the way ... I got stupid.'

*

Walking back along Gecko Street now, hauling my ladder in my left hand, the concrete apple in my right. I stop at my section of the nature strip to find Hercules taking his mid-morning Friday shit on my manicured lawn. Eight brown orbs of bullmastiff feculence resembling my mother-in-law's Christmas rum balls, minus the coconut flakes. The dog stares at me as if I'm the one who's being rude.

I raise the concrete apple, making like I'm about to throw the projectile at the dog's busy arse. 'Fuck you, Hercules, you loose-bowelled cretin,' I spit. I wind up my throwing arm and fake-peg the apple at his head.

The dog doesn't even blink, just drops two more rum balls from his evil anus.

I hear a whistle in my left ear. Turn to find Jim England standing in his driveway, three doors down, next to his Triton, in grey work suit and tie.

'Wrap it up, buddy,' he calls to Hercules.

Hercules skips away towards his owner.

'You gonna clean this mess up, Jim?' I ask.

'No,' Jim says.

'Why not?'

'Because I gotta go to work, Cork,' he says. 'I gotta go find the arsehole who left a message in some muckraker's mailbox. You mighta heard of the case?'

'Yeah, I know that case,' I say. 'That's the one where the police haven't made a single breakthrough in six months.'

'Don't believe everything you read, Cork,' he says. 'See, unlike some tabloid crime hacks I know, us cops like to find out what the story is before we share it with the world.'

'You hear about the woman who tried to run me over?'

'I heard.'

'And?'

'And a partridge in a pear tree, Cork. What the fuck do you mean, "And"?'

'*And* what are you gonna do about the woman in the red Toyota Hilux?'

'I'm gonna give you a cuddle, Cork,' he says. 'And then I'm gonna sing you "Twinkle Twinkle, Little Publishing Star".'

He hops in the Triton, turns on the engine. 'You want answers from us,' he says. 'Call Georgia Long at police media.'

He points at the droppings left by Hercules on my lawn.

'I'll clean that mess when it dries,' he says, before barrelling out of Gecko Street.

I turn and walk into my front yard, pass a blue metal outdoor table setting on the front porch where, out of the corner of my left eye, I see Tamsin's skeleton sitting. She shakes her head at me. Tries to say something.

'*Sssssssss* …' she says. She can't get the word out.

'Honestly, Tamsin,' I reply. 'Not right now, please.'

*

When I walk through the front door of our house, Rita is still sitting at the end of the dining table. I take a seat beside her. A table corner between us. Our kneecaps touching under the table. I place the concrete apple on the table. Sit in her silence for so long that I lose track of how long the silence lasts. I close my eyes. See Tamsin briefly wedged into the kitchen oven of my mind. Then a warm hand presses gently against my forehead. Rita's hand. I immediately place both of my palms upon her hand because I don't want her hand to move away from my face. And Tamsin disappears from my mind.

Rita's hand slides to my left cheek and then towards my eyes. I see only Rita in my mind now. Rita from years ago. Our housewarming party. Rita with that haircut that I said made her look like Demi Moore in *Ghost*. Rita laughing with our friends and family as she sits at this very table, opening housewarming gifts. Rita posing for a photo taken by her younger sister, Mardi. She's just opened up the box that was holding the silly concrete apple. She's laughing at the apple, asking her sister what the hell the apple is for.

'It's not for anything,' Mardi says. 'It's ornamental. Its beauty is its purpose.'

'Nah, apples exist to be eaten,' Rita says.

And Mardi snaps a shot of her sister pretending to bite into the concrete.

Rita's hand cups my bruised eye. Her fingers rest upon the puffy pouch above my cheekbone. And for the first time in days I realise there is no more pain in the bruising.

'I remember the first word I ever heard come out of your mouth, Rita,' I say. 'It was an "S" word. The word was "Stop".

'You didn't want me jumping on the train tracks that night. Then you asked me if I was crazy. I remember the sound of your voice through the phone when I called you up three days later. The phone line was crackling because you were still living with Mardi in that flat in Indooroopilly, and Mardi had that dodgy phone that was a plastic replica of KITT, the car from *Knight Rider*.'

Her thumb runs along my right eyebrow.

'I remember that word "Yes" and how it came out of your mouth on that platform when I asked you to be my wife,' I say. 'That sound meant you were gonna give your life to me and I never thought I was worthy of such a gift. Your voice cracked for a moment because you were crying when you said it.'

Her fingers move down across my nose and her hand moves down further and settles upon my mouth.

I stay silent. Eyes still closed. Her hand moves down to my chest. My heart.

'I remember the last word you said to me,' I say. 'It was the night before you and Clem had the school excursion to Fernvale. It was the night of the meteor shower. The night before everything seemed to go all funny. We were talking about the hotel room. We were talking about Georgia Long.

I stormed off and went to the bedroom like a spoilt little boy who didn't get his ice cream after dinner. You and the girls stayed in the yard and watched that meteor shower. I stayed in bed looking at my stupid fucking book. Do you remember the last word you said to me? It was an "S" word. You said, "Stop". You told me to stop.'

I shake my head. Another full minute of total silence. Use it. Don't waste the precious silence. Put some value on your noise.

'I don't know what exactly it is that you want me to stop, but I'm gonna stop, Rita. Whatever it is, I'm gonna stop.'

I grip her forearm. 'You devoted your life to me,' I say. 'And I devoted my life to a fuckin' laptop.'

I grip her wrist. 'I'm sorry if I ever used this voice of mine to hurt you,' I say. 'I'm sorry for every word I ever said to you that wasn't, "Thanks, I love you." I'm sorry I talked about myself so many times when all I meant to say was, "Thanks, I love you." I know you think I never listen. But I heard every word you ever said. I can hear your voice in my head, Rita. I can see you in there, too. I can see the very moment you first held that concrete apple. I could tell you about every movement that I ever saw you make. I can recall every picture I ever saw you pose for. I was always watching over the snapper's shoulder. I know you so well, Rita, and I know I still don't know you well enough at all.'

Breathe. Think. Feel. Speak.

'I miss your voice, Rita, but I don't mind. You stay quiet as long as you want. I love your voice, but I can live without it. I still have your smile. And your breath. And your brain. I still have you near me. I still have your touch.'

I rest my right hand upon the hand that rests upon my heart.

'Touch beats talk, doesn't it?' I ask. 'Any day of the week.'

Think before you speak, Noah Cork. Don't waste your noise. Don't waste her silence.

'I'm sorry I'm so loud,' I say. 'I'm sorry I talk so much. All I was ever trying to say was, "Thanks, I love you." I'm sorry, Rita. I'm so sorry if I ever used these fool lips of mine for anything more than kissing yours.'

Rita remains silent. I press her hand against my heart and shut the fuck up, too, just this once. Breathe in with her hand on my heart. And stop.

ELEVEN

Avoid clichés like the plague. Corect spelling is esential. Only arseholes resort to swearing.

– Rutledge, *Journalism Practices and Principles*

'So, what's the secret to a good profile, Dad?'

Clem wears a straw Bunnings hat. The red suede Adidas Gazelles on her feet. Her notepad and a pencil case inside the white canvas tote bag over her shoulder that used to belong to my sister, Meg: *Cool Aunts Club*. A Taylor Swift shirt with a single word stretched across it: *Lover*. We're walking through the Jubilee War Memorial park on Noonan Street, heading towards Drake Bridge. We pass five sandstone pillars dedicated to fallen locals who fought in the world wars. Clem's eyes briefly fix upon a Mexican stand-off between a water dragon and a brush turkey, but it's the rainbow lorikeet over her right shoulder that wins her attention.

'You need everything you already have in spades, Clem. Enthusiasm. Curiosity. A love of people and things with wings. You need just one good ear and at least a two-litre tank of tears inside you. You need to remember that actions speak louder than quotes, but tattoos and framed living room photographs speak louder than actions. And, above all else, you need a museum pass.'

'A museum pass? What's a museum got to do with anything?'

I shake my head.

'It's Rutledge,' I say.

'What's Rutledge?' Clem asks.

'*Who's* Rutledge,' I say. 'Professor Lionel Rutledge. He wrote the Bible for young journos like me in the 1990s. *Journalism Practices and Principles*. Required reading for a thousand young Aussie hacks hoping to change the world in one fell *scoop*.'

Clem spots an empty can in the grass and stomps violently on it until it resembles an aluminium pancake. She slips the crushed can into her tote. She made $72 last weekend at the Containers for Change drive-through depot in Banyo.

'Sorry,' Clem says. 'Go on.'

'Rutledge said every profile subject has a great big museum inside their mind. You remember we did that virtual tour of the Natural History Museum in London?'

'Yeah, Erin said it looked like Hogwarts.'

'Well, everybody's got a big museum like that inside their brain and it's the feature journalist's job to go as deep inside that museum as we can. There'll be all kinds of exhibits in glass display cases that your profile subject will be dying to show you. All the moments of their lives that they keep inside these cases, unfolding like cinema showreels. There's that first kiss. There's that wedding day. There's that brave thing they did, that unexpected moment of pride, that hard-won success. Cases like that are always well-lit and easy to find in the museum of the mind. These are the flashy moments that they're proud to exhibit in gallery rooms one through five, just near the cafeteria and the welcoming gift shop with the polished teaspoons and the shortbread boxes. The truth of human conversation is this: we all want people to exit through our gift shops. But it's not the journalist's job to exit through the gift shop. It's not *your* job to exit through the gift shop. It's your job to find the place in the museum that ain't so easily found, you hearing me?'

Clem nods, scribbles in her notepad: *No museum gift shops.*

'You want to get to the storage room,' I say. 'You want to get to the storage place at the very end of the museum, that room that's dark and covered in cobwebs that nobody wants you to enter. The place where they store the cases made of nailed-down plywood. These are the storage rooms of our lives that never see the light of day. The ones we always keep locked. The rooms you gotta open with a crowbar.'

Clem nods, scribbles: *Get to the storage room.*

'So the storage room is where they keep their secrets?' Clem asks.

'Sometimes,' I reply. 'But sometimes it's just a single moment. That one revelatory moment of their life that speaks to who they really are, not just who they say they are.'

'But why would anyone let a journalist bring a crowbar into their museum?'

'Well, time is a crowbar. Trust is a crowbar. Enthusiasm is a crowbar. Understanding is a crowbar.'

'Love is a crowbar,' Clem says.

'How so?'

'I'm only ever gonna let the people I love bring a crowbar into my museum.'

'Sounds pretty smart to me, kiddo,' I say.

Clem scribbles more notes. Then she looks up at me, eyes squinting in the sun, face filled with thought.

'Maybe that's all we gotta do, Dad,' Clem says. 'Find someone we love enough to hand them the crowbar.'

That makes me laugh. 'Maybe, indeed.'

Clem sees seven white stone pillars standing like a Stonehenge formation at the end of Drake Bridge on Wicker Road. The collective title of the formation is fixed to one stone: *The Pillars of Jubilee.* A public art installation paying tribute to the physical environment of Jubilee – blue quandongs, black wattles, lungfish, pythons in our parks and in our guttering – and the outstanding contributions of its residents. Clem darts between the pillars like a mouse in a lab maze, reading each white square plaque as she goes.

Cary Wright (1934–2008) owned the Wright Family Jewellers shop on the corner of Stuart Street and Edgar Road for 42 years (1958–2000) and sold thousands of engagement rings, wedding bands and anniversary necklaces to the residents of Jubilee and beyond. Cary is also remembered as the driving force behind the construction of the Jubilee Skate Centre on Edgar Road in 1986.

Jill Leggett (1943–2016) moved to Jubilee in 1962 and established the Friends of Jubilee Community Association in 1963, which thrives to this day and has been responsible for countless community projects, including the Teaneck Creek Rehabilitation Project and the annual Jubilee Darkness to Daybreak walkathon for victims of domestic violence. Jill was a dedicated member of St John's Anglican Church and, in 2007, her faith called her to establish the Volunteer Refugee Tutoring and Community Support Program, operating out of her own basement in Bush Crescent, Jubilee.

Clem hops on the spot when she finds the plaque dedicated to her mother.

Rita Munro (1979–   ) was raised in Jubilee from the age of six months by her parents, Bill and Deborah Munro, who ran the Jubilee Realty agency on Wicker Road (1981–1995). In 1996, in her senior year at Jubilee State High School, Rita single-handedly saved the lives of three siblings – Adam, Tenille and Leah Duncan – who were trapped in a deadly house fire on Pike Street. With little regard for her own safety, Rita entered the blazing inferno on three separate occasions, carrying each sibling to safety on her shoulders. Upon finding the youngest child – eight-year-old Leah Duncan – unconscious and without a pulse, Rita recalled the first-aid skills she had learned in her childhood as a member of the Drake Bridge–Jubilee Girl Guides and successfully brought young Leah back to life. One month later, in a formal ceremony held in the Drake Bridge Reserve amphitheatre, officers from Jubilee Police Station presented Rita with the Department of the Prime Minister and Cabinet's Star of Courage, awarded for acts of conspicuous courage in circumstances of great peril.

Clem runs her finger along the black lettering of her mother's name at the top of the plaque. 'You ever been in a circumstance of great peril, Dad?'

'Well, I took a wrong turn into Bracken Ridge once, but other than that …'

'I wanna get myself in a circumstance of great peril.'

'Please don't.'

Clem scribbles again.

'So what have you learned so far about your profile subject?' I ask.

She flips back through her pages, considers the question. 'Well, she's brave,' she replies. 'Humble, too.'

'What makes you say that?'

'She never shows anyone her Star of Courage. She keeps it in her second drawer, in the box with all the earrings she never wears.'

'What else?'

'She never tells anyone she was adopted.'

Clem taps her right forefinger on the first sentence of the plaque. 'The only reason she wasn't raised in Jubilee by Bill and Deb Munro for the first six months of her life was because Bill and Deb Munro didn't know her for the first six months of her life. That feels like a storage room box to me.'

'Maybe.'

'Maybe? Dad, she's a foundling. Who knows who her parents are? Her parents could be billionaires. She could be a Kennedy for all we know. Better yet, a Kardashian. Or maybe she's from some place much further away than we think.'

'And what place might that be, Clem?'

Clem bites the end of her pen. Her eyes turn slowly up to the blue sky above us. My daughter doesn't explain herself. Just stares up into the sky. Then she turns her eyes back to me and raises her eyebrows as if I should know what she's thinking. Something conspiratorial in the way she raises those eyebrows.

'You pickin' up what I'm puttin' down, Dad?' she whispers.

She looks to the sky again and I look up at it as well, just to see if I'm missing something up there in the endless blue.

'Clem. Mum's told you all this before. She was left at the doors of the Mater Mothers, most likely by a couple of deadbeat druggos.'

'Yep,' Clem says, nodding while still facing the sky, 'and Clark Kent was just a Kansas farmboy.' Clem whips her head back to me. 'Surely, that's my intro for the story?' she suggests.

'Where we've come from doesn't always tell us who we are,' I say.

Clem scratches her head, takes a deep breath, studies the plaque.

'So where to now?' I ask.

'You reckon the Duncans still live in Jubilee?'

'Nobody ever really leaves Jubilee.'

Clem closes her notebook, heads back across Drake Bridge in the direction of the Jubilee Plaza shopping centre. I catch up and we walk together in silence, back past the Jubilee War Memorial, to the Yaris that's baking in the sun of the Jubilee Diamonds soccer club carpark.

I can tell Clem is thinking deeply about something. Her quiet tells me this. Usually, Clementine Cork's thoughts shift straight from her brain to her mouth in the same instant. But all her deeper thoughts take a longer route to her lips, the route that detours to her heart.

We get into the car.

'Hey, Dad, can I ask you a question?'

I start the engine, give it some revs. 'Sure,' I say.

Clem's head's hanging over her lap. 'Did you ever hand Mum the crowbar?'

TWELVE

The journalist must maintain a professional physical and emotional distance from the subject at all times.

– Rutledge, *Journalism Practices and Principles*

Did you ever hand your wife the crowbar? Huh! Punk kid. What kinda question is that, Cork? Smart kid. Pure journo brain. She cut straight to the bone, huh? But let's not get started on *bones* again. Besides, it's ridiculous. As if there's anything about you that Rita doesn't know. She got it all, heart and soul. You've been married to Rita for twenty-three years. You can't stay that close to someone for that long without handing them the crowbar. Right, Cork? *Right?*

A still afternoon now. Driving alone now. Taking sharp rights and lefts through the streets of my suburb. On my way to right some wrongs. What was that thing Rutledge said about caring for your sources? *Always leave them better than how you found them.* Ain't that just your problem, Cork? You're like some kinda curse with a computer, some kinda contagion with a keyboard. Have you ever left anyone better than how you found them, Cork? A thousand innocent sources falling through the cracks between your black ink words. A hundred criminal subjects who would love to see you cut into pieces and stuffed inside an oven. What were you needing from them all? What were you searching for all this time, Cork? Your three reasons for living. Clem and Erin? *Rita?* They were perfect how you found them. But how have you left them lately?

Left, right, left again through the streets of Jubilee.

Did you ever hand your wife the crowbar? Huh! I mean, how hard would it be, Cork? Just to take Rita's hand and hold it tight as you walked to the end of that museum at midnight when the ceiling lights were out and you coulda walked right past them memories with the girls and the train platform at Bowen Hills and the big fat kiss on your wedding day and the arguments in the kitchen and the make-up sex in the bedroom and the hours you spent showing Rita every last exhibit box, every last room inside your museum … except … except … *except* … that one. That one room right at the back. That one room with the locked door marked *STORAGE*. What do you think might have happened if you had handed her the crowbar? Did you think it would be the end? The end of the only story that ever really mattered to you. That's it! Of course. You think it will die if you hand her the crowbar, so you will die before you hand her the crowbar. Here's a page-one lead for you, Cork. Call it a hunch, call it a seasoned crime journo's instinct. Or maybe just call it a question. Are you the skeleton? Are you the walking dead? Are you the skeleton in your closet?

I drive by a bus stop where I see Tamsin's skeleton with her right foot propped upon her left knee, waiting for the bus as she reads a broadsheet newspaper. A big bold headline stretched across page one: GRAVITY LET HIM GO. Tamsin's sinister black-orb eyes follow me across the top of her newspaper.

'Stop!' I scream.

I slam the brakes on the Yaris and turn my head to find the letterbox of 56 Fletcher Street, Jubilee.

Breathe. Breathe again.

*

I'm walking up the stairs of Tamsin Fellows' two-storey house. Peeling gunmetal grey paint on the steps. A rusting metal rail that moves five centimetres when I grip it. The steps lead to a timber veranda and a front door off the veranda that is wide open, I assume, because it's hot enough today to make the simple task of ascending a staircase cause a drop of sweat to roll gently down my left temple. This is Brisbane storm weather. Muggy and maddening. This is the slow build. Summer's come early this year. The great summer suck. The seething swelter. The suffocating climatic prelude to storm season. There was a story in the paper this morning about how every fifty-dollar pedestal fan in every Kmart across the city has been sold. Ellis told me yesterday of a radio report about an eighty-year-old grandmother in Deagon who died alone in her house from heat exhaustion. He said the woman had been dead for four days and the neighbours had no idea because, Ellis said, the world is filled with eight billion self-infatuated, self-serving isolationists who know more about Kim Kardashian's preferred undergarments than they do about their eighty-year-old neighbour's agonising and lonely death. I didn't want to know how the woman might have passed but Ellis told me anyway. 'Head starts to pound,'

Ellis said. 'Muscles seize up. Dizziness. Vomiting. She woulda been too confused to even dial the police. Your insides heat up and your heart works overtime to pump blood to your skin. Boom. Heart attack.'

In my left hand is a child's gift bag featuring cartoon images of all the planets of the solar system. I found the bag in Rita's box of birthday cards and gift bags.

Raising my knees to climb steps is still causing an ache in my balls, still tender from Operation Twisted Olive. A lazy old black labrador fights the summer heat in the far corner of the veranda. The dog's too heat-weary to even bark at the stranger at the top of the stairs. Tamsin loved this dog. What was he called again? Jed? Ted? There's a name on the metal tag hanging from his collar: *Ned*.

I knock twice on the open front door leading directly into the living room. No movement inside the house. I poke my head through the entrance and see an impressive, ornately carved homemade wall unit filled with small woodcarvings – a dolphin, a horse, a perfect wood sphere the size of a lawn bowl jack. I look deeper into the living room and find the back of a man's head sticking up from an oatmeal-coloured three-seater suede lounge that's facing away from me. I think that head belongs to Neil Fellows. All I can see is the dark, grey-flecked hair on the back of his head. He's watching something on a flatscreen television, volume up too high. Some kind of YouTube tutorial video where a man in America's Deep South is turning a thick tree trunk into a large wooden grizzly bear with nothing but an axe and a chainsaw.

'Neil,' I say, leaning my head through the doorway without

stepping a foot inside the house. 'I'm sorry to bother you. It's Noah Cork.'

Neil's head does not move.

I knock twice again on the front door. 'Excuse me, Neil.'

Nothing. No movement. I put one foot inside the house. Can see the framed family photographs on the wall unit. There's that one photo the family released to the press in November 2022, days after Tamsin's disappearance. She looks to be at a daytime backyard barbecue and she's wearing a crushed green paper crown that she might have just acquired by pulling one end of a Christmas cracker. She has hair like Olivia Newton-John, golden hair, blue eyes. I've never properly seen the other shots of Tamsin. A photo of her in a red netball bib, wing defence. A picture of Tamsin and Neil Fellows, kissing beside the Trevi Fountain. Tamsin and her children, John and Helen, when they were young, on a Queensland Rail train, their hands filled with show bags from the Royal Queensland Show.

The living room flows to a kitchen and a hallway. The chainsaw in the video quietens long enough for me to hear death metal music coming from the backyard and a toilet flush from the end of the hallway. I step back outside onto the veranda, head still peering through the open door. A man emerges from the hallway singing, in a death metal voice, something about the four horsemen of the apocalypse. It sounds as though he's trying to cough up an apricot seed wedged in his larynx. A flash of his black clothing as he disappears into the half of the kitchen I can't see. Sound of a fridge door opening. Bottles clanging. Fridge door closing.

I walk back down the front staircase and follow the death metal music around the side of the house to a large galvanisedsteel work shed that occupies most of the backyard. There's a sliding glass door built into the side of the shed and I knock loudly on it, twice, to cut through the music. A curtain is pulled open behind the door and a young man, tall and pale and thin as a chalk stick, eyeballs me from behind the glass. He's wearing tight black jeans and a black shirt with the word 'Succubus' written in a font designed for the angry and the dead. The young man snarls at me and draws the curtain closed again. The music stops. I wait in silence for almost sixty seconds before a disembodied hand reaches behind the curtain and opens the door. Curtain still closed.

A voice beyond the curtain says, 'Come in.' The voice might belong to John Fellows, but it's difficult to tell.

'Is that you, John?'

'Yeah, it's me,' the voice says. 'Come in.'

I look back over my left shoulder, checking my surroundings. Not a person in sight. Nobody even knows I'm here. I didn't tell Rita where I was going. Didn't tell nobody. Had nobody to tell.

I pull the curtain back and step inside the shed.

John Fellows lunges at me immediately, pressing something sharp against my Adam's apple. Spits at me when he screams, 'You dare come into my fucking house, Cunt Money?'

My eyes drop down and catch a glimpse of the woodcarving chisel in his hand. The blade is fine and maybe three inches long. Three of John's friends circle around me. All long-haired metalheads, bony and under-nourished. All three of them carrying woodcutting tools with pointy metal ends. Another friend remains on a couch on the far side of the shed, a juice bottle bong in his hand, still bubbling with water and smoke.

My eyes scan a coffee table by the couch, filled with beer and whisky bottles, vape pens and two syringes resting on a saucer.

'John, John,' I stammer. 'Just wait a second. I came to give you something.'

I raise the gift bag in my left hand. He screams in my face again. 'There's nothing I want from you, Cuuuunt Money!' And he knees me in the balls and I drop straight to the concrete floor of the shed like a felled tree ready for Neil Fellows to turn into a grizzly bear. I wail in agony, twisting snake-like along the concrete, hands clutching my aching nut sack.

John and his friends are momentarily puzzled by the apparently unexpected intensity of my pain. 'What the fuck is wrong with you, Cork, you pissant?' John barks. 'I barely tapped you.'

'You fuckin' brute,' I say, my back curled, knees to my chest to absorb the pain. 'I just had surgery on my balls.'

'What happened to your balls, Cork?' John asks.

'My right testicle twisted upon itself,' I explain. 'The surgeon recently stitched it to the side of my ball bag. He saved my life and he saved my balls.'

'Faaarrrrrk me,' one of John's friends says, wincing.

'Yeah, my thoughts exactly, thug,' I say. 'Fuck me.'

I take a deep breath and find my feet. I extend an I-come-in-peace open palm, like an earthling meeting four invading metalhead Martians. 'Just gimme a second, please,' I say. I hold the gift bag up for John.

'I came to give you this,' I say.

'What the fuck is that?' John asks.

'It's twenty-five thousand dollars in cash,' I reply. 'It's what I got paid for writing the book. Every cent I got paid by the publishers. No more, no less. I don't want it anymore.'

John's puzzled face.

I take three more breaths as I step closer to him. 'I want you to have it, John,' I say. 'That's enough to get your dad into rehab for six months. You could get him off the booze. Maybe somethin' good could come from what I wrote about your mum.'

John moves towards the gift bag, snatches it from my hand. He looks inside it. Bends his back and laughs at me. Then he throws the bag at my face. It bounces off my nose and into my open palms. I rub my nostrils and check my fingers for signs of blood.

'I don't want your money, Cork,' John says, his face so close to me I can smell the whisky on his breath. 'That money's cunt money. I don't want your cunt money, Cork.'

He turns to his friends.

'Drag this cunt over to the bandsaw,' he says.

John's metalhead mates rush me, woodcutting tools raised for combat.

'What?' I exclaim, raising my palms. 'Wait, wait, fellers. Stop. Don't do nuthin' stupid now. There are many important people who know I'm here.'

The boys wedge me into a corner of the shed with no exit routes.

'Nah, I don't believe you, Cork,' John bellows across the shed. 'Who gives a fuck about what happens to cunt-money hacks like you?'

The tallest metalhead collars my shirt, the two others grip my elbows. John pulls a safety visor from a hook on the wall and slips it over his head. His fist bangs a bright yellow power button by a work bench and then he slaps two more buttons on a large orange and black stationary bandsaw that stands like a stallion rearing wildly back on its hind legs. The metalhead thugs grip my wrists and bring my hands to the square cutting plate as the beastly machine roars into whirring life.

'I don't need your money, Cork,' John screams over the sound of the raging fourteen-inch steel blade that is whizzing patiently in place, waiting for something to sever. 'What I need is for you to never write another word about my mum. What I need, Cork' – the metalhead thugs slap my open right hand palm-down on the cold surface of the cutting plate – 'are your fingers and thumbs.'

'Stop this, John,' I say. 'I'm letting it all go. I don't want to be a part of Tamsin's story anymore. I came to tell you I'm letting it go. You don't have to do this. I won't write another word. I'm letting the story go, John.'

'Starfire burns in the eye of the serpent,' screams one of John's friends.

'Nocturnal torment in the ages in your eye,' screams another.

'Arise, o ancient one,' screams John.

Fingers inching closer to the blade. The rabid looks on the faces of these troubled boys. They want my blood. They want my fingers removed from my hand. I know for certain now that they want this. This is not a game. This is real. This is evil cult shit beyond my pay grade. This is me bleeding to death on a concrete floor. This is the end of the story for a story with no end.

'Arise red beast,' roars John. 'Here be Noah Cork. Receive his selfless sacrifice.'

My right thumb is only a centimetre from the raging saw blade.

And then the motor on the bandsaw cuts out. John flips back the shield on his visor and whips his head towards the yellow power button.

'John, you fuckin' freak,' says Helen Fellows, her hand over the button. Her hair is golden like her mother's. She's twig thin. A white casual maxi dress. Bare feet on the concrete. She shakes her head at her brother. 'Stop fuckin' around, Johnny. You're gonna give him a heart attack.'

She rushes towards me.

'What?' John asks. 'Nah, he's all right. He knows we're just fuckin' with him, don't ya, Cork?'

John gently slaps my cheek with an open palm. 'I was only gonna take one of his fingers,' he says, winking at me. He howls with laughter and his metalhead friends share in the mirth.

Helen Fellows drags me by the shirt, away from the bandsaw and the band of Satanic brothers.

'Well, maybe just one thumb and one finger,' John says. 'But that's all I was gonna take, Cork, I promise.'

John's friends keel over, laughing again; one slaps John's shoulder blade, *Congrats on a job well done.*

'You're fuckin' nuts,' I say, staggering to the shed's sliding door, with Helen Fellows helping me stay on my feet in the insanity of the moment.

'The ancient one can't wait to meet you in the abyss, Cork,' John shouts. 'You two have so much in common.'

Helen walks me out of the work shed, towards the rear stairs of the Fellows family home.

'Please forgive my brother,' she says. 'He climbed out of his cot when he was a baby. Poor boy landed on his head.'

She takes me by the hand and leads me up the back stairs of the house. I stop halfway up the staircase.

'Thanks for your help, Helen,' I say. 'But I need to go home now. I'm not feelin' too well. Bit rattled or somethin'.'

I pull my hand away from hers, but she won't let go. Her fingers are sweaty and bony. Freckles across her forearms. A scarlet birthmark at the base of her neck. I'm sure Tamsin Fellows looked just like her when she was eighteen. Then I see her necklace. A tin heart with the name Tamsin hanging from the chain.

'Don't be silly,' she says. 'I don't want you to go. Lemme fix you a cup of tea, Noah Cork.'

She places a second hand on mine and pulls me back up the stairs. The summer sun shines through her white dress and I realise now how thin that dress is. It's easy to see in this light that she's not wearing underwear.

'Come on,' she says. 'There's nothing to be afraid of, Noah Cork. I've actually been wanting to speak with you.'

'I'm not sure you should be speaking anything to me, Helen,' I say. 'What if something I say makes you … makes you …'

'What, Noah Cork?' she asks. 'Sad? A wee bit maudlin? A wee bit wanting to take a shower with my toaster again?'

I know my face betrays my fears. My face says I have helped to ruin this young woman's life.

'Relax, Noah. The rumours of my suicidal tendencies have been highly exaggerated. I'm not suicidal. I'm not even that gloomy. I'm death-curious, at best. John got all sour at you at that book event because he's a big fat drama queen. Come to think of it, and maybe this is just my weird internal thought processor, but I do wonder sometimes if John wasn't just putting all that fuss on inside that auditorium, you know … to throw us all off his murderous scent. Doesn't it make you wonder, Noah?'

'You think … you think your brother could have …?'

'Do I think John could have chopped my mother into pieces and burned her bones inside an oven? Yes. I've got suicidal tendencies. My big brother's got parricidal tendencies.'

'Parricidal?'

'One who kills their parents,' Helen says. 'You saw all that devil guff in Monaco House, didn't you? You saw him just now at the bandsaw. Tell me that kid couldn't have done that to Mum. He's not human like you and me. He's something more erratic. *Unpredictable.* I tell ya, if I was one of them idiot gumshoes trying to solve this thing, I certainly wouldn't be scratching that psycho off my suspect list.'

Helen sits on the stairs, three steps from the home's rear balcony, elbows resting on her kneecaps, which are now just below my eye level.

'And who else shouldn't be scratched off the suspect list, Helen?'

'My Uncle Grant,' Helen says. 'Definitely Unky Grant. Dad's little brother. He always loved my mum. I'd always see the way he would look at her across the dinner table. Straight-up potential crime of passion right there, Noah Cork.'

'Anyone else they should be taking another look at?'

Helen runs her hands through her hair. She tugs at the chest of her dress, airing it out, trying to cool down in the heat. Sweat across her neck and where her forehead meets her hair.

'Well, there's me, of course,' she says. 'Mum and me weren't on the best of terms when she disappeared. I hated the woman, in fact.'

'Why?'

'Well, for a start, like everybody else, she was a phoney. Just another counterfeit human. Another copy of a copy of a copy. My mum was the plastic version of the flesh and blood wonder-mum she thought the world wanted her to be.'

'You told the papers she was the best mum in the world,' I say.

'Yeah, because I'm a big fat phoney, too,' Helen says. 'I told all you salivating scribblers that shit because I knew that's what you wanted to hear.' She chuckles to herself. 'All those heart-tugging feature articles you and all your hack friends wrote about what a loving woman she was,' she says. 'The poor dead mother with a heart of gold, taken too soon by a monster in the suburbs. Fuck, I had to laugh at how you all just dived head-first for the easy narrative. The palatable narrative. The bullshit narrative.'

'What's bullshit, Helen?'

'I am,' she says without hesitation. She laughs. 'I'm a compulsive liar,' she continues. 'You shouldn't believe a word I say.'

'What? Wait … Helen. I'm confused.'

She leans forward and runs her hands down her closed legs. She whispers to me, 'I want you to take me to my bedroom and fuck me on my Snoopy sheets.'

I study her face for a moment. 'Excuse me?' I must have misheard her.

She leans back on the step, smiling. 'See, that was a lie,' she says. 'These horrible lies just burst out of me. Don't trust me for a second, Noah Cork. Put that in your notebook.'

'I don't have a notebook, Helen,' I say. 'I didn't come here to take notes. I didn't come here for information about your mum's murder. I'm stopping. I'm letting it go. I shit you not. I'm not gonna write about your mother no more.'

'I don't believe you, Noah Cork,' she says. 'I think you'll wring every ounce of blood you can out of this story. You'll bleed the story dry. You'll strip the flesh off the bones of it. And then you'll lick your fingers after every bloodthirsty paragraph you punch into your laptop.'

I hand the now-crushed gift bag full of cash to Helen. 'I came here to give this to your family,' I say. 'It's twenty-five thousand dollars in cash. It's what I was paid to write *Anonymous Source*. I want your family to have it. It might be enough to put your father into a quality rehabilitation centre. It could be the fresh start he needs. I thought maybe something good could come of the book I wrote.'

Helen does not take the gift bag from my hand.

'Is that what you thought, Noah Cork?' she asks. 'You could give us this money and everything would be just peachy again for the Fellows fam?'

Sounds shallow when it's verbalised.

'You wanna know what I think?' she asks. 'I think this is a new low for you, Noah Cork. I think you're more full of shit than I am. I think you're using that filthy cash as a way to get inside our house again. I think nothing on this planet could make you let go of this story. Not your guilty conscience. Not your fear. Not even the nightmares in your head.'

'What do you know about the nightmares in my head?'

'I don't know, Cork, what should I know about the nightmares in your head?'

I look into the young woman's eyes. 'I wasn't lying to your

brother, Helen,' I say. 'I'm letting the story go. I don't want to write another word about Tamsin Fellows.'

'Okay.' Helen shrugs.

'Okay what?'

'Okay nothing. Just okay.'

She smiles. Something sensual in the way she smiles, or maybe just something troubled. Something dangerous. I see fire in that smile, the kind that burns down primary schools.

She stands. 'Come on,' she says, 'lemme make you a tea.'

Then the spark of a new idea in her eyes. She's eighteen years old but sounds like a seven-year-old when she says her next sentence, with her eyes alight. 'Then we can watch *The Wizard of Oz*.'

And she turns and skips up three more steps and scurries into the house.

*

Helen sits me on the middle cushion of the oatmeal-coloured lounge, beside her sleeping father. Drool spills from Neil Fellows' mouth and the smell of dry piss emanates from the crotch of his shorts. An empty Smirnoff vodka bottle lies on its side at his feet. Helen says he sleeps here most days. Drinks through the night, sleeps it off in the daylight, slowly falling onto the left edge of the lounge. She doesn't hate him for it, as long as he leaves enough space for her to sit on the couch and watch *The Wizard of Oz* on Blu-Ray. She says she used to watch the movie at least once a week with her mother. Now she watches it once a day.

It was Helen who bought Tamsin the 'Over the Rainbow' music box. Just a random gift she found in the South Bank markets one Sunday morning. Helen told her mum that she could play the music box when she was lost or lonely. Tamsin carried the music box around in her handbag, always. The sound of 'Over the Rainbow' is, Helen says, like her own personal sonic Yellow Brick Road, a way to get back home when she is lost.

Helen sits to my right on the lounge, so close that our shoulders rub. We sip English Breakfast tea with milk and eat straight from a half-eaten packet of Arnott's cream biscuits. Helen hears the woodworking machines start up in the work shed and says I don't have to worry about John and his friends seeing me in the house anymore because the machines starting up means they're taking a hit of smack. The sound of machinery, she says, helps the boys in black pretend they have heroin-sunk down through the earth to a particularly industrial layer of hell, where they are jointly building Satan a new throne out of Sunshine Coast forest wood.

'Here's to healthy choices,' I say, raising my teacup.

On the television, Dorothy Gale suggests to the Tin Man that he might care to join her and the Scarecrow on their journey to the Emerald City. Dorothy suggests the heartless Tin Man could ask the Wizard of Oz for a heart.

'What would you ask the wizard for, Noah Cork?' Helen asks. She licks the pink and white cream from half a Monte Carlo.

'I don't know,' I say. 'Never really thought about it, I guess. What would you ask him for?'

'I'd be like the Tin Man,' she says. 'I'd ask for a heart. A replacement one. I think the one I got is a bit broken. It doesn't work like it should. It doesn't seem to care about things like it used to. Doesn't seem to feel anything anymore.'

'I reckon it still feels something for *The Wizard of Oz*,' I say. 'I was watching you when Judy sang "Over the Rainbow" before. Tell me you didn't feel that in your heart?'

Helen smiles. 'Yeah, I guess I did feel that,' she says. 'Good point, Noah Cork. Come on, out with it. What's the one thing you'd ask the wizard for?'

I think on this for a moment. 'Can I ask the wizard for things on behalf of other people?'

'Well, I'm not really sure,' Helen says. 'I don't know if you've seen this movie before but, spoiler alert, turns out the wizard of Oz is full of shit and can't give you much more than an empty promise. But, for the sake of the exercise, hell yes, you bet you can ask for things on behalf of others.'

'Well, in that case I'd ask for my wife's voice back,' I say.

Helen sits up in the lounge. 'Where did it go?'

'I don't know. It's gone inside her for a bit. Don't look like it's gonna slip out again anytime soon. She hasn't said a word all week.'

'No communication whatsoever?'

'Well, she sometimes writes things with her finger in the condensation on the bathroom mirror,' I say.

'What sort of things?'

'Well, only one thing, really,' I say, biting into my second Delta Cream. 'Gravity … let … me … go.'

Helen turns her head from me here on earth back to Dorothy Gale in the Land of Oz. She ponders the mirror line for a moment. 'Gravity … let … me … go.'

She nods her head, as though she understands something in the sentence. 'That's a nice thing to write with your finger on a mirror,' she says. 'Sounds poetic. Sounds … *revelatory*.'

'What do you think she's trying to tell me?'

'What makes you think she's even trying to tell *you* anything whatsoever?' Helen asks. She takes a long breath, shakes her head. 'Why do you assume that it's all about *you*, Cork? Bloody men! You do know, Cork, that we women very often experience the most deep and labyrinthine emotions and are often forced to navigate complex phases of our lives that have nothing whatsoever to do with the idiot men in our lives.'

'Thanks for the reminder.'

Helen bites into the last Kingston and I kick myself for letting it sit for so long unclaimed.

'I think your wife is making a very powerful statement,' Helen says. 'I think she's saying that she feels untethered by this place. Like she's been let go of.'

'I have never let her go,' I say. 'I *will* never let her go.'

'I'm not talking about you, Cork. I'm talking about the earth. The universe. Life. This whole fucked-up place. Maybe she feels like it let her go.'

'So what do I do about that? How do I make her feel like she's ... I don't know ... *tethered*.'

'You go home, Cork,' she says. 'No place like it. You go home and you remind your wife about everything she's always had inside her. You go remind her of her courage and her brains and her heart. And you never stop reminding her. For as long as you live and for as long as you say you love her. And then she'll feel like she belongs to this place again. She'll feel like she's home again. You know ... *tethered*.'

We watch much of the film in a surprisingly comfortable silence, aside from a few moments of film theorising from

Helen. She tells me she likes the film because all the men in it are either fraudulent, brainless, heartless or cowardly. All the women in the film are brave, whip-smart, magical, powerful, feisty and hopeful. She likes how the film can be read as both an endorsement and an indictment of religious faith. 'Dorothy and co take their path to enlightenment – the Yellow Brick Road – doing their best to avoid all manner of threats and sinful temptations on their way to heaven – the Emerald City – where they hope to speak to God, our dubious wizard,' Helen says.

She says her mum was a bit like Dorothy. Wandering wide-eyed through life, in search of some wizard who was gonna make sense of it all, taking her Yellow Brick Road up to the Jubilee Uniting Church twice a week. She didn't click her heels to get back home. She drove a Hyundai Elantra. 'Of course, the atheists among us would tell you it's a treatise on the falsity of all gods,' Helen says. 'The power to change our world and our fate can only come from things we keep inside our mortal bones.'

The film ends and I need to go home because Erin and Clem will be back from school and Clem asked for help on a science project she's doing. It's all about the infamous Jubilee microburst of December 2009. She was asked by her teacher to find a firsthand source who could recall the great storm and she realised last night that she had two firsthand sources sitting across from her at the dinner table.

Helen walks me down the front stairs and across the front yard to my car. I get in and turn the engine of the Yaris on and she studies me through my side window. She taps the glass and gestures with her forefinger for me to open the window.

'That thing I said about being a compulsive liar,' she says. 'That was bullshit, Cork. I lied to you about being a compulsive liar. I'm not a compulsive liar. I'm just a little untethered myself right now. Maybe I should go talk to your wife.'

'She's not talking, remember.'

'Yeah, they're the best people to talk to.'

I nod twice.

'I thought your book wasn't all bad, Cork,' she says. 'I've always liked your writing. Mum and me used to read your crime pages in the *Courier-Mail*. It was kinda strange having the great Noah Cork write a book about my little ol' tragic family. Then I read the parts about finding Mum's body. Those parts were gross, Cork. And hurtful to me and my family. They were unnecessarily offensive to my mother's memory. I truly wish the world didn't have to see those visions of her. You gave the world those visions, Cork. It's important that you know that. I used to only see my mum in my head as the woman she was. I used to see her in my head as the mum who took me to the school fête. I used to see her with a cowboy hat on, walking kids around on the pony rides. I used to see her looking down on me before she kissed me goodnight. Now all I see are her bones. Stuffed inside that awful oven.'

She begins to cry. Standing right there at the window of my car. She weeps. I can't seem to form a sentence that could satisfactorily speak to the unspeakable traumas she has endured in the past two years. I settle for the truth. 'I see her, too, Helen,' I say. 'She's all bone. Just a skeleton in my head.'

'What's she doing when you see her?'

'I see her doing all sorts of things. Standing in my closet. Lying in bed. Walking dogs down the street.'

'She ever say anything to you during these visions?'

'No,' I say. 'Well, she's always trying to get this one word out. An "S" word. But she can't get the word out because she's got no muscles to speak or something. No voice box. Her lower jaw keeps falling off when she tries to talk.'

'What do you think the "S" word is that she's trying to squeeze out?'

'I have no idea,' I say.

'Sssssssinner!' Helen says, pointing her finger at me, smiling. She thinks of another word. 'Sssssssave me, Noah Cork!' Then she sings. 'Sssssssomewhere ...' She laughs, waves her arm at me to suggest she's going to stop.

'Can you see her now?' she asks.

I scan my surroundings, look up and down Helen's street.

'No,' I say. 'She comes and goes.'

Helen frowns. Looks left and right along her street, taps her fingers on the car door.

'I'm sorry, Helen,' I say. 'I'm not gonna write about her anymore. I'm done.'

'You sure about that, Cork?' she asks. 'Or are you just another bullshit wizard making empty promises?'

I think on this. 'I guess you'll just have to wait and see,' I say.

She kneels down and leans through my window. Whispers, 'But what if you discovered something so compelling that you couldn't help but tell it to the world, Cork?'

Her blue eyes on me. There's a glowing white ring circling her sapphire irises. A whole Antarctic ice shelf floating in those eyes.

'What exactly do you mean by compelling?'

'Well, what if I put your wizard's promise to the test, Noah Cork?' she asks. 'What if I told you something about my mum that nobody knows?'

'It would make no difference to me, Helen,' I reply, 'because I'm letting the story go. I'm letting Tamsin go. I don't want her in my head anymore.'

Helen smiles at me, taps a knuckle on my door. Studies my face. 'Okay,' she says, standing. She turns around and walks back across the street.

'Well … hypothetically speaking,' I call to her, 'supposing I was still interested in the story … what would you have told me?'

She turns and smiles. Glides back to my car on a gentle breeze. Looks up and down her street. Not a soul in Jubilee. Not a soul on earth.

She crouches back down by my window. 'Tell me, Cork, didn't you ever think it was a little strange that you ran into your friend Miles on that path that day you found Mum's shoes?'

I say nothing.

Her eyebrows rise. 'Honestly,' she says, 'what the hell is a guy doing on a path like that, on a day so miserable and muddy and wet?'

'Miles was down there that day because his marriage was falling apart,' I say. 'He needed to clear his head. He's always going down to the reservoir.'

'Oh, I know, Noah Cork,' Helen says. 'I know all too well. I saw him down there once. I spied on him through the bushes. Sitting on that birdwatchers' seat. Right beside my mum.'

'What?! You saw your mum sitting there beside Miles?'

'Yup.' She folds her lips inwards like she's spreading lipstick.

'What are you saying, Helen?'

She shrugs her shoulders. 'I'm saying I once saw my mum sitting beside your mate Miles De Jonge on that viewing seat by the reservoir. Same place you two found her red shoes.'

'Have you told the cops this?'

'No.'

'Why not?'

'Because I didn't want you scribblers splashin' all my family's dirty secrets across the morning news.'

'You have to tell the cops, Helen.'

'No, I don't,' she says. 'And you don't either, Noah Cork. You made a promise, remember? You're gonna let the story go. You meant what you said, didn't you? Didn't you, Mr Wizard? You meant what you said?'

She shakes her head. 'You don't believe me, anyway, do you?' she asks. Flat and broken and disappointed.

'I believe you, Helen.'

'You really shouldn't.'

'Why not?'

'I told you, because I'm a compulsive liar.'

'You just told me that was a lie.'

'Yeah, I was lyin'.'

Helen stands again. Shrugs her shoulders again. Looks up to the sky. Shakes her head. Closes her eyes and clicks her bare heels together three times. 'There's no place like home,' she says. 'There's no place like home. There's no place like home.'

She keeps her eyes closed for a moment. Opens them again and studies her surroundings, immediately disappointed to find she's still standing in Fletcher Street, Jubilee.

'Damn, thought it would work that time,' she says.

She slaps the car door twice. 'Goodbye, Cork,' Helen says. 'Thanks for watching the movie with me.'

She walks back towards her front yard. Turns around once more.

'Sssssssay g'day to Mum for me.'

*

I check the messages on my phone as I drive to Miles De Jonge's house on Butcherbird Close. Three missed calls from my sister, Meg. Two missed calls and a voicemail message from Sherry Sharp.

'Noah Cork, you absolute wizard! Nielsen BookScan figures just in. Guess whose book has just cracked the national non-fiction top ten! You're a star. Great job, you. Call me. The *Today* program still wants that live cross. I thought we could do it from outside Monaco House, where you found Tamsin's body. Really raise the chill factor, right after the weather report. Ha! Boom! Call me, call me, call me.'

I call my sister, Meg. She picks up after two rings.

'Megs!' I say, before she can even speak. 'I'm soooooo sorry. I'm a prick. I'm a big selfish arsehole. I'm so sorry I haven't been to see Dad yet—'

'Noah ... you don't—'

'Just had so many things come up with this book. Kinda had the craziest week since I last spoke to you. Really actually fucking bizarre on about five different levels. Is he still crook? I feel like I'm cursed or something. Then I just heard my book has made the top ten non-fiction list, that's from all non-fiction books across the country. And I don't know how to feel about that—'

'Noah … let me talk—'

'Yes, yes, sis! I promise I'm gonna go visit Dad soon. I just needed a little window, but I kept on getting distracted. I don't know what's wrong with me. No matter how hard I try, I can't seem to prioritise the most important people—'

'Noah, just shut the fuck up for a second!' Meg shouts into the phone. Then she weeps down the line. She wails. Meg is not silent. Meg is loud and broken and raw and verbal.

'He's dying,' she says. 'He's fucking dying, Noah.'

THIRTEEN

Corrections are as inevitable as they are essential. It is never too late for the journalist to publicly admit to a mistake.

– Rutledge, *Journalism Practices and Principles*

Dad lives in a small one-bedroom flat in a block of twelve units on the calm side of Bribie Island. The flyscreen mesh on his front security door is split in three places.

His in-home carer hears my footsteps as I reach the door. 'That you, Noah?'

She opens the door. A tag on her St Vincent's Home Care polo shirt says *Carmen*.

'He's in bed,' she whispers. 'He can't wait to see you.'

'Thanks, Carmen.'

The unit smells like pumpkin soup. And the smell of pumpkin soup is masking the smell of something rotting in the flat.

'What's that smell?'

Carmen hauls a duffel bag of used sheets up over one shoulder and a bag of medical supplies over the other shoulder.

She tries to say it tenderly. 'That's your dad, hon'.'

Maritime décor through the flat. For two decades, before the emphysema kicked in, Dad ran the Reel Life bait and tackle shop on Bribie Island, the one next to the Bellara boat ramp off Marine Parade.

A ship's wheel hanging on the living room wall. Framed paintings from the 1950s. Giant-sized marlins and sharks being hauled onto fishing boats. Two crab pots in the laundry off the kitchen. A framed oil painting of a mangrove jack, Dad's favourite fish to catch in the green-brown creek systems of Bribie Island. The jacks like to eat in stormy weather and Dad likes to fish in stormy weather.

I open Dad's bedroom door. He's lying flat on his mattress. Looks like he's shrunk in size, shrivelled up like a fallen frangipani leaf curled and aged by the sun. A grape withering on the vine of life.

'Jesus, Dad, you look like a skeleton.'

He laughs and the laughter makes him cough three times. A wheezy rattle in his chest like there's nothing beneath his thin skin but air and a single dried-up pea seed.

'Flattery will get you nowhere,' he says. His breathing is laboured, movement slow as tar pitch.

'Meg says you're dying?'

'Meg's spot on, as usual,' he says.

'She said Dr Fielding has given you a month at the most. There's a bed waiting for you in Caboolture Hospital, Dad. I can take you there right now.'

'They gimme the penthouse suite?'

'Yep, bar fridge full of XXXX Gold. Nightly spa bath wash from a nurse named Inga.'

'Fuck me, does sound inviting. Trouble is, hospitals an' me are a bit like oil and water, Israel and Palestine, Abbott an' Gillard – we're best kept at a distance.'

'You can't just rot away here in bed, Dad.'

'I'm not gonna. Fair warning, mate, some night soon I'll be chugging down that box of Oxycodone on the bedside table there.'

'Please don't do that,' I say, resting my backside on the edge of the mattress. 'I don't know how I would explain that to the girls.'

'Just tell 'em I got eaten by a bull shark in the Pumicestone Passage. They'll love that story.'

He leans over to find a piece of paper he has slipped inside a paperback copy of *Hogfather* by Terry Pratchett.

'Here, take this,' he says.

A list of names on the paper, scribbled in a visibly weakened hand.

'I don't want a funeral, but if you're doing one, then that's a list of all the people I don't want coming to it.'

'Dad, if anyone wants to come to your funeral to pay their respects, I'm not gonna stop 'em.'

'I want nuthin' but the Stones playing at the wake, but don't play anything from *Bridges to Babylon*. That album's a piece o' shit.'

'Stop it, Dad.'

'Stop what?'

'Stop acting like your death is a fait accompli.'

'Well, I'm afraid death's a fait accompli for all of us, Noah,' he says. 'Mine's just gonna get *accompli-ed* a little sooner than later.'

He hacks up a mouthful of phlegm and spits it into a coffee mug emblazoned with an image of Marilyn Monroe standing on an air vent.

'Meg's already said her last words to me,' he says. 'Maybe you should also think about what you want to say to me before I go the full stiffy.'

'What did Meg say?'

'She told me she loved me and then she told me I was a selfish prick and then she told me she wouldn't have wanted anyone else to be her dad, except maybe Kerry O'Brien from *The 7.30 Report*.'

I laugh. Drop my head. A tiny son-of-a-bitch tear runs from my left eye, but I rub it deep and quick into the soft baggy skin.

'I love you, Dad,' I say, softly and carefully. 'You were a selfish prick sometimes, but I never wanted anyone else to be my dad. Not even Kerry O'Brien.'

Dad nods. His lip trembles and he acts all tough and stoic and hard, but he's only beautiful and nearly dead.

'I love you, too, Noah,' he says. 'I'm not bullshittin' ya. One day soon you're gonna get that news from Carmen that I'm gone and, when you do, you better believe that the last thing that went through my mind before I croaked was you and Meg and your mum. You'll know that will be true because you know that you three are all I ever think about.'

He wipes his own left eye now, sits up in his bed.

I nod. 'Yeah, I know,' I say.

'Well, now we've got that outta the way,' he says, wiping his lips with a yellowy arm he must have stolen from a stick insect, 'tell me about the girls. When's the last time you brought 'em up to see me?'

'Not sure. I'm sorry for not coming up sooner. I've been … a bit tied up … Tamsin and everything.'

'Of course, Tamsin and everything,' he says. 'Well, don't go beatin' yourself up over me. It's your job. The scoop of a lifetime landed in your letterbox. Journo's gotta make hay when the sun shines. How's Rita coping with all this mayhem in Jubilee?'

'Not the best, to be honest.'

Dad rubs the stubble on his chin.

'She's stopped talking,' I say.

'The ol' silent treatment,' Dad says. 'Your mum used to do that. She'd throw me that cold shoulder for hours.'

'Rita's stopped talking to everyone.'

'The girls?'

I nod.

'The neighbours?'

Nod.

'Her parents?'

Nod.

Dad smiles. 'I told you she's bloody special, that Rita,' he says. 'She reminds me of your mum, you know. A bloke will go one of two ways: they'll marry the exact opposite of their mum or they'll flat out marry their mum. You married your mum.'

'Bullshit. Rita's nothing like Mum.'

'Nah, your Rita's special. Just as special as your mum.'

I turn to the framed photograph of Mum he has hanging above the bed. I remember her posing for that picture at a pop-up photography studio in the Sands Shopping Centre on the Sunshine Coast, in 1989. The photographer insisted on surrounding Mum's whole face with plastic sunflowers.

'I see the way Rita is with Clem and Erin,' Dad says. I realise now that he's looking at Mum's portrait, too. 'They got that unspoken thing going on, like they could read each other's minds, they're that close.'

'Via the feminine hormonal plane,' I mumble.

'Huh?'

'Nuthin'.'

Dad turns to me now. 'You and your mum had that kind of connection. Remember?'

'No.'

'What do you mean, *no*? You two weren't just joined at the hip, you were joined at the leg and the elbow, too. You were like one being. I used to get jealous of the way you seemed to know exactly what she was thinking some days, how you'd go up and give her a hug when she was feeling sad for some shit I'd no doubt done to her that I was too blind – or just too blind-drunk – to see. You'd get all angry, remember?'

I remember the anger.

'Feisty little fucker you were,' Dad says, laughing, 'always protecting her. Always warning me about all the terrible things you'd do to me if I ever broke her heart.'

'All piss and wind.'

'Nah,' Dad says, 'all minerals, mate. All love.'

I take three steps to Dad's bedside table, run my fingers through a blue two-litre ice cream container carrying a pharmacy of random pill packets with no boxes. I check the names on the backs of the silver packets. Prednisone. Ibuprofen. A blue inhaler. A grey inhaler. Corticosteroids to reduce the inflammation and swelling in Dad's airways. I grip the box of Oxycodone, wave it in front of Dad. 'This shit's evil,' I say.

'Nah, it's like free jazz,' Dad says. 'Okay in small doses.'

Dad changes the subject. 'Why's Rita stopped talking to everyone?' he asks.

'I don't really know for sure. Sometimes I feel like I've never really known her at all.'

'Bullshit. You know her. You might not be familiar with who she is right now, what she's feeling right now. Don't go doin' what I did and expect her to stay the same woman you fell in love with when you were about as old as a raindrop. Women aren't like us blokes. They don't just stay the same ol' lumps of meat and brain matter, decade upon decade upon decade. They ... *transform*. They ... *evolve*.'

'I just wish I could understand her better. No matter how hard I try, I can't quite fully understand her.'

'Has any man ever truly understood the woman he loves? How would a being as feeble as you comprehend a thing of such profound wonder as your Rita? Answer: don't even bother. Just remove your dick from your hand, you lucky cretin, and wrap your arms around her and say, loud and often, "Thank fuck for Rita Munro."'

'Thank fuck for Rita Munro,' I say.

'That's it.' Dad nods, the way he used to nod at me when I tied a swivel to my fishing line with the right number of twists and loops. 'Good news is, son, you don't have to know what's really going on inside her mind. All you have to do is hold her hand and not let it go.'

'Hold her hand and don't let it go,' I say, nodding.

Dad points to an old Mathers shoebox at the end of the bed. 'Open up that box there, will ya?'

I reach for the box, lift the dusty lid. It's filled with all my old editions of the newspaper I made about my street when I was Clem's age.

'The *Bega Street Bugle*,' Dad says. 'Where it all began.'

I flip my fingers through twelve editions of my crudely designed community newspaper. Old typewriter-printed and cut-and-glued pieces about Bega Street marriages and war stories and flashes of fishing good fortune and acts of neighbourly kindness. I dig to the bottom of the shoebox and find the cover story of the last ever edition.

'Where it all began,' I say. 'And where it all ended.'

Dad raises his eyebrows, shakes his head. He's shirtless and his belly has been sucked in towards his backbone, turning his bony ribcage into a bowl I could drop my car keys and wallet in. His chest tattoo is fading with age, the smiling grim reaper waving his sickle on the bow of the ghost ship he guides through treacherous seas. I loved that tattoo when I was a boy. 'Has he seen land, Dad?' I once asked. 'Is that why he's so happy?'

'Nah, all that guy sees is death,' Dad said. 'Death's what makes him happy.'

Now I read the first five words on the cover headline for the last *Bega Street Bugle* ever published: BRIBIE ISLAND HUSBAND PHIL CORK—

I can't bring myself to read the rest of the headline. Turn my face to Dad. 'Do you know I've never told Rita the reason why Mum went swimming that afternoon?'

Dad offers nothing but silence.

'I've pulled out every bit of myself and put it on display for her,' I say, shaking my head. 'Every bit except that bit. That bit stayed in the storage room. I never quite brought that bit out.'

'She went for a swim, Noah,' Dad says. 'People go swimming all the time on Bribie Island.'

'I couldn't let go of the story, Dad. Maybe if I'd let it go … Mum would …'

'Maybe the Broncos will win the GF next year,' Dad says. 'Maybe those mountains of Antarctic ice won't crumble into the sea. Maybe the whales will finally tell us why we're here. Maybe nothing can stand between a woman and a sunset dip in the ocean.'

Keep talking, Dad. Tell me somethin' I don't know. Tell me I'm not the worst son in the long and storied history of the worst sons in all the world. Cain, son of Adam. Adolf, son of Alois. Noah Cork, son of Phil and Alison.

'Gravity let me go,' I say.

I say the words again. 'Gravity let me go, Dad.'

'What the hell's that supposed to mean?'

I say it again because it feels good to say that sentence. 'Gravity let me go.'

Dad leans over to me. 'Noah, what the hell's going on with you?'

I say it again until tears fall from my eyes. 'Gravity let me go.'

'Noah?'

Sink my head into my hands. 'Gravity let me go, Dad.'

And then I fall into the stick-thin arms of my dying father. I rest my head flat against the reaper's boat. I can hear the dried-up pea rattling inside his broke-down chest. I stay there for ten seconds. Fifteen seconds. Twenty seconds.

Dad keeps making the same 'S' sound. 'Sssshhhh. Sssshhhh. Sssshhhh.' He pats my back three times. 'C'mon,' he says, 'you're taking me for a drive.'

I sit up and rub my eyes. 'You're not up for a drive.'

'I said I'm dyin'. I didn't say I was dead.'

'Where are we going?'

'We're gonna go see yer mum.'

*

I'm holding my father's bony left arm as he lugs his rubber-gripped, four-legged burgundy folding walking frame through the Woorim Beach sand on the rough surf side of Bribie Island. He coughs and spits and pauses for a moment to catch his breath.

'You're gonna get sand in the wheels,' I say.

'Not gonna need the cursed thing much longer,' he says. Splutter. Cough. Spit. Dad gazes along the beach. Two boys fishing with surf rods, knee-deep in foamy whitewash.

'Fez says they're catchin' swallow-tailed dart off Skirmish Point, half a metre long,' Dad says.

'You shoulda brought your rod down,' I say.

'Can't even cast a line out no more. Barely get the bait off the sand.'

'I could cast out for you,' I say.

Dad grips my hand and leaves the walker on the higher, drier part of the beach and we walk towards the damp sand that's been touched by the tide. 'Well, wouldn't that be the sweetest full circle moment,' he says. 'I cast the line out for you when you were just a pup. You cast the line out for me when I'm a bag o' bones sinkin' into the sand.'

Dad reaches the edge of the water, which laps at our feet. He says a line he's been saying to me since I was six. 'Don't get stung by no bluebottles.'

He nearly falls over into the wash, but finds his balance after digging his feet into the wet sand.

'You ever talk to your mum, Noah?' he asks.

I pull the legs of my jeans up to my kneecaps. Take two steps into the wash. Don't know how to answer the man. I think about her almost every day. Always something reminding me of her. A Vegemite and cheese sandwich I'm making for Clem's school lunch. Any old magazine image of Princess Diana – Mum loved Princess Diana. A bird in the sky, a pale-headed rosella or a red-backed fairy wren, any bird with enough colour to steal Alison Cork's attention. Sometimes I'll look at a bird while I'm out on the Gecko Street nature strip and it will feel like she's standing beside me, admiring that bird with me. Sometimes I want to say something. Sometimes I want to open my mouth and say something only she could hear.

'How could I talk to Mum, Dad?'

'Fascinating process, not sure if you're aware of it,' he says. 'You get a thought inside your head and then you decide to speak it and then some kinda complex interplay between your lungs and larynx occurs, forcing something out your mouth sometimes known as … *talk*.'

'No, Dad, I never *talk* to Mum,' I say.

'You should. Be good for ya.'

'And how exactly would I talk to Mum? She's not listening, Dad, because she's not around no more, remember?'

Dad nods at the ocean. Waist-high waves folding into whitewash. 'She's around,' he says. 'I can feel it in my bones. Where do you think she went, Noah? Hate to say it, kid, but she didn't go to no cloud farm in the sky. She went into this drink right here. She went in deep and got herself recycled by the universe. She might not be listening with her old ears, but the universe is. The universe is always listenin'. That means she's listenin', too.'

Dad takes a deep breath and opens his arms to the sea, like he's ready to be dragged away by it. 'Wanna hear somethin' real nutty?' he asks.

I scratch my head, wave a squadron of sandflies away from my face.

'I used to come down here to fish at sunset,' Dad says. 'I once caught this bream, maybe the fullest and prettiest bream I ever caught. She was so pretty this fish that I thought for a second it was your mum coming back to me. I felt bad for putting that hook through her lips, so I gently pulled that barbed steel out and told her how much I missed her. I told her about you and Meg and all the things you were getting up to. I told her about Erin and Clem and Rita and how happy you all were in Jubilee, how happy you all made me. I told her what a great dad you were. "Alison, you should see him … You taught him good … He's twice the dad I ever was."'

I put my hand on Dad's shoulder. 'You were a good dad,' I say.

He shrugs. 'Good dad,' he says, 'shithouse husband.'

His eyes well with tears. He laughs. 'I got so caught up talkin' to this fish that I realised the poor thing was drowning in the air,' he says. 'I slipped her back in the water where she belonged and then I was done. Could never keep a fish I caught after that. Not one. They all went back in the drink. Just in case one of them fish was your mum.'

He lets a tear run down his cheek, laughs again, and the effort causes him to wheeze and cough and spit and cough again. 'Now, as fate would have it, it's me who's drowning in the air,' he says.

He takes two steps further into the sea and I pull him back towards the shore.

'You're gonna bloody fall in, Dad.'

He turns to me. 'Listen to me,' he says. He squeezes my right collarbone with his bony fingers. 'Noah, I want you to do something for me. It's the only thing I need you to do when I'm gone. You're not gonna wanna do it, but I need you to do it.'

'What is it, Dad?'

He turns his head back to the sea. 'I wanna be with her again, Noah,' he says. 'When I go, I need you and Meg to toss me in the cheapest furnace you can find and then I want you and Meg and Rita and the girls to come and throw my ashes in this drink right here.'

'Dad ...' I shake my head. Fight the tear that's forming in my eye. Hide the tear. You know what I speak of, Dad? Some kinda complex interplay, Dad, between your heart and your head, forcing something out your eyes sometimes known as ... *crying*.

'I wanna be with Alison again,' he says. 'Even if she doesn't want me, that's where I'm going. She's the only place I ever belonged.'

'You don't deserve to be with her,' I say.

'I know,' he says.

I study the sea. Whisper something so soft that even the universe would struggle to hear it. 'Maybe I don't either.'

A beach stone-curlew, the shyest shorebird on Bribie Island, flies into our view, hovers on the breeze, eyes cast down, scouting for afternoon grub. The bird dives in a long arc towards the sand on shore, looking like a World War II fighter plane. And the arc turns into circles. Round and round and round the bird flies. Then it glides off in the direction of the two boys surf fishing further along the beach. And then I see Tamsin. My ever-present skeleton. She made it all the way to the surf side of Bribie Island, all the way from my closet in Gecko Street, all the way from my dreams. Her skeleton marching along the sand, right by those boys with the fishing rods. They don't even give her a glance. She just powers on along the beach, towards my father and me. I rub my face with my palms, cold salty water on my fingers. Slap my face. But the vision does not vanish: Tamsin's skeleton and its shaky forward motion, bone footprints in the sand.

I tap Dad on the shoulder. 'C'mon, time to go,' I say.

I pull him by the arm, too hard and too fast and he almost falls in the whitewash.

He coughs and splutters. 'But we only just got here,' he says.

I keep pulling Dad onwards, our legs sloshing in the wash. Tamsin's skeleton thirty, twenty, ten metres away from us.

'What the hell's got into you, Noah?' Dad barks.

Then I hear a whisper on the beach wind. A hissing 'S' sound.

'Sssssss.'

I turn my back on Tamsin's skeleton and tuck my shoulder under Dad's arm as we trudge back up through the thicker, drier sand towards his walker.

'I don't wanna go,' Dad says.

That dark whisper again. '*Ssssssss.*'

'We've gotta go, Dad.'

An aching in his voice. Something childlike in it. A sorrow. A burden. 'Whhyyyyy?'

'*Sssssss.*'

'I gotta get back home.'

He's crying now. My father is *crying* now.

'I don't know if I'll ever get back here again, Noah.'

Some complex interplay between his past and his present, between his place and his time, what little remains of it.

'*Sssssss.*'

'I'll bring you back here, Dad,' I say, breathlessly heaving him along the sand. 'I'll bring you back.'

FOURTEEN

Sometimes it will be days, even years, after the story is written when you will fully understand why you wrote it in the first place.

– Rutledge, *Journalism Practices and Principles*

Three cars parked in front of my house. The black Toyota Land Cruiser belongs to Rita's mum and dad, Deborah and Bill Munro. The white MG4 belongs to Mardi, Rita's younger sister, and Mardi's partner of seven years, Rick Bright, who runs a highly profitable business selling lilypad-shaped deodorised men's-room urinal anti-splash pads – 'WilyPads' – to pubs and clubs across Australia. The electric-blue Volkswagen Golf belongs to Gemma Leader, who has been both Rita's and Mardi's shared best friend since primary school.

Out of the corner of my eye I see Ellis Towers and his front-yard hedge. Ellis and his cordless hedge trimmer, the one my neighbour switches off as he marches across the nature strip to meet me before I enter my home.

'The sign's just for show,' Ellis says.

'Whassat?' I reply, distracted by the thought of how all these people ended up at our house at the same time.

Ellis pulls a deep green hedge leaf from the trimmer's still blades, nods at the *For Sale* sign in front of Carol's house next door.

'Spoke to the real estate agent,' Ellis says. 'The house has already been stitched up by a buyer. Paid a pretty penny, too. The new owners are desperate to move in. People can't wait to slip into our little patch of paradise, Noah.'

I smile at Ellis, turn my gaze to the *For Sale* sign.

'Best street in the world,' I say.

Ellis says something else, but I don't hear it because I'm thinking about my dad and the vision of Tamsin on the beach.

'Noah?' Ellis says. 'You there, neighbour? Knock, knock.'

I snap back to the real world, not the place where skeletons take afternoon strolls along the beach.

'Sorry, Ellis, I was thinkin' about …'

'About?' Ellis asks.

'My dad,' I reply. 'He's on the way out. Doctors have given him a month, tops.'

Ellis sucks a breath between his teeth. 'Oh, Noah,' he says. 'I was wondering why all the cars were parked in the street.'

He plants a hand on my right shoulder and grips it tight. I'm unexpectedly moved by the gesture and, without thinking, I reach for his hand and hold it there.

'My deepest sympathies, lad,' he says. 'Father-shaped holes are not easily filled. When the time comes, grieve long and grieve true, my friend. In times of loss, our beautiful grieving is the only glue that sticks our broken hearts back together.'

I look into Ellis's eyes and see that he is weeping. His bottom lip quivers.

I don't know where the words came from. But they're the words I need to hear. 'Thank you, Ellis,' I say. 'Where'd you hear that stuff about loss and glue?'

'My father, George,' he says. 'Best man I ever knew.' He shrugs. 'He told me about loss just before we lost him. His final lesson. How to say goodbye.'

I see now that Ellis is looking at something over my shoulder. A voice behind me. Clem's voice.

'What are you two talking about?'

I turn to find my daughters standing by the yellow letterbox.

'We were just talking about Pop,' I say.

'What about Pop?' Erin asks.

I study their faces for a moment. No sorrow in them. 'Did Meg call here this afternoon?' I ask.

'Not sure,' Erin replies. 'Mum's been tied up in some kinda court hearing in the dining room, where they're quizzing her on why she's gone all chatty as a chimney. It's like an intervention in there, Dad. Everybody's attacking Mum. You need to go help her.'

'I'm going in now,' I say. 'Where are you two going?'

'Grandma sent us over to Ellis and June's for a Milo chocolate drink,' Clem explains. 'She said they needed to talk "grown-up stuff" with Mum. I was personally offended by the implication that we couldn't handle grown-up stuff, but I can't say I wasn't taken with the idea of one of your Milos, Ellis.'

Ellis smiles proudly.

'You drink too much Milo, Clem,' I say.

'Please don't judge a woman by what she chooses to do with her body, *Dad*,' Clem says. 'Some women just need a Milo sometimes, *okayyyy*.'

'What about Pop?' Erin asks.

And the question makes me mute. The weight in my belly. The thought of what's to come. The thought of explaining it to my girls. Maybe I really could tell them he met a bully of a bull shark in the Pumicestone Passage.

Ellis marches up to the girls, places a gentle hand on Clem's shoulder.

'I guess *one* more Milo might not be the death of the wee lass,' Ellis says, chirpily. 'Why don't you girls come with me? I'll fix you a drink and then you can all reconvene after your visitors have gone.'

Ellis throws me a brief nod of understanding. I nod back to my neighbour in thanks. Clem falls in with Ellis immediately. Erin follows, reluctantly, studying my face as she goes.

'If you're lucky,' Ellis says, 'June might cut you a slice of her carrot cake.'

The girls can't stand June Towers' carrot cake.

'Oh, she really doesn't have to waste her carrot cake on us,' Clem says.

*

I hear the sound of raised voices beyond the front door. Think for a moment that heads will turn towards me when I open that door, but it's not the case. Six adults seated at our dining room table, around the concrete apple at its centre. Five adults talking at once. The only adult not speaking is my wife. Rita sits at the end of the table where she always sits, arms folded across her chest, staring at the apple, as her mum and dad and her sister and her best friend and her sister's partner shout random sentences at her. They think they're just talking, but in trying to have their voices heard, they've resorted to shouting.

'It's absurd, Rita,' barks her mother, Deborah. 'It's childish and it's downright disrespectful. After everything your father and I have done for you. How long do you intend maintaining this ridiculous experiment in silence?'

Rita's father, Bill, builds on his wife's attack. 'Don't you see how worried your mother is, Rita?' he asks. 'What happened to our sweet and compassionate daughter? Who is this ... alien we see before us?'

Deborah places two open palms on the table. Trying her best to stay calm, stay understanding, stay Deborah.

'It's about your bioparents isn't it?' Deb adds. 'How many times do I have to tell you, Rita, there's no pot of gold at the end of that rainbow. There's nothing good to find at the end of that search. Only tears and regrets and heartbreak.'

Deborah falls back in a heap of tears and regrets and heartbreak.

Rita's sister, Mardi, drops a bomb from the left edge of the table. 'You can be so fucking self-absorbed sometimes, Rita,' she spits.

Bill now builds upon Mardi's attack. 'Look, child, look at your mother. You know she has the arrhythmia? Did you even consider the arrhythmia, Rita?'

'What's an arrhythmia?' Rick asks. 'Is that like a menopause thing?'

Deborah Munro finally acknowledges my presence. My existence. She turns her head towards me but refrains from making the extra effort required to turn her head a further ten centimetres to her right to actually look at me.

'Did you see the girls, Noah?' she asks.

I nod.

'They don't need to hear all this grown-up stuff,' she says. 'I sent them to Ellis and June's for a Milo. I hope you don't mind.'

'No, of course not, Deb. I always appreciate it when my mother-in-law gives instructions to my daughters, who we have raised in a house where there is no delineation between grown-up stuff and child stuff, only family stuff.'

'Clem seemed fairly keen on the Milo,' Deborah says, shrugging her shoulders and smiling at her husband, who reliably smiles back at her.

I turn my eyes to Rita, who remains silent. Pull my pants half-a-centimetre up my waist like I always do when I'm about to say something controversial. 'Clem ... drinks ... too ... much ... Milo,' I say.

Rita remains silent, but says enough with one raised eyebrow.

Her mum speaks for her. 'Weren't you the one who gave Clem her first glass of Milo, Noah?' Deborah asks.

I'm about to give a PowerPoint TED Talk response to Deborah about my thoughts on drinking Milo in moderation and why I wanted my daughter to experience the innocent domestic joys of an ice-cold glass of said beverage, when Gemma Leader wails in tears, 'It's my fault, isn't it? Just tell me, Rita. It's me, isn't it? You can't forgive me, can you?'

Gemma then addresses the table. 'Six weeks ago,' she says, struggling to spit the words out, 'it was a Sunday afternoon, we were … having a few wines at the Bardon bowls club. We were sharing a few home truths, because that's how we've always been with each other. Brutal honesty, no matter what.'

Gemma snorts. Wipes tears from her eyes. 'I just came out and said it,' she says. 'I just had to tell the truth. I called Noah a total fuck-up.'

'You called me what?' I ask, pacing to the edge of the table, without anyone but Rita acknowledging my presence. Rita rolls her eyes at me, suggesting I'd do well to not listen to the words that are a half-second from exploding from Gemma's mouth.

'I said it,' Gemma continues, wiping her tears away. 'I just came out and spoke my truth. I told Rita straight that Noah was a dead-set fuck-up who had made her life a misery. I told her she could have done better than Noah. I told her she never should have broken up with Julian Azzopardi.'

Gemma turns to Deborah. 'You know they used his home in *Anyone But You*?'

Deborah nods knowingly, closes her eyes and aches for what might have been.

'I had to come clean,' Gemma says. 'I just had to. I told Rita Noah was just one of those born losers who seem permanently magnetised to misfortune.'

'What … the … royal … fuck … Gemma?' I say, pointing my right forefinger at the circle of people surrounding my wife. 'What the hell is this?' I shout. 'What the fuck is going on here? Rita doesn't need an intervention.'

Deborah turns to me over her shoulder. 'It's not an intervention, Noah,' she says. 'Erin told me about her mother's seemingly sustained vow of silence and I asked Mardi and

Gemma to join us here today to see if we could talk some sense into her or at least get to the bottom of what's causing her to give us all the silent treatment.'

'Well, I'm fairly certain shouting at her will get to the bottom of jack shit,' I reason.

Mardi stands at the table and leans in to speak to her sister. 'You can never allow me to be happy can you?' she says. 'Just when things are going great for me.'

Bill Munro tugs at my arm. 'Oh, by the way, Noah, I took the liberty of inspecting the gutters on your roof,' he says, between Mardi's thoughts. 'How long's it been since you cleaned them out? You've got leaves and dirt clogging your water flow. Storm season's comin', mate. We didn't buy you that new roof only to see it blow away to Birdsville again.'

I'm momentarily stunned by Bill's conversational timing.

'I've been a little busy, Bill,' I finally say. 'The book an' all that.'

'Oh, of course, the book. I started reading it yesterday.'

'You did?'

'Not my cup of tea. Speaking of which, you got any English Breakfast?'

Mardi continues addressing Rita. 'I've managed to establish my calligraphy business,' she says. 'I've just hit forty-five thousand followers on Insta.' She puts a hand on Rick's shoulder. 'The WilyPad is now the third highest selling urinal pad in Australia. We just bought the unit in Yamba. And you didn't even phone to say congratulations. You have always resented my successes. Remember when I got the role of Mary Magdalene in *Jesus Christ Superstar* and you had a big hissy fit because you had to play Pontius Pilate? Remember when I saved up to buy that Hypercolor shirt and you got so jealous of it that you *accidentally* spilled a bottle of nail polish over it? What exactly is your malfunction, Rita?'

Deborah drops her head on the dining table. Howls. Hands over her eyes running with tears. 'She knows, Bill!' she wails.

Bill places a hand on his wife's shoulder. 'She knows what, petal?'

She shakes her head and spits words at her husband, words summoned from the pit of her stomach, where they've seemingly been buried for the past three decades. 'Youuuuuuu knowwww!' she howls, pointing a crooked forefinger at her husband the way a Salem priest might have pointed out a witch in a circle of wives. Her wailing makes her cough, like she's choking on her own agony. 'Your little indiscretions from the summer of ninety-six!' She screams the word 'six' like she's screaming at a devil who has temporarily taken possession of her husband. 'I knew you would ruin her with your … *great betrayal*,' she says.

Rita rolls her eyes again. Takes a deep breath.

'I told you Rita sees everything,' Deborah continues. 'You took all your guilt and you took all your … ssss … ssss … ssssin … and you dropped it straight upon your daughter's shoulders! How … *dare* you, Bill Munro!'

'Deborah Jean!' Bill bellows, blood rushing to his cheeks and temples, face as red as a cheap tomato. 'You will not speak of this! You will indulge no such memory. You forget yourself.' He bangs his closed right fist on the table and Mardi jumps in her seat.

'What the fuck is wrong with you, people?' I gasp.

Deborah turns to Rita. 'Look at what you're doing to us, Rita,' she says. 'Please stop this. Please. Please. Say something.

Say … *something*.' Deborah reaches out and grips the collar of Rita's white cotton shirt. 'For fuck's sake, say something!' she screams.

Rita remains silent.

No sound for almost ten seconds. Then only the sound of adults breathing.

'I want you all to leave,' I say.

No reaction from the adults at the table.

'Please get out of our house,' I say. 'This is not helping.'

Bill takes a folded handkerchief from his pocket and dabs at the pockets of sweat spread across his forehead and temples. 'Noah, with the greatest respect to you as the man of the house,' he says, 'we cannot leave here with our daughter so clearly in the grip of some kind of nervous breakdown.'

'Bill, with the greatest respect to you and your handkerchief,' I say, 'you're an idiot. Nervous breakdown? Are you fucking kidding me, Bill? Rita's the only person at this table who is perfectly at peace.'

I look at my wife, who looks back at me.

'In fact, I can't remember the last time I've seen her so peaceful.'

Something close to a smile begins to spread across my wife's face.

'You're all talking *at* her,' I say. 'You're not talking *with* her.'

Deborah scoffs. 'Ridiculous, Noah!' she says. 'How can one possibly talk *with* someone who refuses to talk back?'

'There are more ways of talking than out your mouth, Deborah.'

Deborah leans back in her chair, arms folded across her chest. 'Okay, if you're such a communication expert,' she says, 'you say something to her. Please, go right ahead. Chat away. Let us all witness how she talks back.'

I shrug my shoulders. Take a deep breath. Stare at my wife, who stares back at me. Stare into those eyes that speak their own language. Stare into that smile that has its own dialect. Say what I've been wanting to say to her. 'Dad's been given a month to live.'

Silence in the dining room.

Rita stands up. Her mother and father and her sister and her best friend and her sister's partner watch her slowly move around the table. She meets me in my future sorrow and my future grief that is true glue for a broken heart. She stands before me and grips my arms before she turns her head to the side and rests her head upon my heart.

We don't need words anymore. All we need is this.

FIFTEEN

Get up off your seat. Pound the pavement. Knock those doors until your knuckles bleed. Walk those streets until you can see your big right toe sticking out of your shoe.

– Rutledge, *Journalism Practices and Principles*

Sunday morning. Sleeping. Fingers on my closed right eyelid. Fingers opening my right eye. This is how I wake sometimes, flat on my back in bed, with my younger daughter, Clem, prising my eyelids open at dawn. Her face in full close-up. It's like waking up halfway through a dental appointment.

'Rise and shine, Noah Cork,' she whispers. 'I need you to drive me to 16 Cairo Street, Nundah.'

'What?' I reply.

She puts a forefinger to her mouth, turning her face to her sleeping mum. 'Ssshhhh,' she says. 'Don't wake Mum up.'

'What's at 16 Cairo Street, Nundah?' I whisper.

'*Who's* at 16 Cairo Street, Nundah,' Clem says, excitedly.

'Who's at 16 Cairo Street, Nundah?'

Pride across her face. Light and wonder and summer sun through our bedroom window.

'Adam Duncan,' Clem says.

'Who's Adam Duncan?'

'He's the boy Mum saved from the fire. I tracked him down on Facebook. Found his address through *White Pages* online. He's all grown up now.'

Clem consults her notepad.

'Works in the Cannon Hill slaughterhouse,' she says. 'Plays second row for the Brothers St Brendan's men's over thirty-fives. Drives a 2017 Holden Commodore SV6 that he's trying to sell on Facebook Marketplace to fund a trip to Hawaii with his latest girlfriend, Shyann—'

'Wait, Clem, I can't do this today. I've got to go speak with Miles De Jonge this morning,' I say. 'It's kind of important … You know … it's about …'

'Tamsin?' Clem asks.

'Yeah, Tamsin.'

'Mum said you weren't going to write anymore about Tamsin. She said you were stopping. She said you were letting go of the story.'

'Mum told you all that?'

'Well, she told me without telling me. I told her that I was worried about you and the way you get so distracted whenever Tamsin comes up and then she put her arm around me in a way that told me that I had nothing to worry about because you must have told her something about how you were slowing down on all that Tamsin business and I thought that would be a really good thing because it would mean you would have more time to spend with me, Dad, and then I thought about how fun it would be if you and me went out to Nundah to interview Adam Duncan about the time he was saved by my mum.'

Clem pulls on my hand. 'C'mon, Dad, we got a yarn to get! Clem and Noah Cork, writing exclusively for the *Gecko Street Gazette*!'

I rest my head back on my pillow, close my eyes for a moment. Clem still pulling on my hand. You did this to yourself, Frankenstein. You made this beautiful monster. She's alive, Frankenstein. She's alive!

*

The Yaris takes a left exit off the Inner City Bypass and joins the morning traffic on Abbotsford Road, skirting Brisbane's sleepy Breakfast Creek.

'So, how do I get him to let me inside the house?' Clem asks from the front passenger seat.

'You show him who you are,' I reply. 'You show him why it's safe to talk to you. He'll give you about sixty seconds at the front door and, inside that sixty seconds, you'll have to convey to him that you are, at once, professional, trustworthy and, critically, not there to rob him at knife-point.'

Clem scribbles notes. I turn the Yaris into Sandgate Road at the Albion McDonald's. Pass a series of restaurants that I remember eating at when Rita and I were first dating. Sitar Indian Restaurant. Thaiways. The Albion Hotel garden bar.

'If he goes to close the door on you, ask him for advice,' I say. 'Quickest way to build a connection with someone – *anyone* – is to ask them for advice. You ever watched someone's eyes light up after you asked them for advice? It's as if they've got a spotlight pointed right at their noggin. You just told them without telling them that you feel they are wise and they are learned and they are worthy. "Before I go, would you mind if I just asked you for some advice … How would you tell this story? Who would you speak to next? Where would you go from here in this tricky thing called life?"'

We motor on towards Oriel Road, Clayfield, pass the Clayfield Lodge and Clayfield College. Drive for two or three minutes in silence. Clem turns the Yaris air-con up, but the vents have about as much blowing power as Clem's dying grandfather. She winds her window down instead.

'Dad, can I ask you something?'

'Sure.'

'I was interviewing Ellis and June the other day about Mum.'

'Ellis and June?'

'Yeah, I've been interviewing all the neighbours. They all had great stories about Mum.'

'What sorta stories?'

'Just things I didn't know about my own mum. It's actually kind of amazing, when you think about it, all the things you don't really know about the person who sleeps every night in the room right across the hall from you.'

'What didn't you know about your mum?'

'The pot plants.'

'The pot plants?'

'All those pot plants that Mum grows. Did you know that she's been giving them away to all our neighbours for the past five years? Six different neighbours told me stories of Mum just turning up on their doorsteps and handing them some beautiful plant she'd raised herself from nothing. Did you know that?'

'No,' I say, sheepishly, 'I didn't know that.'

Clem consults her notepad. 'Did you know that when Cherry Harms in number 23 had that lump cut out of her breast, Mum took three tubs of food – macaroni chicken, beef stew, minestrone soup – to her house every Tuesday morning for two months straight?'

I shake my head.

'Did you know Mum helped Les Schubert in number 12 quit drinkin'?' Clem asks. 'She drove him to a dry-out centre in Spring Hill. Les says it was on that drive when he was talkin' to Mum about his rotten life that he decided to quit drinkin' for good. He can't even remember exactly what Mum said, but it was somethin' about purple heart plants that continually die and continually come back to life again. Les said this is how he leads his life now, letting some parts of himself die and letting other parts of himself come back to life again. Did you know about Mum and Les?'

'No,' I say, squirming. 'I didn't know about your Mum and Les.'

'Honestly, do you know anything about your wife at all, Dad?'

'I know plenty about my wife, thank you.'

Clem's ballpoint pen is hooked through the loops of her notepad. She takes the lid off, presses it against the notepaper. Ready for work.

'All right, shoot.'

'Shoot what?'

'Shoot your mouth off. Tell me what you know about Mum. Tell me all the things you know about her that I don't know.'

I think for a moment. Think for another moment. 'Well, I know exactly where she was when she found out she was pregnant with you,' I say.

Clem beams. She wants more.

'She told me you existed through the crack of the open toilet door and she handed me the pregnancy test. I know how loud she wailed for you in the RBWH labour ward. Her screams seemed to come less from her throat than from some kind of deep-time place. That wailing was primal and ancient and I've never heard a sound more powerful or promising. That wailing had as much of the future in it as it did the past.

'I know how she carried you to the car after you had that seizure when you were three years old. She sat in the back seat, holding you like you were formed from strings of glass. The doctors said you had bacterial meningitis and you spent two nights in hospital. Mum refused to let go of your hand, the whole time. She slept in this plastic chair beside the bed, squeezing your hand in her sleep. If she had to go to the toilet, then she ordered me to take her place in the chair, holding your hand. "Permanent contact," she called it. "Permanent love." The day after you got out of hospital she was in the kitchen baking a Dora the Explorer cake for Erin's sixth birthday party. I didn't understand how she could switch like that, from life-threatening disease to purple icing and sponge cakes.

'I know the way she smiled at you from the side of the running track when you ran that hundred-metre dash on Sports Day in a moon boot, after you broke your toe kicking the white concrete breeze block in the dog park.'

'I thought it was a piece of Styrofoam,' Clem says.

'She was laughing and crying at the same time as you ran along looking like some kind of pirate with a peg leg. She was so proud of this little creature she kindly made and gave to the world. You lost that race by about eighty metres, but you won the day.

'I know what your Mum's voice does when she sings the high notes on "Dancing Queen". I know the sound she makes when she slips into a hot bath. I know she likes to sleep on her side. I know her favourite Beatle is George. I know her favourite film is *The Princess Bride*. I know she's a sock-shoe-sock-shoe woman. I know she likes what's known as "train-track lacing" on her shoes. I know she prefers only two thin arches of red onion on her ham and salad sandwiches. I know when she runs she likes to keep her arms up like she's a zombie extra from the "Thriller" video. I know the exact way she slides a bookmark into a copy of *Jane Eyre*. I know the way she sat with that kid Eddie Marsh on Crabbe Road when his bike hit that parked car. I know how she peels a boiled egg. I know the way she eats an apple. I know the sound of every song she ever sang in the shower. I know the sound of her laughter after a glass of red wine, which is different from the sound of her laughter after three vodka cranberries. I know the way she speaks in front of ten men in suits, and I know the way she speaks in front of thirteen ten-year-old girls dressed like Taylor Swift. I know the sound of her whispers in my ear. I know the sound of her anguish and her aching, and I know what happens to her eyes and her lips when her heart breaks.'

The Yaris brakes by a gutter in front of a low-set worker's cottage at 16 Cairo Street, Nundah. The car idles in place.

'Why did you say that?' Clem asks.

'Say what?'

'"Her heart breaks."'

'I don't know. That's all part of her, too.'

'Ellis and June said they heard you and mum having an argument down by the side of the house on the night of the meteor shower,' Clem says. 'That was the night before Mum and me went panning for gold. That was the night before she stopped speaking.'

'And does the esteemed editor of the *Gecko Street Gazette* have a question in there somewhere?'

'Well … what were you two arguing about?'

'Good question.'

I turn the engine off. Gaze through my side window at Adam Duncan's home. A silver Holden Commodore SV6 parked in his driveway. The words 'For Sale' and a mobile phone number scribbled in white marker across the rear window.

Thoughts of the late Lionel Rutledge: *Sometimes the trickiest thing about the digging is actually finding what you were looking for.*

'You wanna be in the business of asking good questions, Clem, then you better be willing to hear good answers.'

'I'm willing.'

I tap my right hand fingers on the steering wheel. Deep breath. The car is getting too hot to sit in, so I decide to keep it brief.

'We were arguing about a woman named Georgia Long,' I say.

'Who's Georgia Long?'

'She's an old journo friend. Do you remember five years ago Grandpa Bill and Grandma Deb came around to babysit you guys because your mum and I were flying to Sydney to attend the big annual journalism awards?'

'Yeah, I just remember Mum's black dress and she had the haircut that made her look like Black Widow from *The Avengers*.'

'Yeah, that sounds about right.'

How to put this? How to say it right to a twelve-year-old newshawk?

'Your mum left the afterparty early that night because she was tired. We were staying in the hotel where the party was taking place, so she could just duck upstairs no problem. Then she woke up at about two a.m. and she was worried about me because I wasn't beside her. She sent me two texts that I didn't respond to like a dumb a-hole, and then she checked the Find My Phone app and she could see I was nearby but not in the room. She thought I might have passed out or something from too many free wines and came looking for me. She gets halfway down the hall of this hotel and she sees me walking out of someone else's hotel room. She sees a woman waving goodbye to me from the doorway of this room. This woman's standing barefoot in a one-shoulder silver sequin mini.'

'Georgia Long?' Clem asks.

I nod.

Clem turns her head from me to the car windscreen in front of her. A suburban street filled with picket fences and parked cars and wheelie bins.

'Why are you telling me this, Dad?'

'Because you asked.'

Clem's right thumb starts to scratch her thigh. Her face reddens. I watch a tear fall from her left eye.

'Nothing happened, Clem,' I say. 'I promise you.'

Clem makes a fist with her right hand and rubs her left eyeball.

'You promise?' she replies.

'I promise.'

'So what's the big deal? If nothing happened, then it's not worth arguing about.'

I shrug my shoulders. 'Maybe. Maybe a lot happened that night when nothing happened.'

'What do you mean?'

'I mean that something happened to your mum and me that night,' I say. 'She slipped away a little from me. When you're as close to someone as I am to your mum, Clem, the slightest slip feels like a drop down the bottom of a hole.'

'Georgia was your friend, wasn't she?' Clem asks.

I nod. 'We went to university together,' I reply.

'So you were catching up with a friend in a hotel room, what's the big deal?'

What's the big deal? That's what I kept asking myself. Rita saw Georgia in the doorway of the room that night and she turned on the spot and walked silently back to our room. She didn't say a word to me that night, nor over breakfast the next morning. No matter how many times I told her nothing happened, she refused to speak about it.

'Georgia had no shoes on,' I say.

'So what?' Clem replies. 'What difference do shoes make? On or off, who cares?'

Maybe it's another fact of life, kid. Maybe I'm just overthinkin' it. Nothing good happens when a married man is alone in a hotel room at 2 a.m. with an unmarried woman in a silver sequin mini and no shoes on. Our rooms were on the same floor. Rita knew the layout of the rooms. Rita knew the rooms were small. Rita knew there was only one chair to sit on in that cramped hotel room and the only other place to sit was the queen-size bed with the white sheets and the four pillows and the ruby-red throw rug. Rita knew I wouldn't have sat on the bed. Of course I'd take the chair by the thin office desk with the room service phone and the hotel notepad, sipping a Crown lager and then another Crown lager from the beer fridge. Rita saw it all without seeing it. Georgia Long sitting on the side of the bed with a vodka-tonic, silver heels still laced to her feet beneath the silver mini. A text lands in my phone from my wife and I don't text back because … because … because … I don't want to lie to my wife. A second text lands and I don't text back because … because … because … Georgia Long just took her heels off and lay back on the bed in the silver mini dress. And now something *is* happening. It's not nothing. Something in the air of this small 2 a.m. hotel room just turned from university friendship to barefoot intimacy. So why the fuck am I still here? So why am I stuck like this in the intimate slip … *slip* … *slip*. 'Fuck,' I tell myself. 'Time to go.' But a slip is a slip is a slip and Georgia Long knows it. 'One more drink,' she says. Okay, Beelzebub. Just one more drink.

Now look at all that confusion across my daughter's face. Of course it makes no sense to her. Because you're not telling her the full story, Cork. Because that hotel room story is really all about the things we carry in our blood. The things we see when we're young and the things we almost do when we're old enough to know better. The things kids learn from their fathers.

'Trust me, Clem,' I say, 'shoes make all the difference.'

Clem shakes her head, opens the passenger door. 'Jeez, Dad, if this is an example of your museum storage room, then I think I'll stay in the cafeteria.'

*

Adam Duncan's thigh-high front steel gate has lost a hinge and scrapes along the concrete path when Clem swings it open. She leads us to Adam's front porch. A pair of steel-cap boots by a worn doormat, still wet with sweat and what smells like animal guts and blood. An ashtray resting on the arm of a two-seat sofa with torn upholstery on the porch and an old metallic-blue ten-speed racing bike with two flat tyres leaning against a concrete porch wall, painted forest green. Clem pulls on a flyscreened security door that nearly falls off its hinges, and knocks three times on the white wooden front door.

A man in a State of Origin 'Queenslander' tee opens the door.

'Yeah,' the man says.

'Adam Duncan?' Clem asks.

'Yeah.'

Adam has a thick grey-brown beard shaped like an icicle hanging from his chin. Breadcrumbs and mayonnaise on his beard and – let the journalistic dot-joining commence – a half-eaten Red Rooster Rippa Roll in his right hand.

'Mr Duncan, my name is Clementine Cork …' She raises a right palm in my direction. 'And this is my father, the groundbreaking Brisbane true-crime journalist Noah Cork.'

'Nice to meet you, Adam.' I nod.

Adam takes a bite of his Rippa Roll. 'Yep,' he says.

'Mr Duncan, I'm the editor-in-chief of a local street paper named the *Gecko Street Gazette* and for issue thirteen of this august community broadsheet, I am piecing together an in-depth profile of a longtime resident of Jubilee named Rita Munro, who, to my good fortune, happens to be my mother.'

'Yeah, I know Rita,' Adam says.

'Yes, I know you do,' Clem says. 'That's why I'm here this morning. I was wondering if you might be able to share any recollections you have of that amazing night when my mother saved the lives of you and your siblings, Tenille and Leah, from the devastating fire that ripped so savagely through your home in Pike Street in 1996?'

Adam takes another bite of his roll and takes his sweet time to chew this mouthful and swallow it before replying to my daughter. 'Yeah … nah,' he says.

'I'm sorry,' Clem says, 'I don't know what that means.'

Adam grips his front door and moves to close it. 'I don't really talk about that night,' he says. 'But thanks for asking, anyway. Please say hello to your mum for me. We all think she's amazing for what she done. But … yeah … nah.'

Adam starts closing the front door.

Clem blocks it with a stiff left arm. 'Yes, I think she's amazing too, Adam, and I was just wondering if maybe you might have some time to take me back to that night.'

'Sorry, darlin', I work nights,' he says. 'I'm fucked. Gotta get my beauty sleep. Good luck with the story.'

He tries to close the door again, but Clem sticks her left foot in front of it.

'So sorry to be a pain, Mr Duncan, but I wonder if you might have some time just to give me some … some … *advice* … on what angles I should explore when revisiting this extraordinary moment in time?'

Adam Duncan laughs. 'Advice?' he asks. 'You want advice from me on how to write a story about your mum?'

Clem beams a smile. 'You bet I do,' she replies.

He takes another bite of his roll. Kinks his neck in a kind of nod and leaves the door open as he walks back into his house.

*

It's a beautiful scene for a dad like me. My daughter taking notes at the kitchen table, from an interview subject whose home she found her way into without a lick of assistance, as Adam polishes off what looks like a Red Rooster roll, chips and Pepsi combo meal.

'Trouble was, Pike Street's in the hills a bit,' Adam says. 'The houses are all spread out. I was twelve years old and was supposed to be the man of the house that night. The oldies were down at Twin Towns for the weekend. It's Saturday night and it starts getting late. You know how all them old Jubilee houses have them 1960s basements and rumpus rooms?'

Clem nods.

'My little sisters go to bed upstairs and I have the bright idea to cook myself a big pot of potato gems in hot oil and then go downstairs to the rumpus and watch *Bad Boys* on video. About an hour into the movie I fall asleep on the bean bag. Suddenly I wake up coughing my guts up and the whole rumpus room is filled with smoke.'

Adam slaps his forehead. 'Bozo's left the oil frying, hasn't he,' he says. 'I don't know where the fuck I am. I can't even find my way upstairs in the smoke. There's one little window in the basement that opens on the side of the house, but it's got security bars on the outside and I can only open the window a crack just to get some air, and then I'm screaming out like a fuckin' nutter for help but no one can hear me cuz the neighbours are miles away. Maybe I scream like this for a minute, two minutes, tops. And then I'm out.' Adam clicks his fingers. 'Everything goes black.'

He shakes his head. Cleans his mouth with a Red Rooster wet wipe and tucks the wet wipe into the empty chips box. And then he takes a deep breath and begins to weep. It's as though he hasn't thought about that night for decades and those words – 'everything goes black' – are an emotional trigger, the pulled valve of a memory fountain in the deepest corner of the darkest room in his museum. His shoulders move up and down with his sobbing. His breasts wobble beneath the Queenslander tee. He wipes his eyes.

'And that's when I woke up in my front driveway, staring into the eyes of the most beautiful woman I've ever seen in my life,' he says. He points a finger at Clem. 'Your mum.'

He laughs.

Clem beams.

'She was riding her bike home from Tiffany Bight's seventeenth birthday party,' Adam says. 'She told the firefighters that she saw the flames first in the kitchen windows and then she heard me screaming from the basement before I passed out. I don't know. Even that all sounds like a miracle to me, just the fact she was there at exactly that moment. But that's not the half of it.

'Then I come to and I tell your mum that my sisters are upstairs in their bedrooms.' Adam is so into the story that he re-enacts Rita's movements inside his kitchen. He stands and turns slowly, looking towards a space in his mind. 'I swear she stands up and she stares into this fuckin' inferno of a house and she thinks for maybe one second and then she takes this denim jacket that was tied around her waist and she wraps it around her face like she's some camel walker in the Sahara and then she just fuckin' … *sprints* … into the house.'

Adam gets down low in the kitchen and pretends to run like Rita ran. 'I just watch her disappear and I think for all money that this … *beautiful* …' Adam can't get words out. Tears come instead and he cups his mouth. 'I think, She's just fuckin' chosen to kill herself because nobody could survive going into that place. But she goes in.'

Adam looks at me and I realise he's made me cry.

'That's Rita Munro,' he says. 'That's your wife.'

And I'm weeping openly now because I love the woman at the centre of this story and I've never heard the story told like this before. Rita's only ever spoken in shrugged-off fragments about that night. Impossible story pieces that never join to form anything beyond what's already written on a community pillar at the end of Drake Bridge.

'Sixty seconds later, she barrels out the front door with my kid sister, Tenille, on her right shoulder. She dumps her on me and screams, "Check she's still breathing." And my sister and your mum's all black. They look like them old blackface singers. All I see is her eyes and then she runs straight back into this fuckin' hellfire to find Leah. I check Tenille's breathing and I slap her face and, thank God, you know, she's wheezing and coughing and spluttering and she's still alive. Then fuckin' two minutes go by and I think for sure your mum's a goner and Leah is too, you know, and then, like some kinda fuckin' dream, your mum emerges from the side of the house, this time with Leah on her shoulder.'

Adam's voice drops to a whisper. He pulls his chair in closer to Clem. 'You asked me to give you advice on how to write a story about your mum,' he says.

Clem nods her head. 'Uh-huh,' she says. Her right foot is tapping the linoleum flooring of Adam Duncan's suffocating kitchen.

Adam taps his forefinger on Clem's notepad. 'I advise you to write about how everything you have read about that night is bullshit,' Adam says. 'Your mum told those firefighters that Leah was unconscious. She wasn't unconscious. She was fucking dead. I saw her face. She was gone. Your mum told the firefighters that she was unconscious for about one minute. She was fuckin' dead for three.'

He shakes his head. 'I told my parents,' he says. 'I told the cops what I saw. Leah was gone for good and your mum brought her back somehow. Nobody believed me. They all said I was foggy and traumatised and confused. Bullshit.'

He points to his front door. 'I didn't want to talk to you before, Clementine, because every time I've ever told the truth about your mum, the world wants to tell me I'm crazy,' he says. 'They all told me I was crazy back then and you'll tell me I'm crazy now.'

Clem shakes her head. 'I won't, Adam, I promise. What's the truth, Adam?'

Clem turns to me, eyes of fire. Turns back to Adam. 'What's the truth about my mum, Adam?' she asks, urgently, pen pressed against her notepad. 'She's special, isn't she? She's really, really special.'

Adam shakes his head. His eyes are so alight and he leans in so close to Clem that I put a comforting hand on her shoulder.

'Special?' he whispers. 'Your mum's fucking miraculous.'

SIXTEEN

Always tell your editor where you are going. Give your editor a rough estimate of the time in which you expect to return to the office. In the event of your sudden disappearance, the nation's most kind-hearted editors will make some effort to uncover your whereabouts. The nation's best editors, however, will forget you even left the office and will continue to produce tomorrow's paper.

– Rutledge, *Journalism Practices and Principles*

Sunday afternoon. Digging. Digging for the answers I told myself I didn't need to find. Digging for the story I promised to let go. Just one more itch to scratch before I stop for keeps: Miles De Jonge.

I reverse the Yaris out of the carport on this sweltering summer afternoon and see, in the rearview mirror, my daughter Erin talking to Seb Cavendish in the middle of the cul-de-sac. Shoulder bags on the black tarmac by their feet. Seb's hair is dyed black and scarlet now. Erin laughs at something Seb says and stabs her forefinger playfully into his belly button.

I continue reversing the car, then turn the wheel so my window is two arm lengths from my daughter. I bring my window down. 'Seb,' I say, by way of greeting.

To my surprise, Seb responds. 'Mr Cork,' he says with a nod. I might be mistaken, but there's warmth in that half-smile.

Seb brushes Erin's right elbow. 'Talk later, all right,' he says.

She nods, smiles at him in a way she's never smiled at me. Watches her lanky young neighbour disappear into Jon and Rose's garage at number 40.

Erin takes a breath and looks to the sky to exhale, then pads over to my window. For ten or so seconds, we watch a magpie dig for worms in the grass in front of Anushka Burman's house.

'Soooo … you're talkin' to Seb again?'

She nods.

'Soooo … I take it that's lover boy?' I add.

Erin rolls her eyes. Looks down at her feet, digging the toe of her right shoe into the tarmac.

'I don't think he threw that brick, Dad,' she says. 'It was an accident. He wasn't lying. He's got a good heart, Dad. Didn't you always tell me to look for the good hearts? I found one right across the street from me. How lucky am I?'

I grip the fingers she has curled around the bottom of my window. I have a vision of these fingers when they belonged to a month-old baby sleeping on my chest.

'He's managing the head stuff?' I ask.

'He's super diligent about it,' Erin says. 'He's got a whole healthcare team sorting him out. He gets scared sometimes about stuff and he hears the odd voice in his head now and then, but who doesn't hear voices now and then?'

I, personally, hear the hissing skeletons of murdered mums. Who am I to judge?

I squeeze my daughter's hand. 'Go slow,' I say. 'Go smart.'

Erin turns this hold into a handshake. An unspoken agreement. Then she drops the rules for life. 'Be kind and don't do drugs,' she says.

'I promise I'll be kind,' I say.

*

This must be the beginning of my ending. The story's ending, I mean, just to be clear. My story's demise, not my demise. Not to skip ahead or nuthin', but the long and winding red Boral-brick road to my story's certain demise begins here. Standing on the porch at number 34 Butcherbird Close, Jubilee. Miles and Stephanie De Jonge's house. A mid-century mauve-coloured stucco-walled cottage, not far from the Jubilee Tavern on Kenning Place. The De Jonges have a novelty doorbell that plays the Indiana Jones theme. It sounds ridiculously upbeat in contrast to the look upon Steph De Jonge's face when she opens the front door and sees me standing on her porch. She tightens the knot on her dressing gown belt and audibly sighs.

'He doesn't live here no more,' she says.

'Where's he live?'

'Why do you wanna know?'

'Because I want to ask him something.'

'Whaddya wanna ask him?'

'I wanna ask him if he knew Tamsin Fellows before she disappeared.'

Steph De Jonge chuckles under her breath.

'Something funny, Steph?'

'Yeah, *you*. You're somethin' funny, Noah Cork. You're somethin' fuckin' hilarious.'

'What's so fuckin' hilarious about me?'

She shakes her head and grips the front door, moves to close it. 'Cops told me not to talk to you,' she says.

'They give you a reason, by any chance?'

'Yeah, they did,' Steph says. 'They said you are a kind of hazardous waste. The head cop, Jim England, likened you to a litre of concentrated weedkiller.'

'Jim says the sweetest things. Where's Miles living now, Steph?'

She rests her weight on the front door. 'I hear your wife's giving you the silent treatment?'

'Where did you hear that?'

'My hairdresser.'

'Where'd your hairdresser hear that?'

'Her hairdresser.'

I tap the back of my heel three times on the tiles of the porch.

'What did you do to her to make her so pissed?' Steph asks.

I give this more thought than Steph expected me to. What *did* I do? What *did* I do? *What did I do*?

'I don't even think she's pissed, Steph,' I reply. 'I think it's something deeper than anger. She's just … silent.'

'So what did you do to her to make her so silent? You must have done something.'

'Is that true?' I ask. 'Do you honestly think that? Is it really true that I must have done something? Could I possibly be the root cause of it all? Or could it be possible that a husband is not, for once, the sole reason for a wife's dismay?'

Steph seems to ponder this for a moment. 'Nah,' she says. Shakes her head. 'It's always the husband.'

I rub my chin with my thumb and forefinger. 'I guess it makes sense,' I say. 'If it is all my fault, then I honestly don't know what it was that I did to her. It could be ten things, it could be none.'

I smile at Steph, whose face suggests she is struggling to follow my thoughts.

'She hasn't told me yet,' I say.

'Did *you* know Tamsin Fellows before she disappeared?' Steph asks.

'No. Did your husband?'

She chuckles again, clutches the edges of her dressing gown where they meet at her chest.

'He's staying at his grandparents' old house,' she says. 'Big ol' timber place on Gettysburg Street.'

'The one that's on the lean,' I say. 'Like it's about to fall over?'

'Yeah, that's the one,' Steph says. 'And with any luck, that prick will be having a snooze when it finally collapses.'

*

Storm clouds gathering in the silver-black sky. This must be the middle of the beginning of my ending. Gettysburg Street runs off Stackhouse Road, which snakes through hectares of bushland hills separating Jubilee from the neighbouring suburb of Glen Forrest. Miles De Jonge's grandparents' home is a three-storey timber pole house that looks like it could collapse under the kind of gust that comes from a five-year-old blowing out candles on a chocolate cake. I recall Miles telling me something over a beer at a school fête. Something about how he inherited the crooked house on Gettysburg Street from his late grandparents. Something about it being a burden he and Steph didn't have the time in their schedule to accommodate.

Termite-ravaged timber steps climbing four metres to a front door. The house is secluded. Not a neighbour to be seen through the surrounding eucalypts. Deadwood branches scattered across the forest floor. Dry-baked powder-keg forest just waiting for some idiot to flick a cigarette butt into it. A dozen tall and unpredictable widowmaker gums that rise eighty feet to the sky and will each cost Miles $2,000 to have professionally lopped and removed from the property – $500 per tree if he went with one of the half-dozen unlicensed tree loppers who door-knock Jubilee on the regular.

I knock twice on the front door and it opens slowly because, I realise, it wasn't fully closed.

'Miles?' I call through the doorway. 'It's Noah Cork.'

Music playing loudly inside the house. The heavy bass sound of a pre-2000s living room stereo system. The song is 'Don't Bring Me Down' by Electric Light Orchestra.

'Miles? You there? It's Noah.'

I lean in through the front doorway. A 1980s kitchen. Timber veneer doors and cabinets. On the wall above the stove is a framed faded print of an oil painting showing a stuffed turkey at the centre of a banquet table with a flower in its mouth, surrounded by oyster shells and wine and sliced bread and a bowl of grapes and apples. Dishes left unwashed in the sink. Empty beer bottles on the kitchen benchtops. Empty spiced rum and ginger ale cans. A crushed paper Uber Eats delivery bag.

'Miles, you there?' I call, then step gingerly through the kitchen, my shoes squeaking on a brown and orange linoleum floor that's gone sticky from a dried pool of red wine. ELO build a wall of noise in the living room off the kitchen and I follow that sound. What the hell's that guy even saying in that song? He doesn't want *who* to bring him down? … *Bruce*? *Groos*? *Vamoose*? *Belarus*? More framed oil painting prints in the living room. Dutch artists, maybe. Vermeer. Rembrandt. A group of Dutch men in one print with hair like the members of Iron Maiden, dressed in formal black gowns with white lace collars. A series of colourfully painted eggs – eggs the size of emu eggs – lining a brown timber-veneer wall unit. The eggs are Mexican themed – Frida Kahlo meets Old El Paso taco kit.

An empty space in the wall unit where a television would normally be. A dated Panasonic CD and record player on the lowest shelf of the unit. That's where the music's coming from. Other shelves in the wall unit lined with old green and amber and clear glass tumblers and shot glasses and sherry and brandy glasses. I startle myself briefly when I catch my own reflection in a mirrored wall hanging depicting what looks like some kind of family crest, a knight's battle helmet above two red lions bumping claws in triumph. Then my eyes fix upon something impossible. Something on the living room carpet. At first I think it's a large living room rug that's been rolled up for transportation. A bright orange rug, pushed to one side of the living room. But then my eyes and my brain work hard to make sense of the vision. That is Miles De Jonge's head sticking out from a torso that's been wrapped in a thick orange plastic film that has ensnared his body like shrink-wrap. It looks like he's in the process of metamorphosing, wriggling his head out of some kind of plastic cocoon. An orange plastic chrysalis. Except he's not moving at all. His eyes are closed. His face is white as oat milk.

'Miles,' I whisper to no one but myself.

Then I hear a single footstep behind me, a sound from the kitchen I just stepped through. Look up to see the flash of two eyes inside a black balaclava reflected in the mirrored family crest wall hanging. Whip my head around sharply, just in time to absorb the full force of a heavy and blunt instrument connecting with my left temple. And in my head I see Adam Duncan from this morning, talking to my daughter at his kitchen table. 'Everything goes black,' Adam says, and clicks his fingers.

Then everything goes black.

SEVENTEEN

Physical injuries are a common occurrence when reporting in the field and should be reported immediately to your chief of staff or appropriate department head. You may be entitled to compensation. Impacts to your mental and emotional health, however, can sometimes seem far more difficult to report. Remember, few problems are ever solved through silence.

– Rutledge, *Journalism Practices and Principles*

A dream about my mother. Alison Cork. The age she was when she died. She's standing underwater. A school of bream swimming around her and she's standing, impossibly, at an ironing board. She's down in the deep blue-green sea with a Sunbeam iron and a smile on her face. What's that black cloak that she's ironing? Looks like she's ironing Dracula's cloak or something. No, wait a second. That's no cloak. That's the black gown I wore when I graduated from university. That's what I wore when I got my journalism degree.

'What are you staring at, Noah?' she asks with a smile. 'You'd better get dressed, love. Don't wanna be late for your graduation.'

And now I'm awake. Everything black again. But waking black. Black in the real world. I'm lying on my side. Where am I? That's right, the house with the lean on Gettysburg Street. I saw Miles in the orange plastic chrysalis. I saw a flash of a balaclava in the reflection of a mirror. Then I turned and then I saw nothing.

I blink three times. Silence in the house. Nighttime summer crickets outside. A crashing, sickening throbbing in my head. I want to vomit. Reach my fingers to my temple and feel a bruise that's swollen to the size of half a tennis ball. I think I'm going to vomit. Stomach sick rushes up through my throat and I rest my weight on my right elbow and turn my head to the living room carpet and cough a ball of vomit up the way a dog might hack up a jagged bone.

I wipe my mouth with my shirt sleeve. Need water. Need answers. Need my wife to speak to me. Need my wife. Need Rita Munro in the dark. I check the time on my phone. It's half-past midnight. I must have been unconscious for more than eight hours.

Moonlight breaking through a living room window, allowing my eyes to adjust. I crawl to the place where I swear I saw Miles De Jonge wrapped in orange plastic. Pat my hands on the carpet in the moon-blue darkness. Nothing. The orange chrysalis has disappeared. The body is gone.

*

I bang on the doors of the Jubilee police station. A light is on in the station, but nobody answers the door.

I jump back in the Yaris and drive as fast as I can without dying in the direction of my home. I realise now that the streets of Jubilee are covered in debris. Wind-snapped branches in the gutters of Wicker Road. Leaves and sticks scattered across streets. A Coles shopping trolley upturned by the entrance to Jubilee Plaza. A heavy storm has passed through; the summer storm season arrived while I was dreaming of my dead mum under the sea.

I call Rita as I drive. She answers her phone but says nothing. Lets me do the talking.

I tell her I'm driving to Jim England's house to report a crime. 'I'll explain when I get home, Rita. I'm sorry to make you worry, Rita. I'm so sorry for everything.'

Erin takes the phone from her mum. 'Dad, where the hell have you been?' she asks.

'I'm so sorry honey, I got … a bit stuck … on a story,' I say. 'Go to bed, honey. I'll explain when I get home.'

'We thought something happened to you in the storm,' Erin says. 'Mum's so pissed at you. You better get home quick, Dad. Clem's kinda flipped out.'

'What? What happened to Clem?'

'She's acting all weird again,' Erin says. 'Mum and Clem got stuck in the storm. The storm hit them just as they were walking to the Corolla, which was parked on the rooftop carpark because they couldn't find a spot under shelter. You should see the Corolla, Dad, it's all shot to hell with hail damage. Two big hailstones burst right through the back window. It looks like they were in a Compton drive-by.'

'Jesus Christ.'

'Nah, not his work, I'm afraid. This one was Zeus, I reckon. God of lightning, thunder and microbursts in Jubilee.'

'Listen, Erin, tell Mum I'll be home soon. I just gotta drop in and see Jim England about something.'

'This about Tamsin?'

'I can't say, honey. Just look after your sister for me, all right. I'll be home soon.'

'Can I take the day off from school tomorrow?'

'Why?'

'Mum's giving Clem the day off.'

'Why?'

'Storm trauma.'

'But why do *you* need to take the day off? You weren't caught in the storm.'

'I think I've got astraphobia.'

'What's astraphobia?'

'Fear of thunder and lightning. It's the third most prevalent phobia among children in the United States.'

'Erin, can we discuss this when I get home?'

*

I pull into my own street and slam the brakes in front of Jim England's house. Trip on the gutter outside Jim's house and nearly crash into his front gate. Rush up a set of six steps and bash six times on his front door with my closed fist. No noise inside the house. Bash four more times with my fist. Then I feel a presence behind me – the growl of a post-midnight monster. Turn to see Hercules, the loose-bowelled bullmastiff, bane of my suburban existence, licking his teeth at the bottom of Jim's front stairs. His low-dwelling growl sounds like a truck engine stuck in neutral. He bounds up four steps and barks so loudly at me that I jump on the spot.

'Hercules, buddy,' I plead. 'It's me, Noah. From up the street. I let you shit on my lawn three times a week. Shhhhhh. Shhhhh. I've just come to see Jim.' The dog moves closer. I hold my palms out. 'Wait, stop, I've come to see Jim, mate.'

A porchlight zaps to life above me. A shoestring of saliva slips from Hercules' mouth as his head moves within biting distance of my increasingly endangered scrotum.

Jim England opens his door in his dressing gown and slippers. He can't disguise his fury. He lets it shine through every 'f' letter he uses in the following sentence. 'Ffffor ffffuck's sake, Cork,' he barks. 'You better have a ffffuckin' good reason ffffor bangin' on my door after fffffuckin' midnight.'

*

I'm standing in the living room now of the Gettysburg Street pole home beside plainclothes detective Jim England. The lights are on. Jim's wearing an old blue cardigan over a white V-neck T-shirt. Loose linen shorts exposing bare kneecaps, and blue and red tartan slippers. He's so tall his head is only two or three feet from the living room ceiling lights. He holds a small notepad and a pen and a black metal torch that looks part illumination device, part baseball bat.

'I swear, Jim,' I say, pointing to a corner of the living room. 'I looked at the mirror crest thing, then I looked down and I saw Miles right there. He was wrapped in that orange plastic stuff that you see on construction sites. He looked like a bug caught in a spider's storage web. Then I heard a noise behind me. I turned around. Boom. Out like a light.'

Jim takes notes. His default facial expression is a closed-lip snarl.

'This person in the balaclava,' he says. 'Male or female?'

'Well, I just assumed male—'

'Why would you assume that?'

'Women don't tend to do this kind of thing, do they?'

'What kind of thing do you mean, Cork? Kill men and wrap them in plastic? Believe me, some women do that kind of thing.'

'Well, I guess I couldn't say if it was a male or a female, then. I only saw a flash across the mirror crest thing there.' I point at the family crest on the wall.

'How tall would you say?' Jim asks.

'Well, about my height, I guess. Like, average height. I mean, not tall enough or short enough for me to notice. I guess.'

'This is a murder investigation, Cork. Do us a favour and leave your guessing out of it. If you're unsure, tell me. If you're sure, tell me. Do not guess.'

He studies the room with his eyelids half closed, as though using some kind of microfocal system that helps him zero in on potential pieces of evidence. He kneels in the corner beneath the family crest and inspects the area I was just pointing to. Gestures towards a small round pool of vomit some ten centimetres from his right slipper.

'Who belongs to that?'

'I do,' I say. 'I did. When I woke back up. Just came out of me.'

Jim turns his body on the balls of his feet, still kneeling, showing strength in his thighs, casts his eyes across the wall unit. Seems transfixed for a moment by the painted eggs lining the shelves. Stands then paces down the hallway beyond the living room. Makes a phone call.

From where I stand, I hear only snatches of the conversation he's having.

'Twelve Gettysburg Street ... De Jonge. Capital D-e-space-capital J-o-n-g-e. No, not Italian. Dutch, I think ... Give Parsons a bell, yeah. Mmmm, let's get FSG down here, quick as you can ... All comms through me.'

He pockets the phone, pads back into the living room. Stands frozen and studies my face for a long moment.

'You did this, Cork.'

'What?'

He repeats words from my book, verbatim. '"You are a deranged and perverted monster who somehow crawled from a bucket of evolutionary slime ... You are a worm-ridden coward." You remember writing that stuff, Hemingway?'

I hold up a palm. 'Wait, no ... no, Jim ... That wasn't what—'

'You sent a fuck-you message to a killer,' Jim says. 'How did you expect a killer to respond?'

He shakes his head and pockets his notebook. 'You can take me home now, Cork.'

*

Jim England says one thing to me on the way back to Gecko Street in my Yaris. 'Is this your wife's car?' he asks.

It's almost 2 a.m. when I pull up in front of his house again.

'Turn the car off,' he says.

Sitting in silence now. Storm clouds have made way for stars in the black sky.

'Listen to me very carefully, Cork,' Jim says. 'I do not want to read a word about this in the press. You have already done enough damage to our ongoing investigations by publishing that so-called book of yours.'

'I was doing my job, Jim,' I say. 'My job is to tell the story. My job is to give the people the truth.'

Jim whips his head around to meet my eyes. 'And my job is to keep the people safe,' he spits. 'Even in the face of glory-seeking hacks hellbent on provoking sick-fuck killers in the suburbs.'

'Correct me if I'm wrong, Jim, but I thought your job was to keep me safe, too,' I say. 'I nearly got run over the other night by some psycho Meat Loaf lookalike woman in a red Hilux and I tried to report it, but your Constable Blake wasn't having a bar of it. My life gets threatened, around the corner from my own house, and the cops tell me to call fuckin' Georgia Long in the media department. You think I wanna keep writing about the Tamsin Fellows story? I'm fucking *done* with the Tamsin Fellows story. The Tamsin Fellows story is a fucking noose around my neck. It's brought nothing but pain and agony to my work and my marriage and my life.'

'Is that right, Cork?'

'Yes, that's right, *England*.'

'You're done with the Fellows murder?' England asks, dubious.

'Yes. I am. I'm done. I'm out.'

'Then why the fuck were you visiting Miles De Jonge's grandparents' house?'

Good question. I shake my head and think of an answer. Settle for the truth. 'I don't know,' I say. 'Because I'm a sucker for punishment. Because I can't live with loose ends. Because Helen Fellows told me something that might have been a lie, but might have been the truth, and I needed to work out which one of those it was.'

'What did she tell you?'

'We talking off the record?' I ask.

Jim shrugs. 'Cork, that means about as much in my world as it does in yours,' he says.

I take a breath. Look up at the stars through the front windscreen. 'She told me she saw Miles sitting with her mum, down on that very seat where we found her red shoes,' I say.

Jim nods his head, allows the sentence to float in the air for a moment. 'We still talkin' off the record?' he asks.

'That actually still means something in my world, Jim,' I reply.

Jim scoffs. 'That day you boys found Tamsin,' Jim says. 'We interviewed Miles about an hour after you. Poor bastard looked like a rabbit in the headlights. We grilled him for an hour and he told us how he went down to that reservoir in the rain that day because he was feeling all sad about fucking things up with his wife, Steph. And he told us exactly what you told us, that you stumbled across him and you had a note from some psycho in your hand that was sending you on some kinda macabre treasure hunt through Jubilee, in search of poor ol' Tamsin in the oven.'

The events run like an old film projector showreel in my mind. Miles resting by the steps on the reservoir track. Miles saying he couldn't bring himself to enter Monaco House. Miles waiting for me in the car.

'We sent Miles home, but we knew there was more to his story,' Jim says. 'You can just tell sometimes. You ever get that in journalism, Cork? When you see the very weight of a story pulling someone down into their seat? The story itself becomes like lead in their pockets. Secrets make people move slow, slow to react. Make 'em seem unnatural. That's how Miles seemed that day. Unnatural.

'Sure enough, he calls me back an hour later. Tells me he went home and did some thinking. And what he was thinkin' about was that thing you hacks like to call the truth.'

Jim pulls his phone from his pocket, swipes through a series of photos on his screen. He zooms in on one photo and passes me his phone. The photograph is an image of a handwritten note.

'You weren't the only one who got a letter in his mailbox, Cork,' Jim says.

I read the words on the note, scrawled roughly in blue ballpoint pen, across what looks like an index page from a textbook.

Hello lemon drop,
Miss u.
Seems I left my ruby slippas by the reservoir.
Could u find them for me, lemon drop?
TF

'What the fuck's going on here, Jim?' I ask.

Jim's right forefinger opens and closes the plastic grille on the side air vent. 'That's what we're trying to find out,' Jim says. 'See, us cops have a thing called police process, Cork.

We don't go publishing books before a case is complete. With patience and care, we pursue every lead. We methodically rule out suspects and we keep as many potential breakthroughs as we can out of the newspapers because – newsflash, Cork – we don't want the killer to know what we know.'

'So what do we know, Jim?'

He sighs, shakes his head. 'Across three months prior to her disappearance in 2022, Tamsin Fellows had sexual intercourse with Miles De Jonge on four occasions inside Tamsin's red Hyundai Elantra. These sexual encounters took place after dark in the Spearwood Reservoir carpark. In the exact parking space where Tamsin's car was found in the wake of her disappearance.'

'We talkin' about the same Tamsin Fellows?' I ask.

Jim nods.

Why am I so shaken by this? Is it so hard to believe that she would like to secretly make love to a man inside her car in a carpark after dark? Too bad if that doesn't fit the suburban angel narrative you so love to regurgitate, Noah Cork, which is starting to look like that circle of sick you left back there on the carpet.

'They met at a dog obedience class,' Jim says. 'Miles and Tamsin were there every second Friday night on the Good Shepherd school oval on Salem Road. They bonded quickly over their disobedient dogs and their disappointing marriages. Stephanie De Jonge had grown bored with a husband she constantly referred to as "vanilla". Neil Fellows, meanwhile, was balls deep in a now well-discussed fuckathon with the highly flexible local samba instructor, Luna Ora. To cut Miles's long and somewhat embarrassing police statement short, what began as a revenge fuck blossomed into something almost resembling love. Then poor Tamsin dropped off the face of the earth. Only to be found again, two years later, by an irritating crime journo neighbour of mine named Noah Cork. We didn't charge Miles for withholding evidence because we didn't want Tamsin's killer knowing what we knew. Now, it seems, it's poor Miles's turn to take the one-way bus to Dodoland.'

Jim holds his palms up. 'That's what we know,' he says.

'You forgot to mention one thing, Jim.'

Jim raises an eyebrow.

'Who's the killer, Jim?'

'What?' he replies. 'I just told you, that's what we're trying to find out.'

'But I know you know. You guys always know. The annoying thing about police work is all that messy space between what you know and what you can prove.'

Jim clicks his tongue. Sighs. 'I wouldn't be so confident in the things I know, Cork,' he says. 'In case you hadn't noticed, this investigation is leaning further each day towards the fucking bizarre.'

'What's that thing you say you do?' I ask. '*Methodically rule out the suspects.* So let's methodically rule out the suspects. Let's start at Mr Nine Times Outta Ten. The husband.'

'Well, I thought for all the money it was Neil Fellows,' Jim replies. 'I didn't doubt for a second that his brother could have verified a false alibi for a brother he worships. We've tracked Neil Fellows for six months, just waiting for him to slip up. The husbands always slip up. It's the arrogance that gets them in the end. The remarkable self-confidence that tells them they actually fuckin' got away with it. Six months, twelve months, forty-eight months later, when they're standing in the soft green grass of *the clear* – boom! That's when everything invariably comes crashing down.'

Jim scratches the flaky top of his left ear. 'But our Neil,' he says, 'he hasn't slipped up yet. Maybe that means he didn't do it. Or maybe that just means he's smarter than we thought he was.'

'Neil Fellows is a drunken mess,' I say. 'He sleeps half the day on his couch.'

'He wouldn't be the first killer I've come across who buried his genius in a visage of intemperance.'

Jim takes his notebook from his pants pocket, opens it in the middle. 'But there's a real big problem with the Neil Fellows angle.'

'What's that?'

'You, Cork,' he grimaces. 'Why get you involved?'

We both place our hands behind our heads and think on this question. Silence in the car for almost a minute.

'Muddy the waters,' I say. 'Spread the scent of guilt.'

'He's caught his wife in a sexual tryst with a local idiot named Miles,' Jim says. 'He kills his wife in a moment of domestic anger. Possible. Believable. I could give you four homicide cases that I worked on myself in the past five years alone where that was the scenario. But why bury the body only to dig it back up again for some sick game where Noah Cork is the poor bastard chosen to hold the dice?'

'Fair point,' I say. 'But only a fool would rule the husband out.' I shrug my shoulders. 'There's you, Jim, of course.'

'Me?'

'Yeah, you hate my guts. Who knows how many screws you got loose in that noggin. Not the first homicide cop to go psycho rogue. And there was the number on the fish and chip shop docket?'

'What the hell are you talking about?'

'The docket number on the killer's second note to me,' I say. 'Number 33.' And point my finger towards Jim England's letterbox and the glowing plastic *33* screwed into the face of it.

'Oh, go fuck yourself, Cork. Think harder.'

Do what the cop says. Think harder.

'All right, here's one for you,' I say. 'The son. John Fellows.'

'He's not wired right that kid, but I don't see a mum killer in him,' Jim says.

'He and his friends tried to slice my fingers off with a bandsaw,' I say.

'Why?'

'John's not the biggest fan of my book,' I say. 'Metalhead crackbrain with a hard-on for Satan. Remember all those symbols in Monaco House?'

'Weak lead,' Jim says.

'Helen Fellows?' I suggest. 'For the killer to drop that note in Miles's mailbox, the killer has to know about Miles and Tamsin.'

'Stronger.'

'Helen told me she used to read my crime pages. So she knows me. Fair chance she'd know where I lived, too.'

'I don't like it,' Jim sniffs. 'But I don't like dismissing it, either.'

'You got anything stronger than Helen?'

'Yeah,' Jim says, 'I got a rather strong and growing group of suspects all linked by one unique characteristic.'

'What characteristic? What group?'

'The group of people who hate your guts, Cork.'

'Like who, Jim?'

'Like Margot Lang,' Jim says, casually.

'Who's Margot Lang?'

'She's the woman who was driving the red Toyota Hilux.'

My hand instinctively grips Jim's right bicep. 'What the fuck are you talking about?'

'Your bat outta hell,' Jim says. 'We ran the plate, Cork. Didn't need a final letter. Only one red Toyota Hilux in South East Queensland with those five letters and numbers. Margot Lang. Loving wife and mother of three grown-up sons. She rehabilitates racehorses on a property in Fernvale. You might be familiar with her middle son? Kurt Lawson. The twenty-six-year-old father of two you got kicked off the police force after your Walkley Award–winning stories about the death in custody of Brandon Curtis.'

Damn, Noah Cork. You really do have a way with words. I mean, you really do seem rather skilled at ruining lives with your powerful sentences.

'Don't worry, you're not the only one Margot Lang has pointed a bone at,' Jim says. 'She's sent death threats to half the Queensland Police Service. She believes her son is a patsy we hung out to dry. She may not be wrong.'

'You think she could be linked to Tamsin?' I ask.

'Maybe,' Jim replies. 'Maybe not. We've got eyes on her, either way.'

'So that's it, then,' I say. 'You still think the killer is someone I pissed off in the press? Someone who wants to teach me some kinda lesson. So we're back where we started. A suspect list of about a hundred anonymous arseholes who have my face stuck to their basement dartboards.'

Jim unbuckles his seatbelt. Slips out of the passenger seat. Holds the door open as he leans in to talk.

'I'm sending a two-person police detail to your house in the morning,' he says.

'Thanks,' I say. 'I appreciate it. Honestly, Jim, what's your feeling on this? How scared should I be?'

Jim takes a long breath. Leans in further to the car. 'My feeling is that the killer is proud,' he says. 'He doesn't mean you harm.'

'You think it's a *he* after all?'

'Nine times outta ten it's a he,' he says.

Jim reaches for his house keys in his pocket. Considers his words. 'He didn't put that letter in your mailbox because you pissed him off,' Jim says. 'He put that letter in your mailbox because he is exactly what he told you he was in the letter. He's a big fan. He will contact you again. He will contact you soon. That's when you immediately contact me. You understand me, Cork?'

'I understand you, Jim.'

'He doesn't want your life, Cork. He doesn't want your fear. All he wants is your writing. All he needs from you is ink. Do not give it to him.'

Jim goes to shut the car door.

'Hey, Jim,' I say.

'Yeah,' he says.

'I didn't know they had a dog obedience school here in Jubilee.'

'Neither did I,' he says.

I smile warmly. 'Maybe you could take Hercules some time?' I suggest.

England grimaces. 'That dog follows orders just fine,' he says. 'He'll do anything I say.'

'He shits on my lawn three times a week, Jim,' I reason.

'Like I said, he'll do anything I say.' Jim smiles. 'Get some sleep, Cork.'

The car door closes.

*

I see the damage on the Corolla the second I pull into the carport. Hop out to inspect it closely. Run my hands along the car's rear window. Two holes in the car that look like shotgun holes. Hail dents across the car that will never come out.

Lights out when I enter the house. I place the car keys on the kitchen bench and rub my eyes. A bluey white light is coming from Clem's room. I slip my shoes off and pad down the hallway silently in my socks. Open Clem's bedroom door.

'Dad,' Clem whispers, as soon as I enter. 'Don't let her go, Dad. You can't let her go.' She's sitting up in her bed with her legs folded. Our Maglite camping torch rests on her thigh, driving light up to her face.

I sit on the side of her bed. 'Let who go, honey?' I ask.

'Mum,' she whispers.

'Mum's not going anywhere, honey.'

'Not yet, Dad. But soon … she will be … She'll be going home soon, Dad.'

'What are you talking about, Clem? What happened today in the storm? I saw the car. What the hell happened to you two?'

Clem pulls her notebook out from under her blanket, her right thumb bookmarking a page. 'We got a blast, Dad,' she says. 'Not a 2009 blast, but it was a blast. Supercell, I think.'

'It's storm season, honey. It probably won't be the last blast we get this month.'

'Dad, did you know the Jubilee storm of 2009 created winds that reached up to 130 kilometres an hour?' she asks. 'That's the equivalent of a Category 3 cyclone, Dad. The Bureau of Meteorology called it the worst storm to hit Brisbane since 1985.'

I run my left palm along Clem's forehead, partly out of affection, partly to see if she's running a fever.

'What will we do if it happens again?' Clem asks. 'I mean, happens again like 2009?'

'Well, we'll be a bit more prepared this time,' I reply. 'The bureau's pretty good at predicting these things these days. We'll be safe enough, don't worry. Ellis and June said we can all shelter in their place if we ever cop another blast like 2009.'

'Ellis told me his house didn't even get a scratch in 2009. They didn't lose a thing.'

'Well, that's not entirely true,' I say. 'They lost their beloved Sherlock.'

'Who was Sherlock? They have a pet or somethin'?'

'No, Ellis's favourite garden gnome. Sherlock Gnomes.'

Clem giggles too loud.

'Sshhhhhh,' I whisper.

Clem covers her laughter with her hand. Takes a moment to think of something new. There's always something new with Clem Cork.

'Don't you think it makes no sense at all, Dad?' she asks. 'That a storm like that would just come along and pick on

Jubilee like that? There are 190 suburbs in Brisbane. Of all the suburbs it coulda destroyed, why did it choose to destroy ours?'

'I guess that's just how it landed, honey. The gods rolled the dice and everything came up Jubilee.'

'Do you believe that, Dad?'

'Believe what, honey?'

'That the gods did it,' she says. 'Zeus and co. Or Jesus's ol' man. You reckon they were responsible?' She points a finger up to the window by her bed, the curtain pulled across to reveal a night blanket of stars beyond two small palm trees and a swelling viburnum bush. 'You reckon someone up there had a bone to pick with Jubilee?'

'No, honey,' I say. 'I was just saying it was … I dunno … our time. Our … fate.'

'Yeah, fate. Exactly. So it was meant to be?'

'Well … no … what I mean is—'

'Were you scared when our roof came off, Dad?' Clem asks.

I think about the question. Think about Rita and me under the bed in the main bedroom. 'Yeah, I guess I was scared,' I say.

'Was Mum scared?'

I think about that question. Do I tell my youngest daughter the truth? That it's a good question because it has a good answer. The truthful answer is no. I really don't think she was scared. All I remember is how awed by the storm she was. It wasn't fear in her eyes, it was admiration. Not for the violence of it, but for the wonder of it. The stuff that the universe can form, the things that it can build and send our way to remind us to love.

I love you so fuckin' much, Noah Cork.

I can't answer the question.

Clem answers it for me. 'She wasn't scared was she, Dad?' Clem nods her head. 'Did you hear the way Adam Duncan was saying that stuff about Mum this morning, Dad? Did you see the look in his eyes?'

Eyes like fire. Eyes like madness, too.

'Yeah, I saw.'

'Adam said his sisters got all burnt up in that fire,' Clem says. 'He said they still have scar tissue on their forearms and ankles. You ever seen any scars on Mum?'

I shake my head in the torchlight.

'Her skin's immaculate,' Clem says. 'She could be in one of those L'Oréal Revitalift ads if she wanted to.'

Clem whispers to me now. Truth teller. Scoop teller. Born digger. 'She ran into that house three times and she didn't get a single scratch,' Clem says. 'Do you remember that time I broke my arm riding my bike down Goldfinch Crescent?'

'I remember.'

'You took me to St Andrew's and my arm was hurting so bad that I thought I was gonna die and all I wanted was Mum but she couldn't get to me because she was at work and they put me on that hospital bed and I told the doctor that all I needed was my mum because she always takes the pain away and then an hour later Mum came into the hospital room and gave me a hug and she told me she was gonna kiss my arm and the pain would go away and she kissed my arm and it did just that. The pain went away, Dad.'

'Clem, sweetheart,' I say, wrapping my left arm around her neck, 'the doctor gave you an anaesthetic five minutes before Mum got there … Half your body was numb.'

Clem shakes her head. Eyes alight. 'And what about the time

I got my head stuck between those two rusty poles going into the old septic tank on Uncle Walter's farm at Kilcoy and I was so scared because I thought I was gonna have to stay like that forever but then Mum said she was going to use all her super strength to push the poles apart and give me the space to slip my head out and then she pushed the poles with all her might and they moved enough apart for me to slip my head out? It was incredible, Dad. I couldn't believe it. I thought she must have been some kind of superhero.'

'Clem,' I say. 'Listen, we never had the heart to tell you before, but you're probably old enough to know now that your mum was just saying that stuff, honey, to give you the confidence to pull your head out a bit harder. That's all that was, sweetie. You were too scared to pull your head all the way out. Mum helped you.'

Clem turns her face to me. Her bottom lip trembles. Tears well in her eyes but they do not run.

'I know you think your mum's special, Clem,' I say. 'You're dead right about that. She's the most special person I know. But, sweetie, she's probably not quite as special as I think you think she is.' And for some reason, there are tears welling in my eyes now. 'She's just … she's just' – and the tears run down my cheeks now – 'a real bloody good mum.'

Now Clem's tears run and I wipe my tears away from my cheeks with my fingers and with my left forefinger I stop a tear from running all the way down Clem's face to her chin.

She wipes her face on the sleeve of her pyjamas. 'She is that special, Dad,' she says. 'I think she might be so special, in fact, that she might not even belong down here with us. She knows things that nobody else knows. When she looks up at the sky, she sees things that nobody else sees. Have you ever seen her looking up at the sky, Dad? Have you ever seen her, Dad?'

I think of Rita's face when she looked out at that Jubilee microburst, that day in 2009. Of the electricity in her eyes when she saw the pulsing blues and emeralds and silvers inside the storm. 'It's beautiful,' she said. The storm wasn't beautiful, of course. But Rita was. Rita was beautiful that day. Rita is beautiful every day.

I shake my head slowly. 'I dunno, honey,' I say. 'I can't remember how she looks, specifically, when she looks up at the sky.'

'I saw her last month, Dad,' Clem says. 'I saw her lying on the driveway, just staring up at the sky. I thought she musta hurt herself, because she was just lying on the concrete like a dead starfish. And I walked right up to her and I was standing over her, waiting for her to see me, but she didn't even see me because she was looking so hard up at the sky. And now that I think about it, I think she might not have been just staring into space, I think she mighta been communicating.'

'Communicating?' I reply. 'Communicating with who, Clem?'

'The people who come from where she comes from.'

Clem flips open her notepad, licks her thumb and whips through endless pages of furious shorthand.

'I think you're chasing the wrong story, Dad,' she whispers. 'What if Mum turned out to be the greatest scoop anyone's ever dug up?' She grips my right forearm so tight I can feel her fingernails digging into my skin.

Clem points to a rough sketch she's done in her notebook. A vision she clearly felt shorthand notes couldn't fully capture.

A good enough sketch for me to know the car she has drawn is our car, the silver Toyota Corolla. I recognise the carpark. It's the exposed rooftop carpark at Jubilee Plaza. I recognise the woman in the centre of the image. The woman is floating.

Clem whispers. 'The greatest page-one exclusive in the history of the world: MY DAD HAS BEEN MARRIED FOR TWENTY-THREE YEARS TO A GENUINE GOD.'

And now my youngest daughter is scaring me. Her thoughts are scaring me. Her sincerity is scaring me. Her belief in her words. Her belief in her mother.

More thoughts spill from her lips. She consults her notes. 'Today, I asked Mum if we could have hard-shell tacos for dinner because, you know, it's Taco Tuesday, and she said we could, but we had no ingredients, so we went to the shops after we dropped Erin at guitar practice,' she says. 'It got so dark, Dad, but it was only four in the afternoon. The sky went dark grey and then it turned green, Dad. Remember when we saw *Wicked*, Dad, and they had all that green smoke surrounding Elphaba?'

'Yeah, I remember.'

'I asked you on the way home how they make green stage smoke and you said the smoke was just normal stage smoke but they shine a green light through it.'

I nod.

'Well, these were Elphaba clouds, Dad. Normal clouds but with Elphaba light shot through them.'

'Elphaba clouds?'

'Yeah, Elphaba clouds. Witchcraft stuff, Dad.'

She runs her right forefinger under a line of notes. 'There were no spots in the undercover levels of the carpark,' Clem says. 'We had to park on the rooftop. Mum grabbed a brolly from the pocket behind my seat and she hopped out of the car and stared at the sky and there was something in her eyes that made me scared, Dad. I don't know what it was. She wasn't just staring at the clouds; it was like she was staring at someone she knew up there. Some enemy or something that she had up there in the green clouds. I called, "What is it, Mum? What is it?" But she didn't say anything. She just turned towards the shops, like she wanted me to know that we had to hurry.'

Clem flips to another note page. 'We could hear the rain when we were in the shopping centre,' she says. 'It sounded heavy but I didn't think it was anything to be too afraid of. We grabbed a taco kit and some lettuce and tomatoes and corn and mince and a couple of avocados, and Mum filled a trolley with some other supplies: apples, milk, some things for school lunches, big thing of toilet paper. And then she was moving so quick that I couldn't even keep up with her. Just pushing the trolley through the shops to get back to the car. It was like she was racing someone. Some … *thing.* Jasmine Peel's mum said hello to Mum by the eye doctor's and Mum just scurried right past her. Didn't even acknowledge she was there.'

Clem's forefinger stops at a word in her notebook. *Rooftop.* She nods her head twice. 'When we went outside, Mum put the brolly up and started pushing the trolley up the ramp to the rooftop, but she couldn't push the trolley with one hand, so I helped her. But the wind was blowing the brolly off our heads and the rain was smashing into our faces. And Mum didn't say anything because she still wasn't talking, of course, but I really, really wanted her to tell me why we were walking so fast. Then we got to the rooftop and that's when everything went potty.

The sky just went loopy, Dad. It was furious. The moment we got to the rooftop, it was like the sky had just spotted us. And we were the only people up there. Then there was a huge thunderclap and then all these hailstones started slamming into all the parked cars. Thwack. Thwack. Thwack. As big as cricket balls, Dad. One got me right in my shoulder blade.'

She pulls her pyjama shirt down over her right shoulder and shows me a black and purple bruise the size of a golf ball.

'Just as we got to the car, two great big balls of hail smashed through the rear window. Bang! Bang!' Clem slams a fist into her palm and it makes me jump in fright. 'It all happened so fast, Dad. It was like a dream. Erin didn't believe me when I told her, and I get it.'

Clem runs her fingertip under more notes.

'Then what happened, Clem?'

'The wind happened, Dad,' Clem replies. 'It just got so hard that we couldn't keep our feet on the ground. It started pushing us along the rooftop. It spun the trolley around and Mum managed to hold on to the handle. And then I realised what was happening, Dad. The wind wasn't pushing me. It was *pulling* Mum. It was pulling Mum away, Dad. It was trying to take her. Just like the birds were trying to take her.'

'What birds, Clem?'

'The birds at the gold-mining creek,' she says. 'The birds that wanted to kidnap Mum and take her away.'

'Clem … maybe you should get some slee—'

'The wind just kept pulling her and she fought it but then the wind pulled harder and her feet were sliding along the concrete. It was like it was pulling a statue or somethin', Dad. And Mum just kept holding on to the trolley and then I grabbed the front of it and pulled so hard I thought my arms might come out of their sockets and Mum would go barrelling along the rooftop and smash into a car or something. But I kept her there … until the wind lifted her up.'

'Lifted her up?' I ask, struggling to mask my scepticism.

'Lifted her up,' Clem replies, nodding, eyes wide.

She hands me her notebook. She wants me to read the shorthand notes for myself.

'This is what it felt like,' she says.

I see the images the words conjure up. A rooftop. A storm. A Coles grocery trolley. A windswept twelve-year-old girl pulling hard on the front of the trolley, her mother, the love of my life, clinging to the trolley's handle, her arms outstretched, day dress billowing in the storm, torso and legs and sandshoes aloft, her feet higher than her head. Floating, held to the earth only by her grip on a ridiculous suburban shopping cart, and the strength of her daughter. If Rita had let go of the trolley, Clem says, she would have flown off into the swirling and violent sky.

Then one last sentence in capital letters and underlined, at the bottom of the page of notes. A sentence I've seen before. *'GRAVITY LET ME GO!'*

'Did your mother say that, Clem?' I ask. 'Did she speak to you?'

'No,' she replies. 'That was moon-time connection, again. She told me that without telling me that. I knew it was what she was thinking.'

Damn, Noah Cork, you got your hands full with this one, don't ya? Kid's not playing with a full deck, is she? Stubbie short of a six-pack. Sanga short of a picnic. Be gentle. Don't dismiss her dreaming. It will only make things worse. She needs your understanding. The least you could do for her is empathise. She is scared, Cork. Her mother has not spoken for a week. Her father communicates with murderers. This is all your fault, of course. Are these not merely all your anxieties passed down from your mother and your father to you and from you, now, to your beloved Clem? Do not dismiss your daughter's dreaming.

'I keep seeing that message on the bathroom mirror,' I say.

'Me too,' Clem says. 'I knew she was saying it without saying it, Dad. And I screamed at Mum to hold on. "Hold on, Mum," I said. "Don't let go. Don't let go, Mum." But then I felt like my fingers were slipping because it was so wet and the rain was falling so hard and the wind was so, so mad and I begged for it all to stop. I begged the enemy up in the sky: "Stop it," I said. "Stop it! Leave her alone. Leave my mum alone!" But I knew someone in the sky wanted her back. I get it. I'd want Mum back, too. And Mum was just staring at me, Dad. She was just so … *normal*. She wasn't even scared. But then I saw her fingers slipping on the trolley, so I screamed, "Nooooo, Mummmm, noooo, don't go, *please* … *don't* … *gooooo*." And just when I thought she was gonna let go, it all … *stopped*.'

Clem looks at me and curls the left edge of her closed lips upwards.

'The wind just dropped and Mum fell onto the concrete like a bag of spuds,' she says. 'Splat.'

Clem slaps the notebook shut.

I wrap my arms around my daughter. Kiss her scalp and fight the tears that want to fall from my eyes.

'She must love us so much, Dad,' Clem says.

'Of course she loves us, Clem.'

'Do you remember all that stuff Erin was saying in the hospital that day? She rattled off all the things Mum does every day just to keep it all going. All those things we never see. She could go anytime.' Clem looks out her window again to the night stars. 'She could just fly away and be miraculous up there where she belongs. But every single day … she chooses to stay. She chooses us, Dad. She doesn't go. She stays.'

'Are you all right, honey?' I ask.

She nods. 'I'm all right, Dad. Are you all right, Dad?'

'I'm all right, Clem. Let's talk more about this in the morning. I really need to sleep now. I can't make sense of anything anymore.'

'Yeah, I know, Dad,' Clem says. 'Ever since Mum stopped talking, nothing's made sense. Mum always makes sense when she talks.'

I rest my head for just a moment on the right shoulder of my daughter.

'Do you think Mum's ever gonna talk again, Dad?'

'Yeah, she'll talk again,' I say. A long yawn. 'We just need to give her time.'

'Time for what?'

'Time for silence.'

I put my finger to my lips. 'Ssshhhhh.' Kiss her forehead.

She turns to her side and sinks her head into her pillow. I take her notepad and her torch and place them upon her bedside table. I yawn again and close my eyes. I'll rest here for just a moment, arm wrapped around my daughter. Just a moment.

'It's not a statement, Dad,' Clem says from her pillow.

'What's not a statement, honey?' I mumble.

'*Gravity let me go.* I thought it was a statement. I thought she was trying to tell us that she felt like gravity let her go. I thought she thought she had been let go by us, let go by the earth. I thought she was making a statement. But it's not a statement, Dad.'

'What is it then, Clem?'

'It's a request.'

The words hang in the darkness of the bedroom.

'Don't let her go, Dad.'

'Sshhhhh, honey. Ssshhhh.'

'You can't let her go, Dad. Please don't let her go.'

'I won't, Clem. I'll never let her go. I promise.'

'Wooooshhh, Dad.'

'Wooooshhh, Clem.'

And then my brief rest turns into a deep sleep that lasts for what's left of the night.

*

At 7.12 a.m., I'm woken by my phone buzzing inside the left pocket of my jeans. Clem is snoring softly beside me. I check the caller ID flashing on the phone screen: *Carmen – St Vincent's Home Care.*

Fuck. The next thirty seconds of my life unfold in slow motion. A simple exchange.

'Hi, Carmen.'

'Noah …' A long moment of silence. Carmen cries.

'Carmen … What is it, Carmen?'

'It's your father, Noah … he's … he's …'

He's gone.

EIGHTEEN

> *Don't be surprised by how many people will be perfectly willing to talk to you directly after the sudden loss of a cherished loved one. They are not talking to you because you are special. It's not because of your warm and comforting smile or your well-crafted questions. They are, in fact, not talking to you at all. They are talking through you. You are the vessel through which they are talking to the loved one they just lost.*
>
> – Rutledge, *Journalism Practices and Principles*

Woorim Beach at sunset. Wind blowing the quarter flaps of an old navy-blue suit that's too small for me. Me and every person on this planet that I love lined up at the edge of the rolling surf like soldiers before a firing squad, all of us hoping this will be over quick. Rita. Clem. Erin. My sister, Meg, who gave a touching eulogy for Dad inside the Little Flower Church at Bongaree on the calm side of Bribie Island. Meg spoke about a one-armed mud crab that Dad caught in a pot in the Pumicestone Passage. This mud crab's single remaining claw was the size of a sledge hammer, and Dad certainly pondered the gastronomic joy he would experience in devouring the salty white flesh inside that claw, but he couldn't bring himself to end that indefatigable crab's life, awed as he was by the efforts of any creature that could survive with only one fighting arm in the underwater maximum-security prison yard that is the Pumicestone Passage mangroves. Dad likened the feat to climbing the cliffs of Gallipoli armed with a butter knife. He left that crab in the pot for two months. Fed it a wholesome diet of frozen mullet heads and raw kangaroo meat. Gave him a name. Milo. Just another 'armless joke at the Venus de Milo's expense. Milo attracted a dozen sorry muddies into the pot, all of which felt the wrath of his Tysonesque right hook. Then Dad felt his plucky prize fighter deserved his retirement. He set Milo free, only to catch him two more times in the same crab pot over the course of the following year. 'Milo missed me,' Dad said.

I'm holding my father in my hands. We went with the biodegradable urn for $22.95. It looks like the kind of cylindrical cardboard container you'd normally see holding a quality whisky. Meg leans forward from the line of loved ones and nods at me. I nod back and roll the legs of my suit pants up to my kneecaps. Look to my wife and my daughters. Rita nods in silence. Clem weeps in silence, rubs her red eyes. Erin offers three words to the beach wind. 'Love you, Pop.'

I make my way into the whitewash. Hold the urn in two hands and nearly lose my footing in a stingray hole beneath the water. I need to go deeper because I want to reach a place where the waves will swallow Dad up in one crashing gulp and not a series of bites that will leave his leftovers spreading across the water in full view of my daughters.

The waves are now reaching my waist. This cheap navy suit has had it. Some complex interplay occurs between my lungs and larynx. Something between my heart and my soul and my past and my present coming out of my mouth as words. *Talk.*

'Hey, Mum,' I say, the sound of my words mercifully drowned out by the crashing waves. 'It's me, Noah. Dad said you might be listenin', so in case you are, I just wanted to tell you that … ahhhh … Dad asked me to do this. I'm doing it for him, because I told him I'd bring him back and … you know, you always told me to keep my word. He said he wanted to be with you. He said you were the only home he ever had, which I thought was a nice thing to say. I told him he didn't deserve to be with you, but … I don't know … maybe he earned the right. All that drinkin' he did for you. *All that thinkin'.* He kept your picture above his bed for thirty years. I don't know if that means anything to you' – a flood of tears from my eyes – 'but it meant something to me.'

I take a deep breath. Turn back to see my family on the shoreline. Rita smiling at me. Clem raises a closed fist in encouragement.

I turn back to the water. 'Anyway, we're all going good,' I say, and let that line sit for a moment.

'No, that's not true, Mum. My life's a mess. I wrote a book, Mum. It keeps climbing the book charts while my life keeps sliding down the toilet. Four nights ago I was struck on the head by an anonymous killer. Ten nights ago, I was nearly run over by an aggrieved mum who looked like Meat Loaf. Clem's believing in fantasies and Rita's flat-out stopped talking to me.'

I shrug. Laugh at the sea.

'Clem asked me the funniest question the other day. She asked me if I'd ever handed Rita the crowbar. I didn't know what to say to her, Mum. How could I tell my kid that I never did hand her mum the crowbar? How would Clem ever understand that some crowbars are just too heavy to hold, ya know? How could I say what I did, Mum? How could I say that to Rita and expect her to understand? I get paid to string sentences together. That's what I'm supposed to know how to do. I tried to say it, Mum. I tried a hundred times to say it out loud. I've edited that sentence down a dozen times over the course of two decades. I've cut that sentence back to four simple words. *Just four friggin' words.* And not once have I been able to say those words to my wife.'

And I try to say these words out loud now to the sea, to the universe, to my mother. And still I fail.

I drop my head and stare into the ocean water. The flash of something silver – maybe even a healthy-sized bream – swimming past my bare feet. A wave builds before me and I scatter Dad's cremated remains across the surface of the water. The stuff looks like grey-coloured sand. Not fine, but coarse and gritty, a bit like Phil Cork, I guess, back when he was flesh and blood.

'I love you, Dad,' I say, emptying every grain of his remains into the sea. I check the bottom of the container, shake out some leftover grains stubbornly wedged into a fold. 'Don't get stung by no bluebottles.'

I wade back through the whitewash and join my family once more on the wet sand. A line-up of my loved ones looking out to a loved one lost. Me next to Rita next to Clem next to Erin next to Meg. Five of us staring blankly at the sea.

And now a sixth among us.

'*Ssssssss* ...'

I turn my head right to find Tamsin's skeleton standing beside me. She, too, stares at the sea. Then turns to me and tries again to speak. '*Ssssssss* ...'

And now I need to walk away. And now I need to run. Feet trudging through white sand. Clem calling after me, 'Dad! Dad!'

I run all the way to our car, parked at the Bribie Island Surf Club. The Corolla has been baking in the heat of the midday sun. I slip into the driver's seat and slam the door behind me. Drop my head in my hands and rub my eyes. Now my hands are wet with my tears. I lift my head and turn to the skeleton sitting beside me in the passenger seat. And I say the four words I will never say to my wife.

'I killed my mother.'

NINETEEN

Sometimes you'll want to give up on the story. Sometimes things won't make sense. Sources contradict sources. Information negates information. Discoveries dismiss discoveries. But you will stand firm in all the inevitable storms of self-doubt and self-recrimination. The storms will pass and there, like a light shining through the blackest cloud, will be truth.

– Rutledge, *Journalism Practices and Principles*

The curry-powder dust has disappeared from the leaves of my frangipani tree. The leaves are sunshine-strong. Summer-strong. These are days of fear and silence. Days of nothing and everything. Summer days of heat and lightning. The news speaks of predicted storms and floods. Unprecedented summer destruction. Insurance ads every ten minutes on the telly. Ready your houses. Don't go near fallen power lines. If it's flooded, forget it.

The news speaks of the disappearance of Miles De Jonge. Jim England and Georgia Long keep their investigative cards close to their chests. Jim gives a bizarre and awkward press conference in the Roma Street police headquarters, where he brazenly withholds all mention of the fact that I saw Miles wrapped in plastic on the day of his disappearance. He doesn't mention me at all.

'Until we establish the exact details surrounding Mr De Jonge's disappearance, we will be referring to this as a missing persons case,' Jim informs the gathering media. 'This is not a murder investigation.'

And that's precisely when the gathering media know that it is very much a murder investigation. The circus returns to Jubilee. Morning show crosses from outside Miles's house on Butcherbird Close. Press photographers papping Steph De Jonge as she exits Poseidon's seafood shop with a kilogram of Moreton Bay prawns. I wake each day to find a police car parked in front of my house, two officers sipping coffees and eating ham and cheese toasties and acting like there's nothing at all unusual about a police car parked in the same spot in my street, eight hours a day, seven days a week.

Ricky Waverly knocks on my front door at 7.15 a.m. on Friday morning.

I do my best to avoid Ricky Waverly whenever possible because he's an ambitious freelance-journalist snake charmer who would wedge a foot inside the devil's door if he could just convince one of his many criminal contacts to dish the dark lord's address. I avoid Ricky Waverly because he reminds me of myself, and I do my best to avoid myself whenever possible.

'That patrol car's been out front for a few days now, Cork,' he snarls.

'Just precautionary, Ricky,' I say.

'Precautionary … because the cops fear the killer's had a crack at Miles and now you're next?'

'No, just precautionary, Ricky,' I repeat.

'Precautionary enough for the cops to make regular patrols of your daughters' school?'

'Where'd you hear that, Ricky?'

'Little birdy. Same little birdy who told me you visited Miles on the day he disappeared.'

'Chirpy little birdy you got there, Ricky. You workin' up a feature?'

'Always. You know how it is. The story never ends for us, right, Cork?'

'Well, I wouldn't be so sure about that, Ricky. You want some help with your ending?'

'Sure.'

'Here's a final line for ya. Write this down.'

Ricky whips a pen to his notepad.

'*It was then that Mr Cork slammed the door in my face*,' I say.

And I slam the door in Ricky Waverly's face.

*

The Gecko Street neighbours start to complain about a police car being parked in their street each day. Ellis wants answers, but I can't give him any.

'You must know something, Noah?' he asks, standing in his pyjamas on the nature strip.

'I don't know anything, Ellis,' I insist, opening my letterbox to find nothing inside it but an energy bill.

A removal truck pulls up outside the house to our left, the home once owned by the late Carol Myers-Ryan. Two men in fluorescent yellow polos begin hauling a fridge into the house at number 37.

'Have you met the new neighbours yet?' Ellis asks.

'Not yet, Ellis,' I reply.

'Lovely couple,' he says. 'Think they'll fit in nicely.'

He looks at the police car.

'Not the nicest welcome you're giving them, Noah, I must say,' Ellis says. 'Leafy street. Mountain glimpses. And our very own police surveillance unit.'

'It won't be here for too much longer, Ellis,' I predict. 'It'll be gone as soon as they find Tamsin's killer.'

'Well, I hope they find the killer before the Gecko Street Christmas drinks,' he says. 'We're hosting this year.'

*

A brief World War III erupts in the hallway between Clem and Erin. The hallway is the traditional location for most fights between my daughters. It's an elbow-rub thing. Close quarters. Too many opportunities for mortal combat.

'You wore them, didn't you?' Clem screams. She has one arm and a thigh holding Erin's bedroom door open. Clem has forgotten where she put her red suede Adidas Gazelles – the ones with the unicorn stickers – and she's accusing her sister of leaving them at the house of her best friend, Isabella Dyer, who had her sixteenth birthday on the weekend.

'I didn't wear your stupid Gazelles,' Erin says, forcing the door closed with two hands. 'How would I even squeeze my feet into your shrimp shoes?'

'Bitch!' Clem howls.

'Hobbit!' Erin replies, slamming her door shut.

Clem weeps at the end of the hallway and turns to me, pointing her finger. 'This is all *your* fault,' she screams.

'What did I do?' I ask.

'You didn't discipline her enough,' she replies, wiping her eyes. 'You raised a fuckin' shoe stealer, *Daaad.* Too caught up in your precious stories to get caught up in being a real dad. It's no good, Dad. It's all bad. It's all real *baaadd … Daaad.*'

Clem marches into her bedroom, slams the door shut.

*

Clem hasn't been herself lately. Not to deflect from potentially valid accusations of poor fathering, but she really *hasn't* been herself lately. Clem won't leave Rita's side. She follows her mum everywhere. Down the hall. Down to the shops. Into bed. I tell her three times a day that her mother is not going anywhere. I tell her that nothing is going to happen to her mother while she's at school, but she doesn't believe me. I tell her not to be scared by the police car outside our house. I tell her not to bend for the butcher who has, at once, ruined my life and handed me a bestseller. I tell Clem to be brave in the face of the depraved and anonymous sicko bully who has, quite perplexingly, so far managed to evade the apparently quite short and stubby arm of the law.

'I'm not worried about him, Dad,' she says.

'Then what are you worried about, Clem?'

'You wouldn't believe me if I told you, Dad,' she says. 'You'd just call me crazy.'

'I would never call you crazy.'

'I *heard* you call me crazy, Dad.'

She's got me on a technicality. She's got me where it hurts. Three days ago, she heard me arguing with Rita by the clothesline in the backyard. I thought we were alone, me and my absurd one-way talking behind a hanging white bed sheet.

'This silence has to end, Rita,' I said. 'I think it's gone too far. You're scaring Clem, you know. You're putting all kinds of thoughts in her head. You're gonna send the poor kid round the bend.'

'I said "round the bend",' I say to Clem. 'I didn't say "crazy".'

'I looked up what "round the bend" means, *Daaad*,' Clem says. 'The roads leading up to English lunatic asylums were always bendy, as opposed to English estate driveways, which were always straight! You think I'm on my way to the loony bin, *Daaad*? Well, at least I don't go around picking fights with murderers! If I'm goin' round the bend, then you better be coming with me, bro.'

*

We receive a phone call from Petrina Boyle, guidance counsellor at Clem's school.

'Mr Cork,' she says. 'Your daughter, Clem, has been caught trying to leave the school grounds.'

Clem put her hand up in modern history class and asked to go to the toilet. She walked past the toilets and right on to the school gates.

Petrina Boyle asks for a meeting. I blame my wife. Because I'm too stupid and proud and blind and tired and confused to blame myself.

'How did you expect her to react?' I ask Rita, driving to Clem's school. 'How fucking terrifying must it be for a twelve-year-old child just to see her mum go mute one afternoon? You know she thinks you're some kind of hero or something? She thinks her mum can bend steel poles. How the fuck do I explain that to some guidance officer head shrink? *I'm so sorry our daughter was found leaving your hallowed school grounds. You see, her mum recently engaged in a season of selective mutism, for reasons which remain a mystery, and it seems Clem has responded to such disturbing parental behaviour by convincing herself that her mum is, quote unquote, special. She has come to believe that her mum's some kind of superwoman who needs protecting from those who dwell beyond the clouds, where her mum might also belong. No, Petrina, we have never consumed hallucinogenic drugs of any kind, why the fuck do you ask?*'

Rita stares out her window at the clear blue sky. This is how she looks when she looks at the sky. Rita remains silent.

Petrina Boyle informs us across her office desk that our youngest daughter is suffering from an acute form of 'school refusal'. 'Well, to be more nuanced – this is, after all, a nuanced world, is it not – I would say she is suffering more from a case of what I call *school can't*,' Petrina says. 'I believe she's experiencing a kind of separation anxiety.'

She nods at Rita across the desk.

'It seems to be driven by something more than Rita's ongoing selective silence,' Petrina says. 'Have there been any incidents lately that might have made her anxious at the thought of separating from her mother?'

'Clem and her mum were caught in a vicious hailstorm on the rooftop carpark of Jubilee Plaza,' I say. 'I think she believes that storm was sent to carry Rita away.'

'Away where, Mr Cork?'

'Away to where she believes Rita came from.'

'Where did Rita come from?'

'Well, nobody really knows,' I say. 'She was left at the door of the Mater Mothers when she was six months old.'

Petrina leans in closer to her desk. 'So, perhaps, presented with a void inside the troubling mystery of the origins of a woman she cares for deeply, she has chosen to fill that void with her own fabulous interpretations.'

'Yeah, somethin' like that. So what should I do about this *school can't* issue?'

'Well, a few days off school is not going to do her much harm,' Petrina says. 'But it is very important that days don't turn into weeks and weeks don't turn into months. Prolonged school refusal can often lead to entrenched school refusal. Separation anxiety can become separation *panic*. That can be somewhat … *testing*.'

Rita blames me. She doesn't openly say it's my fault because she's still not talking. But I know she thinks it's my fault. There are more ways of talking to your husband than just talking to your husband. She tells me it's my fault by the way she brushes her teeth beside me at the bathroom sink. She tells me it's my fault by the way she stirs sugar into her tea.

*

A few days off school is not going to do her much harm. So it's been a few days now. Three full school days in a row. *Separation anxiety can become separation panic*. This is all my fault. This is all my anonymous source's fault. This is all my fault.

I stare into the bathroom mirror after my morning shower. The condensation message has vanished from the bathroom mirror. But I can still see it in my head.

Gravity

let

me

go

I turn on the ABC news app on my phone, which is leaning on a packet of make-up remover pads on the washbasin. A severe thunderstorm warning has been issued for the Gold Coast, Brisbane and Sunshine Coast regions. An Irishman from the weather bureau is speaking about the summer's most devastating supercell, due to sweep into Brisbane from 3 p.m. this afternoon.

'This is a high-end phenomenon,' the meteorologist says. 'Damaging winds expected to exceed gusts of a hundred kilometres per hour. High likelihood of hail and extreme rainfall. We urge all residents of South East Queensland to take appropriate safety precautions.'

I tug on a jet-black nose hair that's hanging from my left nostril like the rope on a church bell and whisper necessary words to the bathroom mirror, fearlessly eyeballing the blue-eyed man who is solely responsible for all that is terrifying and wondrous in my life. 'Noah Cork, you jittery, loose-tongued kook,' I say. '*Do not pussy out on me now.* You have done nothing wrong. The scoop of your lifetime landed in your letterbox and you did what you were supposed to do. You did your job. So you go out there now and fix this shit. This is not your fau—'

How in fuck is it possibly not your fault, Cork? You were dancing with the devil while your angels forgot how to fly. You don't understand them. You never have. You're just another stupid bloke always leading with your mouth when you shoulda been leading with your heart. You don't understand the very love of your life. You barely even know her. How could you possibly get it so wrong with Rita, Cork? How could you possibly miss all this? You don't have the faintest clue about her, do you? Who she is. What makes her tick. Where she's going. Where she wants to go and who the fuck's not letting her go there. Maybe you should just let her go, Cork. *Gravity let me go.*

And sorry for the wake-up call, you pitiful and blind hack, but have you considered for a single second that it might be you she's been directing her request to all this time? *Let me go, goddamn you, Noah Cork!*

Noah

let

me

go

Or could it be a request from someone else, Cork? Hang on a dang second here! Are you sure it wasn't you who wrote those words on the mirror, Cork? Are you sure it's not you, Cork, who feels so unbound, so released, so detached, so … let go?

Noah

let

me

g—

*

I dress for the day in my bedroom: blue jeans, white T-shirt, sneakers. Look through the blinds of the bedroom window. See Rita watering a dozen pot plants she's gathered into one easy-to-soak grouping. Study her movements between two slats in the blinds. What was it that my dying father told me? Could any man possibly ever know what's really going on inside the mind of the woman he loves? *All you have to do is hold her hand and not let it go.*

I won't let her go, Clem. I promise.

I stop in the hallway outside our bedroom. Guess Clem is sleeping. Guess Clem is taking today off, too. That'll be four school days off in a row. I guess her mum has decided this. She hasn't told me. I haven't said a word to Rita in three days, either. See how she likes it.

I carefully open Clem's bedroom door. I like to see her when she's sleeping. The peace of it. The calm of it. She is untouched by the world when she sleeps. Unchangeable and unburdened. I like to stare at her cheeks and her temples and wonder what vivid dream she is conjuring in her busy imagination factory of a brain, what wondrous dream I will later see depicted in Posca paint pen on the door of the fridge. But when I open her bedroom door, I see that she is not sleeping at all. She's lying flat on her belly on her bed. Elbows up, carving something into her wooden bedhead. A message. She sees me enter. Stiff white rabbit in a morning headlight. Then she slips her hands under her blanket. Drops her head on her pillow. Closes her eyes. *If I can't see him, then he can't see me.*

I lean down to read the sentence she has carved into the bedhead.

Gravity let m—

Knife carved. Blade carved. Something small and pointy that I didn't catch sight of.

'Give it to me, Clem?'

'What?' she asks, eyes still closed.

I put my hand out. 'I won't ask again, Clem. Give it to me.'

She keeps her eyes closed as her hand slips out from beneath her blanket. She hands me a small red Victorinox Swiss Army knife.

'I'm sorry, Dad,' she says. 'It's to keep Mum safe. It's to keep us all safe.'

I stare at the knife in my palm. Tiny flecks of wood still stuck to the tip of the blade.

'Put your uniform on, Clem,' I say. 'You're going to school.'

Clem's eyes open. Clem sits up. 'What?' she exclaims. 'But I can't. I've got *school can't.*'

'Bullshit,' I say. 'You're going to school.' I hold the Victorinox up. 'And I'll be talking to Ashton Gillan's parents about how we can organise a refund for this piece of junk.'

I slip the knife in my pocket and leave the room, closing the door harder than I intended behind me. I hear Clem's scream halfway down the hallway.

'All your fault! ALLLL. YOURRRR. FAULT.'

Then a knock on our front door. Too early for a knock on our front door. Deep breath. March to the front door. Open it, just a crack.

'Hello, neighbour!'

A man and a woman standing on our porch. I know that man's face. Pure white hair. Bowl cut, parted down the middle. Sixty going on six. White eyebrows. The tip of his tongue hangs out his mouth when he smiles at me. A woman by his right shoulder. Her hair is the same white as the man's. Long and flowing, not styled. She's wearing a yellow singlet top, blue denim shorts and gardening clogs, the soles of which are covered in black soil. Both of them are wearing yellow leather rigger gloves, also covered in black soil. Sweaty faces and pale, sun-reddened skin. Nordic skin.

'Good to see you again,' the man says. He hands me a jar of homemade jam wrapped in a bow of gold ribbon. An old Nescafé coffee jar, white square sticker on the brown plastic lid: *Wild Plum*. 'We just moved in next door,' the man says, beaming. He points at the jam jar now in my hands. 'Where I come from, it's the newcomers who bring gifts to the neighbourhood they're moving into.'

I know the face, but I can't remember where from exactly. Something in his eyes and his smile causing my spine to tingle.

Then he laughs and it's the laugh that colours in my blank memory spots.

'You don't remember me, do you?' he adds.

I remember. I recall. I see him now. The man with the pure white hair laughing in the carpark of the State Library.

'It's me, Axel,' he says, pointing at his own chest. 'Axel Olsson.' He points at the woman standing at his side. Her hand is now resting on his shoulder. 'This is my wife, Deirdre.'

'Hello, neighbour,' she says.

I'm too confused to form a satisfactory sentence in my mind. One sentence comes out as two.

'Hi, you … neighbour … *too*.'

Axel beams. 'Remember, we met in the State Library carpark,' he says. 'You signed a copy of your book.'

'*Jubilee forever!*' Deirdre giggles, punching the air with her fist.

'I see that *Anonymous Source* has been storming the book charts!' Axel says. 'Congratulations on all your success. You must be over the moon.'

I don't respond. With as little expression on my face as possible, I'm silently trying to understand the reasons why Axel Olsson, sole survivor of the 1983 Kidwell Street massacre, has decided to be my next-door neighbour.

'I hope you're giving that anonymous source a cut of the royalties,' Axel says. He winks.

I stare into his wide blue eyes. Why did you do this? Why did you move into my street?

'Noah?' Axel says. 'You there? Noah?' He clicks his fingers in front of my face the way a hypnotist might.

'Sorry,' I say. 'I'm just a little … Axel … You moved … into the house next …'

He nods twice, tongue hanging from his bottom lip like a puppy dog's.

'You better believe it,' he says. 'We had the big five-bedroom dream home in Barley Close and that was good for a lifetime of raising the kids, but then they flew the coop and then Deirdre just woke up one day and said she didn't want to look after such a big place anymore. We started looking at places to downsize to and, wouldn't you know it, a gorgeous little three-bedder popped up on beautiful Gecko Street. Imagine how delighted I was when we discovered, upon closer inspection, that the place was right next door to my favourite Brisbane true-crime writer!'

Axel wraps his arm around Deirdre's waist, shakes his head over his good fortune.

'It was meant to be,' Deirdre says.

They rub the tips of their noses together. I can't bear to give this display of affection more than a fleeting glance.

'Did you read my book?' Axel asks.

'Your book?'

'My book, *Improbable Cause*,' he says.

A flash of a book cover in my head. Themis. Goddess of justice.

'Yeah … umm … of course … your book,' I say. 'The one about all the … unsolved … suburban Brisbane murders.'

He waves a forefinger in front of my face. 'You didn't read it, did you?' Axel asks.

'I … ummm … yeah …'

'You didn't read it!' Axel says.

'No … well … I've been—'

'You've been a busy little bluebird,' Deirdre says.

What did she just call me?

'Excuse me … What did you …'

Axel shakes his head at me. 'Naughty little lemon drop,' he says. 'Never mind, maybe one day you can read it and give me some feedback. I'd be so honoured to hear the thoughts of a bestselling true-crime writer.'

'What did you just call me, Axel?'

'What?' Axel asks.

'You just called me "lemon drop".'

'Did I?'

Axel turns to his wife. A puzzled look on her face.

'Yes,' I say. 'You did.' Eyes to Deirdre now. 'And you just called me "bluebird".'

'Did I?' she replies. She puts a hand to her mouth. 'How careless of me.' She giggles, embarrassed. 'It's just what we call you at home. We've become quite the fans of your work. We can't get enough of this Tamsin Fellows case. It's all just so … umm … so … so … oh, I'm so lost for words … What would you call it, Axel?'

He turns to me with a smile, something knowing in it. 'So close to home,' he says.

He almost laughs but works hard to bury his laughter. And something about this inner work makes me shiver. I want to close the door. I want these people to leave my porch. I want to move out of my house immediately. I want to float off beyond the clouds.

Gravity

let

me

go

'I see your patrol car is a little late to arrive this morning,' Axel says.

'It is?' I reply. 'I hadn't noticed.'

Gravity

let

me

go

I stare into Axel's turquoise-blue eyes. Silence for now. We both nod.

'Welcome to the neighbourhood, Axel,' I say. I go to shut the door. 'Sorry, my daughter's running late for school.'

'Yes, of course,' Axel says. 'Feel free to come on over, anytime. We'd love to fix you and your wife dinner sometime. We could talk more about the note I gave you.'

'The note? I'm sorry, what note?'

'The note I left in the book for you,' he says. 'The list of names.'

'Yes!' I say. 'Of course. The list of names. Yeah, yeah. I will very much look forward to that.'

Close the door, Cork. These people gimme the creeps. Close the door. Close the door.

'Okay, bye,' I say. 'Welcome to Gecko Street.'

And as the door swings shut, Axel and Deirdre Olsson remain standing in place, staring at me, their smiles fading to a strange and hollow blankness just as the door closes. Hollow. Like a tin man without a heart. Hollow. Like a rattling skeleton moving with nothing inside it. Hollow. Like a true-crime writer without a clue.

I close the front door and rub my eyes. Keep them closed and shake my head. Open my eyes again to find Clem standing before me in her Harry Styles nightie.

'Who was that?' she asks.

'Our new neighbours.'

'They sound weird.'

'Don't worry about them,' I say, then point at her nightie. 'Why aren't you in your uniform?'

*

An hour later, Clem drags her feet as I lead her to the school administration block. Her head is down when we reach the late-arrivals sign-in desk. The school attendance officer, Kat Price, wears a telephone earpiece and chews gum as she taps on her keyboard.

'Hi Kat,' I say. 'Just gonna need a pink slip for Clem. We're running a little late this morning.'

Kat spends ten full seconds running her eyes over Clem. 'I

thought she was assessed as having school refusal disorder,' Kat says.

'*Disorder* seems a little strong, doesn't it?' I reply.

Kat chews her gum, shrugs her shoulders. Turns her head back to her computer screen. Taps her fingers on her keyboard. Points at her screen. 'Yep, there she is. Clementine Cork. Year 7 Blue. "Displaying signs of school refusal behavioural disorder. Indefinite absence."'

'Well, it would seem, Kat, that I've come down with an indefinite case of daddy refusal disorder. There is no reason whatsoever that Clem can't go to school today.'

Clem leans over the sign-in desk. 'Truth be told, I don't really have a disorder as such, Kat,' she says. 'My biggest problem is that my father is weird. He's more interested in dead people than me. Just gimme the pink slip so I can get him off my back.'

Kat Price turns to me for some kind of parental explanation.

I smile defiantly. 'I came for the love,' I say. 'I stayed for the gratitude.'

*

I pull the Yaris back into the carport on Gecko Street. Our police surveillance car arrived while I was driving Clem to school. I nod to the two young patrol officers as I scoot across my driveway.

Now where did I put that book? I rush inside the house to the kitchen table. There's a stack of books and letters that have piled up over the past month, towering and unstable, pushed against the wall on the left edge of the kitchen bench. Self-published books sent by readers to the publishers of my problematic debut work of non-fiction. They come with typed and handwritten letters. Theories on who killed Tamsin Fellows. Some letters written by nuts and kooks and cranks. Story ideas for my next true-crime book. Essays on why Neil Fellows should be placed behind bars immediately. Essays on why I should be placed behind bars immediately. Not the worst idea in the world. The publishers didn't send me the letter they got from a fifty-five-year-old recently divorced Port Adelaide man who confessed to Tamsin's murder. That one was handed to the police.

Not here. So where the hell did I put that book? Honestly, Cork, you'd lose your noggin if it wasn't stapled to your neck. The glovebox, you clod. Remember? You said you'd read the book, and you made a big show of placing it safely in the glovebox of the Yaris and that's exactly where it has stayed for a month, ya big fibber. Ya big falsifier. Ya big storyteller.

The glovebox. I rush back out the front door to the carport. Sit in the front passenger seat of the Yaris. Open the glovebox and see the image of the blind goddess, Themis, and her scales of justice. *Improbable Cause* by Axel Olsson. I flip open the softback self-published book and land upon the dedication page.

For my mother, Abigail Olsson.

A folded note falls in my lap.

Dear Mr Cork,

Did you know 38,000 Australians go missing every year?

Greer Payne.

Shane Meakin.

Peter Renwick.

Three inexplicably missing persons from Jubilee across the course of thirty years. Three names readily found on the Australian Federal Police's Missing Persons search engine. Each name unfortunately and unofficially relegated to that useful police officer's catch-all closer: 'suspected suicide'. Maybe your anonymous source deserves more respect, Mr Cork, than you have hitherto afforded him.

With thanks and admiration,

Axel Olsson

I rush back into the house. Flip my laptop open at the dining room table, hold the concrete apple in my right hand as I wait for my home screen to load. A single word bouncing through my brain. *Respect. Respect.* What the fuck does he mean by *respect*? Who the fuck does this guy think he is? That look upon their dumb faces when the door was closing. Aliens. Invaders. Aliens from beyond the clouds. My new Gecko Street neighbours. A home-screen image of Rita and Erin and Clem in beanies, posing for a photograph I took of them by the balancing rock at the summit of The Pyramid, a granite peak that towers over Girraween National Park in Queensland's granite belt.

Three names in Axel Olsson's letter. Three former residents of Jubilee.

I google the first name. *Greer Payne.* Hyperlinked blue headlines from newspapers and online websites.

UNIVERSITY PRIZE WINNER, MISSING.

COMMUNITY PRAYS FOR GREER

My eyes clocking keywords and sentences.

Home in Todd Street, Jubilee.
4 September 1989.
Divers and blood-detection dogs to continue search.

A grainy 1980s photograph of Greer Payne and a profile on the Australian Federal Police's Missing Persons web page. Bright smile. Big hair. Hairspray and curls. The sort of all-business photograph found in the top left corner of a résumé. Her name in blue block lettering.

GREER PAYNE
Missing since: 4 September 1989
Last seen: QLD
Responsible jurisdiction: QLD
Year of birth: 1968
Age now: 57
Gender: Female
Height: 167 cm
Build: Thin
Hair: Brown
Eyes: Brown
Complexion: Medium
Circumstances: On the afternoon of 4 September 1989, three days after winning the inaugural Williams Rayner Prize for Queensland's architectural student of the year, 21-year-old Greer Payne was last seen by a student walking along Albert Street towards Queen Street Mall's underground bus station. She never made it home to her house in Todd Street, Jubilee, where she lived with her parents, Harry and Noelene Payne, who were travelling abroad at the time of Greer's disappearance.

Greer has not been seen since, nor has she made contact with family or friends. There are grave concerns for her welfare.

I keep this page open. Open another search page and type the second name on Axel Olsson's list into the AFP Missing Persons search bar.

SHANE MEAKIN
Missing since: 22 May 2004
Last seen: QLD
Responsible jurisdiction: QLD
Year of birth: 1968
Age now: 57
Gender: Male
Height: 170 cm
Build: Slim
Hair: Brown
Eyes: Brown
Distinguishing features: Scar above the right eye; tattoo of tiger carrying a rose on left shoulder blade.
Circumstances: 36-year-old father of two Shane Meakin was last seen leaving the Just Cuts hairdressing salon on Gallagher Street, Jubilee, around midday on 22 May 2004. At the time he was wearing a brown and black flannel shirt and blue jeans with white Nike running shoes.

I open another search page. Type Axel's third name into the AFP search bar. A profile image of a short-haired man in a red sweatshirt. A silver necklace around his neck with a cross hanging from it. Green eyes. Father of two, Peter Renwick.

Former resident of Ngungun Close, Jubilee. Missing since 18 June 2017. He texted his mum before he disappeared: *A thousand suns will stream on thee; a thousand moons will quiver.* Police said it was from a Tennyson poem, 'A Farewell'. Peter's wife, Louise Renwick, said in the months before his disappearance her husband had been visiting Hibiscus House, a psychology service found on the upper level of Jubilee Plaza. Peter was an Australian Army veteran who had been suffering from suspected PTSD after two tours to Afghanistan. I remember when Peter Renwick went missing. A topic of discussion in the neighbourhood for approximately three days. His car was found by the Indooroopilly boat ramp on Meiers Road. He was believed to have swum into the Brisbane River sometime between midnight and dawn. Never seen again.

Rita sits at the opposite end of the dining table. She wears a red and white striped shift dress. I remember laughing with Rita about how much she looked like Wenda in that dress, the girl from *Where's Wally*. I remember laughing with Rita about a lot of things. She's eating a cheese and salad sandwich. It must be lunchtime already. I look at the clock on the kitchen wall. I've been on my laptop for ninety straight minutes. Rita stares at me. Rita remains silent.

I toggle between each AFP search page. The faces of three missing persons. Three people missing from my suburb across a period of twenty-eight years. Some 38,000 Australians go missing every year. Not that strange that three would go missing from Jubilee across almost three decades. Or maybe three is a lot for thirty years? I tap on Greer Payne's AFP profile. Something familiar about that name.

Oh, here we go! Hear that rusty crunching metal sound, Cork? That's the creaky old cogs and wheels of your pea-sized lump of a brain waking up. Look at little Sherlock Gnomes with his eyes closed, trying to take himself back, back, back. To the day your balls ached. To the day you were running late for that book event where you rolled around on stage like a drunkard trying to dance The Worm. Remember? Remember, Cork? You nearly killed her. You nearly ran her over in your Yaris, ya big fuggin' nitwit. Come on now! Get in your car. What are you waiting for? Drive, Cork. Drive!

*

The Yaris turns right out of Boodua Street into Lamb Street and my tyres brush against the gutter when I park in front of Jean Rooney's house. I leave the car unlocked and run towards her front gate. Three brick steps to the front door. Three taps of my right middle knuckle. No sound for half a minute. I knock three times again. Then Jean appears at a front window, studying me from behind a pulled curtain.

I smile and raise an open palm. 'Hi, Jean,' I say. 'It's me, Noah Cork. I walked you back to your home last month … We had tea … and … you gave me an Iced VoVo.'

Jean looks pained. Maybe her brain is struggling to remember my face or maybe she just stood on a loaded mouse trap. The curtain closes. A minute later, the front door opens.

'Yesssss?' Jean says through a gap in the door the width of my shoe.

'Jean, it's me, Noah Cork,' I say. 'I live in Gecko Street. I found you in the street last month and I got you back to your home. Gwyn thanked me for looking after you?'

'Yes,' she says. 'I remember you. You were going to have scones with Kenny and me under the bridge. I took your picture.'

'Yes, that's right, Jean,' I say.

'It was a beautiful picture,' she says. 'You have an interesting face. You hide parts of yourself from the world. It shows in your face.'

'Nice of you to notice,' I say. 'Listen, Jean, remember we came back to your house that day and we ate Iced VoVos and I mentioned the book I was working on. I said my book was about that terrible business with Tamsin Fellows and you and Gwyn started talking about a woman who had the name of "Greer"? Do you remember that, Jean? Do you remember that? I remember you said the name Greer.'

Jean pulls a hanging vine of grey hair away from her eyes. Brushes an eyelash from her upper left cheek. 'Greer?' she ponders.

She leaves the name to the air, a tossed tennis ball of a name that refuses to come down again for a bounce.

'Yeah,' I say. 'Greer? I think maybe you'd mistaken Tamsin Fellows for Greer Payne? They both went missing, you see. Except Greer went missing a long, long time ago.'

Jean nods, pushes the door open with her left hand. She turns and marches down her hallway, disappears into her lounge room.

'Jean?' I say.

A call echoes along the hallway. 'In here, Bradley.'

'Bradley?' I say. 'I'm not Bra—'

I step through the doorway. Pad through the hall. Black and white photographs on Jean's hallway walls. A waitress with a pencil and pad in an American diner. An old man on a ride-on mower. Identical twins in pink swimming togs at what looks like the beach at Burleigh Heads.

Jean sits on a three-seater lounge. Gold-coloured velvet with white lace sunflower-patterned doilies. A framed oil painting on the wall. Sheep shearers in an outback tin shed. A flat screen television that's too small for the wall unit that occupies one entire wall of the lounge room. Jean flips through a photo album that rests in her lap.

'Oh, there you are,' she says.

I join Jean on the lounge. The photo album is open at a collection of scenes from what looks like a birthday party.

'Greer had three aunts,' Jean says. She elbows my arm. 'But she had no qualms at all about telling the world I was her favourite.'

Old and yellowing photographs under clear protective plastic.

'I didn't always have the spare cash, then, for gifts, so I let my photographs be my presents,' Jean says. 'Best gift of all, wouldn't you say? Memories.'

Images of Greer Payne standing by a table filled with birthday presents and a raspberry and cream chocolate cake affixed with a wax *21* candle.

'It was a beautiful party, wasn't it, Bradley?' Jean says.

'Jean,' I say, as tenderly as I can. 'My name is not—'

Jean turns a page of the album to find an image of Greer Payne wrapped in the arms of a young man in a black coat and stonewashed jeans. Nighttime, maybe, at the same party. Greer and this young man, beaming for the camera.

'You made such a cute couple,' Jean says. 'We all knew you would have spent your whole lives together.'

I feel my phone vibrating on silent, but I don't check it because I want to hear what Jean will say next. She turns another page of the photo album. My phone vibrates another four times then stops. Jean's left forefinger settles on a photograph of Greer in the middle of a circle of dancing friends. A hall of some kind. Fifteen or so friends, arm in arm, their legs raised in a kind of can-can dance. The photographer must have been standing inside the circle to take this shot.

'She was so happy,' Jean says. 'I just refused to believe she could have chosen to leave like that. I never believed it, Bradley. I never believed what they said.'

Tears well in Jean's eyes. I place a calming hand on her wrist that rests upon the open photo album. And that's when I see the face of the young man who is staring across at Greer Payne, four body spaces from the birthday girl. The tip of his tongue sticks out from between his teeth as he smiles. Blond eyebrows. Long, straight blond hair, parted neatly down the middle of his scalp. Something cold running inside me. Something cold like the truth. Something like an answer.

I tap on the blond man's face in the photograph. 'This guy, Jean,' I say. 'Do you remember this guy?'

My phone vibrates again.

'Of course I remember him,' she says. 'He was your friend wasn't he, Bradley? Greer's friend from university. He never strayed too far from your side, did he? What was his name again? Adam? Abel?'

My phone vibrates again.

'Axel,' I say. 'His name was Axel.'

I slip the phone from my pocket. Check the screen to see who's calling. It's the school administration number.

I put the phone to my ear.

'Noah Cork speaking.'

'Mr Cork, it's Kat Price.'

'What is it, Kat?'

'Before I say anything else,' she says. 'Please know that we have already notified the police.'

'What is it, Kat?'

'It's Clem, Mr Cork,' she says. 'Did you arrange for anyone to pick her up from school at lunchtime?'

'*No*.'

A coal-black one-tonne lump of dread immediately sinks to the bottom of my stomach.

'At the end of lunch break, Mr Cork,' Kat says. She struggles to spit the words out. 'It … seems … as though a car pulled up … by the fence of the back school oval. They said it was a blue or possibly black SUV. Two Year 8 boys in the cricket nets said they saw Clem from across the other side of the oval. They watched Clem climb the school fence. They tried to call out to her.'

Kat's voice breaks. She pauses.

'Please, Kat …'

'She … she … she hopped in the car, Mr Cork.'

TWENTY

You should never be expected to report on a family member or anyone with whom you share a personal connection. You should inform a senior member of the newspaper of said connection immediately and respectfully request for the story to be reassigned.

– Rutledge, *Journalism Practices and Principles*

Two police cars with lights flashing in front of my house. Rita stands in the middle of our driveway. I see her through the windscreen of the Yaris. Blue and red light bouncing off her face. Red and white striped shift. White Kmart sneakers. And fear. So much fear. In the way she turns her right foot inwards. In the way her right hand grips two fingers of her left hand. In the way she locks on to my gaze, makes it feel like we're staring at each other through two open ends of a cut pipe. The intimacy of true love. Tunnel vision. *Tube vision.* Nothing surrounding our eyes. No sky. No trees. No neighbours. No street. No suburb. No killers. No cops. But then I see Jim England standing beside her. I don't even bother parking the car in the carport. I leave it running by the gutter as I burst from the car to hug my wife. Tears in her eyes. But other things in them, too. Rage. Power. Love.

Jim's talking before I even look at him. 'We've got four patrol cars already searching for her, Noah,' he says. 'We've sent out an amber alert. And we have a car bringing Erin from school, as we speak.'

Our neighbours have all come out of their houses to grab a front row seat at the darkest circus that ever rolled into our town. A high wind barrels up the cul-de-sac. Too cold for a summer wind. With my wife in my arms I feel the sky darken above us. The driving wind makes Rita's day dress blow at her kneecaps. One side of her hair curls over in a wave. The dead and fallen leaves beneath my frangipani are being blown across the street towards the Cavendishes' home at number 40. I watch a wheel-flattened pancake of a cane toad slide along the tarmac like an ice hockey puck.

'Noah, do you know anyone who drives a blue or black SUV?'

'Yeah, Jim, every second person in Jubilee.'

I feel Rita's chest move as she sucks in a deep breath through her nose. She doesn't seem to let all that air back out.

'I'm gonna find her, Rita,' I say. 'Don't worry, I'm gonna find her.'

I take Rita's hand and pull her towards the Yaris. 'Let's go find our daughter,' I say.

I've almost reached the car when I hear my name echo through the driving wind.

'Noah, wait a second.'

I turn around to see Axel Olsson pacing warily across the nature strip. He holds up a pink square of notepaper in his right hand. 'I just found this note in my letterbox,' he says.

He shakes his head slowly in a gesture of what I guess I am supposed to take as confusion or disbelief.

'What … is … that … Ax—'

I can't finish the sentence because the disappearance of my daughter is real and unchangeable. It's a part of my story that I cannot rewrite and edit and delete and backspace and backspace and backspace. Every muscle in my face fights the urge to weep. I point to the note. Turn the tears to anger.

'What the fuck is that, Axel?' I spit.

Axel keeps walking towards me. Deirdre follows, an arm's length behind him. She's crying, with her right palm covering her mouth. People do that when they've witnessed something horrible. People do that to contain the fear that wants to erupt from their mouths in wailing and gasping and howling.

Why is she doing that? *Why the fuck is she doing that?*

'I'm so sorry, Noah,' Axel says. He shakes his head. Despair and disorientation.

Six neighbours circling me now. More emerging from their homes further down the street, drawn from their porches by the flashing blue and red lights.

Axel wants me to take the pink piece of notepaper from his right hand. He wants me to carry the burden of it. He wants me to see it. He wants me to feel it. Tears form in my eyes and I squeeze my eyes shut.

'What the fuck is that, Axel?' I ask again.

'I just found it in my letterbox, but I think it was meant for you,' he says.

His white hair. The whites of his wide eyes. The whites of his teeth. I turn to Jim England, who takes a step towards me.

He puts a tender hand on my shoulder. Kindest gesture I've ever received from Jim England.

I snatch the pink notepaper from Axel's hand. Wipe my eyes and read the message. A lined sheet of paper the size of my palm. A single fold across the middle. Rough blue pen scribbling. Misspellings and awkward spacings.

Hello lemon drop
Loved   ur book
Might have found the sequel for   ya
Seems I left ur   dawter by the reservoir
Could u find her for me,   lemon drop?
She wants to go   home

And time slows. And the earth crumbles around me. And all that I know of physics and gravity and motion falls away as the molecules in my making disperse. Then rage and hate and fear put me back together again. I take two steps towards Axel Olsson. Nothing making sense in my fool head. That image from Jean Rooney's photo album. The white-haired man looking across the dance floor at Greer Payne. The look of desire in his eyes. The look of intent. The look of a killer.

This fool head of mine. These fool lips with the fool words falling out of them. 'What the fuck is wrong with you?' I shout. 'Are you deranged? Are you sick in the fucking head?'

I hold the note up. 'Why would you do this to me? Do you think this is funny? Why are you even here? Why did you move in next door to my house? Who the fuck are you?'

Jim England steps towards me and gently takes hold of my right forearm.

'Noah,' he says, calmly.

All my fear, all my fury, directed at Axel. 'You twisted fuck,' I say. 'You *sick* fuck.'

I launch myself at the wide-eyed man with the tongue between his teeth. Clutch the collar of his shirt. There's spit in my words and there's hate in my words. 'What did you do with my daughter?' I scream. 'Why are you doing this to me?'

My arms have a rage-strength that surprises me, that scares me. I lift Axel off his feet and drive him down onto the manicured grass of the nature strip. Gasps echo around the growing circle of neighbours as I scream in his face, 'If you harmed a hair on her head, you fuckin' animal, I will fucking kill you. Butcher!'

Deirdre Olsson pulls at my arms, trying to protect her husband.

Then Jim England barks at me. 'Cork!' he bellows.

He pulls me off Axel with two strong hands under my armpits.

'I will fucking *slayyyyyyy* you, butcher,' I spit again.

Jim pulls me away and pushes me hard against the side of a cop car, its lights flashing in our eyes.

'Calm down, Cork, for fuck's sake!' Jim says.

I push back against Jim, arms flailing, fingers pointing at Axel Olsson, who's being helped up from the grass by his wife. I'm crushing the pink note in my clenched left fist, which I want to stick through Axel's cranium.

'There's your killer, Jim!' I scream. 'Fucking weirdo orchestrated it all.'

'What are you talking about?' Jim asks.

I keep eyeballing Axel over Jim's shoulders.

'Why don't you tell him, Axel?' I say. 'Why don't you tell us all about what you did to Greer? You knew her. You fucking knew her. You probably knew 'em all. Crazy as your fuckin' mother. Did you know Tamsin, too?'

Axel stares at me. Face lost in confusion. 'Are you out of your mind?' he asks.

Jim shouts in my face, 'Cork, control yourself. Get a fuckin' grip. We have to focus on finding Clem.'

'Greer?' Axel says. 'Of course, I knew Greer. We went to university together.'

'Did you hit Carol as she crossed the street that morning?' I ask.

'What the hell are you talking about?' Axel gasps.

'The hit an' run,' I say. 'You had it all worked out. One big fucked-up plan to move in beside your favourite true-crime writer so you could start fucking with me and my family up close and personal. You're obsessed. You get your kicks out of ruining my life. You sick fuck. I'm gonna fucking kill you!'

'I have no idea what you're talking about, Noah,' Axel says. 'I think you might be having some kind of mental breakdown.'

Don't mind if I do, butcher! The red mist falls again, and I puff my cheeks and I flail my arms, pushing with all my strength against Jim England. 'I'm gonna fucking kill you, Axel!' I scream.

Then I hear someone say my name.

'Noah,' says my neighbour, Ellis Towers, standing on an empty patch of nature strip behind my left shoulder. 'Noah, please.'

He places a hand on my shoulder. 'I got one, too, Noah,' he says.

Jim sees it first. Then I follow Jim's eyes. And what Ellis Towers raises in his left hand turns me to stone. Freezes my legs and stills my heart. A pink square of lined notepaper.

'I found it in my letterbox, Noah,' he says. 'I just … don't … *understand*.'

Jim eases the pressure of his grip on me. He's as mystified as I am.

I breathe. 'What?' I reply. 'Why do … *you* …?'

Ellis reads from the note. '*Hello lemon drop*,' he reads. '*Loved ur book. Might have found the sequel for y—*'

I rip the note from Ellis's hand. Finish reading it myself. Same blue scribble. Same rough handwriting. Same single fold.

Seems I left ur dawter by the reservoir
Could u find her for me, lemon drop?
She wants to go home

'I'm so sorry, Noah,' Ellis says. He's crying behind his spectacles. 'Why are they doing this?' he says. '*Little Clem*.'

Dizzy now. Weak at the knees. Gonna collapse right here in the road and could collapse for good, but then I hear my neighbour Rose Cavendish calling to me from her letterbox at number 40, directly opposite my house.

'We got one, too, Noah,' she shouts. And then she reads from the pink square of notepaper in her hands as her only son, Seb, grips her shoulders. '*Hello lemon drop. Loved ur book. Might have found the sequel for ya. Seems I left ur daw—*' But Rose can't finish reading that word. 'What's it mean, Noah?' she asks. 'Not … Clem … please … not our Clem.' She weeps into a cupped hand. Seb wraps his arms around his mother.

Then Anushka Burman paces towards me from the nature strip in front of her house at number 36. She holds her own pink notepaper and she picks up where Rose left off. '*Could you find her for me lemon drop*?' she reads. '*She wants to go home.*'

Two more neighbours circle around me with pink notes in their hands.

Jim England's husband, Hua, enters the scene with yet another pink note. Says to Jim, loud enough for all his neighbours to hear, 'We got one, too.'

Jim shakes his head. No words from the seasoned cop. No words from our brave local gumshoe. He looks at me in case I have some to offer.

I have none.

Hua walks over to me and puts his hands on my shoulders. 'Jim will find her, Noah,' he says. 'Jim will find that beautiful kid.'

I turn to look for Rita. Where'd she go? She was standing right beside me. But now she's standing in the middle of the dead-end turning circle, her back to her neighbours, who are scattered around the street in the most bizarre tableau of suburban Brisbane life. Rita is staring at the red poinciana tree that rises above the park bench beside the round concrete water tank at the end of our street. She watches as the red flowers are blown clean from the tree in their hundreds. And the birds. Hundreds of birds now. Where did they even come from? So many birds circling above Rita in the sky. Crows and magpies and mistletoe birds and a dozen sulphur-crested cockatoos squawking in something that sounds like excitement or fear or maybe even exultation. Rainbow lorikeets and crested pigeons and red-capped plovers. All circling above my street and above my wife.

And now a furious wind drives through my suburb. One by one, the branches of the poinciana bend and then break from the tree's trunk, flipping like tossed tomahawks before crashing violently into the concrete water tank.

A police patrol car pulls up in the cul-de-sac. Erin slips out of the back of it, still in her school uniform, runs to her mother, wraps her arms around Rita's waist. Rita puts a loving arm around her daughter and stares at the same thing we are all now staring at. The sky. We can't take our eyes off it. Throbbing as it is with an electric emerald-green light that's pulsing from a place that might be beyond all of our human understanding. Then a hard and heavy rain drives into Jubilee along with further gusts of wind that bring leaves and sticks and debris with them.

Rita remains silent. I'm walking towards my wife when I hear my name again.

'Cork,' Jim calls through the rain. I turn to see the detective, who has one leg inside the driver's door of a police car. 'Let's go find your kid.'

I nod and rush around the bonnet of the police car. Slip into the front passenger seat. My shaking hands try to insert the seatbelt's tongue into the buckle, which is stuck between the seat and the car's central console. I hear someone slip into the back seat and I turn to see Rita buckling the central seatbelt around her waist. Rita remains silent.

Erin runs to my window, just as Jim starts reversing the car. My elder daughter slaps her palm frantically on the window glass. 'Wait, wait,' she says. 'I'm coming with you.'

I bring the window halfway down. 'No, Erin,' I say. 'You go inside the house and lock the doors. Do not open those doors for anyone but your sister.'

Erin begins to weep, her tears lost to the rain smashing against her face.

'Fuck that, I'm coming to find my sister,' she screams.

'Please, E,' I say.

I reach out the window and she grabs my hand like she used to grab it when we'd cross a busy street or when we'd jump over footpath cracks together. Some fifteen years of held hands flash through my mind. Hands held on roller-coasters. Hands held on busy Sydney city streets. Hands held for balance as a girl in a purple tutu twirled upon a council park boundary log.

Then the sweet young man who lives across the street, Seb Cavendish, puts his hands gently on the shoulders of my daughter.

'I'll stay with her, Mr Cork,' he says. 'She'll be safe with me, I promise.'

I'm eye to eye with the boy with the black and scarlet hair.

'Thank you, Seb,' I say.

Erin wails again and our grip is severed as the police car speeds out of Gecko Street, siren wailing through the safest suburb in the city of Brisbane.

TWENTY-ONE

If fate sees fit, you may find yourself in the centre of a truly dramatic story, a once-in-a-lifetime scoop, perhaps, destined for page one. The natural excitement and momentum inherent in such a story may cause the journalist to drift into exaggeration and hyperbole. Please avoid excessive verbiage in stories of great drama and consequence. Whether on page one or page forty, adjectives are weak, sensational, superfluous and lazy.

– Rutledge, *Journalism Practices and Principles*

The boy running from his front door to drag his BMX out of the walloping rain. The corrugated plastic election sign for our local Greens member doing wind-driven backflips from one side of the road to the other. The old man tying down the ropes on the silver tarp that covers his parked caravan. Three magpies sheltering under someone's front porch. Drains overflowing. Rivers of rainwater in gutters dammed by piles of brown leaves big enough to conceal a body. A thick fallen branch in the middle of the road. An elderly woman bringing her terracotta pot plants inside from the porch. My suburb bracing for the worst of it.

'We shouldn't be drivin' in this shit,' Jim England says, yanking the police car's steering wheel hard right to avoid another fallen branch. He pulls the windscreen wiper lever down one more notch, but the two blades still struggle to shift sheets of rain from the glass. I can barely see where we're heading.

'What the fuck's going on here, Cork?' Jim asks. 'C'mon! Think it out. Let's interrogate this. Why are they doing this to you?'

I stare out the side window.

Go on, Cork, spit it out. Tell him the truth. This is payback, is it not? For what you did to Tamsin? For the way you splashed the gory, whorey details of her demise across 317 pages of tabloid true-crime slime? Or maybe it's payback for what you did to your dad? For what you did to your mum? Or maybe they're just doing this because you asked for it. They are giving you everything you ever wanted, Cork. An end to the story. You made this, Frankenstein. You built this awful monster of a story. What was it you said to Erin? That's right. *Not the first bloke to create something he was repulsed by.*

'Cork,' Jim says. 'Tell me why they're doing this to you.'

'I don't know,' I say. 'Some kind of lesson, maybe.'

'What lesson, Cork? What do you need to learn?'

'I don't know,' I say. 'I haven't learned it yet.'

Jim pulls the police car hard left into Wicker Road. It feels like the tyres are going to slip on the wet road.

'That psycho Axel Olsson is a good place to start, I'm sure of it,' I say. 'He asked me to sign his book a month ago. He said I was his favourite writer. He gave me a book with a list of names of missing persons from Jubilee. He knew one of 'em,

Jim. He was close with Greer Payne. Maybe obsessed with her, too, for all I know. He's trying to fuck with me.'

'So that's the best you got, Cork?' Jim asks. 'And you think he somehow found out where Carol Myers-Ryan would be going for a morning walk in Indooroopilly and he clipped her with his car in a staged hit-and-run because he knew he would then be able to move in next door to his favourite true-crime writer?'

'People like Axel do all sorts of crazy things when they're obsessed,' I propose.

'You think he's obsessed with you now?' Jim replies. 'Fuck me, Cork.'

Jim shakes his head and leans in closer to his steering wheel to see the road, then accelerates into a bend.

'We found the car that clipped Carol, Cork,' he says. 'Three brain-dead kids from Ipswich, souped up on meth. Car was stolen. Carol was crossing the wrong fuckin' street at the wrong fuckin' time. That is all. Wake up, Cork. You're seeing things that aren't there.'

Hearin' things, too. Tell him the truth, Cork. You're not fit to make a single sound judgement because you've more than likely lost your mind. Tell him, Cork. Tell him.

'I don't think I'm well, Jim,' I say.

'Huh?' Jim says, eyes fixed on the road, weaving the car through more fallen debris on Wicker Road.

I turn to Rita in the back seat. 'I said I don't think I'm well. Ever since I saw Tamsin's bones in that oven, I've been hearing her voice in my head.'

Rita nods. Closed lips. Understanding in that nod.

'I think it's damaging me in ways that I'm not yet fully aware of,' I say.

The car swerves hard and sharp on the road and my body slams into the door.

'The fuck you talkin' 'bout, Cork?' bellows Jim. He weaves between two fallen tallowwood branches at the entrance to the Spearwood Reservoir carpark. Where I think Jim will slow the vehicle down, he accelerates, bashing through another barrier of leafy hoop pine and red cedar branches. Not a single car in the carpark. The park rangers from the Teaneck Creek Discovery Centre, the wildlife sanctuary attached to the reservoir, have all wisely closed shop and gone home for the day. A suburban fringe forest crowded with windblown widowmakers is no place to be during a supercell storm. And yet that's where we find ourselves. In a wind so strong it makes the reservoir's welcome sign flap in and out like a wobble board. *Thwump. Thwump. Thwump.*

Jim pulls the car up at the start of the five-kilometre Hickory Wattle walking trail that circles the reservoir.

'Jesus Christ,' he says, staring through his windscreen at a towering forest that looks like some kind of wild native-tree headbangers' ball, a violent rave party of crazed acacias and drug-addled ironbarks shaking their tops in cyclonic winds. A branch the size of a cricket bat flies out of the forest and smashes into the top right corner of the car's windscreen, leaving a crack in the glass shaped like a bent drinking straw.

'Fuck!' Jim says, jumping in his seat.

Then the sound of the car's left rear door opening and slamming closed behind me. Through the windscreen, I watch my wife sprinting towards the forest. Not a second thought. Falling debris all around her. Wind whipping through her hair, blowing the bottom hem of her red and white striped day dress across her kneecaps. My wife charges into the grey and green wall of rain and wind and nature, and disappears into the forest.

I open the car door. Call as loud as I can to my silent wife. 'Rita, wait!'

*

Flashes of Rita's red and white striped dress as my wife sprints along the dirt walking track. I forgot how fast she can run. She was a born runner. And here she is, running for her life. Running for her daughter's life.

'Rita, wait!' I call again.

The forest canopy thickens above us and darkens in kind. Rain still hammers through the trees that bend and snap around us. Rita must be thirty metres ahead of me, her shoes landing in mud puddles on the track. Nothing slows her frantic forward momentum.

'Rita, you're gonna slip,' I shout. 'You're gonna break something! Rita! Slowww dowwn.'

We cross the small rock and concrete bridge, with Jim England calling, metres behind me, 'Coooorrrrk! Stop her! We don't know what's waiting up there!'

We pass the clearing on the forest floor where someone built a teepee out of branches and paperbark sheets. The branches are now scattered across the forest floor, the teepee ravaged by a storm that is only strengthening. I watch Rita bound effortlessly up the series of stone steps where, months ago now, I found Miles De Jonge sitting in the rain. Miles De Jonge. The dead man in the orange cocoon who knew so much more than

I thought he knew. The sad and sorry vanilla butterfly in search of his colour.

Rita follows a sharp bend in the track, turning behind a cluster of thick brush box trees. I lose my footing in a puddle of mud and almost roll my ankle. Adrenaline pushes me on, down a gentle slope then right through an avenue of bootlace bushes with blooming white flowers that look like popcorn to eyes on the run. The track then runs gun-barrel straight towards the viewpoint on the outcrop, where I find Rita sitting on the wooden bench where hikers normally sit and admire the blue-winged kingfishers that gather on the exposed limbs of semi-submerged eucalypts. She is soaked to the bone. Her wet hair hangs over her face. Sheet upon sheet upon sheet of hard rain and still my wife sits, with a grey-black rock in her left hand shaped like a large serving of mashed potato, staring at a notebook that rests in her lap. A Spirax notebook. A name and a title scribbled across the front cover of the notebook: *Clementine Cork, editor-in-chief, Gecko Street Gazette.*

Rita stands and begins to walk back to the car. Robot-like. Machine-like. Detached somehow. She opens the notebook to the last page, hands me the Spirax as she passes me. I try to look into her eyes, but she refuses to meet my gaze. I hold the notebook as I watch my wife march back along the walking track. She passes Jim England, who keeps walking till he reaches me by the seat. He sucks in three breaths. Coughs twice. Wipes rainwater and sweat and mud spots from his eyes.

'Where's she goin'?' he asks.

I turn my eyes down to the open notebook in my hands. There's a message someone has scribbled in blue ballpoint pen.

Hello   lemon drop
Almost done, ya   wunnerful one
Seems I left ur dawter   in Monaco's place
Could u find her for me,   lemon drop
She wants to go   home

TWENTY-TWO

If nothing else, be brave.

– Rutledge, *Journalism Practices and Principles*

'Faster'.

Jim England ignores me.

'*Faster.*'

Police sirens sounding above my head. Cars doing their best to move out of our way on the wet and busy road. Lounge room windows smashed in every fifth or sixth house along Wicker Road. We speed past one two-storey home where the top half of a grey ironbark tree has snapped and fallen upon a now-exposed family kitchen. Someone's cream-coloured letterbox has blown onto the driveway of the 7-Eleven on the corner of Wicker and Salem roads. A fire engine crew attends to a fallen power line outside Jubilee State High School. An ambulance is overtaking cars in the oncoming traffic, its own sirens howling.

Jim speeds around a blind bend.

'Look out!' I scream, as we narrowly avoid crashing into a white Holden Colorado that's inexplicably stopped in the middle of the road with its hazard lights on. As we pass the car, I see why it stopped: half a tree trunk is resting on its bonnet.

It can't be much past 4 p.m., but the day is as dark as night and all the cars have their headlights on in the vicious rain. The Mobil service station is ahead. The Jubilee Golf Club is ahead. Giancarlo Monaco's abandoned family home is only one sharp right turn away now across two lanes of oncoming traffic. Jim pulls the wheel hard right and the police car is nearly clipped by an 804 council bus that emerges from a blind rise in Wicker Road. The car barrels hard over a gutter and I bounce so high in my seat that my head hits the roof.

Jim kills the engine and reaches for the handgun he has holstered under his jacket. He stares through the windscreen at the fenced and rambling grounds of Giancarlo's abandoned three-storey mansion. Multiple long and imposing strips of police tape run along the perimeter of the property. Signs cable-tied every metre along the security fence: *Trespassers will be prosecuted.*

Jim checks the bullet chamber in his gun. Sees that it's full.

'You expecting to use that?' I ask.

'Bloke hangs around Noah Cork long enough, he learns to expect anything.'

He slots the bullet chamber back inside the gun. Reaches across me and opens the car's glovebox, clutches a black metal hand torch that he slides into his left jacket pocket.

He turns to Rita in the back seat. Turns to me. 'You two stay in the car, you hear me?' he orders. 'Keep the doors locked. I have two back-up cars on the way. They'll be here in minutes. There is nothing you can do now. Let me do my job. Let me find your daughter.'

'I'm coming with you, Jim,' I say, releasing my seatbelt.

That's the straw that breaks the gumshoe's back.

'You. Will. Stay. In. The. Fucking. Car. Cork.'

My heart is thick and thumping inside my chest so loudly I think I can hear it in my head. Might be the beginnings of a heart attack. Might be the beginning of the end. I breathe. Nod understandingly at the man with the lump on his forehead and the gun in his hand.

Jim gets out of the car and Rita leans over the central console. Through the windscreen, we watch Detective Jim England, husband to Hua, father to Hercules, walk to the security fence surrounding the abandoned home.

'We just have to be patient, Rita,' I tell my wife.

We watch Jim holster his gun as he crawls through a hole someone has cut in the fence.

'We'll find her, honey, I promise,' I say. 'We just need to have faith in police procedure. Trust in the people who are trained to do this stuff.'

Jim disappears into the overgrown foliage surrounding the property.

'We just have to let Jim do his jo—'

Rita opens her side door and closes it gently behind her. She doesn't even look at me as she scurries to the hole in the fence.

'Rita, what the *farrrrrk*!' I whisper.

I open my own door and shut it as softly as I can before running to catch up with Rita, who is already through the hole. As I crawl through it, my loose shirt catches on a piece of fence wire.

'Rita, wait, goddammit!' I whisper, my words lost in the heaving rain.

I watch Rita squeeze through a brown snake sanctuary of overgrown weeds, thorny plants, crowded palms and a mess of fallen palm fronds. She finds a faint path that leads to the concrete front courtyard covered in broken dinner plates and upturned drawers and snapped planks of wood. Broken window glass everywhere. I remember seeing that used fire extinguisher the first time I walked into this shithole drug den.

Rita stands by the front entrance to the sprawling home, looking into a darkened living space offering maybe two corners of natural light at best. I see the copper wire hangman's noose blowing in the storm wind above the entrance, like some kind of warning sign for unwanted intruders. Spot a rusting black metal fence post sitting on the courtyard floor beside the cut-basketball syringe disposal unit from last time. I pick up the post and grip it with two hands. Practise swinging it across the temple of the twisted leech who has my daughter. Short of a broad sword or a submachine gun, this will do nicely.

I finally catch up with Rita and tap her on her shoulder. We peer inside the front door, to the floor covered in old books and magazines.

'I'll go first,' I whisper.

We hear Jim's voice beyond the entrance hall. He's calling from the bottom of the staircase that leads to the upstairs kitchen. He can hear the same thing we can. Glass and porcelain and tin banging and crashing violently.

'This is Detective Jim England from the Queensland Police Homicide Investigation Unit,' he hollers into the void beyond him. 'Please be aware that I am carrying a loaded handgun. Please do not make me use it.'

Rita and I enter the house carefully. I catch glimpses of the graffiti on the walls. Satanic pentagrams. The number 764 again. Stains of shit and mud and blood. Filing cabinets by the walls. The portrait with crosses for eyes. The shopping trolley filled with empty boxes in the corner of the foyer. The hubcap filled with cigarette butts. The other hubcap, the one filled with disposable syringes.

Rita follows behind me with a hand on my shoulder that's making me feel brave and needed and wanted. We come to the bottom of the staircase and when I take my first step my fence post accidentally bangs against the wobbly wooden banister. I hear the click of a pistol locking bolt and look up to find Detective Jim England adopting a shooting stance at the top of the stairs, with his pistol aimed squarely between my eyes. He mercifully clocks my face and eases his aim, breathing deeply and silently as he does so. He shakes his head and mouths something that's hard to lip-read in the dark but looks like *Cork, you stupid fucking fuck.* Then he puts a forefinger to his lips. *Sssshhhh.*

Jim holds his gun out with two stretched and strong arms and steps gently through the archway between the stairs and the living room that's connected to the kitchen.

The sound of more glass breaking. Movement in the kitchen.

'This is the Queensland Police,' Jim calls again. 'If you are armed, I suggest you lay your weapons down now.'

Rita and I scurry up the stairs to be close to Jim, the smell of human or animal shit stronger with every step. We move through the archway and stand shoulder to shoulder with Jim in the upstairs television room that is covered in dust and ancient DVDs.

Heart fat and bursting. Heart attack imminent. Sweat building in my fingers that grip the useless post in my hands. Jim raises three fingers. Three fingers turn to two and two turn to one and then I watch my neighbour move catlike from behind the wall to stand with his pistol aimed into the kitchen. He immediately ducks down beneath something white that flies towards his head.

'Fuck,' he says, pointing his gun at what we all realise now is a white cockatoo. The bird shrieks in fright and I enter the kitchen to see maybe thirteen or fourteen soaking wet and shivering white cockatoos flying from the storm-sheltered safety of the kitchen island bench. Some birds bash their heads against the ceiling, others seek freedom through windows that are closed and bash their heads against glass. Panicked birds swirl in circles above us, some crashing into old plates and jars that still rest on kitchen shelves. The squawking madness of their collective noise makes the room sound like a zoo enclosure for a dozen monkeys crazed on cocaine-dusted banana bites. The cockatoo cacophony ends only when one wiser bird finds the gap between the doors onto the ornate balcony.

Jim drops his head and takes a deep breath. Holsters his handgun, studies the makeshift weapon in my hand. Raises his eyebrows. The three of us look around the kitchen. No signs of life. No signs of anything.

It's Rita who first walks towards the built-in silver oven, drawn by the two words still written in spray-paint on the oven door. *Cunt money.*

Back where it all began, Cork. This is where it all started to go wrong, isn't it? Let's be honest. It all started in this shithole kitchen. You thought it was all going so well. You got such a thrill from the story, didn't you? Remember that? How electrified you were by the sight of Tamsin?

The howling wind rattles around us. The storm thunders outside. I want to join my wife at the door of the oven but realise, to my surprise, that my feet are refusing to move. My legs feel exactly the same way. My hands, too. My mouth. Speak, dammit. Say something to your wife.

Rita steps to the oven door and her right hand reaches slowly and cautiously for the rusting handle.

'Rita,' I say, 'don't.'

She leaves her hand where it is as she turns to me and slowly shakes her head. *No*, she says in her silence. I can read her so well now. I know everything she wants to say without even having to hear it. I am so practised. I am so versed in her non-verbal. I know this because I can feel her from three metres away. I know this because I love her. *No*, she says. *I have to*, she says. *Turn away now if you need to, Noah*, she says.

Her right hand brings the oven door down and her left hand flies immediately up to her mouth. I can't see what's inside the oven from here. It's too storm-dark to see.

Jim England moves past Rita to the open oven, pulls his torch from his pocket and shines a circle of white light on whatever has mesmerised my wife.

Finally, I move. One foot after the other. Left, right, left, right, until I'm standing by Jim's shoulder, following the terrifyingly honest beam of torchlight illuminating a pair of red shoes sitting on the middle tray of the oven.

A pair of red suede Adidas Gazelles. White and purple unicorn stickers lining the edges of their thick rubber soles.

Rita pulls the shoes from the oven. Finds a folded piece of notepaper inside the left shoe.

Jim shines his torch upon the note that's now open in my wife's palm. A message scribbled in blue pen.

There's no place like home
There's no place like home
There's no place like home

TWENTY-THREE

The job will be the death of you. The job will bring you back to life.

– Rutledge, *Journalism Practices and Principles*

Exposed roof beams. Storm-blown holes in tiled roofs. Black voids where sheets of tin roofing have blown to the hills. This storm is worse – it must be worse – than the microburst of 2009. This storm is the worst of everything. Worst of rain. Worst of wind. The worst of another bullying blast from the great beyond.

Jim England speeds home to Gecko Street along Wicker Road.

There's no place like home
There's no place like home
There's no place like home

In the grey-green sky we watch a silver panel of aluminium – maybe one full side of someone's garden shed – spinning through the air like an Olympics discus. The deadly metal sheet flies over our police car and smashes into the roof of the C & K Community Kindergarten.

'Faster,' I say.

Jim listens to me. No cars on the road anymore. Nobody dumb enough to drive in this. Only debris on the road now. I see kitchen furniture. Tree branches and a blue and white plastic high chair. White plastic balcony chairs being pushed along the road like they're being manoeuvred by invisible bobsled teams.

Jim speeds into the corner of Gecko Street. Brakes hard in the middle of the road. 'Jesus *fucking* Christ,' he screams.

He looks through the windscreen of the car to his home at number 33. The whole right side of his tin roof has been lifted from its fixings and curled back upon the left side. A crashing wave of tin, revealing a fractured mess of cracked and exposed rafters and collar beams. Strips of silver insulation are hanging haphazardly over his house, like it's being gift-wrapped by a two-year-old.

'Stay on your phone, Cork,' he says. 'I've gotta check on Hua.'

He bursts from the car and runs into his house. 'Hua!' he screams, right forearm over his eyes to protect his head from debris.

Rita's already out of the car. I follow her up the street to our house.

'Clem!' I scream through the smashing rain. 'Cleeeemmm!'

There's no place like home
There's no place like home
There's no place like home

Rita runs past the letterbox. The letterbox. Where it all began. The killer will end it all where it all began.

'Rita, the letterbox,' I call.

Rita stops, almost slipping on the nature strip grass as she does.

She joins me at the letterbox. We lean down to it, frantically open the rear flap. Nothing. It's empty.

'No,' I say, broken and desperate. Breathless and confused.

I scan the street. Scan the house. Scan the driveway. Nothing but wind and rain and sky-born violence.

Then I hear my name across the nature strip.

'Noah!'

Then I hear Rita's name across the nature strip.

'Rita!'

I look up to find where those names are coming from in the madness of rain and debris.

'Noah, she's here!' shouts Ellis Towers. He's standing on his front step, holding the door open. 'She's sheltering downstairs!' He waves us over, beaming in the rain.

My heart swells and my worry eases instantly. We run to Ellis and barrel into the mudroom. Stop on a rug by a wooden coat rack holding an umbrella, a woollen cardigan and one of Ellis's tweed sixpence caps. Ellis waddles in after us, shuts the front door and shakes water from his hair.

'I found her standing up there on your driveway,' Ellis says. 'Just standing there in the storm, looking up at the sky!'

I place a grateful hand on Ellis's left shoulder.

'Thank you, Ellis!' I say. Panting now. Gathering my breath. 'Where is she?' I ask. I call through the house. 'Cleeemmm?'

Rita is scanning the hallway before us. She needs to run to her daughter but doesn't know where to run.

'She's in the work studio downstairs,' Ellis says in a calm voice. 'She's perfectly fine and enjoying a cold glass of Milo as we speak.'

He paces down the hallway. 'Follow me,' he says.

The smell of roast lamb is baked into this place. It's warm. Insulated brick, the walls so thick we can barely hear the end-of-days storm that's currently destroying half of Jubilee. Cream-coloured décor ageing to yellow. Framed family photographs on the hallway walls. A print of Frederick McCubbin's *The Pioneer*, the great bushland triptych about the selector and his wife with their new patch of land and then the same couple in the middle image with their baby and a cottage to call home in the background, and then the all-things-must-pass final panel in which a figure inspects a gravestone where the couple once sat, and a city is emerging in the distance.

Ellis leads us through his living room. No sign of his wife, June, anywhere. Antiques and ornaments on floating shelves throughout the house. A bone china teapot. Some kind of sheathed blade from Nepal or India. An antique German beer stein filled with fake daisies. A yellow and brown shield resting in a corner of the living room. The four frames on the shield feature the same illustrated dragon raising its claws in both attack and defence.

'This way,' Ellis says.

He darts through an archway off the living room and comes to a closed door, which he opens and then ushers us through.

'Go down the stairs,' he says. 'Be careful. It's a steep descent.'

In my rush to see my daughter, I almost lose my footing on

the second step. Rita grabs my shoulder and waist from behind me, stops me from falling. Four steps down. Eight steps down. Ellis's workshop comes into view. This is less a studio than a basement hideaway. A polished concrete floor painted green. Brown-brick walls. Only one thin half-basement window built into the wall on the left. I can see the edge of Ellis's lawn brushing up against the window glass and a thin strip of grey sky outside. The smell of glues and paints and turpentine. The smell of work.

And this is what my neighbour has been working on. His suburb. All six-by-four metres of it. A sweeping painted polystyrene and wax dioramic re-creation of Jubilee, from Spearwood Reservoir to Hazel Park, including the roads I've just been driving on with Jim England and my terrified wife, and the shops and houses of my suburb that I've just watched being throttled and walloped by a storm that, even now, makes the basement window rattle like a snare drum.

Then I see my daughter.

Clem is directly opposite where I'm standing below the bottom step of the basement stairs. She's sitting on a white wooden stool on the other side of the diorama, sipping a glass of Milo through a straw. She beams when she sees me and points a finger at Gecko Street in the diorama.

'Look, Dad,' she says, 'it's our house.'

Then I hear a thump behind me. I turn around to find Rita collapsed and unconscious on the stairs.

I look up to see my neighbour of sixteen years, Ellis Towers, staring blankly into my eyes.

Ellis lifts his left forefinger to his lips. 'Sssshhhh,' he says.

And then he swiftly brings his right hand from behind his

back and drives a syringe hard into my neck. As he keeps his hand there I grab his wrist and try to pull the syringe away. But he squeezes it before I've even comprehended the meaning of his actions.

He yanks his hand away and begins to stumble back up the stairs. I clutch at the syringe dangling from my neck as I take one, two, three steps after him.

'Ellis,' I say. 'What … are … you—'

Doing, Noah. The word is 'doing'. I know it is. But I can't say it. I can't say anything, in fact. For my mouth is made of jelly. For my mind is made of marshmallow.

Ellis trips on a step and falls back hard on his arse.

I hear the voice of my daughter. 'Dad?' Clem says.

My daughter is confused. My daughter is frightened. Then I hear my daughter scream. Hear her glass of Milo smashing on the basement concrete. Feel myself collapsing on the basement stairs. See my neighbour laughing at me. Watch my neighbour turning on the top step of the basement stairs to close and lock the door we just walked through.

Everything goes black.

TWENTY-FOUR

Believe the impossible. The impossible is as much a part of life as death and air and blood and ink.

– Rutledge, *Journalism Practices and Principles*

'*Sssssssss*'.

The voice of Tamsin's skeleton in my dreams. I'm standing in the museum of my mind. The museum has been flooded. I look down to see water up to my kneecaps. All the glass display cases around me are cracked and broken. All the memories these cases once held now lost to the murky floodwater.

Something heavy in my left hand. Something made of black steel. A crowbar.

'*Sssssss*.' The voice of Tamsin's skeleton reaching my ears from that room with the white door at the darkened far end of this floor.

'*Sssssss*.'

I slosh through the floodwater and come close enough to the white door to see the word in black stretched across it: *STORAGE*.

The door handle rattles. Tamsin's skeleton thumps on the other side of the door. She wants to get out of the room. Someone's locked her in there. Someone's trapped her in that room for the longest time.

'*Sssssssss.*'

I'm scared now, but still I move through the water.

'Tamsin, I'm coming,' I say. 'I'm gonna get you outta there. I'm gonna save you.'

Fists banging on the other side of the door. I slosh through the flood, dragging my legs in water that feels as thick as treacle. Or are these just my dream legs? My dream legs never move as fast as I need them to.

I reach the storage room door and wedge the crowbar's vicious front teeth into the thin gap between the lock and the frame.

Pull. *Crack*. Pull. *Crack.*

The doorframe breaks. I push the door open.

A storage room about the size of my backyard garage. Walls of shelving. Cardboard storage boxes sealed with silver duct tape. Some boxes have fallen into the floodwater.

And a woman standing in the centre of the room. A woman of flesh and blood. She looks roughly the same age as Rita. Same size. Same coloured hair, but this woman's hair curls more than Rita's. Water up to her kneecaps. She wears a plain blue T-shirt, the sort of round-the-house shirt you'd pick up for six dollars at Best & Less. A silver wristwatch on her left arm. Bermuda shorts, a faded apricot colour.

The woman smiles at me. And a simple and perfect three-letter 'S' word falls from her lips. 'Son,' she says.

The crowbar drops from my hands. Splashes into the water below me.

'Mum?'

Tears flooding into my eyes the way the Pacific Ocean once flooded into this museum. Left leg moving. Right leg moving. Sloshing towards my mother. And I fall into her arms, which have opened to catch me, and I'm weeping before I even touch her.

'I'm sorry, Mum,' I wail into the space between her left collarbone and her left ear. 'I'm so sorry.'

'Sssssssssshhhh,' she whispers. 'Sssssssshhhh.' She pats my back. 'You gotta wake up, Noah,' Mum says. 'Looks like you've got yourself into quite the circumstance of peril.'

'Ellis Towers?' I gasp. 'It's not possible, Mum.'

'You of all people should know that anything is possible in the suburbs of Brisbane,' Mum says. 'All the signs were there, kiddo. You were just so caught up in where the story was going that you missed who was tellin' the story. But hats off for finding him, my brave little newshawk.'

'I didn't find him, Mum,' I say. 'He found me.'

Mum shrugs her shoulders.

'You've been living next door to a sick and twisted killer for the past sixteen years,' she says. 'Never a dull moment in Jubilee is there?'

'He's going to kill me now, too, isn't he?' I ask. 'He's going to kill Rita. He's going to kill Clem. And it's all my fault. I did this.'

'Well, Ellis did the lion's share of this, let's make no mistake. But, yeah, you did your bit, too, truth be told.'

'How do I undo what I did, Mum?' I ask. 'How do I fix this? How do I save my wife and daughter?'

'Well, you just need to wake up.'

'But I can't. That's the problem. He drugged me, Mum. He filled me with something. Feels like a horse tranquilliser's running through my veins.'

'My guess is dimethyltryptamine,' Mum says. 'Same thing the Beast of Bismarck used, remember?'

'You read that piece in the *New Yorker*?'

'No, you did. I am you, remember. Dimethyltryptamine. Go-to knockout drug for serial killers the world over. Need to absolutely positively send your victim to Nodsville pronto? Accept no substitutes.'

'It's got hallucinogenic properties,' I say. 'Might explain why you're here.'

'Why *we're* here, love.'

'But you've been with me for a while now, Mum. I thought you were Tamsin.'

'I know.'

'It's some kind of trauma manifestation, I think,' I say. 'A weird mental reaction to seeing Tamsin's bones in the oven like that. It triggered something in me. Something I buried so deep that I never even told Rita about it.'

'You never handed her the crowbar,' Mum says.

'*I never handed her the crowbar.*'

'Clem's right about you,' Mum says.

'Right about what?'

'You've been so caught up in the scoop of a lifetime that you've missed an even greater scoop of your lifetime,' she says.

'Rita?'

Mum nods.

'She's … *special* … isn't she?' I add.

'Oh, you wouldn't even believe how special she is.'

'I've gotta save her.'

'Yes, son, you do.'

'How do I save her, Mum?'

Mum thinks on this for a moment. She pulls the black crowbar from the water, smiles, hands it to me. 'She wants all of you. The light, the dark, the good, the bad. She wants all of it.'

She kisses me on the forehead, runs a gentle hand through my hair.

'I couldn't let the story go, Mum,' I say.

'Of course you couldn't let it go,' Mum says. 'Why would you ever let it go? It's our story.'

Mum sloshes past me. I watch her walk out of the storage room.

'Wait,' I say. 'Don't go.'

'I've gotta go, Noah,' she says, wading out into the main hall of my museum. 'And you've gotta get back to your girls.' She pushes on through the thick floodwater. 'You've gotta wake up and save the ones you love the most. And maybe then you gotta save yourself.'

'But we only just got here, Mum,' I say.

She stops and turns back to me. Looks at her wristwatch. 'Not me,' she says with a wry smile. 'I've been here for years.'

She turns round again and wades on through the museum.

'Wake up, Noah,' Mum says, over her shoulder. 'Wake up.'

*

'Wake up, Noah.'

An open hand gently slapping my face.

'Noah, you there, neighbour?'

My eyelids opening. Darkness flecked with wedges of grey-blue light. The sound of a rattling basement window. Hailstones from outside smacking into the glass. A head now filling my view. Big bushy eyebrows. The lashes of a rockhopper penguin. The face of Ellis Towers.

'There he is,' Ellis says. 'Welcome back, neighbour.'

I'm sitting on a wooden chair. Drool running down my jaw. Something in my mouth, pulling hard on my lips. Cotton on my tongue. I look down. There's a gag in my mouth. My shoulders ache because my arms have been pulled hard behind my back, and my wrists are bound behind the chair with something that's cutting into my skin. A thick plastic cable tie, I think. Instinctively, I move my legs and realise that my thighs and torso have been strapped to the chair – seven, eight, nine loops – with heavy-duty duct tape.

I turn my face to my right to find Rita beside me. Her mouth gagged, hands bound with a cable tie, legs and torso strapped to a chair just like mine. Rita is unconscious. Needle in the neck like me, I'm guessing. The vision of my wife like this causes me to bounce furiously in my chair, screaming muffled words through my gag. 'Kill. You. Fucking. Monster.'

The whole chair lifts up when I force my body upwards, then the chair falls over and I fall with it. My whole world turned sideways.

I see Ellis's thick-veined, hairy legs. His white socks and old brown leather shoes, his tan-coloured dress shorts and white buttoned short-sleeve business shirt with a folded hankie in the chest pocket. The thick glass lenses of the spectacles that he adjusts when he bends to study my actions like a scientist observing the movements of a drugged rat in a lab maze.

'Oh, look what you've done to yourself, Noah,' he says. 'You can rock and roll in that chair all you want, Elvis, but you aren't going anywhere until you've heard the end of our story,' he says. He pats my face. Smiles. 'Silly billy. We've come so far, neighbour. Don't you want to know how it all ends, Noah?'

He lifts my body up and the chair sits upright. 'There we go,' he says. The effort causes him to have a brief coughing fit. Wheezing. Sounds like fluid on his lungs. I realise now how pale the guy looks. I haven't noticed that before.

I search the room for signs of Clem. Discarded slabs of plastic for model bases. A work bench full of tools. Power saws. A small, square surveillance monitor on the work bench running a live feed of the view from Ellis's front door. One thin half-basement window. How do I get to that window? How do I scream for help? How do I save my wife and child?

Again I try to push words out. 'Clem. Clem. Where's. Daughter. Fucking. Kill.'

'Quit your bleating, hack,' Ellis says. He places a white wooden stool in front of my chair, casually parks his backside on it like he's sitting down to catch the nightly news. 'Clementine? I wouldn't harm a hair on her pretty head. Juney and I love that girl. Your sleeping beauty's upstairs in the guest room sleeping off that Milo.'

He raises an eyebrow. 'That particular Milo had quite the kick,' he says, with a wink.

'*You. Fuckin. Animal,*' I try to yell.

'What's that? Animal? Beast, more precisely. But aren't we all? Aren't you, Noah Cork? I've been watching you for so long now, Noah. One might even say you have been my greatest sociological study. I know you better than you know yourself. I know the beast that dwells inside you. The animal that hungers to fill the hole that won't be filled.'

He shakes his head. Laughs. 'The lengths I had to go to, Noah Cork,' he says. 'Just to get you to come down here and see my life's work.'

He scratches his head. 'How many times did I invite you down here?' he asks. 'All those times you said you were too busy chasing your stories about the dead and the severed and the chopped and the burned and the buried. Not very neighbourly, Noah, I must say. You know, someday you might consider putting as much focus on the living as you do on the dead.'

A phone in his right trouser pocket buzzes and vibrates. He pulls it out and checks the caller ID. Same green-apple-coloured phone case as mine. I look at my pants pocket and realise my phone is gone.

'Detective Jim England,' Ellis says, eyes on the phone. 'I think we'll just let that one go to voicemail, hey neighbour?'

He waits for my reaction.

'Fuck. You. Ellis. Let. Me. Gooooo. *Hellllpppppppp.*'

'Sorry, I really can't understand a word you're saying, Noah,' he says.

I rock furiously in my chair. Nearly fall over again, but Ellis keeps me upright. 'Woah there, cowboy.'

He swipes through several screens on my phone. 'Let's see now,' he says. 'You're a journo. I'm guessing you got some kind of voice recorder on this devil machine.'

He adjusts his glasses for a moment, brings the phone to his eyes. 'Aaahh, there we are,' he says. 'When in doubt, tap the big red dot.' He makes a show of tapping the recorder button and places the phone on the edge of his sweeping polystyrene diorama. Waves his right hand in a flourish.

'So … shall we begin?'

*

He says he's about to gift me the greatest true-crime story ever written. A story in which the writer will prove as essential to the narrative as the subject. He says he wants his words recorded because he wants his quotes to be exact. 'None of that bullshit paraphrasing that you guys do,' he says. 'Just print the quotes, unadorned. This is not literature, Cork. This is social science.'

He moves to the left edge of his sprawling diorama. A scale replica of our suburb, Jubilee. Parks and shopping strips and hills and valleys and houses by the thousands. Street signs for the streets I drive through every day. Little plastic people and little plastic pets.

He points his finger at a miniature replica of the Jubilee Uniting Church. 'There she is,' Ellis says. 'Our Tamsin. This is the first time I saw her. Sunday morning mass. Eleventh of August, 2019. She was my longest study, Noah. Three years in total.'

Tamsin in the red Sandler slippers. Tamsin with the handbag over her left shoulder. The handbag carrying the music box that her daughter, Helen, found in the South Bank markets. The handbag carrying Tamsin's pocket Bible.

'Don't you understand, Noah?' he asks. 'This is what I've been wanting to show you all this time. I wanted to show you exactly what I have done.'

There's no place like home. There's no place like home.

He tells me the whole story and he shows me the whole story, like a bubbly schoolboy who's brought a diorama to show-and-tell. I see the whole story in painted and glossed polystyrene. The trees, the houses, the people, the blood. Some kind of stop-motion horror movie comes to life in my mind. Die-cast figurines of real people in die-cast figurines of real cars moving through plastic and Styrofoam models of real suburban landscapes.

'This is where she did part-time work at the early learning centre on Spain Road,' he says.

'This is where she met Miles De Jonge at the dog obedience school.

'This is where I saw her sitting with Miles by the birdwatching bench,' he says.

This is where the killer watched her disembarking from the 804 bus from the city.

This is where she sat inside her house watching a daytime *Seinfeld* rerun as she returned emails on her laptop.

This is the back door he walked through. This is where he laid her down after the tranquilliser needle.

This is the pumpkin patch in the backyard where he so boldly buried her severed limbs.

'And this is us, Cork,' Ellis says. 'We're trying to dig that infernal Chinese elm out of your backyard and you're pissing and moaning, like always, about how your great and noble journalistic search for the truth got those cops kicked off the force and sent your crime-writing career down the toilet. You told me about the house payments, Cork. You told me about the debts. You told me how scared you were of having to leave the best street in the world! I asked you if there was any way June and I could help, remember? Remember that, Cork?'

I remember.

'Do you remember what you said?'

I remember.

'You said: "I don't need any help from you, Ellis. What I need is a big ol' crime scoop."'

Ellis claps his hands. 'I nearly burst out laughing in your face, Noah,' Ellis says. 'You were standing ten feet from Tamsin's body, scattered beneath the pumpkin patch! You were standing beside the scoop of a lifetime! You were, in fact, standing beside a remarkably accomplished murderer.'

Still groggy. Still dizzy. Still catching up with the real world. I focus on the woman tied up beside me. On Rita. On getting us out of this basement. I need to scream out of that rattling basement window and maybe my wife might be riding past on her bicycle, aged seventeen, on her way home from Tiffany Bight's birthday party.

Ellis continues his macabre presentation. His great reveal. It feels like a hoax of some kind. Some grand and elaborate prank. Get my wife and me down here in hell, tie us up for a laugh, start rambling about a sociologist sociopath killing women and men in the safest suburb in the world.

He points at a replica of Tilbrook Road State School, Jubilee. 'Tilbrook school fête,' Ellis says, 'spring 1989.'

The twinkling eyes of a man looking through a high school yearbook and stumbling upon past glories. 'The morning of my eureka moment.'

He has artfully constructed a suburban school fête on Tilbrook's rear oval. A yellow super slide and kids on potato sacks. A jumping castle. A candy floss stall. A stage filled with dancers. A small crowd enjoying the show.

He points at the performers on the stage. 'It might not be so easy to see this from where you sit, Cork, but these children are midway through the most god-awful and ill-timed dance tribute to the music of Michael Jackson.' He points at a couple in the audience. 'That's June and me,' he says.

Ellis laughs and the laughter causes him to wheeze and cough again. 'Such an absurd setting, upon reflection, for me to be struck with the most profound and motivating idea of my career. A simple, solitary idea that would define my life's work.'

He grips his bottom lip with his thumb and forefinger. 'I remember sitting right there in that seat with my arm around my June's shoulders. I started looking around at all the residents of my suburb going about their business with their loved ones. Time seemed to slow down around me, Noah, and I could suddenly see them all for what they were. These creatures of routine and habit. These slaves to accepted human behaviour. Eighteen thousand suburban Brisbane convicts imprisoned by their own customs. I looked around me and I could observe, with microscopic focus, all this utterly predictable human order. I wondered how often these people questioned the profound precariousness of their good fortune. To somehow find themselves in the luckiest suburb in the luckiest country tucked safely away at the bottom of the luckiest cosmic miracle in the entire universe. Have you ever had these thoughts, Noah? Do you ever find yourself looking around at this suburb of ours and pondering the meaning of it all? What on earth could we all possibly be trying to achieve here? The Michael Jackson performers made their merciful exit from the stage and then June and I watched the school's brass band defile Beethoven's "Ode to Joy".'

Ellis's eyes light up behind his spectacles. 'And then I had my eureka moment,' he says. 'What if I was to add what we scientists call a "covariate" to the ongoing behavioural experiment that was the very suburb I was living in? What if I was to add my own independent variable to the suburb of Jubilee? If one is searching for dramatic test results, it is, of course, always useful to make one's added independent variable something dramatic. Something really unexpected … something … *out of the box*!'

He points at the replica Todd Street on the sweeping Jubilee diorama, at a small blue sedan parked beside a wattle tree, four houses down from Greer Payne's family home at number 47.

'That's me watching Greer Payne through her kitchen window,' Ellis says. 'Fourth of September 1989. Greer was my first. You never forget your first. I was stronger then, but I was clumsy.'

He laughs at himself. 'Absolute amateur hour. Awful wrestle in Greer's kitchen. Scratches across my face, the whole bit. Took an age to cover my tracks. Mercifully, she succumbed after I struck her left temple with an academic award that I had received from the Australian and New Zealand Anthropological Society, recognising ten years of sterling service to the University of Queensland's School of Social Science.'

He smiles at me. 'Same thing I clocked you with in Miles's living room, in fact,' he says. 'Big metal rod this thing is, shaped like a rolled academic paper tied with ribbon. Weighs as much as a shot-put ball.'

He motions the striking of a blunt object against, presumably, my head. 'Thwump!' He beams. 'Isn't that remarkable, Noah? The sheer sweep of my study. The length of it. You're lucky I've lost a fair whack of strength since eighty-nine, neighbour. Might have done you in, too, with just one swing! And you never would have made it here, Noah, all the way to the end of the story. You never would have met the man behind the curtain!'

*

Look at his eyes. Rita hates that look. It's the sign of a man completely obsessed with the story he's telling. Rita sees that look in me all the time. That distracted storyteller look. She says I always look so far away, so many miles away from her. Lost in the past. Lost in the promise of a story I haven't written yet. Lost in everywhere but where I need to be now. I've been temporarily mesmerised by Ellis's story, too. But I must remember why I came back from the darkness. I must remember why I clicked my heels three times and wished for home.

Save my wife.

Save my daughter.

Get the fuck outta this basement.

There's no place like home.

There's no place like home.

Feeling returns to my fingers. Ellis is still lost in the wonders of his precious diorama.

I use this time wisely. Use it to flex my arm muscles and pull my wrists hard from the cable tie that's cutting into them. Snap the tie, I tell myself. Snap the tie. Snap. The. Tie.

I can't. It's impossible. The tie is too tight. The cable is too thick.

I wiggle my fingers as if they are moving across a piano keyboard. Something hard pinching the left side of my arse. I shift my torso as much as I can beneath the tape straps. I'm sitting on something. Something hard in my pocket. The back left pocket of my jeans.

Ellis's eyes are still fixed on the diorama. He reaches across it, removes the roof of the miniature house at 47 Todd Street, and plucks a die-cast miniature Greer Payne from the home's kitchen.

'The ripple of panic I witnessed spreading through Jubilee in the months following her disappearance,' he says. 'An entire ordinary, run-of-the-mill, middle-class community asking itself one terrifying question: how does a bright young woman just disappear without a trace?'

He grips Greer Payne in his closed fist. 'Planning plus effort plus belief,' he says. 'The scientific observer drives his car into the driveway of 47 Todd Street, parks around the back by the laundry door. The observer takes the queen-size bedsheet from the boot of the car, the army-green one that he took from the bottom of the folded bedsheets in the linen cupboard, the sheet that the observer's wife, June, never uses. The observer wraps the subject in the sheet, along with her keys, her backpack, her headphones and her Sony Walkman. Observer drags body through hall into laundry. Observer scouts for signs of life from neighbours. High wooden fencing on both sides. Observer transfers body to Nissan Sentra boot. Observer returns home with one hour remaining before wife returns home from dropping children at high school musical camp. Transfer subject to basement workshop. Transfer subject to pre-prepared 390-litre waterproof hard plastic basement storage box. Cover subject with two kilograms of Vm3 Zero odour neutralising powder. Open lids of paints and glues and turpentine to also neutralise potential odour of subject's rotting flesh. Across following fortnight, laboriously remove limbs from subject with butcher's bone saw.'

He turns to me. 'This was pre-power-saw days, Noah, you must understand.' Ellis shakes his head. 'Brutal business. Not for the queasy. Observer patiently and progressively buries subject in four phases – arms, legs, torso, head – in four different national parks across South East Queensland. Abracadabra. A bright young woman from Jubilee disappears without a trace.'

Ellis rubs his chin, reaches down to reassemble a trio of miniature plastic journalists with microphones camped outside Greer's miniature home. He's like some god reaching his hands through the diorama's invisible exosphere.

'And, almost immediately, I was able to observe the most remarkable social phenomena,' Ellis says. 'The shot of life that my great independent variable brought to the citizens of Jubilee. The injection of horror and fear. The shock of one family's loss and the way it temporarily united us all. Reminded us, in the worst possible way, of the value of our good fortune; reminded us, through blood and severed limb, my dear Noah, to cherish and protect the ones we love the most. There were candlelight vigils. Countless prayers said in Greer's name. There were national newspaper headlines. Political grandstanding calls to do more to keep the locals safe. Political pressure on the police to dig up the answers that simply refused to sprout back up from four and a half metres down in the cold, hard earth. To be honest, Noah, it's all so long ago now that I couldn't even tell you where I buried that pretty girl's limbs in those forests. Put a loaded gun to my noggin, I wouldn't have the faintest.'

Then the rumours started, Ellis says. The growing voids of investigative answers from the police were filled by whispers and assumptions. An architecture student from the University of Queensland named Bradley Cabrera claimed to the press that he was Greer's long-term boyfriend. He said Greer had wanted to marry him. But in the days before her disappearance, he'd sent her a letter saying she was moving too fast. He wanted to take a break. He was too young for a love so strong.

'That's true, of course,' Ellis says. 'I found the letter in her backpack. Poor Brad, perhaps carrying an inflated sense of his own importance, said it was all his fault that she disappeared. Remind you of anyone, Noah? Bloke was making it all about *him*! Young Brad said he was convinced that his girlfriend was out there somewhere nursing a broken heart. June and I saw him that night on the idiot box; we were eating beef burgundy and mash by the telly. Brad looked into the TV cameras with the face of a daytime soap opera star: *If you're watching this, Greer, please come home. We miss you. We love you.* I chuckled so hard to myself I nearly choked on a half-moon of carrot.'

'After the Bradley Cabrera statement,' Ellis tells me, 'the good citizens of Jubilee were confronted with a hitherto inconceivable notion: what if Greer Payne had actually wanted to go missing from Jubilee?

'A remarkable research question presented itself,' Ellis continues. 'Would a community be less inclined to mourn the disappearance of someone who always wanted to disappear?'

He places Greer Payne back inside the plastic kitchen, inside the plastic Todd Street house.

'But that wasn't the only question raised by my experiment, Noah,' he says. 'I had tapped into a whole lifetime's worth of theoretical inquiry. What role did Greer's youth and attractiveness play in harnessing the community's sympathy? At what point did the nation's media lose interest in the disappearance of Greer Payne? Why exactly was it that, within the space of the six months in which the police investigation reached its tragic and inevitable dead end, her community abandoned Greer Payne to that black hole of a metaphorical out-tray marked "suspected suicide". A decade later, I found myself slipping her name into conversations with my golf buddies in the bar of the Jubilee Golf Club. "I wonder whatever happened to Greer Payne?" I asked. "Who?" they replied, scratching their sunburnt foreheads.'

*

I maintain eye contact with the basement academic psychopath. My extended left-hand fingers can feel the denim lip of my rear left pocket. I look across at my wife in the chair next to me – no sign of waking. Arch my back as Ellis moves around the diorama, piecing his dark oration together in his mind. He might as well be giving a lecture to his UQ anthropology students. All he's missing is a PowerPoint screen and a laser pointer.

I shift my numbing arse an inch along my chair. Fingers digging into the pocket now. Fingers touching something at the bottom of the pocket. I wriggle and shake the thing closer to my fingers. Something that's plastic and metal at the same time. A vision of Clem in my mind. My youngest daughter etching a message into her bedhead.

Gravity

let

me

go

That punk kid Ashton Gillan's useless Victorinox pocket knife. I take it all back, Clem. Dad's sorry, yet again. That's the best twenty-five bucks you ever spent. If I can just get a hand on it.

Reach, you worm-ridden hack. Reach, you blind and narrow-minded nitwit who ruined everything. It's all your fucking fault. *Reach.*

Ellis points now at a row of shops on Gallagher Street, Jubilee. 'Just Cuts salon, twenty-second of May 2004,' he says. 'Last known location of thirty-six-year-old father-of-two Shane Meakin.'

There's a die-cast miniature model of Shane, standing outside the hair salon. Slim build. Brown hair. Brown and black flannel shirt. Blue jeans. The haircut was for a court appearance he was due to attend the day after he disappeared. He'd been charged with possession of a Schedule 1 drug.

Ellis grips his die-cast miniature. 'Now Shane here,' he says, 'nobody gave a fig about poor Shane. Estranged junkie father of two kids. Known ties to the Bandidos outlaw motorcycle gang. Observer encounters subject at eight thirty a.m. on a Monday morning in the day and night pharmacy on Wicker Road. Subject seen consuming methadone from a small medicine cup, part of the subject's opioid dependency treatment program. Observer studies subject from afar for a period of two months. Observer notes subject living temporarily with parents, Roger and Carmel Meakin, of 65 Jacobsen Street, Jubilee. Observer notes semi-regular afternoon visits by subject to a ramshackle low-set home on Belcher Street, Jubilee. Observer notes subject's tendency to drive from Belcher Street to secluded carpark at the foot of Jollys Lookout in the D'Aguilar National Park. Observer notes subject regularly sleeping inside car anywhere from thirty to seventy minutes after apparent consumption of Schedule 1 drug purchased from house at Belcher Street. Observer quietly slips into back seat behind sleeping subject. Observer silently fixes leather waist belt around subject's neck and headrest. Observer inserts hypodermic needle into subject's neck, plunges twenty-five grams of potassium chloride into subject's bloodstream. Observer notes brief and violent struggle by subject. Lack of pulse noted within ninety seconds of injection. Subject disappears from the face of the earth.'

Ellis moves along the diorama and points at an exquisitely detailed plastic facsimile of Jubilee Plaza. He lifts the whole roof off and points at a small clinic on the centre's upper level.

'Here's poor ol' Pete Renwick,' he says. 'Sitting for his bimonthly therapy session in the Hibiscus House psychology centre. Purging himself once again of the trauma and blood of war. There's his seasoned psychologist, Aurora Berg, lending an ear. Poor Pete had a winter habit of drinking himself to oblivion every Saturday night in front of a fire pit in the backyard of his home in Harris Street, Jubilee. Pete's maroon-coloured

Mazda sedan was found empty on the frigid winter morning of the eighteenth of June 2017, in the foothills of Springbrook National Park on the Gold Coast. His wife, Louise, told the police that she woke in her bed at one a.m. that morning to hear her husband pulling out of the driveway. She recalled cursing her idiot husband for once again driving drunk to his brother's house in Glen Forrest, one suburb across from Jubilee.'

Ellis points at a miniature model of a woman standing by a trolley in the cereal and bread aisle of Coles in Jubilee Plaza.

'There's poor lonely Louise Renwick, shopping for groceries for the kids and wondering if she could have done more to help her husband.'

Ellis points at a miniature version of himself, holding a box of muesli in the same aisle.

'There I am just dying to tell Louise that it was me, Noah,' he gasps. He beams. 'It was me who was driving that Mazda out of the driveway! Stone cold Pete Renwick tucked under a blanket in the back.'

Ellis wipes a skerrick of dust from the Jubilee Plaza section of the diorama with the fleshy bottom of his right palm.

'Do you know the disappearance of Peter Renwick received a total of two mentions on the Jubilee community page on Facebook?' Ellis adds. 'He didn't make a single newspaper. Can you believe that, Noah? Father of two disappears off the face of the earth. Barely makes a ripple in the community. Human sorrow is just too blasted sad to talk about, I guess.'

My phone pings with a text message. Ellis snaps back to the present, checks the message. Shakes his head when he reads it. Beams again. Removes his spectacles. I think he just wiped a tear from his right eye.

He holds the phone up to read the message again. 'We did it, neighbour,' he rejoices. The guy's giddy. One would think he's just received news of a loved one's newborn baby. 'Someone named Sherry Sharp says: "News just in from a strictly anonymous source – haha – guess whose book just hit number one on the Nielsen? Big bottle o Bolly coming ur way mister!"'

Ellis adjusts his spectacles as he moves swiftly to a work bench beside the diorama. 'Well, this surely calls for celebration,' he says. He sets two port glasses down in the centre of the bench. Presents a bottle of port to me.

'Galway Pipe Grand Tawny from South Australia, don't mind if we do!' he gushes.

From a thin wooden drawer beneath the bench he takes a black zipped leather pouch – not much bigger than a spectacles case – and tucks it under his left arm. He brings the port glasses over to his stool and sits down an arm's length from me. He places the black pouch on the edge of the diorama.

'Please know that if you start hooting and hollering' – he nods at the black pouch – 'I have ways to make you stop. You understand me, neighbour?'

I nod. He puts the port glasses down, stands and unties the knot of the gag. It loosens, falls around my neck. I suck a deep breath of dank basement air that smells like paint fumes. Stretch the aching muscles in my jaw. Ellis wipes a river of drool from my mouth with an old rag that smells like turpentine. I stare at him warily as he brings my glass of port to my mouth. I sip willingly and the stuff tastes good, but a shot glass of pickle juice would taste good at this point because I'm so thirsty.

Ellis raises his own port glass for a toast. 'To us, Noah,' he says. 'Here's to life at number one! Let's hope it's not too lonely for us at the top.'

He takes a thoughtful sip. 'Mmmmm,' he says. 'Dried pear. Raisins.' Thinks for a moment. 'Grilled nuts.' He takes a second sip.

'Why, Ellis?' I ask.

'Why what, neighbour?'

'Why me?'

'Puh!' he scoffs. 'Why does the wind blow, my friend? Why does the moon glow? Why did fate bring you and your beloved Rita here to Gecko Street in the first place? You can choose your friends, Noah, but you sure can't choose your neighbours!'

He takes another sip.

'You need to end this, Ellis.'

'I know,' he says, 'that's exactly what I'm saying. This is the end. We're in it, Noah.'

'You need to stop this right now, Ellis. This isn't you. This isn't who you are.'

'It's not?' he ponders. 'Then who the hell am I, Cork? Please tell me. I'm dying to know. Well, more precisely, I'm *killing* to know.'

He giggles for a moment. Shakes his head. 'In sixteen years of living side by side,' he says, 'you haven't shown the faintest interest in who I am. You know nothing about me beyond what I have tried to tell you about myself in a hundred awkward conversations in the street, which you did your very best to retreat from. Oh, how many times did I watch you squirming in your shoes, just aching to run back to your latest story, to get away from me? Am I really that repulsive?'

He looks at Rita, bound and gagged in her chair. He shrugs.

'Well – newsflash – clearly yes. In fact, you really wouldn't believe me if I told you, Noah, who it is exactly you've been living next door to all this time.' He giggles again. Then his giggle turns into a belly laugh and then his belly laugh turns into a coughing fit. Deep and rattly. Hollow, like a tin man missing a heart.

'That cough doesn't sound good, Ellis.'

'No,' he says. 'Not too good at all. Truth be told, Noah, I'm not long for this world. It's clear to me now that our beloved neighbour, Detective Jim, and his boys and girls in blue will never catch up with me. My despicable crimes will go unpunished. But rest assured, Noah, the cancer in my blood wrapped a noose around my neck long ago.'

He raises his glass again and takes a longer swig of port.

'It's why I brought you down here, Noah,' he says. 'I didn't want to leave our beloved street without you seeing what I've been able to build down here. I didn't want to go without you knowing the end of the story.'

'Where's June, Noah?'

His big eyes turn up to the ceiling. 'Let's just say my Juney has enjoyed her last Milo. I'll walk upstairs soon and lie beside her in the great beyond. Perhaps we'll get to continue our social studies amid the fires of the eternally damned. But first I need to tell you about Tamsin.'

'I don't wanna hear a word about Tamsin, Ellis,' I say. 'I want you to cut these ties, Ellis. I want you to let me go upstairs and see my daughter.'

'I have every intention of letting you do that, Noah!' he says. 'But first, I need to tell you about the conclusions I have come to, now that I have reached the end of my study. I need you to know the end of the story, Noah.'

'Why?'

'Because you're gonna write about it,' he says. 'Don't you see, Noah? I'm ready for my close-up. I can step into the spotlight now. My study is complete. No longer will your best source have to remain anonymous!'

*

I'm holding Clem's pocket knife in the fingers of my left hand. Watching Ellis Towers walk excitedly to the right side of his grand diorama. My fingers search for the notch on the cutting blade, but I need a longer nail on my right forefinger. I pull at something metal. Damn, you idiot, that's the bottle opener. I try the other side. My stubby nail finally gets a grip on the knife's short blade. I gently pull it out. Slowly turn the blade in my right hand and rest it against the cable tie that binds my wrists.

Ellis tells his story. The one about the disappearance and discovery of Tamsin Fellows. The other side of the Nielsen BookScan number-one bestseller by yours truly. The killer's side. He continues his basement lecture. Offers the macabre findings of his dark study.

There is the pumpkin patch where he dug the limbs back up. He did it for me, he says. He did it all for me. This is Monaco House. These are the books that were so randomly scattered around the home. The Brownie annual. The Lionel Rutledge text. The Satanic books were there already. 'Left behind by some local devil worshipper creeps who were always lighting fires inside that place,' he says. 'Great colour for my purposes, Noah, don't you think? Smoke and mirrors, my friend. Smoke. And. Mirrors.'

One brief blade cut along the cable tie. Keep him talking. Two brief blade cuts. Keep him talking. Three brief blade cuts.

This is the oven with those awful words. *Cunt money. Cunt money. Cunt money.* 'The words were on the oven when I got there,' he says. 'It was breathtaking to see those words for the first time. What could they possibly mean? Well, I thought, maybe I'll leave that for Noah to work out.'

The observer brought the copy of *The Wonderful Wizard of Oz* with him. Found it in the Archives secondhand bookshop on Charlotte Street. Tamsin's music box had provided the observer with a theme tune. Red shoes and bluebirds and no place like home.

'I just knew your readers would love that stuff,' Ellis says, beaming again. 'My little themed trail of breadcrumbs. You wouldn't believe how many times I rewrote those stupid little breadcrumbs.'

He takes two steps to his left and points at a replica of Spearwood Reservoir, the real-life 380-metre dam wall reproduced as a thirty-centimetre wall of polystyrene, painted grey. Some four thousand real-world megalitres of rippling dam water recreated with three folded sheets of blue cellophane.

'Look, here's our friend Miles De Jonge,' Ellis points out. 'Sitting on the stone steps of the Hickory Wattle walking track. He's sitting there wondering why on earth someone dropped that note in his letterbox. He's cursing himself for never telling the police about his regular reservoir liaisons with Mrs Fellows. How did it come to this?'

The killer points to a small figurine of a man at the start of the Hickory Wattle walking track.

'And here comes brave Noah Cork, about to stumble upon the scoop of a lifetime.'

He points at the asbestos-walled garage in the backyard of the replica of our house.

'Look, Noah, here you are again,' Ellis says, 'furiously tapping away at your soon-to-be numero-uno bestseller.'

Ellis rubs his chin as he shakes his head, awed by something. 'You certainly held up your end, Noah,' he says. 'I could never have done what you did. Put it all into one seamless narrative like that.'

He points at a miniature woman standing on our driveway. 'And here's your long-suffering Rita,' he says. 'Staring up at the sky like she always does, wondering when on earth her husband will ever stop writing his precious stories. Poor, poor Noah Cork. Filling his pages with all the details of the past while missing all the little details that really matter in the present. Like a wife neck-deep in a mental breakdown.'

'It's not a mental breakdown, Ellis,' I say.

'Oh, stop kidding yourself, Noah. A woman is seen regularly staring up at the sky like some kind of deranged lunatic. That woman just decides to stop talking overnight. Does that strike you as a person of sound mind?'

'Says the man with the two bound captives in his basement,' I say.

He laughs. 'Fair point.' He gestures to a model of a girl entering Ellis and June's house in the diorama.

'All the little details you missed, Noah,' Ellis says. 'Like young Clementine Cork here, walking over to her neighbours' house for a Milo, wearing the red shoes that she'll leave under the sofa in our media room.'

He points at a man by the letterbox of Jonathan and Rose Cavendish's house at number 40 Gecko Street.

'Like me here, after midnight, avoiding the gaze of that infernal surveillance camera of yours, as I do my little mail drops to every house in the street except yours!'

He shakes his head. 'Oh, the things I've done for you and your story, Noah. But what results! Did you see what we created together? Your words and my actions combining in one grand sociological impact study. The circus we created. We're the only thing the community is talking about, Noah. Everywhere I go, the things I hear them saying. The whispers in the shopping aisles. The speculations in the doctors' rooms. Tamsin this and Noah that. And now a number-one national bestseller!'

Ellis smiles, raises his palms in the air, takes a bow. 'No need to thank me, Noah,' he says.

Keep him talking. Keep on cutting. Keep him talking. Keep on cutting.

The pocket knife slips out of my left hand. I catch it with my right. *Cut, cut, cut.*

'Why kill Miles?'

Ellis ponders this question for a long moment.

'Mmmm,' he says. 'Why ... kill ... Miles?'

He moves around the diorama, meanders back to the stool. Sits down once more.

'Well, I guess that brings me to the conclusions of my study,' he says.

He checks that my phone is still recording on the diorama table. Nods. Takes a deep breath and exhales.

'I have now murdered a total of five people in this community across a study period of thirty-six years,' he says. 'I have noted countless behavioural changes within this community throughout that time. I have witnessed a community grow and fracture and grow again under the unifying, life-affirming spectre of one seemingly ordinary suburban man's senseless acts of butchery and evil.'

Ellis leans towards me and places a gentle hand on my left knee.

'But do you know what single experimental factor has changed the most throughout my study, Noah?'

'Please tell me, Ellis,' I say. *Cut, cut.* 'What has changed the most in your sick and twisted study?'

He smiles. 'Me,' he says. 'The observer. The very observation changed the observer. The most remarkable and unexpected phenomenon began to reveal itself.'

Just a whisper now. 'I started to enjoy it, Noah,' he says. 'Every terrifying and impossible independent variable I added to the study. Every thrilling time I got away with it. Every word I ever read about my actions. Every rumour that spread through my suburb. With every new study I came closer and closer to the most profound scientific truth ...'

He leaves the truth in the turpentine air for a moment. Adjusts his glasses. Turns his head and stares at my unconscious and bound wife as he says, 'I am a monster.'

'No you're not, Ellis,' I say. 'You're just a very troubled man. You just need to stop doing what you're doing.' Keep talking. Think. Lie. Cheat. Deceive. Live. 'There is a good man in you, still, Ellis.'

Cut, cut, cut.

Ellis shakes his head, still staring at Rita. 'No, I'm afraid not, Noah,' he says. 'That last page of your book was the truest page you ever wrote. I'm a deranged and perverted monster who somehow crawled from a bucket of evolutionary slime to end the life of a good and loving Brisbane mother of two teenaged children.'

He reaches his left hand out and lifts Rita's chin.

'Get your hands off my wife,' I say. 'Why are you looking at her like that?'

'You really did hurt my feelings in that book, Noah,' he says. 'It hurt, what you wrote about me, because it was true. You were so right about me, Noah. I killed them because I wanted to. I killed your friend, Miles, because I wanted to. I killed him because I could. And I'm afraid that's how this story of ours is going to end.'

He stands and turns his back to me. I hear him unzipping the black pouch.

'What are you doing, Ellis?'

His head is down, hands working on something. 'In the end, the greatest revelation is the darkness,' he says. 'The only conclusion we are ever left with is conclusion itself.'

Cut, cut, cut, cut, cut, cut.

I scream at my wife next to me as the blade in my hands makes another feeble notch in the impossibly thick cable tie. 'Rita, wake up! Rita! *Ritaaaaa!*'

Ellis turns back around. In his right hand he holds a dripping syringe filled with a clear and unidentifiable liquid.

Cut, cut, cut, cut, cut, cut.

'Oh come now, Noah,' he says. 'What do you care? Surely you won't miss her. You've been acting like she doesn't exist for years.'

'That's not true.'

'Puh! She might as well be invisible to you. It's how she feels, isn't it? Why do you think she stopped talking? Because she knows it's no use talking to a husband and a father so caught up in everything else except his own bloody family!'

Ellis takes two steps towards my wife.

'Rita! Rita! Ritaaaaaa! Wake up, pleeeeease.'

I plead with Ellis. 'Wait, wait, Ellis! Don't do this, pleeease.'

I bargain with Ellis. 'I'll never write about this,' I stammer. 'You … you do this … if you hurt her, Ellis … I will not write another word for as long as I live. Nobody will ever read a word from me about your grand study. I will never write about what you did.'

He nods his head knowingly. 'Oh, you'll write about it, Noah,' he says. 'This chapter will be the most painful thing you ever write. It will almost be the death of you, but you will write it. It's too good a story not to. And it will be the greatest first-person true-crime story ever written.'

Cut, cut, cut, cut, cut. This fucking tie will not be severed. Please. Please. Please let this tie break.

Furious cutting now. Back and forth in small cuts. Hacksaw cuts. I feel the friction heat of the blade on my skin. I'm cutting so frantically that on every third cut the blade is slicing through my skin.

Ellis leans over my wife, puts two fingers on her neck, searching for the ideal insertion point for the needle.

Ellis drives the needle into the flesh above Rita's left collarbone. His right thumb moves to the plunger base.

'Ellis, *waaaiiiit*!' I scream.

Ellis holds his thumb over the plunger.

'Ellis, *please* … no!'

And then the sound of the doorbell echoes through the basement. Ellis pauses. His eyes snap to a square speaker fixed to the basement wall, which is clearly connected to the doorbell upstairs. He pulls the syringe from Rita's neck, carries it as he moves to the small black and white surveillance camera monitor on his bench showing a live view of his front yard.

Detective Jim England is frantically pressing the front doorbell.

The speaker rings again.

Ellis spits out a word I can't quite catch and then he slaps the syringe on the bench. Points at me. 'Should you be thinking about making a sound while I am attending to Mr England upstairs, I would ask you to first consider the welfare of your younger daughter,' he says.

He scurries up the stairs, opens and then closes and locks the door behind him.

I cut, cut, cut at the cable tie. Turn to my wife. 'Rita,' I say. 'Rita. You must wake up. Please. Please wake up.'

Cut, cut, cut. I've lost all sense of where I'm cutting now. I'm too exhausted. Too spent. Too rough. Too frantic. *Cut, cut, cut.* Breathe. Catch my breath. *Cut, cut, cut.* But it's no use. No matter how many times I slice away at the plastic, it seems to make no difference. Maybe Ashton Gillan sold my daughter a fugazi. A dodgy blade that wouldn't cut through a ripe tuckshop apple. I catch my breath. Hang my head. Maybe this is how the story was always going to end. A small room in hell at number 41 Gecko Street. This was supposed to be the best street in the world. But it's the street with the room where Ellis Towers stores his biggest secrets. Ellis Towers and his personal crowbar space. Did he show this room to June? Did he hand his wife the crowbar?

Some crowbars are just too heavy to hold.

And I think of my mum in my dreams. I think of the woman standing in the centre of my flooded storage room. Nothing but a drug dream. I made it all up in my mind. She was me and I was her. My mum's dreamspeak echoing in my head. My dreamspeak. *She wants all of you. The light, the dark, the good, the bad. She wants all of it.*

'Rita,' I whisper, sucking thick basement air into my lungs. Breathe in, breathe out. 'I need to tell you something.' Breathe, breathe. 'I never told you why Mum went swimming that day. I always told you and the girls that she drowned in the Woorim Beach surf. I told you she got carried away by a rip and we never saw her again. That's the truth of it, but it's not the whole truth of it. I never told you why she went swimming that day. I never let you open up that room. I don't know why. I'm sorry. I just never … I never gave you the crowbar. I thought it would be too heavy for you to hold, so I kept that room closed. I shoved all my guilt and shame into that room and then I built my museum as big as it could be so anyone who entered it wouldn't have the faintest chance of finding their way to that secret space. I filled that museum with every yarn I could get my hands on. Box after box, story after story. Level upon level of this golden repository, built by stories and bricks, nailed together by my insatiable ambition, by my need to be everything I thought you thought I was, Rita.'

I rub my thumb along the pocket-knife blade. Keep trying to cut the cable tie. No use. I look around the basement. It's not so different from the storage room in my dreams.

'See, you keep a story locked away for too long, the story starts to grow without you really even knowing it,' I whisper.

'The story grows bigger than it was when you first locked it away. Twice the size. Three times the size. It gets so big inside you that it starts to break free. The thing starts rattling the lock, banging on the door. Then it busts loose. Starts huntin' you down in the outside world, seeking vengeance from you for all the time it spent on the inside.'

And I hand my wife the crowbar. Because there's nothing to lose now. There's nothing to hide after certain death.

I keep my eyes on the surveillance camera monitor, where Ellis Towers is telling lies to Detective Jim England, and the lies he's telling make me want to tell my truths. I watch Ellis walk back to the nature strip with Jim. Ellis is making gestures that suggest he wants to help Jim with his search. If I'm quick enough, I might have time to tell Rita the whole story, crack open this room with the crowbar, kick down the door, let the story flood this basement in hell.

TWENTY-FIVE

And the scoop shall set you free.

– Rutledge, *Journalism Practices and Principles*

I became a true-crime journalist when I was thirteen years old. At least that's how old I was when I covered my first crime. No qualifications whatsoever. No cadetship. Just a burning desire to report the facts of the things I saw as I was growing up on Bribie Island.

I was already into journalism by then. Dad always slid the *Courier-Mail* across to me at the breakfast table and we both liked the grisly crime stuff. Bodies pulled from rivers. Corrupt cops caught up in the affairs of underworld gangsters. Mum and Meg called Dad and me a couple of ghouls. But I was sure I'd found my calling. For years, I'd been drawing and scribing fake newspapers for my family, documenting the most mundane family activities and milestones. The *Bega Street Bugle* I called my newspaper. The *Bugle* never featured any crime stories because there were, much to my disappointment, never any crimes in my home or neighbourhood to report.

Then one day I had a break between school lunch and afternoon touch football and decided to ride my bike down to the Reel Life bait and tackle shop to surprise Dad and help him out. But when I got there, I saw my old man from afar, locking the shop doors and then hopping into a green Volkswagen that appeared to belong to a woman with big and curly brown hair, who I'd never seen before. When my dad and this mystery woman drove off, I tried to ride my bike fast enough to follow them to wherever it was they were going. I pushed those pedals so hard that my thigh muscles turned to stone. And I still couldn't ride fast enough. I lost them.

I spent the next hour riding around the streets of Bribie Island, searching for the car. Eventually, sure enough, I found it parked in the driveway of a small blue weatherboard box of a home, in a nothing street on the calm side of Bribie Island. I wheeled my bike up to the gate. Rested my bike on the front fence and padded slowly and carefully to the front door. I was about to ring the bell when I heard moaning coming from a room at the back. I crept round the side of the house, down the driveway, and came to a bedroom window that was half-open. Beneath that window, I kneeled and prayed that it wasn't my father making that embarrassing moaning noise. And I told myself to run away. Even at the age of thirteen, I was wise enough to tell myself that nothing good or useful could come from confirming the truth of the scenario that was forming in my mind.

But I couldn't stop myself. I simply could not resist pulling on the thread of this extraordinary real-life crime story. I had to see where it went. I silently and carefully pulled a black trash bin beneath the window and I climbed atop the bin and slowly peered in through the gap between the half-open window and a flapping white cotton curtain. And in that view I saw my naked father wriggling between the legs of the mystery woman with the big brown hair. For some reason I was immediately struck by the thought of the first full-size legal fish I ever caught, the first time I went fishing with my dad. My father's body, I realised, was flapping between those smooth white female legs the same way that flathead had flapped, gasping for water, on the shores of Woorim Beach.

A week later, skipping afternoon sport again, I returned to the back window of the blue fibro house. I'd brought a camera with me this time. Rented it for a fiver from a kid in my biology class named Eric Flyger. A 35-millimetre Canon SLR that Eric usually used to shoot and self-develop competition-level images of Bribie Island birds and insects. I shot twenty-four photos of the naked forty-five-year-old flathead fucking for dear life. Beneath that window of the blue fibro box home of the woman with the big brown hair, I realised I had stumbled upon a page-one crime scoop for the ages.

I set about building my story. Spent days on my bicycle, riding around Bribie Island, piecing together the identity of the mystery woman with the big brown hair. I discovered that her name was Trish Pembroke. She was a thirty-five-year-old bartender at the Bribie Island RSL. One Saturday morning, a month later, I presented my latest edition of the *Bega Street Bugle* to my family at the breakfast table. My dear mum, Alison, was at the kitchen stove, cooking scrambled eggs with slices of fried luncheon meat. My older sister, Meg, was at the table eating cornflakes. My father, Phil Cork, was biting into a piece of Vegemite toast. The word 'SCOOP' stretched across page one of my amateur newspaper. The headline was clear and unmerciful: BRIBIE ISLAND HUSBAND PHIL CORK BETRAYS WIFE IN SHAMELESS SEX ROMP. The story was an eight-hundred-word feature written in first-person by 'Noah Cork, *Bega Street Bugle* chief reporter', a gripping and salacious tabloid account of how I came upon the scoop of my young life, complete with the damning photographic evidence, the series of shots developed by Eric Flyger in his family's garage, still smelling of Clag glue.

> *Bribie Island small-business owner and father of two, Phil Cork, has been caught balls-deep, fucking his brains out with the bargirl from the Bribie Island RSL. The* Bega Street Bugle *can confirm that the suburban tryst has been going on for at least a month. On no less than four occasions, your fearless scribe witnessed his father's flabby white arse pounding for queen and country as he went heels to Jesus with his taproom tart in a dank and featureless bedroom on Mule Street. Cork's mysterious alehouse harlot, Ms Trish Pembroke, could not be reached for comment yesterday as her mouth was fused to the lips of another sexual conquest.*

Dad tore the newspaper in half after he'd read it, then rushed me like a Wallabies prop. He tackled me to our living room floor and slapped me across my face three times with his open hand. 'What have you done?' he asked. 'What have you done, you stupid fucking boy?'

I spat back at my father as he placed his hands around my collar. I spat back in journo speak. 'Comment for the press, Mr Cork? What do you have to say to your loving wife, Alison, who gave her whole fucking life to you? What do you have to say to your children, you pitiful cunt?'

My first great pulling of the thread. My first big dig.

Thoughts of the late Lionel Rutledge: '*Sometimes the trickiest thing about the digging is actually finding what you were looking for.*'

My father moved out of our house after my story. He set about punishing himself for his crimes with a solitary drinking binge that lasted thirty years. My mum punished my father – and maybe punished me, too – with her silence. She didn't seem to say a word for a month after my story. Her words came back eventually, and she started to talk to me again, but I knew something had been stripped from her. Something to do with love that was lost to her, something that was replaced by something sad and irreversible. I barely saw her laugh throughout my whole high school life. She swore to me that I wasn't the cause of her sadness but we both knew I had a hand in it. She swore to me that she was proud of what I did, of my adherence to the truth. But I still felt like I had something to square with her, something to make right.

I tried to make everything right by working hard at my studies. Three weeks from the end of my senior high school year, I won a scholarship to study journalism at the University of Queensland. Opportunity of a lifetime. Mum and Dad attended the scholarship ceremony. They posed for photographs together. They cried together. Tears of pride. I told them both that I never would have won the scholarship in the first place if it hadn't been for that crime story I'd written when I was thirteen years old. They seemed to agree with me.

But a week after the ceremony, on a Sunday afternoon at sunset, long after the lifesaver patrols had packed their things and gone home, Mum went for an ocean swim at Woorim Beach, on the surf side of Bribie Island. She left her towel and her beach bag on the sand. The next day that towel and beach bag were handed in to the Bribie Island Surf Club as lost property. I never saw my mum again – until I started seeing her skeleton in my closet.

*

'That's it,' I say. 'That's all I wanted to tell you, Rita. That's all that's left in the storage room. That's all. That's all of me.'

My eyes are fixed on the CCTV monitor. Just an empty black and white yard on the screen with nobody in it.

I turn from the monitor to see that Rita has her eyes open now. Tears welling. The gag still in her mouth. I don't know how long she has been listening to me. Something peaceful about her. Something calming. I don't know how much of the story she heard. I don't even know how it happened like that, how my little story woke my wife up.

That's how it is with Rita Munro. She's special like that. How did Adam Duncan put it? *Your mum's fucking miraculous.*

'I love you so fucking much, Rita Munro,' I say.

Rita stares into my eyes. And she talks to me without talking. Something deeper than moon-time comms. Something closer to love.

Then her head whips up to the sound of the basement door opening once more. Ellis Towers thumps down the stairs. Moves straight to the work bench and reaches for the loaded syringe that he placed there minutes ago.

'Now, where were we?' he says.

He steps swiftly to Rita and stabs the syringe hard into her neck. Rita convulses with panic, fury maybe, in her chair.

'Ellis, *nooooo*!' I scream.

Ellis pauses for a moment, turns to me.

'Just think for a second, please,' I say.

I turn to Rita. She's breathing hard. Sweat and panic on her face. Struggling for clean air with the gag in her mouth.

'Breathe, sweetie,' I say. 'In through the nose. Please do not move. Just stay still, sweetie.'

Ellis's thumb moves once more to the plunger. Rita's eyes roll south and clock the syringe sticking from her neck.

'You kill her, Ellis,' I say. 'And I'll tell the world the real reason why you killed Tamsin Fellows.'

'What real reason?'

I resume hacking away at the cable tie with the pitiful pocket knife covered in sweat from my palms.

'You know the reason,' I say. 'The real reason you killed all of 'em. Your dad. What was his name again?'

'George,' he says, his eyes back on Rita now.

'Yeah, that's right, George Towers,' I say.

Cut, cut, cut, cut, cut. Maybe it's working, I think. Maybe I'm almost through the cable. Something about Rita's face a few minutes ago has charged me with hope. I can feel it now. Maybe a millimetre more of hard plastic to cut through. Might as well be a mile. But keep going. *Cut, cut, cut.*

'I remember what you told me about him when we were digging out that Chinese elm,' I say. 'It all makes sense now.'

Ellis turns back to me. 'What did I tell you about my father?' He's confused.

I shake my head, full of sorrow. Full of understanding. 'I'm so sorry for what he did to you.'

'What the hell are you talking about?'

Cut, cut, cut, cut, cut.

'The beatings, remember. The things he did to you in the dark.'

Ellis shakes his head. 'That's not true,' he says. 'My father was a great man.'

'That's not what you told me, Ellis, by the elm tree. You told me he was the reason you have dark thoughts. You told me he was the reason you could never go home again to England. He did it to you, didn't he? He was your own Victor Frankenstein, wasn't he? He made the monster.'

Ellis's face is going red. 'Lies,' he gasps. 'You're telling lies. That's all bullshit.'

Cut, cut, cut, cut, cut.

'Only bullshit until it's believed,' I say.

Ellis's right kneecap is bouncing, because, I realise, he's nervously tapping his right foot on the basement's green concrete.

Cut, cut, cut, cut … cut.

'Won't be lies once I write about it, Ellis,' I say. 'Psycho just don't cut it no more for a public who've seen it all. All those loyal readers are going to want a deeper explanation. I'm gonna have to give 'em one, Ellis. Guess poor ol' George is gonna have to take the—'

I don't get to finish the sentence, because the pocket knife slips from my fingers, drops to the concrete. Ellis spots it between my feet. Some kind of angry frothing emerges at the corners of his mouth as he pulls the syringe from Rita's neck. He holds the syringe the way he would hold a spear as he drives the needle point down in the precise direction of my left eyeball. With the little strength I have left inside me, I force my wrists apart and the cable tie snaps free, just in time for me to grip his descending wrist, stopping it mere inches from my eyeball.

The force of his attack pushes me over in my chair. Flat on my back now, my legs still fastened to the chair. Only my arms for protection. Ellis is much older than me but he's heavier, too. He forces all his weight on top of me. My only defence is my arms and they're busy stopping the needle that's moving closer to my iris. I'm pushing, pushing, pushing back against the force of his wrist. Now he's got two hands pressing on the syringe. Two hands plus the weight of his chest and legs against me.

Hold. Hold. Hold. But the needle moves closer. I can see a drip of the fluid emerging from the tip.

And then I hear it.

A scream from my wife so primal that I wonder if it does not, in fact, come from the very centre of the earth. I wonder, at first, if I'm only seeing things, if I'm still woozy somehow from whatever hallucinogenic drug Ellis Towers recently injected into my bloodstream. But as I lie here on my back, fighting for my life against the quintessential neighbour from hell, I witness, out of the corner of my right eye – the one not staring into the dripping eye of a needle – what could only be described as another of my wife's miracles.

I've read about this kind of thing before. Never believed it for a second. Texas mum of three deadlifts car to save trapped baby. Brazilian mother of two breaks windscreen with bare fist to rescue baby from flooding car. Mum in northern Canada wrestles a polar bear to save her six kids. They call it hysterical strength, when adrenaline and love combine to possess an individual with a physical strength beyond natural human capacity. But this feels different from all that. What was that word Ellis used a while back to describe my wife? Yeah, that's it. This feels like something far more … *mystical.*

Mystical is the total calm in which I watch my wife, Rita Munro, snap the cable tie that binds her wrists, then lean her chair back – with the controlled balance of a circus performer – to reach for the pocket knife on the ground. Mystical is the ease with which she cuts through the silver tape that binds her legs.

The stunned look on my face is enough to make Ellis turn his head back towards my wife, just to see what I have seen. And that's his fatal mistake. To look at her.

Rita stands from her chair and now stands above him. Reaches down with two hands and clutches her neighbour by the collar. Heaves the killer up to her eye level in a display of terrifying strength. And all I see from my vantage point down here is the back of Ellis's head. And all I hear is a banshee scream from my wife that forces me to bring my hands to my ears in fear and awe. She roars into his face with such force that I see Ellis's hair blow back, as though he's standing in front of a violent cyclone. The roar makes the basement window rattle. A month of silence, I think for a moment. A month of stored noise, released in one awful sound. It makes Ellis's spray-paint tins wobble on his work bench. It makes several little lifelike figurines of Jubilee residents fall over on the diorama.

The roar lasts for almost thirty seconds. Feels like something's gonna burst inside my eardrums, like the arteries in my brain are swelling. I can't find the words inside my head that I could use to beg my wife to stop. The furious shrieking comes to a merciful end and Rita releases her hold on Ellis Towers. His body falls backwards like a felled tree and his big head smacks hard against the green concrete basement floor. I'm still lying flat on my back, legs fastened helplessly to the chair. Ellis's face falls directly in line with my eyes down here on the ground. I'm a handspan from my neighbour's nose. His face is frozen, white as oat milk. It's like he stared for too long and from too close at a lightning bolt. Like he stared too long into the electric-blue eyes of God. I can't see his eyes clearly because the thick lenses of his spectacles have shattered into splintered webs. But I can't take my eyes off him.

I feel Rita cutting through the tape around my legs. Pressure eases on my thighs and then my legs move freely. My head is still resting on the concrete when I feel my wife's calming hand upon my forehead. Brushing my hair back with her thumb. Holding my cheek with a loving palm.

'Rita …' I say. Thoughts in my head that defy understanding. 'What … *the fuuuuck*?'

She smiles, rubs my forehead tenderly once more. Brings a forefinger to her lips. 'Ssshhhhhhh,' she says.

She pulls me up from the ground and holds my hand as she leads us back up the stairs we descended into this hellish basement. The door is closed at the top and Rita reaches a hand out to turn the knob. The door is locked, so my wife takes a half-step back, then kicks the door clean off its hinges.

TWENTY-SIX

The world is an ever-turning wonder. The world is a dark and terrifying place. The world is bursting at the buckle with light and love. And it's your job to witness it. That's all you have to do. Hear it. See it. Feel it. Now write it.

– Rutledge, *Journalism Practices and Principles*

The smell of rain on tarmac. I open Ellis's front door to stare at the eye of the storm. I've seen this before. The blue-green colours in the sky like the colours in my wife's eyes. The dome of a mini cyclone like a glass bell jar placed over Jubilee. The strange peace in it. The deception of it. A meteorological phenomenon pretending to sleep. I don't trust this thing for a second. Sly bastard acting as if it hasn't just destroyed the suburban street my family has lived in for sixteen years. The flashes of blue and green popping behind the gun-metal grey clouds. Signs of intent. Promises of further punishment.

'I think we can go,' I say. 'But go quick, Rita.'

Rain is still falling hard, but there's no hail in it. I hold the door open for Rita to pass me, carrying our sleeping daughter,

Clem, in her arms. Clem's head bounces on Rita's shoulder as she pads quickly along Ellis's tiled front path. We reach the nature strip and take in a full view of what happened up here in the cul-de-sac while we were in that strange hell, way down there at the bottom of the steep basement stairs.

The sweep of the destruction stops us in our tracks. So many leaves and branches across the tarmac that you could squint and believe it was a forest floor. Curled and ripped sheets of tin and plasterboard among the leaves. Everything wet. Everything blowing. My frangipani bald and broken. Rita's pot plants that once surrounded our yellow letterbox now spilled and cracked and scattered across the cul-de-sac. A wattle tree has fallen and broken Anushka Burman's front fence. Several hail-dented cars at the bottom of the street have broken windscreens. A free-standing basketball hoop with backboard from a neighbour's driveway six doors down has crumpled Jon and Rose Cavendish's garage door.

A violent thunderclap wakes Clem from her sleep. She rubs her eyes and slides down her mother's side to the ground. Turns her head up to me. 'Is this a circumstance of great peril, Dad?'

I look at my daughter. 'Not anymore, Clem,' I say.

Rita grips Clem's hand, shakes her head. Then she pulls Clem quickly along the nature strip and I follow my wife and daughter to the front door of our house. Clem runs ahead and taps the doorbell six times fast, like it's the shoot button on a gaming controller.

'Who is it?' Erin calls from inside.

Clem has two hands pressed against the front door. 'Harry Styles,' she says.

The door flies open.

'Clem,' Erin exclaims. And she exhales a breath she's clearly been holding for hours. She cries and smiles and squeezes her younger sister with such force that the two girls would have fallen flat on the front porch, if not for their mum kneeling to break their fall. Now it's a three-person hug. A human shelter. A cave formed by the ones I love the most.

Seb Cavendish stands in the doorway now, smiling at the embrace, breathing hard. He nods at me and I nod back at him.

I take two steps towards my wife and children, but a noise from the clouds makes me freeze. A thrumming sound. A sound that is, impossibly, as silent as it is deafening. A noise that echoes in our souls before it echoes in our eardrums. *Thrrrrrruuuuuuuummmmmmm.* Rita stands up and looks up at the sky like she knows it. I don't understand why, but she's looking at that sky like they have a history. It's something like the way a woman might look at a violent ex-lover through a café window. *Thrrrrrruuuuuuuummmmmmm.* I remember this now, too. The devil thrumming. The sound of the earth rebelling. The sound of the wind waking up on the wrong side of the bed. And now the sound of the panels on our glass doors exploding into a thousand pieces as a violent gale crashes into our home, lifting picture frames from the walls inside the house, turning kitchen appliances on their sides. I'm not immediately sure whether to run inside to shelter the family in the bathroom or to stay out here on the porch where there are no porcelain vases breaking against walls. I wrap my arms around my wife and kids. Then hear the tearing sound of nails and metal being ripped from wood. Like a rip in the wall between space and time. Rita looks up and I follow her gaze to where a corner of our roof is being torn from its fixings.

'Get down low and get into the bathroom,' I scream. The girls and I hunch over and scurry into the house. But I stop in the doorway when I notice that Rita is still standing frozen on the porch, staring up at the roof. Transfixed by the violence and the noise and the fury of the storm.

'Rita!' I scream. 'Get inside.'

And then a new light floods our home as, above me, the entire flat tin roof, along with the white ceiling plasterboard underneath it, is peeled off our small and insignificant house by a force of nature I can't possibly understand. The storm pulls our roof away as casually as you might ring-pull the lid from a can of baked beans, and the wind and rain smash into our faces where we stand inside our home with no top, our shoebox without a lid. We're like lab rats in a domestic maze of walls and roofless rooms.

Flashes of blue and green in the sky behind the clouds. I snap my head right to see my wife again. But she's gone. She's not standing where she stood one simple second ago.

'Rita,' I scream.

And I run back through the front doorway and stand on the porch to lay my eyes upon the impossible sight of my wife desperately clinging to the prop pole of our yellow letterbox, her legs suspended in the air by a wind that wants to take her away. A wind that wants to blow her into the sky. A force that wants to steal Rita Munro from us. A gravity that wants to let her go.

'Ritaaaaa!'

I run to my wife, shielding my eyes from the heavy rain and the flying debris. She surely can't hold on to the letterbox much longer. Her strength seems to be ebbing away. Her fingers are slipping from the pole. Too wet. Too loose a grip. Too impossible is this moment.

Her right hand slips from the pole just as my two hands reach her right wrist.

'I got you,' I say. 'I've got you, Rita.'

The force of the wind pulls my wife and me along the nature strip, my shoes sliding along the wet grass, but I lean back against the push and pull of the cruel and tyrannical storm and I don't let go. I will never let her go.

Do not let her go. That's all you have to do, Dad said. Do. Not. Let. Her. Go.

My wife is a kite now, legs pointing up towards the sky, and connected to the earth only by a grip that her husband knows deep down he's about to lose.

'I've got you, Rita,' I scream. 'Don't go.'

Aching now. Pain in my arms and legs. Heart beating too fast. Can't catch my breath now. Tears in my eyes. My feet sliding further along the grass.

'I've got you, Rita,' I scream. 'Please ... *don't go.*'

But I'm sliding. I'm slipping. Can't stay on my feet. I'm losing this grip. I'm losing my wife.

She stares into my eyes. She's like an astronaut floating inside a space capsule that is the very earth surrounding her. Weightlessness. Zero gravity. Arms losing strength.

And I can't keep pulling. Can't keep holding on. Fingers slipping.

'Rita, I can't—'

Then two more sets of hands grip mine, pull hard against the bullying wind. The hands of my daughters, Erin and Clementine Cork. Rita's girls. My girls.

'Don't let go, Mum!' Erin screams through the driving rain. '*Don't go.*'

The girls drop their weight back towards the ground, try to pull their mother back to the earth.

'Heeelllp!' I scream into the rain. 'Please help us!'

My feet are still slipping in the relentless pull. The girls and I slide a foot along the grass as Rita rises another foot into the air.

Then I see Seb Cavendish's arms around my chest, and, out of the corner of my eye, spot Axel Olsson rushing to join the strange and impossible street scene and wrap his arms, in turn, around Seb's chest, pulling him back hard towards the earth. And there's Jim England, brave bullet-slug-in-the-head detective, running to us from his own storm-battered home.

'Jesus Christ!' he exclaims, reaching up for a two-handed grip on Rita's forearm. 'Puuulll,' he screams. '*Puuulll!*'

A human chain of good-hearted neighbours pulls on the woman in the sky. A tug-of-war between six suburban mortals and a greedy sky. And no matter how hard we pull her down, the sky keeps pulling her up. The sky is winning. We can't keep holding her like this. Somebody's gotta win. And somebody's gotta lose.

A gentle voice behind my left ear.

'You can go if you want to, Mum.'

I look down at Clem, who is crying as she says the words, but still pulling as hard as she can. 'You can go if you need to, Mum,' she howls.

I shake my head. No. No. *No, Clem.* No.

'Noooooo, Rita. You can't do that. You're not allowed to do that,' I shout, squeezing my words out through the tears and the pain and the rain. 'I'm sorry, I'm sorry. You are not allowed to go. YOU. ARE. NOT. ALLOWED. TO. GO.'

And I pull harder and harder and harder and I pull so hard that I worry I'll pull her whole arm clean off. But she can take it. Because she's strong. Because she's made of things I don't understand. Because she's Rita Munro.

Yet still her wrist slips beneath my fingers.

'No.'

Still she rises into the air.

'No.'

My wife stares into my eyes. Not a hint of fear there. Only fate. Only miracles. And she speaks to me without speaking to me. That look in her eye. That voice in my troubled head. I can hear her.

I love you so fucking much, Noah Cork.

In the sky over Rita's shoulder I watch a flying piece of scrap paper abruptly lose height and start falling towards the ground. Falling. Falling. Leaves falling now, too. Dipping and swaying on their descent. In an instant, the wind has dropped. Physics. Necessary collapse.

With nothing to pull against, six suburban mortals fall back hard onto the nature strip. And my wife, Rita Munro, falls back to earth.

Falls back into me.

*

Zoom in on all my rain-soaked gratitude, if you think you can stomach it. Use that satellite-eye view from outer space. Zoom through that layer between humanity and the universe, look through that exosphere where atoms skip loose from earth's embrace, see through all that blue-hued illusion and the shifting ghost clouds veiling Asia and North America, look further south, look all the way down here to the northern suburbs of Brisbane, Queensland, Australia – and find me here in the thick of it, in the swelling consequence of breathing. See the bodies flat on their backs on the grass in the cul-de-sac. See those neighbours catching their breath in the still aftermath of another earthbound story, just another neighbourhood rumour. See the teenaged girls with their hands still gripping the right arm of their mum. See the mum with her head on her husband's chest that rises and falls with every heavy breath he takes. Can you see her now? Can you feel her? Can you hear her now? Can you hear what she says?

'Gravity let me go,' she whispers. 'But you didn't.'

THE GECKO STREET GAZETTE

Volume 1, Issue 13

Clementine Cork | *Editor-in-Chief*

Well, dear readers, wasn't that just the craziest summer you've ever seen in Gecko Street? Thanks for all the letters and photographs you sent in to Gecko HQ, letting us know about the storm-recovery efforts happening in your little patch of paradise.

Thanks again to Anushka Burman from number 36 for organising last weekend's working bee to help build Celia McIndoe her new and totally unbreakable brick fence at number 7. If you're feeling a little low at the moment, as we all endure the long wait for appraisals from the insurance companies, I urge you to turn to page 6 and read Celia's deeply moving reflection, in which she thanks all you indefatigable Gecko Street neighbours for reminding her of something her old friend Albert Camus once said: 'In the depth of winter, I finally learned that within me there lay an invincible summer.'

Thanks to Harry and Miriam Barker from number 21 for this month's photo essay capturing the extraordinary arrival of an eastern koel bird that sat for a rest on their backyard clothesline just moments before the devastating storm tore their garage roof clean off its fixings. Harry says that the eastern koel is sometimes known as the 'stormbird' because some twitchers believe these birds can predict when a storm's about to hit. Harry wonders if that koel came to Gecko Street this summer to warn us all to batten down the hatches. So if anyone sees a black bird with big beady red eyes in the street in the future, do please spread the word!

Recipe of the Month is from our beloved Detective Jim England from number 33, who shares his delectable Sticky Date Slab Pudding with Salted Treacle Sauce.

And, finally, don't miss our page 9 cover-story profile of Rita Munro from number 39. I have been made aware of the many theories and rumours that have developed in recent days, regarding what some of you are now referring to as 'the miracle of Gecko Street', the apparent meteorological anomaly that caused my mother to be pulled from the earth by a force unbound by any realm of human understanding. As you will soon discover in our four-page global exclusive, there is a perfectly valid explanation for the events that took place and we can finally lay all rumours to rest. As we here at Gecko HQ have always suspected, Rita Munro is miraculous. Rita Munro can fly with the birds. Rita Munro is a god.